Multispecies Cities

Solarpunk Urban Futures

Editorial Masthead:
Christoph Rupprecht
Deborah Cleland
Norie Tamura
Rajat Chaudhuri
Sarena Ulibarri

World Weaver Press

MULTISPECIES CITIES

MULTISPECIES CITIES

CONTENTS

...before you dive into the stories, might we ask for your help?

This book is both a collection of stories and a small research project.
We (the editors) want to understand how stories might contribute to
building better futures for humans and nature alike.
You can help us do so!

Simply visit the link below and fill out our reader survey:

https://presurvey.multispecies.city

After reading the book,
we will ask you to tell us what you thought in a second survey.

Thank you in advance —
It really means a lot to us!

Christoph (responsible for the survey) & the editor team

This research is supported by the Research Institute for Humanity and Nature (RIHN).

Introduction

Christoph Rupprecht, Deborah Cleland,
Norie Tamura, and Rajat Chaudhuri

What If Stories Could Plant the Seeds of Hopeful Futures?
It has been less than a decade since the movement and speculative
fiction genre solarpunk set out to imagine futures worth living in.
Story after story refusing to surrender to the temptation of violent,
dystopian post-apocalypse imaginaries. Seeking ways of practicing
solidarity, embracing human ingenuity from traditional ecological
knowledge to scientific research, celebrating diverse forms of being in
the world, from personal expression to relationships. Planting these
seeds of hopeful futures is hard work, especially amidst a constant
stream of news about the challenges between now and better
tomorrows: accelerating climate change, species extinctions,
(re)emerging fascism, lasting legacies of imperialism and colonialism,
and the ongoing struggle to overcome an economic system based on
the exploitation of living beings. As daunting as these are, solarpunk
has inspired many of us engaged in overcoming these challenges, its
art and stories finding their way into classrooms and everyday lives.

Yet among the hardest things to reimagine in the process of
worldbuilding are those engrained the deepest, those not-so-obvious
assumptions we take for granted. Unnoticed, they threaten to stymie

solarpunk's roots, keeping them from spreading wide and deep. This book exists to tackle one of these assumptions: that we as humans can and must face the crafting of futures worth living in alone. Looking with wonder and awe at the myriad ways plants, animals, microbes, rivers and other more-than-human actors on this planet shape their environments with ingenuity and resourcefulness, who could think of better allies and companions in facing uncertain futures? The stories in this book explore what shape such alliances might take, the joys to be discovered, the negotiations and compromises required, and most importantly, the more-than-human ties, relationships and kinship on which such alliances might be built. They do so in places where another assumption tells us not to look: cities, which even ecologists deemed "outside of nature" until the 1980s.

We have also sought to look for authors from, and stories set in, a place that has been underrepresented in the solarpunk movement up until now: the Asia-Pacific. With its rich bio- and cultural diversity, mega-cities, and exposure to the effects of past colonialism and current and future climate change, the region provides fertile ground for asking deep questions about what our urban future will look like, how and where we will be living and whose company we will be keeping.

Nevertheless, we still see this collection as a first step in a rich journey of discovery and imagination. We would love to see more alliances (human & non-human) described and depicted through fiction (and art, and all the various ways solarpunk is expressed). While these stories made great strides in terms of representing a rich array of urban possibilities, it would be wonderful to have a more-than-English collection that fully captures the linguistic and cultural diversity of the Asia-Pacific and beyond. Collaboration between authors, artists, futurists, scientists, geographers and sociologists may also yield fruitful pathways, as we question and tussle with the opportunities and constraints of technology, urbanity and the earth's biophysical systems. Through this collection of authors from around the globe, we sought to contribute to disrupt the way published speculative fiction, dystopic and otherwise, too often reproduces patterns of exclusion and oppression. Commissioning and platforming diverse writers is the surest way to authentically grapple with these issues, and so we look forward to continuing the journey with further collections bringing in more voices and perspectives from around the globe.

Why Multispecies?

Why are we, as humans, thinking we can or should face ecological crises alone? Some of the most eminent natural science research today is engaged in trying to create systems to measure and control physical and biological processes, all to support human well-being. That is also what the concept of sustainability itself is about. Plants, animals, fresh air, and clean water are seen only as resources that need to be managed correctly. As a result, it is easy to forget the ecological basics: species in the webs of life depend on each other in complex ways, even those in extreme environments such as deep sea vents. No happiness is to be found on an Earth devoid of more-than-human life. Add capitalism and colonialism, and it becomes clear why we find ourselves in a world where profit is more important than fulfilling basic needs, where land and people are exploited by those in positions of privilege and power. The reasons that have been historically used to justify exploiting nature and people are eerily similar. Be it skin colour, culture, religion and beliefs, consciousness, brain complexity, mobility, the ability to feel pain, or indeed being alive—distinguishing someone or something as different, other, and often somehow less, is to this day used to perpetuate injustice. To decide who may be controlled. One of the deepest lines in the sand among these is the question of agency: whose actions shape our world?

The multispecies concept argues that we can only truly understand the world if we look at the many ways humans and other life forms

3

are entangled, in a way that cannot be easily separated. For example, one could not possibly write a human history of the year 2020 without considering another organism: the novel coronavirus. The consequences of this shift in thinking are mind-boggling: imagine a stage, just a second ago with nothing but a single spotlight shining on a lone human actor before an unmoving set, now fully lit, suddenly overcrowded and teeming with actors animal and vegetal, fungal, bacterial and viral. The human actor is still moving with intent, yet in all the whirl, dance, pull and shove, it becomes clear that the too-bright spotlight hid from us what was really going on all along. Each actor affects the world around them, regardless of their characteristics. Just like this, the doors open to whole new worlds of stories. This book embarks on a wide-eyed journey to explore where these doors might lead.

Why Cities

Since its beginnings, solarpunk has reimagined the places most children born today grow up in: cities. Defying the glowing dystopias of cyberpunk, skyscrapers are painted with living green, plants and trees against the grey of urban existence. But take a look at ecomodernist dreams of smart cities, efficient and clean in their celebration of green growth and capitalism. Built solely for humans, yet no people to be found. The trees and vertical gardens uniform and functional, deployed as green infrastructure, used and discarded as required. There are no more-than-human heroes here. Without the radical changes required to transform cities, such urban designs may simply serve as green-washing, a polished corporate makeover to attract customers for new real estate developments.

Yet so many urban issues require solarpunk's attention, most prominent among them the question: whose cities? Just as cities were seen as outside of nature, they present us with a challenge to grow from: the highest ecological footprints, the hearts of capitalism and power. In re-imagining cities as gentle, as contributing to the ecosystem and landscape, as more-than-human habitats home to diverse forms of life, we can learn to negotiate, coexist, and flourish together. As we learn more about ourselves, we find that cities with healthy ecosystems and green spaces are also vital to human health: a view of trees from our windows, dirt and plants as kids' companions during daycare, the endless joys of chance encounters with multispecies neighbours. In jointly caring for and about place as more-than-human stewards of urban landscapes, we may find ourselves to be cared for in return, each place reflecting our beliefs, values, and cultures, each of us reflecting the places of our lives.

More-Than-Human Kinship

In reflecting on the many ways multispecies care was illustrated in these stories, one striking aspect is how familiar and everyday so many of these encounters are: a curious bird accompanies a teenager as they discover the deep satisfaction of gardening; a butterfly is briefly captured and released; a tame rat enjoys a scratch behind the ears. These moments capture the under-appreciated fact that all human settlements inevitably contain a myriad of life forms—plants, animals, fungi and more. What sets these stories apart is the foregrounding and focus on examining and including these relationships as a core element of world-building.

Anthropologist Deborah Bird Rose described these interspecies bonds as a kind of kinship, where kinship is "mutual life-giving," with our responsibilities for each other enduring over space and time. Perhaps the strongest and most touching example of "mutual life-giving" in these stories is in "The Mammoth Steps" between Roomba (mammoth) and Kaskil (human). The story opens with a list of the reciprocal obligations between mammoths and the Siberian communities—stretching from basic needs like safety and food to the spiritual comfort of the mammoths' "sly humor". Kaskil and Roomba then embark on an epic quest, deftly reversing the human + companion animal trope to animal + companion human. Along the way, we see the scope and scale of the care and love in this friendship, as well as the challenges of bridging differences in communication and physical needs.

Here, as in a number of other stories, interspecies communication is aided by technology not (yet) available. In other worlds, deep and active listening and receptivity is the key to comprehending that "everything speaks" (Chabria's "Listen"). What is common across all is that translating species-specific knowledge, emotion, memories and concepts is essential for the responsibilities of kinship to be understood and realised.

The greater affinity or receptiveness of children to receiving these messages is a common thread. In "The Songs Humanity Lost Reluctantly to Dolphins", a physical, sensory and emotional transformation of human children is initiated by dolphins, creating hybrid beings who are able to bridge species' divides. Similarly, in "Listen" the ability to hear the beyond-human languages is discovered and is at its peak with the leisure-rich days of childhood—perhaps it is the time taken to truly open the senses rather than innate ability or innovative tech that offers the most opportunity for connection. Again, it is the young people inhabiting the post-apocalyptic world of "Children of Asphalt" who are able to interpret the needs of their new mammalian neighbours and communicate these to the less in-tune adults of their world. Here too, the word "kin" has replaced other words the English language has for the more-than-human, indicating beyond doubt the familial ties we have to our co-inhabitants of the planet.

First Nation communities the world over have long taken as given that humans are part of a family tree that extends well beyond *homo sapiens,* including forests, rivers and oceans. As in "Down the River," we ignore our responsibilities of respect, guardianship, and care of these elements at our peril. Translation and understanding may require skills and technology not yet available, but the imagination goes a long way to helping us know what we need to "get along" as kin in our one habitable world.

This is not a matter of a glib declaration of "we are one" without engaging with some of the uncomfortable ways we do and will continue to interact with our multispecies kin. The delightfully disturbing "A Life With Cibi" by Natsumi Tanaka demonstrates how our need to consume can conflict with any universalist notions of bodily autonomy and individual freedom. Through a world where food called "cibis" walk around and talk to you as you carve off their flesh, Tanaka gives voice and shape to the close relationship between how we eat and how we could be eaten, destabilising any ideas of innocence or ability to separate ourselves from the world of predator-prey relationships. Eco-philosopher Val Plumwood blames the "hyper-separation" that feeds the common perception that humans are somehow "not prey"—but also the vegan's delusion that they are "not predator"—for fuelling the global environmental crisis. In the book *Eye of the Crocodile*, she reflects on the crocodile attack that almost claimed her life and concludes "we are food and that through death we nourish others." In "A Life With Cibi," the protagonist's distaste for eating a cibus that she shares her house with backfires, as the creatures need to be consumed regularly to prolong their life. The cibus withers and dies, reminding us multispecies justice does not simply mean straightforward notions of care, guardianship, and "living and letting live", but rather acting both responsively and responsibly in both life and death.

Narrating More-Than-Human Stories

Right from the time we begin to question progress-based narratives, stories of the individual, the lone hero, people against people and in fact most of what stories are expected to be, we stretch the familiar fabric of fiction. But the calls for "reform of literature" (such as from Nick Admussen) have been growing strident with each passing day while the Keeling curve of our carbon karma rises higher and species extinction rates accelerate as if in concert with speedometer needles of the latest gas-guzzling supercars. Considering more-than-human narratives as a subset of stories of the solarpunk—with its decentralised politics and a hopeful belief in a cleaner and better future—we do place quite a few challenges before the teller of these new tales.

While organised politics or the "moral adventure" of an individual makes for engaging narratives, decentralised action and cooperation do not always lend themselves to familiar modes of storytelling. Also the violence that we inflict on the living and non-living by treating them as cogs in the wheels of progress, be it through capitalist production or a centrally commanded system, happens over extended time periods and the processes through which the more-than-human world responds, revealing our connections with it, can be even slower.

Stories which try to highlight these connections or engage with the slowness of the response on a planetary scale have to employ special narrative strategies to hold the reader's attention. One way to approach the issue of slowness and lengthy time periods is by plotting through narrative leaps across tipping points or catastrophes like the coronavirus pandemic. These are the points of rupture, where an equilibrium is lost and the natural world starts to transform quickly and its impact speeds up the story.

"The Songs that Humanity Lost Reluctantly to Dolphins" is one such story, which while highlighting our connections with the more-than-human, brilliantly employs the above-mentioned technique to bypass slowness and lengthy timescales. Here a curious change in human babies "begins quietly" but spreads fast across the world, as a symbolic acknowledgement of the entanglement of humans, the ocean and its creatures. This serio-comic tale also deserves attention for its carnival-like quality and the deft handling of the collective voice, rather than that of a singular hero. From scientist to mad woman and singing dolphins to clueless parents, a polyphony of voices, spoken and unspoken, sweeps us along in this powerful work resolving into an optimistic fantasyland of a second Creation.

Many of these narratives, without sounding preachy, vividly portray how much we are beholden to the living planet and the obligations we cannot ignore. There have been important debates between Marxist thinkers and literary theorists (Sophia David cites this debate in *Ecofiction; Bringing Climate Change into the Imagination*) about a creative work being consciously political or radiating its politics just by "mirroring society" and many believe that consciously political fiction will be aesthetically weak. While the "society" depicted in these stories breaches the Cartesian barrier of the cogito (the principle establishing the existence of a being from the fact of its thinking or awareness), the tension between aesthetics and politics, and the creative devices employed to address it have no doubt enriched this collection with its bouquet of enjoyable and at the same time inspiring tales.

Some stories keep the politics in the background which still impinges on the plot, some others focus on the micro-level working of beliefs through dialogue and action. In a semi-utopian "Vladivostok," a layered narrative about Amur tigers and a VR game developer duo, the politics is mostly in the past and a better world with multispecies elements has been woven together but the jarring notes of the bygone still rend the air, driving the conflicts of the story, giving it poignancy and meaning.

Elsewhere in "Untamed," the ceaseless work of clearing the vestiges of attitudes, through psychological and behavioural change at the level of the individual, propels the plot as it expands a character's consciousness, easing her switchover to a new role. From disinterest to dedication for an optimistic future, the human character's transformational journey, underscored by that of a mynah companion, is engaging in its details. Often in such journeys, there is a helper coming by—the figure of a guardian or lover, disliked at first but accepted and silently honoured later.

As the creative shoots and vines of solarpunk blossom into

fullness, entwining around an understanding of our closely-knit connections with our more-than-human kin, there is a natural venturing into realms which modernism had partitioned off as the preserve of science. In these stories, as in other hybrid genres like climate fiction, the human and the more-than-human dance to step and tune, rewarding us with unforgettable tales of hope, overcoming, and redemption.

Here a gentle science ("Birdsong Fossil") tries to retrieve the lost worlds and culture of extinct species and the author breaks our hearts with the failures and the possibilities of such an endeavour while elsewhere ("Down the River"), the natural world as character, in the person of a river, moulds and guides the narrative flow.

Like a river in spate the stories grow out, absorbing fresh vocabulary, forms, even on-page layouts to reflect their preoccupation with foreign and long-neglected dominions. Sometimes they take science as a companion to enter the minds of the more-than-human characters. More often, they tap the apparently endless reservoir of the poetic imagination ("Listen") to reveal the hidden canvas of our connections with the web of all creation.

In re-imagining the life of future cities not as dystopic dead ends or aquariums of a smart progress but as possible templates for a hopeful and inclusive multispecies future, the storytellers of this volume serve not only their well-established roles as aesthetes of a stricken time but also of designers and navigators of a tomorrow to look forward to.

Listen: A Memoir
Priya Sarukkai Chabria

This is a true story set in the Earth Dominion era, that continues today.

One sunrise, on a day free of storms, when I was eight —
for I was living with my grandparents of Tamil lineage who tended to awaken early—

—I saw something special from my bed. The mosquito net had just been raised, its soft hazy folds lifting like mists dissipating after dawn, which, after a while, form clouds that looked like rats and peacocks and snails and caterpillars who were my neighbours in the garden that spread around our small first floor home with its huge terrace. The ground floor was unoccupied as few chose the life of Settlers, or Opter-Outs as people like my grandparents were called by the mean-minded though that was not the label given to my parents, Opter-Outs, though they had opted out of raising me like most others did, with their children. But few resolved to live in Protected Zones because technology was kept primitive as it was almost two centuries ago, while nature was abundant and life moved at a leisurely pace —like a chameleon soaking up morning sun which won't stir though you are inches away —

except once you stepped outside the Zone everything whizzed by. Transport. Time. Tension.

Inside our home, far from the receding foam of the city, we lived in safe secure solitude.

As I was saying, once the mosquito net was lifted up by my grandmother I could look out, straight through the door of the hall where I slept, out past the large landing with its rough red paving, past the wide terrace straight at the sky tousled by mango and neem and gooseberry branches and coconut fronds, and somehow on that day the light

was so tender, flowerlike, like a frangipani unfurling, that it scented my heart

and I sang to the sky in syllables unknown to me till that moment and my heart filled

with a delight that I did not know was possible until then.

I was repeatedly called so I waved to the sky, dressed, packed my tablet and was walked to the Pick-Up Point by my grandfather, my hand in his, who waited with me till the glider arrived at our Zone and I boarded to go to school where we learnt Real-Life Social Interaction, at which, incidentally, I was good.

That evening, at sunset, as I sat where my bed would later be unfurled, the sky was brighter, as if colours that were unseen behind the day's blazing blue pushed through the azure membrane to make everything splendid. I sang to the sky again, again in tunes unfamiliar until the moment it tumbled out of me as a sudden gurgling stream.

That's when it happened. The sky sang back to me.

A star, five-pointed, like the marvels we spoke about
during Face-to-Face Communication Class,

appeared in the sky's dome and sang to me. I don't know exactly
what it sang for it sang in star language, pulsing in crimson and pale
yellow, pulsing, pulsing, but not fading away. We sang a duet, we
sang a long long time, singing and singing back as if we were rocking
a cradle of melodies.

The star sings to me whenever I remember it, even at this moment
when I'm at the spaceship's controls, as the skyscape wheels, reels and
falls away, as I survey below me the wilder weather patterns we've
become accustomed to since those of childhood over thirty years ago.

The star sings in the eternal present, dilatating time so no past or
future exists, nor separation of self from the star. I was *rapturous*, a
word I was to learn later. At some point my grandmother called,
'*Priya, what are you doing?*' '*I'm singing to the star, that one, there,*' I
said, pointing, '*Can't you see it?*' '*No,*' she said. '*But it's there!*' We
conversed in Preserved Tamil, the Language of Choice we were
allowed at home in the Zone. '*It's secretly talking to you because you're
a good girl.*'

I felt glad, and not glad.

Not glad because the star sings to anyone and everyone who wants to
hear.

My grandmother couldn't see the singing star because she had much
to do—feed us, clear

the plates, make the beds, safely put away leftovers from the ants—
because keeping bots was discouraged in the Zone. We had the
basics: one ancient Gardner's Friend, one All-Rounder cleaner, one
security bot, and a low-grade sous chef. The garden talked to her in
ways it didn't to me, through its wafted scents. But the mango tree
whispered to me through its arboreal cave of leathery leaves that hung
over the terrace. I would do my homework here, feeling

that I'd somehow been absorbed into its rustling grandness along with the birds and big black ants that ran up and down its trunk, the fungi clinging to its bark—patterned like snakeskin—and the other life forms whose home it was. All the while I would be calm yet surgingly alive and the homework got done well.

After the star talked to me other wonderful things began to happen.

When grown-ups slept during humid afternoons, dragonflies that glinted noisily above the shrubs and small flowers that sprouted without being sown in our garden talked to me in their language. As they conversed, I heard them say, '*Thank you! Lots of food! Let's feast!*' Under the sparkling light their drone over still flowers waiting to be sucked of nectar would send me into a trance of *gratitude* —though I hadn't learnt this word either in any language but the feeling overflowed from me. Even today, if I'm anxious about making a smooth touchdown in rough weather, I recall the dragonflies' hum which lulls me into its plenitude of thanksgiving.

Once, on a shimmering moonlit night, all dripping mercury and black patches, as I walked back alone from the far gate I remembered my grandmother's warning, '*Never step on shadows!*' I hop-scotched my way down the shining path, avoiding splotches of stubbly grass and swaying, smoky leaf shadows. Suddenly, something long and dark appeared. '*Don't step on me! I too am scared,*' the shadow said. I froze. It slithered away. I rushed into the low-light comfort of home, onto my grandfather's lap and into the sound of his singing. On another day, as a mongoose was giving chase to a snake—perhaps the same?—it threw me an aside without glancing at me with its beady red eyes, '*Don't distract me. I'm after food. Disappear!*' I halted; snake and mongoose streaked into the undergrowth. Then, two squirrels befriended me, barking into my face in their high loud voices, especially in the fruiting season, urging, *'Hurry! Slice open the mangoes. You know our tiny teeth can't tear its tough skin!'* But grandfather said we shouldn't interfere so we waited till parrots descended like emerald parachutes, shrieking, *'Stop! This is good. Good. Juicy mangoes. Juicy mangoes!'* and the squirrels waited till the parrots exposed the flesh, ate and took flight again before they scurried to eat, their thoughts blaring, *'Thank you, thank you! I'm stuffed.'* Once, when the tree glistened with raindrops strung on cobwebs, each wee drop dangling a dark, inverted tree inside it, I heard a spider on a soaked branch pray, her hairy legs twitching, *'Make it hold! Will it hold?'* I overheard many such conversations though I can't decipher the exact words.

That's how I know we are not alone, a separate species, separated.

Perhaps what I'm saying is if you listen well you don't need to completely understand a language to follow the speaker. Perhaps this is what Wittgenstein meant when he said of Georg Trakl's poems, *'I do not understand them, but their tone delights me.'*

Many among us read poetry while commuting to the Spacedrome which is close to where I now stay, in the Officer's Quarters, a squat geodesics dome with a solar panelled roof, identical to the entire city's rooftops which, from the air, resemble a fly's composite eyes. Each time I descend to land, the city below looks surprisingly modest, rather like an Old World oil refinery; a huddle of sealed low structures connected by tubular passageways. The sprawl is underground, in interconnected caves, layer beneath layer, beneath layer. Here lie its enchantments, its greenery studded workspaces and living cells, its music parks, factories and essential farms.

My grandmother told me that previously, fundamental rights weren't shared with sky-mirror rivers, with mountains covered and revealed by storms, nor the deserts or the in-between lands, swamps and tidal forests, or even with fellow-creatures. In fact, people used to own, grow and eat animals. As a child I wonder why people wanted to eat their friends. Perhaps because people didn't hear them sing, gossip and lament; didn't know the stories of their lives, big, small, and even smaller, which are much like our own, but oh-so frail.

The authorities offered me the standard choice: live in the outlying buildings of AboveCity or beneath. Most prefer to live underground for the obvious benefits, especially Real-Life social contact, gaming and clubs. I opted for AboveCity as I miss the sun-filled days of childhood, the clouds' dappling light, softness of nightfall, part of which is visible through the window slits that strip the residency walls. Besides, I am at heart a Settler, used to solitude. Also, living in the outer fringes I feel freer, especially on a good weather day when I can see past the city's surrounding barrenness to the horizon's arcs — as if from the large, solemn wings of a soaring bird—as the Earth continues its wobbly rotating through space as it has for billions of years.

In my flat, chillies and cherry tomatoes grow in the two window boxes allotted to me and, next year when I'm shifted to Ground Duty, I hope to cultivate butterflies. While watering the plants I can almost hear them beaming, almost hear leaf pores opening and pale root hairs in the soil quicken but plant language is different from that of animals. We hear their response when wind swooshes through branches or rain drips on leaves or sunlight shafts through green so strongly that even koel's jet-black wings are tinged emerald

— for plants speak through *space*, in the manner they open their leaves, spread petals, turn to the light, hold rocks with roots, drop fruit and leaves, scatter spores and scents through air—

so the old Ikebana masters were right when they said a complete
composition is the plant, its curves and flowering, the soil at its roots
and the space around them,
that halo of living which surrounds each one.

Years later, my grandparents and I were shifted to a house by the sea
in another Protected Zone. I was busy with boyfriends, exams and
ambitions because when you are young you think the world
understands your tongue and that *it absolutely should* because you are
like a sword aflame—
or a rocket with its tail of fire lifting into space and you are vibrating
hard, so hard your eyes shake in your skull till your craft floats out of
the Earth's immediate and beloved gravity.

I believe that Earth's strong gravity is also in place because the Earth
loves us, loves to sustain the life forms that dwell here which The
Ancestors intuited, so they gave our planet goddesses names—'Gaia',
'Umay', 'Prithvi', 'Panchamama', 'Bhu Devi'—and many more that I
recite as liturgy during lift-off as a safeguard for our return. I keep
this theory a secret in case I'm labelled muddle-headed after my long
span in the Protected Zones. It won't do for a person with my
responsibilities, though some colleagues also come from Settler
backgrounds before switching, like me, to become Citi-zens. But as
more and more young people left for the city, Protected Zones
became professionally managed farms, their produce has increased,
they are weatherproofed

—but when you're an adolescent you think the world should
understand your every
word, your entire vocabulary of longing and dreams. But the world
often speaks at cross-purposes, which is difficult to decode, though all

Citi-zens share a common language unlike other species that talk in
varied tongues as they pass through your life
like a splash of colour that dyes you forever and you are changed.

I changed when I met L; he too changed on meeting me.
We met by accident in the Yew Maze, which smells of mystery and
the fragrance of ancient foliage as its closely set hedges blaze viridian
under full spectrum sunlight that filters down to every inch of this
fertile territory. The Yew Maze was the newest of the underground
parks that string UnderCity suburbs together, it is a place to get
temporarily lost in, before switching on Location Finder. Both of us
were lost when we came upon each other at a tall, bristly turn of yew;
in an immediate and unspoken way we decided to remain lost
together for as long as we could, there in the Yew Maze, then at his
house, and at mine, lost in each other.

L is for Lover, L is for Love, L forever, L for the secret shared
Language of Lovers.

He was in the Storm Rescue Corps, flying in supplies; I flew my
routine trips to refuel space stations and provide Real-Life interaction
to their crew; we flew towards each other each moment of our free
time, and into one another, into the most intimate spaces of the
body, heart and mind. We were happy.

One afternoon as we lay together, I don't know why I spoke to him
in snail tongue. *'What did you say?'* L asked. *'That's what a snail told
me one rainy day,'* I replied. *'It was worried its slime trail would wash
away and its mate wouldn't be able to follow...'* *'Not likely,'* L
said. *'This snail knows his way back home.'* He trailed his fingers over
my body, he trailed pleasure and more pleasure, and even more.

When our limbs once again slackened and separated, and the room slowly reconfigured itself around us, we slept. I awoke, alarmed, to storm noises. L was making sounds—of drizzle, downpour, thunderclap, deluge. *'I know languages you don't,'* L said. *'No! You're merely imitating rain sounds. Not speaking its language. You need to listen hard to hear it, like you hear my needs without me asking you!' 'I can do that,'* he said, *'I know what you want.'* We were laughing. One day L flew into a cyclone over the seacoast.

I stopped speaking for a long time.
Words bleached like coral reefs.

After a long while, part of me began to speak in the functional tongue of the city. But I could not look upon the luring oceans of The Blue Planet, nor the discus-like cloud formation with its storm eye, its dead, moving eye at the centre as I flew out on routine missions. Or as I returned, the tarmac rolling out into a swift grey sea.

One day I could again look down at the luminous blue.

I took an excursion to the sea. All day I sat by the seashore, on pale sands, looking at a pale sky reflected in a pale tepid sea with neat pale rows of wind turbine plantations marking the horizon. I slept in the resort's underground bunker. All night, in my ears, the hum of wave turbines, their language without rhythm but persistent, unlike the rise and fall of my lover's breath. However, this too was a sign of life, life happening elsewhere, powering the city. Breaking rules, I wander out at night, to lie by dark waves lapping from a dark expanse on which starlight bobbed; after sunup, spinning dolphins flashed fins, and, as the waters warmed, seabirds swooped and dived, though I could not understand a word they said.

One day, I remembered the star singing to me, it sang to me anew.

One night, in dream, I sang back to the star.

The languages of my childhood friends came back to me in fragments and whispers, blowing through me like passing rain, and leaving like passing rain, each time making me feel more alive.

I remembered the sea speaks. Its voice is gravelly in ebb tide, sometimes it spits stinging Blue Bottles along the beach like a decomposing net, sometimes its breath stinks of sadness; on cloudy days its undulating patchwork of purples, greens, blues and greys suggests underwater meadows and forests at different depths, each supporting a mesh of quicksilver life, while its luminous beauty on full moon nights seems to hush its voice,

so that as you gaze at it you fall into a silent thrall.

My grandparents, who had become frail as dawning light, and I made preparation for the frequent storms. They died in the bunker home at the seaside Protected Zone, one after the other, as if succeeding waves washed them away, like small pearly shells on the beach.

Generations earlier, the ocean had warned, *'All life in me is terrified that the coming monsoon will be rougher than you've known before and everyone's going to have a bad time, know this, and do what you can now to set it right.'*

In school we studied the desperate remedial steps taken though it's hard to believe that anyone with the money could own private transport and mining operations, that they put themselves before the lives of their children—but this happened till the world was forced to speak in one language to the Earth, in *its* language. That's when our era began.

I'm approaching the moon which speaks as slicing crescent, and when bloated, with blessings; it has whispered to children staring at the sky in its net of stars—like dewdrops on dark water— as grandparents told them stories. My grandmother, lifting me to her waist, would say the moon changes its face, sometimes you see a hare, a human face, a frog—

the moon allows you to see what you want to see in it because it reflects light.

The moon's craters enlarge in my face, every inch of it scarred by time, scarred by being a satellite that was landed on and mined—but hear what it says in its own language, in its silence.

Listen with all your senses; listen: everything speaks.

***

Priya Sarukkai Chabria is an award-winning writer known for her radical aesthetics. Her books include speculative fiction, cross-genre non-fiction, a novel, three poetry collections and translations of Tamil mystic Andal's songs and an anthology of translated poems edited by her. Awarded for her Outstanding Contribution to Literature by the Indian Government, her work is translated into several languages. She edits the online literary journal *Poetry at Sangam*.

By the Light of the Stars
N. R. M. Roshak

Cars purred slowly down Kalakaua Avenue. The broad sidewalk between the street and Waikiki Beach was lively with tourists this evening, laughing in groups or strolling hand-in-hand. The sidewalk's concrete was sandy-orange in the mellow glow of the streetlights, and the palm and banyan leaves were burnished green-bronze. The breeze was fresh with the scent of the night ocean, and hinted sweetly of plumeria.

And I had just pulled my hand free of my date's, because she had just said the single stupidest thing I'd ever heard.

Our date had been going so well. We'd shared melt-in-your-mouth maguro sashimi, and Mishael had convinced me to try sea urchin roe. After dinner, we strolled down Kalakaua Avenue eating shave ice and holding hands when it was gone. I'd been starting to think Mishael was the best thing to happen to me since I arrived in Oahu two months ago. She was funny, clever, queer, and beautiful, with lithe muscles under skin the smooth gold-brown of a banyan tree at sunset. Her short, tight-curled hair fuzzed into a soft brown cap, which reminded me irresistibly of the velvety summer heads of cattails back home.

Mishael was in-between, like me: not a tourist, not yet a local. She wasn't one of the surfers that haunted the beaches, either; she was a normal person with an apartment and a job. Better than normal, really. She didn't work in the tourist trade, which felt rare and special to me after a couple of months in Oahu's service industry, but had a solid job as an electrician. Plus, she did a little Parkour in her spare time, and had the physique to match: her body had a compact, graceful strength that put me in mind of both a wrestler and an acrobat.

I had started to hope that somehow, on this island of tourists, surfers, and locals who saw me as a transient, I might have found someone just for me.

Then, in the midst of a conversation about Hawai'i's slumbering volcanoes, Mauna Kea's observatory had come up. And these words had come out of her mouth:

"You know the stars are fake, right?"

And that's when I'd dropped her warm, strong hand.

Maybe I'd heard her wrong. "Say that again?"

"The stars're fake news, Grace," she explained. "It's a NASA conspiracy."

I chuckled. "Ha, right. Just like the 'NASA conspiracy' to make us think they put a man on the moon. Or the 'NASA conspiracy' the Flat Earthers believe in, where NASA's tricking us into thinking the Earth is round, when it's really flat. Good one."

"I'm serious," she protested. "This isn't some Flat Earther garbage, it's just common sense. You go on the NASA website and they're pushing the craziest stuff. Dark matter? Planets with iron rain? Please! So you gotta ask yourself, why do you believe anything NASA says?"

"Mishael, are you messing with me? You can't just not believe in *stars*!"

"Oh, there's a couple hundred stars out there," Mishael said easily. "But NASA wants you to believe there's millions of them. Billions. And that's bull. I mean, just look."

We looked up at the sky together. Night had fallen hard while we enjoyed our shave ice. Hawai'i in September was as warm as

Minnesota summer, where warm days meant long, sunny evenings; but here, the sun had set around dinnertime, and although it was barely eight o'clock, the sky was ink-dark. But between the streetlights, the headlights, and the lit-up storefronts that lined Kalakaua Avenue, I could only make out a handful of stars. I had to admit that from Kalakaua Avenue, the crazy conspiracy theory that Mishael seemed to have bought into wasn't obviously wrong.

Not that it made any sense. "Why would NASA even want...?"

"Funding, right? The Mars mission is just the first step. They want all of us to believe there's plenty of other stars to go to, so they can get big money for fake missions to them." She shook her head. "And NASA's the least of it. If we believe there's other planets out there, we won't care so much about fucking up this one. So industry is way behind this too. The Koch brothers. Big Oil. All the details are on YouTube if you wanna know more."

"Ooookay," I said. It seemed inadequate. "That's... interesting, I guess. But..." I thought about how to phrase this. "Haven't you ever been out in the country at night?"

She shook her head. "City girl," she said with a smile. "You?"

I was anything but. Growing up in rural Minnesota, stars had spilled across the sky every night, the Milky Way stretching overhead. I hadn't even realized how I missed them until now.

But Hawai'i was in the middle of the Pacific Ocean. The Mauna Kea observatory was testament to how dark the sky could be in Hawai'i... if not on Kalakaua Avenue.

"You know what? Let's hit the beach," I said. "Come on." I pulled her off the sidewalk, across a narrow strip of grass, and onto Waikiki Beach with me.

The beach was nearly as busy as the sidewalk, despite the dark. We threaded our way around clumps of tourists, toward the ocean. Fine white sand filtered into our shoes as we walked toward the water.

"Look," I pointed her out over the ocean. "It's darker out over the water, and you can see way more stars..." I trailed off. The demonstration wasn't as convincing as I'd hoped. There was a quarter-moon, and the beach was surrounded on three sides by towering condos, resorts, hotels that spread their glare across the water. We could see a few more stars than we had from the street, but nothing like the glory of the night sky back home.

"I hear you. I do see more stars out over the water," agreed Mishael. "But Grace, can you honestly look at that sky and tell me there's millions of stars?"

"Ugh!" I tugged on my hair in frustration. "We need a darker beach, is all. If you could see the stars where I grew up…"

"Mmm, I'd love to see where you grew up someday," Mishael said. "And I bet I do know a darker beach. One of my Parkour people lives in 'Ewa Beach. I haven't been there at night, but there's none of this nonsense," she gave a wave that included the tourists and the light-blaring towers, "just some little houses. It's gotta be darker." She touched my hand. "Want me to take you there?"

***

I'd known the suburb of 'Ewa Beach was west of downtown Honolulu—the locals used "'Ewa" as shorthand for "west of Waikiki"—but I hadn't realized how *far* west. It was a good forty-minute drive. Mishael drove us up H-1, around Pearl Harbour, and back down toward the coast. We turned into a quiet neighborhood of modest single-family homes in modest yards that ranged from overgrown to bare. In one yard, washing hung between two palm trees, abandoned for the night. Cars and pickups lined the unmarked street. Mishael pulled up behind a dented gold Chrysler and led me down a cracked asphalt sidewalk, wedged between two fenced yards, that ended at the beach.

The beach was a long, narrow strip, barely thirty feet of sand pressed between back yards and the ocean. Downtown Honolulu's lights were just a faint glow from here. The beach was dim, lit only by the house lights and streetlights behind us. And the stars spread over us, not in their thousands, but at least in their hundreds. The

Milky Way was barely visible as a faint light smudge on the sky.

"Okay," I said. "It's not perfect, but look at it this way. It's darker here, and you can see that there's more stars, right? So, the darker it is, the more stars we can see. Now imagine how many stars we'd see if it was totally dark."

"Yea, I see what you're getting at," agreed Mishael. A slow smile stole across her face. "Like a math problem, right? 'If you see one star when it's daylight, ten stars in Waikiki, and a hundred stars in 'Ewa Beach, then how many stars could you see from Mauna Kea?'"

I had to smile back. "Ha! Something like that."

"Okay," she continued, "but think about that for a sec. One... ten... one hundred... *millions?*" She shook her head. "Doesn't add up."

I waved a hand impatiently. "Of course there aren't millions of stars you can make out just with your eyes. But c'mon, Mishael, we have telescopes! Look, if we were out in the country, you'd see the Milky Way. It's like... a fog of stars, more than you can count. All you have to do is look at it to *get* how many more stars there are than you can see just with your eyes. Just because you can't see every star right here, right now... I mean... Do you really only believe what you can see for yourself?"

She shook her head. "No, 'course not. But Grace, I learned to trust my own judgement when I was a kid, and people kept trying to tell me I was straight. I got told girls should like boys, dykes are ugly, and being gay is wrong. And it was all bullshit. If someone tells me something that doesn't fit my experience, I gotta have a good reason to believe it."

"Okay. I get where you're coming from. Growing up bi in rural Minnesota wasn't great, either. But jeez, Mishael, what about all the photos... NASA... Hubble... Uh, I guess all the astronomers are in on this, too?"

Mishael shrugged. "Astronomers need funding," she said. "Did you know they built the biggest telescopes on Mauna Kea with oil money?"

I sighed. If Mishael had bought into this fake-stars conspiracy theory so hard that she believed everyone with a telescope was in on the conspiracy, then what was left for me to convince her with?

And I didn't think I could date someone who didn't believe in the freaking *stars*. Even though she was sexy and interesting and (otherwise) smart. Even though my skin tingled when she touched me.

"Never mind," I murmured. "Well, it was really nice talking with you, Mishael, and thanks for dinner, but—"

"Watch out!" She grabbed my arm and pulled me forward, off-balance. I crashed into her.

"Hey! What the heck?"

As answer, she spun me around and pointed down at the sand. I gasped and pulled my foot up reflexively. "Baby turtles," I breathed. Right where I'd been standing, a tiny turtle was making its way up the beach.

This. This was exactly the kind of thing I'd moved to Hawai'i to see. But I'd been juggling three retail jobs while I worked toward my SCUBA license, which left no time to go looking for turtles. I dropped to my knees in the sand and just watched.

Mishael knelt fluidly at my side. A few feet closer to the water, the sand was shifting and wiggling as another baby dug its way out of the nest, and another, and another. One by one, they headed up the beach toward the houses in a disorganized, clumsy little parade. The narrow strip of beach was steep near the yards; their flippers dug at the sand, they struggled for purchase, they floundered in the scrubby backyard grass.

Mishael's voice interrupted my adoration of the baby turtles. "Shouldn't they be heading the other way?"

She was right, and I mentally kicked myself for not seeing it sooner. They were baby sea turtles, not baby beach turtles. They needed to get to the sea, and they were going the wrong way.

"What's wrong with them?" I wondered out loud. I picked one up gently. It fit in the palm of my hand, cool and surprisingly heavy. The turtle ignored me as I lifted it off the ground, waving its little flippers earnestly, as though it still moved over the sand. I ran a thumb over its tiny shell, already hard as bone. I brought it closer to the water, turned it to face the ocean, set it down.

The stubborn little thing turned itself around and started to crawl up the beach, back toward the highway.

"What's wrong with it?" Mishael wondered in her turn. "You scared of the water, baby?" she asked the turtle.

I shook my head. "That can't be it," I said. "They're *all* headed away from the water. And there wouldn't *be* any sea turtles if every baby turtle was afraid of the water. There must be something drawing them there, instead of down to the ocean."

"Wonder if there's a sea turtle rescue we could call?" Mishael was already pulling out her phone, thumbing it on.

"There's got to be one somewhere in Hawai'i—but do you think they'd be open this late?"

"Probably not, but—oops!" The phone flipped out of her fingers, landed wedged on its edge in the sand. Its screen cast a cool blue light over the sand, like a tiny moon. Immediately, the turtles closest to us turned as one and started crawling toward her phone.

"Whoa!" cried Mishael, snatching her phone up. "That was weird. What do you think that's about? I left my wi-fi on, think that's it?" She glanced up toward the houses. "Might be wi-fi in those houses."

I shook my head, wondering if Ms. I-Don't-Believe-In-Stars was paranoid about wi-fi as well as stars. "I really doubt baby turtles go looking for wi-fi after they hatch..." I trailed off, feeling the glimmerings of an idea.

"Light," I said. "Your phone was lit up when you dropped it, and they went right for it." I turned back toward the ocean. Even with the quarter-moon, the sky over the water was darker than the houses and the street behind them. The nearest house had left their back-door light on, and it was outshining the moon, streaming pale light all down their yard. "Could they be heading for the lights?"

"I can Google that," said Mishael: the most sensible thing she'd said since we'd finished the shave ice. I bit back a snarky question about why she'd believe the search results.

While she was poking at her phone, I picked up another baby turtle and turned it around. "See the moon?" I whispered to it. "Go to the moon, baby." I knelt behind it, my body blocking the light from the houses and street. The tiny turtle shot out of my hand and headed down the beach toward the ocean. So fast, for such an ungainly little creature. I felt a momentary thrill of success. But as the turtle emerged from my shadow, it slowed, confused. "Dang it!" I muttered to myself, as the turtle sketched a broad U-turn and started crawling toward the houses again.

"You called it, Grace," said Mishael, holding up her phone. I felt a little spark of warmth at the respect in her voice. "Baby sea turtles go toward the brightest light. I guess in nature, that's gonna be the moon and the sky. But here…"

"It's the houses, and the streetlights," I finished. "They're never going to figure this out on their own. I wonder if it'll help if we put them right in the water?" I scooped a couple up in my hands. Their tiny, soft flippers paddled urgently at my fingers.

"Wait!" said Mishael, stretching out a hand to stop me. "It says here we're not supposed to pick them up. They have to make their own way to the ocean."

I frowned. "Why? They're not going to make it on their own."

She poked at her phone some more. "Mmmm… Says if we just plunk them in the water, then when they're grown-ups, they won't be able to find the beach again to lay their own eggs."

"Oh," I said. I walked down closer to the ocean, set the turtles down, and watched them turn and struggle back up the beach. The sense of wonder I'd felt on first seeing them was giving way to despair. "Dang it, Mishael, there must be something we can do to help. Is this your friend's house? Can you get him to turn his lights off?"

"Nope, sorry. My guy doesn't have a beachfront home. But don't worry…" Mishael smiled suddenly, a brilliant, mischievious smile that lit her whole face. "I got this. I just need to get something from the car. Wait here, I'll be right back."

She bounded up the beach, crossing the narrow strip of sand in seven long, agile strides. Instead of taking the sidewalk back to the street, she leapt nimbly onto one of the fences bordering it. I felt the tingly little thrill I always feel watching Parkour, like I'm watching Catwoman in plainclothes. Mishael ran along the top of the fence, graceful as a panther, and, if I'm being honest with myself, pretty darn sexy.

It really was too bad she was into this crazy fake-stars conspiracy theory.

I turned back to the beach. I had an idea. I pulled out my own phone, turned on the flashlight, and brought it down to beach level near a baby turtle that was struggling in the sand. Not fake stars, but a fake moon, right at turtle-level.

Sure enough, the little turtle turned toward the light. I backed slowly down the beach, holding my phone about a foot from the little turtle, beckoning it toward the water. And the little turtle followed. It was working!

I kept backing down the beach, careful not to squash any of the other babies. By the time I was near the surf, I had four baby turtles following the false moon of my phone. I hurriedly hitched up my pant legs with one hand and waded into the surf with a death grip on my non-waterproof phone. With a burst of joy, I saw the four little turtles follow me into the water. I thumbed off my phone's light and they were off, away into the ocean.

I looked back up the beach, to where tiny heads and flippers were still scrabbling out of the nest, and farther up to their brothers and sisters still labouring up the beach toward the lights. I'd saved four…

but I had about a hundred more to go.

I thought about the mother turtle that had chosen this beach for her eggs. Maybe the house lights had been out that night, the back-door lights turned off, the moon full in the sky. She had pulled herself out of the surf and given over her eggs to the sand, trusting that her babies would find the ocean. But then, the lights had come back on.

I had always thought of sea turtles as living entirely separate lives from us, ocean creatures I hoped to meet someday on a dive. But from laying to hatching, turtles were land creatures; and the land where turtle mothers had been laying their eggs for millennia had slowly become part of Honolulu's sprawl.

Despite themselves, the turtles were as much part of Honolulu as I was. And while I was irritated by Honolulu's lights outshining the stars, I could live with it. The baby turtles could not.

"We have to do better," I whispered to myself.

The back-door light on the nearest house winked out. An eyeblink later, so did all the other lights in the house.

I stared up at the darkened house. Mishael stood on the beach at the edge of its yard. She waved at me, then jogged toward the next yard to her left. As she reached it, its lights winked out too. She kept going, running lightly down the beach away from me, the lights flicking out in each house as she passed.

How on Earth was Mishael doing this?

"Hey," I called to her, as she came jogging back along the beach toward me. But she only waved and kept going, jogging past all the yards on the far side of the sidewalk, plunging them into darkness as she went.

As my eyes adjusted to the darkness, I searched the beach for little turtles. They were still scrambling confusedly through the sand: some headed toward the water, some not. The houses were dark, but streetlights still glowed behind them.

I lit up my phone again and held it over my head. With the house lights out, I thought, I might be the brightest thing on the beach. A few little turtles turned toward me.

"That's it," I called out. "This way, little guys!" I backed carefully toward the ocean.

The streetlights went out.

"Whoa," I whispered. I let my hand holding the phone drop, turned out its light. With the houses and the streetlights out, the quarter-moon was finally the brightest light over the beach. And every little turtle was turning toward it.

A shadow landed softly beside me on the beach. "Nyagh!" I cried, and dropped my phone. Mishael bent to retrieve it and handed it back to me.

"How's our baby turtles?" she asked.

"Look," I said. A hundred little turtles were headed for the moon and the sea.

We watched together in silence for a time.

"How did you do that?" I asked at last.

"The lights?" Mishael flashed that same surprising, mischievous smile, and pulled a little clicker out of her pocket. It looked like a garage door remote, with cryptic symbols Sharpied onto the two buttons. "This's just a little something I put together for my Parkour nights. Police aren't always happy to see people running up the side of buildings, you know? Sometimes, it's easier if the streetlights happen to go out."

"A little something, to put out the lights..." I shook my head. "Mishael. Can I be frank?"

"Frank's okay, but I like you better as Grace... Naw, I'm just kidding you. Go ahead."

"I can't get a handle on you," I confessed. "On the one hand, you believe this crazy YouTube conspiracy theory about stars, and no offense, but it's the dumbest thing I've ever heard. But on the other hand, you're so smart that you can make an electronic thingy that puts out lights, which is... impossible, actually. And you made it because, even though you have a solid job, you like to run up buildings in the dark like some kind of crazy cat burglar."

Mishael laughed, somehow not offended. "Been getting blowback on my beliefs my whole life," she said. "What can I say? I am who I am. Never promised to make any sense."

"Well, who *are* you? Are you some kind of superhero? Or super-villain?" I teased. "Electrician is just your cover identity, right? And the crap with the stars was just to mislead me, so I wouldn't notice your superpowers?" I didn't believe in superheroes or supervillains, of course. But deep down, the question might've been half-serious. She could run along fences, she had super-gadgets... she *was* just a little bit Bruce Wayne.

"Superpowers? Ha, I wish! I just got a way with electronics."

"That's exactly what a super-villain would say," I pointed out.

"True!" She laughed again, eyes glimmering in the moonlight. "But, would a super-villain save a clutch of sea turtles?"

"No, I guess not," I conceded. "Unless, again, she was trying to mislead me."

"Or unless the baby sea turtles were a key part of her evil plan," she teased back.

I looked out over the sea, whose great dark swells were bearing the baby turtles away to begin their lives.

"No," I said softly. "I can't imagine anything less evil."

If anything was evil here, it was the lights Mishael had put out. There was no malice to them, of course; it was a thoughtless kind of evil, one that chose our comfort and convenience over the lives of the countless animals who lost their way in the glare.

"They're not the only ones, you know," murmured Mishael.

"What?"

"These babies. They're not the only ones to get confused by all the lights. When I was looking up turtles? I found out that turtle rescues spend more time trying to get people to turn off their beach lights than they do rescuing turtles. But people say 'no', or they forget. And all these city lights mess with other animals, too. Not just baby turtles. Baby birds, bats, all kinds of animals... So! I'm thinking I'm gonna start a new hobby."

"Huh? A hobby?" One thing about talking with Mishael, the conversation never seemed to go where I thought it would.

"I'm gonna go round asking people to turn out their lights. And when they forget," she brandished her clicker, "I'm gonna help them remember." She sent me a sidelong glance brimming with mischief. "You wanna join me?"

I looked back at Mishael consideringly. She believed NASA was lying to us about the existence of stars. And, okay, that was pretty weird. But, in a way, she was just another creature who'd lost her way in the skyglow. A city girl, born and raised under artificial light, blinded to the sheer abundance of stars in the sky. I couldn't imagine being so cut off from the natural world.

And whether she was a superhero, a supervillain, or simply super-confused, her heart was in the right place. She could've used her impossible clicker to sow chaos across Oahu. Instead, she used it to save baby turtles.

Mishael needed to see the sky without skyglow too, every bit as much as the baby turtles did. The least I could do was show her.

"Yes," I decided. "Sure. I'd be glad to. And Mishael... We should drive out in the country to see the stars. Somewhere there's no lights at all, like the middle of the Diamond Head crater. I'll show you the Milky Way. You'll see."

She turned toward me. "We should," she said. "I'm open to being wrong, Grace. Show me the stars."

In the darkness, my hand found hers. We stood together and watched the last of the turtles slide home into the sea.

∗∗∗

N. R. M. Roshak writes all manner of things, including (but not limited to) short fiction, kidlit, non-fiction and translation. Her short fiction has appeared in *Flash Fiction Online, On Spec, Daily Science*

Fiction, Future Science Fiction Digest, and elsewhere, and was awarded a quarterly Writers of the Future prize. She studied philosophy and mathematics at Harvard; has written code and wrangled databases for dot-coms, Harvard, and a Fortune 500 company; and has blogged for a Fortune 500 company and written over 100 technical articles. She shares her Canadian home with a small family and a revolving menagerie of Things In Jars. You can find more of her work at http://nrmroshak.com, and follow her on Twitter at @nroshak.

Old Man's Sea
Meyari McFarland

Efe hummed into her rebreather's full-face mask before ducking under the ocean's surface into the blue-green world below. Up on deck, Moana sang old Buddhist chants that droned and shifted in as regular a pattern as the waves rocking their battered old thirty-foot catamaran. The kelp Efe swam through rocked in time with the boat and Moana's chant, great fronds brushing against Efe like curious giraffe tongues as she passed.

The remnants of smoked salmon and pickled seaweed still coated Efe's lips and tongue, the vinegar tang buoying Efe's spirits as she went to harvest from the sea floor below.

The kelp shifted around her in the current like blackberry runners dangling off the roof, slow and ponderous but inevitable in their grand sway to and fro. The water was green today, teal near the surface but quickly going emerald as she slowly flipped her way deeper underwater.

Must be an algae bloom moving through. It was a little bit early but with the weather so warm this year, it was hard to say it was outright worrisome. The schools of slate-blue blacksmith fish with their grumpy old-man mouths and pug nose ridges ignored Efe other than staying out of easy grabbing range. She was through these waters enough that the fish knew not to fear her. The seals darting through the kelp?

All the fish darted away from them.

Efe laughed and gave one of the bolder seals a belly rub when it swam up and floated next to her. He was an engaging seal, big dark eyes, whiskers that shook with laughter as she tickled his spotted sides and flippers that showed far too many signs of hooks getting caught and carefully removed. None there now, thank goodness. Not even a recent wound.

He must spend a lot of time further towards the remnants of Drowned Seattle because he had no fear at all. Not much curiosity, either, other than nosing at her empty urchin bags as if looking for a treat. They did treat the critters well there. A lot better than some places on either side of the greatly expanded Pacific Ocean.

Half a life ago, Efe's mama had said that once upon a time, before the sea rose and the land got swamped, there were cities full of shining glass and steel buildings. People'd spend their lives working and working and working so they could buy trinkets in the stores. There were shows and games and cops who weren't all that different from the land-bound cops who tried to chase any sea-dwellers back out onto the water whenever they dared to come in to dock.

No resources for sea-dwellers because they were floating trash, that was what the cops always claimed. Mama said that people with dark skin or poor people or just those passing through used to be treated the same. Cops were cops, dedicated to serving the rich and powerful instead of protecting everyone.

When she was too little to dive, Efe had believed Mama made the stories about the old world up.

Not anymore. Efe had dived all through sunken cities, seen the glass walls. Those that remained anyway. She'd caught fish and harvested spiky purple urchins that lived inside those old buildings. The trinkets, bits of gemstone and silver and gold, Efe always left in the silt. Moana didn't want them and Efe had no need for them. Let scavengers go after the trinkets. Efe just wanted food to eat and the peace of the sea around her.

As far as she was concerned, it was the land-dwellers who were all messed up, fighting each other for scarce arable land instead of living off the bounty of the sea. There was always a war going on somewhere. Usually several places at once, all of them using up food and fuel and lives like they were endless. Stupid, that's what that was.

All the seals looked off to the left and down. They darted away through the kelp so fast that they left behind streams of bubbles heading up to the surface. Efe tapped her comms.

"Anything big in my area?" Efe asked.

"Wartooth's pod is in the area," Moana replied. "He contacted me when you were getting ready. Apparently, he's in a mood and doesn't want to deal with humans."

"Oh, joy." Efe sighed.

A cranky orca with military spec mods was not what she wanted to deal with today.

Or any day.

Not that Wartooth didn't have cause for his crankiness and PTSD. Any creature who'd been modded against his will, put to work in a war that wasn't his own, and then had his cybernetic limbs torn off after he was deemed too old and too unstable for service had earned a temper. They hadn't even given him new limbs before throwing him back into the sea to live or die.

Didn't mean that Efe wanted to be on the receiving end of Wartooth's spleen.

She pointed her head straight down and swam for the sea floor. It was where she was going, anyway, and orcas generally weren't looking for things down here. They hunted the salmon and seals, the sharks and giant Pacific octopus whenever they could catch one swimming free in the water instead of lurking in caves down on the sea floor.

The water cooled enough that she could feel the chill through her warmsuit. A properly made warmsuit would protect you against the pressures, keep you dry, and as warm as possible. No matter how good it was, though, it wasn't going to insulate you entirely from the cold currents that ran deep along the rocky sea floor.

"See him?" Moana asked. "He's close to you."

"Nope," Efe said as she moved from emerald green water down into clearer, bluer water that turned red polyps on the kelp purple. There was a nice herd of spikey purple sea urchins carpeting the floor. "If he's around, he's hanging off a bit. Probably waiting to see if he can startle me into dropping my catch. There's a lot of nice urchins."

"Oh, good," Moana said. "I can make jewelry out of their spikes."

"I'm looking forward to eating them," Efe said.

She grinned into her facemask at Moana's laughter. It wasn't difficult harvesting sea urchins. Her gloves were armored, protecting her from the venom in the urchin's spines. The bags she used were a nice tight mesh that the urchins couldn't poke through, either. Six urchins per bag, four bags full, Efe paused and looked up.

A shadow longer than the catamaran passed overhead, blocking the sun like a thundercloud about to send down hail and tip-you-over winds.

Wartooth.

His black and white body was striped with scars. Despite not being that old for an orca, something like thirty-five or forty if the stories Wartooth told were accurate, he looked like he was late fifties at least. It was the scars and chunks that'd been taken out of his hide, his flippers and dorsal fin.

And the stiff way he swam, always circling so that he could keep one eye on Efe. She sighed and went back to humming as she filled another two bags with sea urchins. The carpet of urchins was thick enough that she could barely see the red and green algae that coated the rocks under them.

"You don't belong here."

Wartooth's comment came straight into her comms. The voice was entirely human, no surprise. The military wanted their sea-going conscripts to sound like any other soldier. The implicit threat wasn't human at all. Efe rolled on her back, attaching the final two bags to her dive belt.

"I was born in these waters," Efe said. "Literally. My mother birthed me in the ocean. I opened my eyes under the water and swam for the air just like one of your pups would have."

She could see the rest of Wartooth's pod further up the water column, swimming like they were keeping an eye on Efe in looping spirals up and down the water column that let them weave in and out of sight behind the towering kelp.

They were all modded. Every single member of his pod had cybernetic modifications that allowed them to access internet and comms and even hack if they wanted. None of them were warriors. They'd been couriers and spies, curious kids who worked with humans to get the mods they wanted. Wartooth didn't want warriors around him. From what Efe had heard, he drove out anyone with a link to the military.

Wartooth snapped his jaws. Not at her. Just a snap like he didn't like the taste of that.

Which was fair.

Efe wasn't fish and she wasn't orca and she wasn't, really, a land-dweller, either. She didn't fit. Anywhere. Kind of like Wartooth, not that she was going to say it out loud or over the comms.

Since Wartooth didn't have anything else to say, Efe checked under a few rocks. She managed to snag four kelp crabs, nice sized ones that were old and big and slower than the little ones that skittered away faster than she could grab at them. They struggled against being put in a bag, wiggling against the small of her back as she made her slow way back towards the surface, harvesting several long fronds of kelp as she went.

Wartooth followed her.

The ports on his sides were smooth. She'd expected them to be rough, exposed bits of circuitry and nerve connections. Apparently, the military had at least capped his ports before they tipped him back into the sea.

"You still don't belong here," Wartooth said as Efe passed from the clear, cold current up into the slower, warmer, greener one between her and the boat.

"Yeah, so?" Efe said. "You looking to evict me from this stretch of ocean?"

This time Wartooth's jaw snap was a lot more aggressive. A lot harder, a lot faster and way too close for Efe's comfort. She looked around and yeah, the rest of the pod was still there. Not close but swimming at the edges of visibility in a further away circuit. Weirdly, they were swimming slow circles around Efe, a good dozen or three yards off. Efe paused in her slow rise, watching the way they swam. Her breath caught before she tapped her comms.

"Moana, I need you to look for anything dangerous in the area," Efe said. "Weather, sharks, anything you can think of."

"Why?" Moana asked. The comms didn't carry the sound of her working the radio, the sonar, the internet, but Efe trusted that Moana started at it right away.

"The pod's swimming guard duty on me."

"...Oh."

That one word held a world of worry. Fear. Racing pulses that pounded in your ear and acid that burned up the back of your throat. Efe swallowed down her acid and her fear. You panic on a dive and you ended up dead.

She had her rebreather. There was no running out of air. Her suit would keep her warm. It was armored enough that she could take pretty much anything but a great white trying to bite a chunk out of her. Thankfully, when she'd upgraded her warmsuit, Efe had gone for one with bold lime green and black stripes, jagged as a tiger's. Sharks didn't like those patterns. They read like threats.

"Tell me?" Efe asked Wartooth. "Is this shark or what?"

He stared at her, dark eye widening and then narrowing as he snapped his jaws three times and blew a couple of small bubbles.

"It's a what," Wartooth replied.

"You are the most cantankerous, annoying old soldier I've ever had the misfortune to deal with," Efe snarled at him. If she'd had the jaws for it, she'd have snapped right back at him. Twice as hard, too.

Orcas smiled. Gaped their jaws and squinted their eyes while wiggling like a happy seal. The damned thing was that Wartooth laughed like he was tickled pink with her.

"Just tell me!" Efe said.

"Oh crap."

That came from Moana. Efe looked up towards the surface. This close, the patchwork paint job on their catamaran showed in light and dark swatches that weren't all that different from Wartooth's black and white hide. Its twin hulls looked almost fish-like overhead, hidden by the thick clouds of algae.

There wasn't anything else for Efe to see, no vibrations in the water, no current changes or oil blooms or anything like a storm brewing on the surface to make the light ripple and shimmer and shatter instead of drifting down in great emerald beams that barely fluttered in time with the movements of the kelp.

"We got a problem," Moana said. "I've got a military boat on a slow approach. I think they're on exercises or something."

"Fuck," Efe said. She turned to Wartooth. "Get your pod out of here!"

"They don't want me anymore. Too old, too stubborn," Wartooth said. "Besides, the military pod will kill you if you're down here. That's part of their training. Killing any humans they find in the water is standard for training runs. The idiot kids are all excited to actually find someone in the water, not that they're saying it on comms. Only in our language. Military never listens to that so they can plan a murder and make it seem like they're not imagining killing their handlers."

Efe sucked in a breath. So did Moana over the comms. Yeah, no, not dealing with a military pod all full of modded orca who were angry and hurting and being used like puppets by idiot land-dwellers who thought they ruled the world instead of ruined it. Bad enough that they fought their wars on what little arable land the world had left. They had to bring their wars out into the ocean and everyone, marine life and human, suffered for their hubris.

She swam hard for the surface. The rebreather did a better job keeping nitrogen out of her blood than regular scuba gear would have, but she was going to be miserable for a few days. It was inevitable and unavoidable. Wartooth stayed by Efe's side all the way to the surface.

His pod kept their distance, swimming in a formation that didn't look like it was impregnable, but wow, they sure acted like it was. Efe was reaching for the ladder up onto the boat, Moana overhead with her waist-length mop of curls wrapped up in a green and blue turban, when Wartooth suddenly pushed his big head right under Efe's ass.

"Out!" Wartooth ordered. "Now!"

His powerful body flexed twice and Efe screeched as he propelled her right up out of the water and then up onto the deck. He subsided back down into the water as Moana screamed.

A second big black and white shape shot up out of the water where Efe had been, mouth gaped open to show vicious teeth that felt, somehow, small compared to Wartooth's teeth.

He'd been about to hit her from underneath, like a shark hitting a seal pup or an orca surging up and taking out a Great White. She cursed and tore off her flippers.

The military orca thrust hard, pushing himself up like he was about to smack down on top of the catamaran, swamping them.

Efe rolled back to the railing and smacked her fin right down on the other orca's snout, hard as she could.

The military orca, younger and unscarred, with a dorsal fin that curled towards his body instead of standing up straight, barked at her in shock as he slid back down into the water.

There were other fins around, black and tall. Every single one of the ones close to their boat had scars. Old call signs that'd been defaced with tattoos or outright cut off leaving ragged edges to their fins. Further out, the fins were covered with military IDs.

"There're so few," Moana said.

She dropped to her knees next to Efe, not seeming the least bit concerned that her multicolored peasant skirt was getting soaked with seawater. Most of the time Moana batted at Efe if Efe dared to get her clothes wet like this. Moana's eyes were all for the circling orca, not for the water or Efe or even the kelp crabs squirming and snapping against the small of Efe's back.

"How many? Efe asked as she did her own count.

She counted four far away, plus the one that'd gone for her.

Wartooth's pod was twenty-six, including the little pup who was far too young to be involved in a territory battle between military and former military.

The water bubbled and surged with a battle going on under the surface. Wartooth had to be schooling the military orca with the curling dorsal fin on just what you didn't do around veterans like him.

The curling dorsal fin of the military orca surged up out of the water as he leaped nearly all the way clear of the water. Wartooth was right on this tail. They both submerged again.

This time blood filled the water.

Wartooth surfaced and blew, submerging again immediately.

The curled dorsal fin of the military orca appeared a few dozen yards away, then further still, out past the circling line of Wartooth's pod.

Done, then. Wartooth had scared them off.

For the moment.

Efe unsealed her rebreather. Stood on shaky legs so that she could hang it up properly and secure it against anything that might happen. Her flippers got put away properly. The belt with its heavy lead weights came off and Efe's lungs suddenly felt like she could breathe three times deeper than before.

By that point, Moana was there to take the kelp and the crabs and the urchins. Her hands shook. She still kissed Efe's wet cheek before heading inside.

"They going to stick around?" Efe asked Wartooth while staring at the military ship quarter of a mile away. It wasn't moving much, just sitting there.

"Oh, probably," Wartooth replied. "The kids aren't happy with having their fun taken away."

"Too young to know their head from their tail," Efe said.

She made sure to say it over the broadest channel possible, just to be sure the military orcas would hear it. And maybe their idiot military handlers, too. Seriously, how many times did it have to be shown that orca weren't good at dealing with humans? You threw them into a war, and they ended up a mess.

Like Wartooth, paranoid old man that he was.

All five of the military orcas breached, sending up fountains of water. Wartooth laughed into her comms. Off in the distance, the military ship started its engines and swung in a wide circle before powering away.

No comm message. No lights flashing so that the orca couldn't see what their handlers said. No nothing and why would there be? The handlers were land-dwellers who thought anyone on the sea was trash. They probably wouldn't have been upset if the military pup with the curling dorsal fin killed her. Good training exercise.

"They'll be back," Efe said, disgusted, to Wartooth.

"Oh, definitely," Wartooth agreed. "I'd find a different patch of ocean to be on, if I were you."

"Not a bad thought," Efe said. "It's been a bit since we headed up to the Anchorage mooring. Might just make the trip. They tend not to mind outsiders too much, as long as you don't try to head for solid ground."

Wartooth surfaced. He blew a great blast while rolling enough that he could stare at her with one wide eye. Efe flipped a hand at him. It had been a while since they'd been up to Alaska. Or across the Pacific to what remained of Japan. If the military was going to be causing trouble here, well, there was a whole lot of ocean out there that Efe and Moana could go live on. It wasn't like they were tied to a bit of ground. They could migrate wherever they wanted, as long as the catamaran floated.

"Good choice," Wartooth said. "The salmon should be running up there soon. And the halibut are always good."

"I am not fighting a halibut," Efe said, horrified. "Those things are vicious. Salmon, though, that's a good idea. You watch yourself, old man. Those pups will be looking for a rematch."

"Their handlers may be," Wartooth said, slipping back under the waves until only the very tip of his dorsal showed. "They aren't. We don't need tech to talk. We've got our own language. You might try learning a bit of it. You don't sing half bad for a human."

He slipped away, leaving Efe smiling at the green waters. Time to find a new patch of ocean to live on for a bit. The military would be called somewhere else in a year or three as their never-ending wars shifted away from this area. Efe and Moana could find another spot easy enough until then.

At least they had some good food to start the trip.

And, apparently, a cranky old man of a guardian angel out there watching out for them.

***

Meyari McFarland has been telling stories since she was a small child. Her stories range from SF and Fantasy adventures to Romances, but they always feature strong characters who do what they think is right no matter what gets in their way. She has been published in multiple anthologies including Love is Like a Box of Chocolates and Cat Ladies of the Apocalypse from Camden Park Press, and the 2019 Holiday Spectacular by WMG Publishing. Her series range from Space Opera Romance in the Drath series, to Epic

Fantasy in the Mages of Tindiere world. Other series include Matriarchies of Muirin, the Clockwork Rift Steampunk mysteries, and the Tales of Unification urban fantasy stories, plus many more. You can find all of her work on MDR Publishing's website at www.MDR-Publishing.com.

Đẹr, Tiger, and Witch
Kate V. Bui

The road to Núi Hổ wound through a mountain pass flanked on one side by sloping hills of dense tropical jungles and on the other by green terraced rice fields carved into the hillside by industrious farmers long dead and forgotten.

In a better time, this area might be flooded with buses of tourists from all over the world, hungry to see the vistas that swept across these enchanting hills and valleys, but that was a different world, when humanity was a single organism, its cells flowing along arteries made of fossil fuels and electricity.

A lifetime had passed and now Thu was the lone traveler on this deeply rutted road, familiarity and pragmatism having drained any magic out the scenery. Decades of hiking through it had made Thu resent how beautiful the Vietnamese countryside was. Why was it that all the difficult, dangerous, or broken things should be so attractive? All she saw was the distance she'd have to walk on aching feet, the elevation she'd have to climb with calves ready to give out, and the fields full of struggling stalks of rice, weakened by the accumulation of decades of agricultural pollutants.

Despite all her personal aches, Thu actually felt heartened at seeing these tender little stalks: the farmers here hadn't given up entirely yet, but she knew the harvest would get poorer and poorer if nothing changed.

She was readjusting the straps of her worn backpack when a rustling from the jungle caught her attention. *Boar? Wild dogs?* Not taking her eyes off the brush, Thu unstrapped an aluminum hiking pole and extended it with a flick of her wrist. The sections locked into place with a click just as a blur leapt out of the brush, startling her and sending the woman stumbling backward and falling into a seated position.

Thu held the pole in front of her like a shield as four pairs of docile black eyes stared into hers. Once her brain made out the animals' silhouettes, she suddenly felt very foolish trying to defend herself from a family of sika deer, the tawny coats and white spots on their small frames unmistakable.

Unafraid of the woman, the deer inspected her dispassionately for a few seconds before bounding across the road to add further injury to the already ailing rice shoots growing out of the paddies. Thu dusted herself off, watched them nibble on the plants for a few minutes, and then set off down the road.

***

A few minutes after crossing into Núi Hổ, Thu came upon a three-walled roadside cafe on the outskirts of the village. It was indistinguishable from one of the many small rural shed houses she'd seen, other than the battered solar panels on the roof and the hand-painted sign outside promising cold drinks. She stepped under the awning and saw a group of middle-aged men gathered around a low bamboo table as they examined hands of worn paper playing cards.

Thu had seen countless scenes like this in her childhood save for one striking exception: the low plastic stools that used to be ubiquitous seating in every home, store, and restaurant had now been replaced with wooden stumps and cinder blocks. Once commonplace in every part of the country, decades of bio-engineered polymertrophic yeast blooms had eaten away all the stools, strainers, toys, bags and other plastic goods that had previously littered the country, leaving people to improvise. Thankfully that was something her people did very well.

Judging from the empty bottles scattered around and the pile of pipe ashes in the tray, these men had been at their cards and beer for a few hours now. Immersed in their game, they ignored Thu as she pushed her way through the thick cloud of pungent tobacco smoke to the back of the cafe. Behind the door-turned-counter, a woman younger than Thu squatted down next to a small mini-fridge that had begun to weep a pool of fluid from its door, fussing with the electrical cable, as if unplugging it and plugging it back in enough times would fix it.

"Hi Cô," Thu said, eyes darting between the woman and the increasingly rowdier men. "I saw your sign and was hoping you'd have some cold, young coconut to drink."

"This damned thing," the woman spat, giving the side of the fridge a kick. "Sorry Bà, no ice so nothing's cold today. I've got some fresh ones here but they're warm." She motioned to a pile of green coconuts stacked by the counter.

Thu nodded. "I don't mind warm."

The woman picked up a large green coconut and motioned for Thu to follow her out to the side of the cafe, where a well-worn tree stump stood with a machete leaning up against it. In a whirlwind of practiced strikes with the large knife, the woman transformed the oblong fruit into a flat-bottomed pentagonal cylinder. One final flick of the wrist took the top off the coconut, revealing the sweet nutritious water inside. The cafe owner grabbed a reed straw and handed both to her.

Thu greedily drank the thin coconut water. As promised, it was blood warm, but the hydration and sweetness refilled her with life. It took less than thirty seconds for the straw to suck air and Thu was about to ask for a second coconut when one appeared, ready to drink.

"From the look of you, I figured you'd want another," the shopkeeper said with a look of amusement. "My name's Thanh—I own this place."

"Thank you, Thanh, I'm Thu," she replied, taking time to savor the second drink. Midway through the coconut, Thu finally noticed the way the other woman kept staring at her—somewhere between appraising and planning something. It made her nervous.

"You're the phù thủy vang, aren't you? The yellow witch," the other woman said nonchalantly, still holding the machete by her side.

Thu froze. Spending so much time alone in the wilderness had made her forget how much attention her outfit drew and how recognizable it was.

Of course. Nobody else is out here travelling in a bright yellow áo dài and straw hat in this century.

The point is to be recognizable, Administrator Minh had told her, *the point was to remind people of the traditional character of Vietnam, the spirit of the people.* She'd hated it since day one but here she was still wearing it decades later even though he was dead and the government they had worked for was long gone.

Thu's mind raced. Which story about her had this woman heard? *Was it the one about the traveling witch that poisons your crops? The one where the kindly woman saves your harvest? The one where she steals your animals? The one where the villagers all die?* No matter how often she tried to explain herself or her work, the stories, rumors, and urban legends all cross-pollinated until they wove into a mantle that fell heavy on her shoulders and she could not shrug off.

Thu eyed the knife in the woman's hand. "I'm not looking for any trouble." She carefully put down her coconut and began slowly undoing the straps of her backpack before setting the canvas bag gently down on the packed red clay. Unencumbered, she twisted her torso away from the woman to show off the fraying embroidery on the back of her dress—a well-worn logo made up of the profile of Vietnam with stylized green leaves and a drop of water.

"My name's Nguyen Kim Thu, Vietnamese Ministry of Natural Resources and Environment, Bioremediation Specialist in VOCs, methyl tert-butyl ether, and heavy metals," she said with as much authority as she could muster.

The blank look on the woman's face was one Thu was used to getting so she added, "I'm not a witch. I'm a scientist who cleans up polluted water and soil."

"So you *are* her," the woman said, a smile blooming on her face. "Bà Thu, I have to show you something." The woman buried the machete into the stump before grabbing a confused Thu by the wrist and dragging her toward the back of the shed.

The rear of the cafe was not what the old woman expected. Instead of piles of garbage and empty shipping crates, she was led through a series of neatly arranged vegetable planters, all a riot of different leaves and stems, nothing planted in rows, just a mixture of crops but all thriving. This small garden was so much lusher and vital than the fields of crops she'd passed earlier that it was shocking. Even the soil looked healthier than the samples she'd examined earlier on the road.

"River silt? No wonder it's free of contaminants. Are you using a natural fertilizer?"

Thanh led her over to a covered area with small troughs of water and animal fodder: cut leafy branches of saplings, browse, and assorted fruit. Scattered all around were dark round pellets Thu recognized as deer droppings, probably from some relatives of the family she encountered on the road. Off to the side was a large pile where the deer manure was being processed into usable compost.

As they walked back through the rows of planter, Thu noticed some sort of construction peeking out between some dark green herbs she didn't recognize but had seen planted everywhere. "Wow, this is amazing," Thu said, kneeling down to admire the complex bamboo drip irrigation system. She could see home-made hydrometer probes pushed into the soil at regular intervals and followed their wire leads to a wooden panel on the wall with an electronic readout showing the temperature and soil moisture content. The engineering, while executed somewhat crudely with scavenged materials, was ingenious in design. "Did you do this all yourself?"

"I started it when I was younger but my daughter Đông has been the one expanding it," the cafe owner said proudly. "She's only twelve but all the irrigation stuff was her idea and the electronics too—solar panel and everything."

"Đông sounds like a smart girl. Does she go to school?" When Thu was younger, compulsory higher education was a luxury everyone took for granted, but after the climate and political upheavals, it had become desperately rare, especially for women.

This clearly touched a sore spot with Thanh, whose eyes brimmed with tears. "I taught her to read and write, some basic math, but that's all I could do for her; I'm just an uneducated cook and my husband a hunter. Everything else she taught herself from books in the library, and any reading materials traders brought by." The mother dabbed at her eyes. "That's how she heard about you. She's told me every one of your stories a dozen times."

"Not everything they write about me is true, you know."

"You just confirmed it yourself. You're the legendary science woman who my daughter idolizes. You're probably more educated than anyone in this village. Am I wrong?"

Thu shook her head. "No, you're probably not. But I can see where this is going: I'll be done with my work in Núi Hổ in three days and then I'll leave for the next village. I'm not staying so I can't teach your daughter."

Unexpectedly, the woman fell to her knees and took Thu's hand. "Please, I don't need you to teach my daughter, I need you to stop her from killing the town gods."

***

Like many of the villages in this region, the heart of Núi Hổ sat at the crossroads of the main street and the single perpendicular arterial from which a handful of side streets and alleys spidered out. It was different in one respect though: colorful banners and decorations hung from all the narrow cinder block buildings with stylized tiger faces on them. Judging from the orange and black striped banners hung from balconies and railings in every direction, it seemed like everyone was very excited about tigers.

The only exception was the austere whitewashed building that loomed over the crossroads with its Colonial-era columns and arched windows. The French had long abandoned their imperial ambitions for Vietnam but their influence permanently changed the symbolic language of her people. This Colonial design style was now so intrinsically entwined with the ideas of 'authority', 'sophistication', 'intellectualism' and it was impossible to escape the shadow of this context.

Thu dreaded making her requisite stop at the local government office. If the yellow witch had her way, she'd just sneak in under the cover of night, do her work and leave without having to deal with the endless negotiations, the condescending administrators, and tin-pot government officials.

But that's part of why you go on these long journeys, Administrator Minh's voice came to her. *Put a face to the work. Make people understand that the soil and water aren't magically fixing themselves. That it took the effort of a team of real people.* Well, these days the team was reduced to a single tired, middle-aged woman, but Minh wasn't wrong.

Even though her positive reputation preceded her, it still took an afternoon of circular negotiations before Thu emerged from the city hall with a signed contract to begin her work and the addresses of ten local farms. Exhausted, she sat down on a bench next to an ancient woman who was chewing on a betel quid, her red-stained lips and black teeth indicative of a lifetime of usage.

"You're a visitor," the woman stated. It wasn't a question; she undoubtedly knew everyone in the village from birth. "Are you here for our tiger god hunt? It's been years since a tourist has come to watch it."

"I'm just here a few days for work, so I'm unfamiliar with it."

The old woman cackled in reply. "Work? So that means you're single, right? You should meet my daughter Ly. She'll show you firsthand."

"Ma, I told you to stop trying to set me up," said a ruggedly-dressed woman who came up to them. She set down a heavy woven mesh bag bulging with banana-leaf wrapped parcels by the elder's feet, "I'm done shopping so let's not waste this nice lady's time."

The new arrival was around Thu's age but almost her complete inverse physically: where years of daily hiking had made Thu's tall frame sinewy and lean, the other woman was shorter, but with solid, ropy muscles that were beyond impressive for someone in their fifties. Her skin was deeply tanned from working outside and she carried herself with the casual confidence of someone who completely understood their own strength. Thu swallowed hard.

"Your mother was just telling me a bit about the tiger hunt, but I'm still not sure I understand it," she managed to say.

"Yeah? You wanna see this month's hunt?" Ly grinned. "We usually don't let outsiders come along but I'm the head of the hunting committee, so I can make an exception. It's a bit of a hike into the forest but I'd be happy to take you—I was actually just on my way over there."

Thu's instincts told her not to follow this random stranger into the tiger-filled jungle, but the heat rising in her chest and cheeks obliterated any rational objections she might have come up with. "Sure, I'd love to go with you," she said before quickly adding, "to learn about the hunt."

As she followed the hunter away from the village, she looked back at the old woman who winked at her and flashed her a mouth of black-stained teeth.

***

The campsite was not what Thu had expected: the villagers had built an arena-looking structure in a wide clearing. A semicircular ring of net fencing about fifty meters wide was strung up along high wooden poles and lit in the slightly blue cast of bioluminescent flood lights. The center of the arena felt like a theater stage before the curtain rises: empty and waiting for its moment of drama.

Behind this structure was a more prosaic affair, with wooden tables, chairs, and a few tents. Though there weren't any other people visible, the hunters had clearly been here for a few days, judging by the piles of refuse.

Ly dropped the bundle of banana leaf parcels on the table, "Wake up, food's here!"

Bleary-eyed campers came out of their tents, each grabbing a parcel from the table.

Most of the hunters were older, in their forties and fifties, with the exception of a thirty-something man and his daughter, a sullen young girl whose eyes widened in disbelief as soon as she saw Thu.

"This is the crew, except for the lookout, who's in a blind over there, watching for deer," Ly said, pointing to a spot at the mouth of the arena.

"Nice to meet you all." Thu nodded greetings to all of them. "I'm still a little unsure of what's going to happen here, so I'd love it if someone would fill me in before the tigers appear."

The father spoke up, pushing his daughter forward. "My daughter Đông is here to watch us so she can join the hunt when she's older. So why don't you explain to Bà what we're doing here?"

The young girl stiffened, locked eyes with Thu, and began reciting something she'd clearly been forced to memorize: "Our proud village is blessed by the tiger gods. They control the vermin deer who—" Đông paused, taking a few awkward seconds to collect herself while desperately trying to signal something to the yellow witch with her eyes.

"It's alright, Con, you can do it," the father said encouragingly and oblivious.

"They control the vermin deer who destroy our crops, and in their benevolence, herd the deer for us to hunt so that we may provide meat for the village. In exchange we give our thanks, and leave offerings to the tiger gods."

The adults clapped and congratulated the young girl for a wonderful recital and began tucking into their food in earnest. Ly opened a package and shared the pile of sticky rice, mung bean, and venison with Thu.

"So yeah," Ly explained through mouthfuls of food, "every month around the full moon the tigers around here will run around herding the wild deer together and run them in this direction." Ly gestured to net. "We built that net in the game trail they use and snag them as they run. It's a good deal for both sides: we get the deer without having to hunt, and kill a few to leave for the tigers, who don't have to risk being gored by antlers."

"Wow, that's amazing," Thu said, impressed. I've heard of dolphins doing that with fish, but never tigers. They must be very intelligent."

Ly shrugged. "I dunno. Either genius tigers or tiger gods, I don't really care; all I know is that it's been a blessing. With the harvests getting smaller and smaller each year, we can't afford to let these deer run wild and eat our crops, and the meat's really delicious too, wouldn't you say?"

"It is." The meat *was* good, but Thu truly relished the click of her chopsticks against Ly's as they would reach for the same morsel. It'd been years since she'd shared a meal with anyone and it felt so intimate. Too intimate.

"So's the company," Ly said, as if echoing her thoughts.

Thu flushed like a schoolgirl. She was the feared yellow witch but all she wanted to do was stand up and flee in embarrassment. She took a deep breath and tried to change the subject into less dangerous territory. "So, uh, how's this month's hunt going? I thought the full moon was a few days back."

This touched a nerve; the older hunter spat into the fire. "It's the damnedest thing. Even with the dwindling number of deer we've been getting each month, they're late. Very late. Normally we'd be back home making venison jerky by now, but there hasn't been a single sighting all week, not a single tiger or deer. That's why I've got the lookout camped out in the blind to watch for any sign. I refuse to miss this deer run."

Calmer now that the talk had turned to practical things, Thu took another bite of the food and thoughtfully chewed. She could start to see the chain of cause and effect at play here, and her role in it all, but needed to make an excuse to talk to Đông first. Thankfully, Ly did it for her.

"Oh that reminds me. Hey Đông, can you go relieve the lookout for a bit while he eats? He's probably starving after being on watch all day." Ly turned back to Thu and smiled, the firelight dancing in her eyes.

"Actually, would it be alright if I went with her?" Thu asked, as innocently as she could. "I'm something of a student of nature and would like to see more of this habitat and observe some of the wildlife."

Disappointment briefly flashed on the other woman's face, but it was quickly hidden behind the same jovial attitude as before. "Of course. Đông, can you take Bà Thu here with you?"

"Thanks, dear." Thu gently touched Ly's arm as she got up. There was a part of her that regretted leaving the woman's company, but time was of the essence and she needed to know exactly what she was dealing with. "I'll be back shortly, okay?"

Thu and the young girl walked in silence over to the blind, the tension thick in the air. On seeing them approach, the sentry in the blind leapt out, brimming with joy at being relieved of his sentry duty. The young man had barely walked out of earshot before Đông's pressurized excitement exploded into a frenzy of whispering and tears. "Oh my god, are you really here? I knew you'd come. You have to help me— I— I— was desperate and I— And my dad is going to find out— and I—"

"Shh now," Thu consoled the child, drawing her close. "It's okay. It's going to be alright."

When Đông's sobs finally died down, Thu spoke to her carefully. "I think I understand what's going on. You want to protect your friends, the deer, right?"

The girl squeezed Thu tightly, nodding.

"Your mom said you'd made something that would help them?"

Đông bawled, furiously wiping the tears away. She pulled a small glass jar out of her pocket and held it out. Inside was a deep green, almost black liquid. Thu carefully uncapped it, wafting the scent of the liquid to her nose: a sharp herbaceous smell, like a mixture of camphor and mint.

"Đông," Thu addressed the girl slowly, trying to make her understand the gravity of the situation, "what have you been doing with this? What does it do?"

"I— I— couldn't let them catch my friends. I—" The rest was lost to sobs.

"Show me what you did," Thu said, fearing the worst.

The girl nodded, wiping down tears, and led her away from the campsite, down the game trail, and into the dark, teeming forest.

***

They walked for nearly an hour under the light of the waning moon until Đông somehow found a hidden side trail that led to a small clearing in front of a rocky outcrop. It seemed empty at first but Thu froze when she saw what was perched on top of the pile of stones: the profile of a predator yawning lazily against the night sky. The woman gripped Đông's arm tightly, shocked that this girl was either brave or foolish enough to lead them to the tigers' den.

Ready to throw herself between Đông and the animal, Thu was astonished to see the large cat leap down off the rocks and retrieve a white object from somewhere inside its cave. It was hard to see in the dim moonlight, but Thu realized it was a cloth bundle the size of a grapefruit. The tiger pulled it into the clearing with its powerful jaws but dropped the bundle and started to roll around on the ground with it, playfully nuzzling up against fabric.

Both woman and child watched mesmerized as another tiger emerged from the den and joined the first in its game, pouncing on the first with the ferocity of a housecat. Thu and Đông watched in rapt silence as the tigers alternated between swatting the bundle around and rolling lazily together without a care in the world, the two animals acting as if they were drugged.

Because they are, Thu realized, astonished by this girl's ingenuity. Not wanting to press their luck any further, Thu had Đông lead them back to the blind where the cocktail of adrenaline in her system and awe at the girl's audacity exploded into incredulous laughter.

"A bag of catnip!" Thu exclaimed to a weak smile from Đông. "I can't even believe you thought of that."

"Catnip concentrate, actually. And not just catnip either," the girl said more proudly now. "I mixed it with the Russian Sage Mom uses to keep the deer out of the garden. The more the tigers rub it on themselves, the more they'll be covered in deer repellant. They'll smell them coming from far away, no matter how quiet they are."

Thu shook her head, a delighted grin across her face. "Here I thought I would have to figure out how to pump a tiger's stomach."

"I did okay?" The need for approval on Đông's face broke Thu's heart. She knew what it felt like to never be understood by the people around you, not even your loved ones.

Thu was torn. The adventurer scientist part of her wanted to crow this girl's achievements from the mountaintops, but part of her knew she should be the sober adult right now. "Well, I do appreciate your ingenuity, but it's never safe dosing any creature with drugs. I'm sure the tigers will be fine eventually, but you do realize this is only a short-term solution, right?"

Đông tensed, like she'd been expecting this. "I just didn't know what else I could do."

"I understand, and you were very clever and very brave, but you can't be out here every full moon doing this. If the tigers go too long without food, they may decide that *people* are worth hunting, do you understand?"

The girl recoiled in shock. "They wouldn't do that would they? There are wild pigs and monkeys and—"

"Even *if* the tigers stay friendly, if the deer eat the crops, the villagers will eventually starve without the meat to replace them."

"But we can plant deer repellent herbs. They'll leave the rice alone."

Thu shook her head. "Everything is interlinked: deer, tigers, people, plants. If one goes out of balance, so do the others. Do you know why I'm here, Con? Your village hired me because the harvests are failing. That's the root cause for all this—the soil is too polluted. Right now the deer meat supplements the food supplies during the winter, but if the crops fail and there's no deer, people will starve."

Hit by the weight of her actions, the girl began to cry. "I didn't want anyone to get hurt, I just—"

Thu reached down and wiped Đông's tears. "No real harm was done, and you weren't wrong in trying to help the animals. And you've already given me an idea of how we can help everyone. So I think between an old witch and a young genius like you, we can find a solution." She winked.

***

The village meeting was contentious. When Thu explained the situation and suggested her plan of suspending the hunts and introducing Đông's deer-dropping fertilizer, drip irrigation, and mixed planting techniques, there was immediate opposition. The traditional ways were hard to let go of and well ingrained in the culture.

Surprisingly, Ly was their loudest ally. "We all know the hunts have been less productive each year. It's time we ease up and let the deer recover before they're gone entirely. I'm not going to let our children's children grow up in a world without deer or tigers."

There was still one skeptical farmer among the crowd though. "All of these new things are exciting, but even with deer fertilizer, the soil on my farm is still too polluted to grow, and we'd have to dredge the entire river before we got enough silt to make up for it." A hesitant murmur went through the crowd.

Thu opened her worn backpack. "This is why your village leaders originally asked me to come." She drew out one of the metal thermoses inside and uncapped the top, pouring a small pile of white powder onto a piece of paper on the counter. "These are Lentinus squarrosulus spores. They're a bioremedial fungus that naturally degrade toxic chemicals in your farmland into safer compounds. Within six months, there will be fewer toxins and more nutrients available for your plants. I'll show you how to mix these with your rice straw and deer fertilizer and have your farms thriving again before the next planting season."

Ly spoke up. "You've given us a lot to think about, but I don't think I'm alone in saying that it's pretty daunting to do on our own." The crowd murmured in assent, farmers and hunters exchanging glances.

"It won't be easy, but I think it's possible," the yellow witch said cautiously. Was this too much to ask of them? It was a hard sell even in less desperate villages.

"Maybe, but our chances of succeeding would be higher with some expert guidance to help us, right?" Ly said, with a sly grin. The crowd murmured in agreement.

"And if someone were there to teach us more about the science," Đông said casually, trying not to sound too pleading.

Thu sighed, frowning theatrically before finally breaking and beaming with her genuine heartfelt smile. "I suppose it would be pretty irresponsible of me not to help you see this through since I've asked you to disrupt your entire way of life. Okay, I'll stay—at least for the first harvest."

***

Kate V. Bui is a Vietnamese-American trans lady from the Pacific Northwest. Kate has been world building her whole life in role-playing games and visual art, but this is her first published work of fiction. You can reach her at https://katevbui.com/

Vladivostok
Avital Balwit

Ronan had grown up on the other edge of the boreal—in British Columbia. The same undergrowth and soil blanketed her home. Whenever she felt lonely, she'd imagine the roots and rhizomes reaching all the way beneath the ocean, communicating and feeding the trees she'd known. Sometimes she'd place her hands in the freezing sea and imagine the water washing all the way back to her coast. Pangea had squished these landscapes together. The boreal used to be a splotch, more circular than band.

She and Bryan had been traveling for three weeks. Seoul, Beijing, and now northward to these frigid trees to find their real reason for the trip. The Amur tigers had returned to Vladivostok. In this frozen region between Changchun, Vladivostok and Pyongyang, where jungle meets tundra meets boreal, tigers as large as cars wander silently through the woods.

Ronan had read online that you could go and see them now, track them through the forest. Of course you and they were always tracking each other—they knew you were there and watched back. It used to be too dangerous, the tigers violent and massive. They broke into homes and dismembered hunters and loggers in the woods. It turns out they had been violent because they were wounded. Once people stopped shooting at them and the last tigers full of buckshot died, leaving their unmarred cubs, an equilibrium returned.

Right around when she heard about the tigers, Metropolis announced their New Species contest. The winner received 10 million Metro dollars, status badges, and a special reception. Ronan had played Metropolis for years, an engrossing, virtual reality game where you lived and worked in a place which combined all of the world's wonders into one mega city. She had saved part of her state stipend to buy an expensive VR rig so that she could feel everything in it. It's also how she had met Bryan—at a local Metropolis meetup two years ago.

"I spent more time in Metropolis than Vancouver." He'd said, "It's more real to me."

Bryan worked as a 3D artist, so Metropolis had naturally been attractive. After the game became popular, his main work switched from soft drink advertisements to helping people customize their characters. In some of their first messages he'd explained:

"I help them look however they want to look. I find the freedom beautiful. In the physical world, you're born with the body you get, doesn't matter if it doesn't fit you. In Metropolis, you can be old, young, genderless, winged, tattooed, animalian. And you can change everyday."

His own avatar reflected this: He had a sleeve of tattoos that constantly shifted with colors reflecting his emotions, or played clips of movies he loved. They started dating six months after they met, and a year after that, decided to do the contest together. They fixed their hopes for the contest on the Amur tiger—they'd go film and intricately model it, then bring it into the game.

She'd written to the Vladivostok wildlife conservation organization, asking if they had any tiger experts or anyone who had seen the tigers in the city. They'd told her to contact "Alek." That's how she'd found herself at the northeast fringes of the city, near two schools, a post office, and a derelict shopping mall, waiting in an empty juice cafe for a stranger.

Alek was in his late fifties. He had thick gray hair pulled back in a pony-tail and spoke English with a warm smile and a rich accent. He greeted them and led them the few blocks to his house. His wife Marya was several years younger, short, broad shouldered and matter-of-fact. They had four children, all grown but two still in Vladivostok. Alexandra, their oldest daughter, had children of her own, one of which, six year old Anya, was playing in their living room when they arrived. Bryan and Ronan gingerly entered the small house. Heat from the woodstove embraced them. The walls were covered in photographs of the boreal wilderness—snow-capped peaks, towering pines. There were older pictures of logging and hunting perhaps from their parents' generation. Marya made them coffee and handed them heavy ceramic plates bearing thick slices of cake. Alek spoke English, while Marya wore a thin headband-like translator to understand them, then replied in clipped phrases.

Ronan and Bryan were initially embarrassed that in classic foreign arrogance, they had not bought their own translators. Marya and Alek reassured them that translator bands were common in a region where Russian, Chinese, and Korean speakers mingled so often. They told Ronan and Bryan about their family—longtime residents of this region—their children, and the tigers. Ronan and Bryan thanked them profusely. There were no hotels in the so-called tiger neighborhoods, and Alek was one of the city's best trackers. Staying here would make the filming much faster.

Alexandra arrived to say goodbye to Anya and to drop off Mihael, her three year old. Alexandra was tall and darked-haired, with high cheekbones and accentless English, only a few years older than Ronan. She had Marya's strong shoulders, and Alek's twinkling eyes. She didn't find it odd to see the two Canadians in her parents' living room, merely asking what had brought the two travelers to Vladivostok.

"We came to film the tigers. We're trying to build a digital re-creation to take into an online world. Have you ever played

Metropolis?"

Alexandra nodded politely, "I've heard of it."

Bryan continued, "It's amazing. It's every city you could want combined. Every person can fit there, in any body they want. Sometimes it feels more real than here. You can add stuff too, and you get a lot of money and notice if you do—that's why we're here for the tigers."

Marya spoke suddenly, "You know, you aren't the first to scan them."

Bryan's face fell precipitously. Marya continued, "Five years ago, some nonprofit came through. They thought the tigers were almost extinct, so they took all these pictures—like a digital ark. They said they wanted to keep a version for humanity."

Alek explained how the tigers had almost died out. In 2015, there had only been a few hundred left. Shrinking territory and increasing confrontations with humans had left them wounded and starving. It had been the US treaty with North Korea which saved them. The treaty had widened the buffer zone between North and South Korea and spurred the removal of the landmines—the UN had finally gotten to them. It was in this strange, empty landscape with watchtowers framed on the horizon like skinny, unnatural mountains, and the hum of drones far above in the sky that the tiger population recovered. They bred there, undisturbed, and fed on the other returning wildlife. The many cameras watched them slink over areas once lethal to any living thing, paws placed over holes vacated by landmines, cubs playing where barbed wire fences used to jut. From that strip they prowled northward, towards their ancestral home. Now, more than a decade later, they had grown even bolder and had started wandering through cities themselves. They were seen in Vladivostok neighborhoods for the first time two years ago, one even as far as old town, but mostly they stayed in the northeast of the city—near enough to the wild zone to retreat if needed.

Alek shrugged at the nonprofit's efforts, "We didn't get it, to be honest. A picture isn't a tiger."

After a brief panic Ronan and Bryan realized that whoever that nonprofit had been filming for, they clearly weren't using it for Metropolis. They would have uploaded it by now—this wasn't the first species contest.

Marya left her husband and daughter with the grandkids, Mihael now squalling at the prospect of a goodbye, and led them next door to where they would be staying. It was an old convenience store attached to the side of the house.

"We used to serve the whole neighborhood, but now you can get anything delivered by drone. People don't want to make the walk in the winter. I'd put you in the house, but we're watching my grandkids for a few weeks while Alexandra travels."

It looked like the store was mostly used for the family's outdoor gear. Snowmobiles sat next to tent poles and skis.

Marya, like most people, didn't work anymore. "When we started getting the checks in the mail, we thought it was a joke or a mistake. We don't follow politics in Moscow—you can imagine, it's a half a world away. But they kept coming, and it made shutting the store easier."

Now, Marya and Alek seemed to hike and watch the grandkids full-time. Bryan unpacked their backpacks in the corner and brought out their cameras. Ronan startled when what looked like a small, curled-up coat unrolled in the corner. The cat regarded Ronan with liquid golden eyes. At first it looked like a house cat, but as it stretched Ronan saw the webbed toes and the intricate markings.

"That's Asha, she's a leopard cat, sometimes called a Siberian wildcat. Someone ran over her foot when she was a cub. We found her and fixed her up. If you look out into the backyard during the night, you might see her family. We never thought they'd come back for her, but they do."

"And she goes out to them?"

"Yes, she does."

"Why doesn't she just leave?"

"Her back paw never fully healed, she limps. I think they realize she wouldn't survive if she joined them."

The next day, Alek drove them around and helped them set up cameras. Sometimes he'd show them a mark in the thick, frigid ground and explain a track, although none were clear enough for them to make out.

"Some people think they're living in the city, in the old school's basement. I still think they live in the woods, but we do see them almost every night."

"Don't people mind the tigers? Aren't they afraid?" Bryan asked.

"They aren't, surprisingly. As we've gotten less violent, so have they. But still, if one gets too close for comfort, you use a sonic gun. It's only fair, since the tigers themselves use sound to stun their prey—they have a roar so low as to be on the edge of hearing, calibrated to paralyze their victim. You just point the sound-gun and the tiger will freeze and slink away, or just fade far enough into the pines to let you wander on."

"Why did people shoot them in the past? Was it for sport?" Bryan asked, no hint of irony, only a gentle curiosity.

"Perhaps sport for some, but for most, it was necessity. We used to have to log and hunt to live, it meant we were constantly fighting the Taiga." Alek used the older word for the boreal, the Russian one. "Now that the government sends the checks, we don't have to. Food is delivered whenever we need it, and we can always pay for heat. You'd think that would have stopped people going out into nature, but they haven't. The people who stay in Vladivostok love it here. They take their copters to ski, hike, spot whales. They birdwatch and collect mushrooms. Now that we don't need so much from the Taiga, we can love it. And the Taiga knows. That's why more animals have come into the city."

They fell back into silence, walking from block to block to lay and conceal the small, weatherproofed cameras. They had a tiny heatsource to melt the snow and ice that would otherwise quickly cover them. Alek told them that his great grandfather was Nivkh, a member of one of the original tribes that populated the Amur region. His Russian side also came to the region more than a century ago. He said the Taiga was in his blood.

***

Alek said his middle son, Innokenty, would take them on an aerial tour of Vladivostok if they wanted. Innokenty and Alexandra had settled near home, while his other son Boris had moved to Beijing, and the youngest daughter, Tanya, to Moscow. Apparently most children here left for the megacities, more often Changchun, Shenyang, or Beijing, since they were closer, but sometimes Moscow or St. Petersburg. Marya's mother was from Changchun, so Boris had first moved there to see family, and then had made the move to Beijing.

Innokenty arrived that afternoon in a minicopter, a four-seat vehicle made of slick metal with huge windows. Ronan and Bryan had seen them parked all over the city; apparently, they made much more sense than cars and even trains with the ground icy most of the year. Innokenty was taller than Alek, with a warm smile and his mother's dark eyes. He greeted the Canadians with a firm handshake, and began to chat cheerfully in Russian before making a look of horror and switching on his translator. The device took his voice and reformatted it in English. Thankfully the days of the eerie digital assistant voices were over, at least as far as translators went.

"Welcome to Vladivostok. I'm sorry, you can tell I don't use translators often. Have you ridden in a copter before?" They explained they hadn't, although Ronan had taken a slightly larger version over London on a tour once.

Innokenty saw Asha and scooped her up. The cat eyed him with a resigned expression. He explained how once he'd stepped on her tail accidentally and almost lost a toe. Asha seemed to smile at the memory.

The copter ride was icy and beautiful. Innokenty first flew north towards the Sikhote-Alin mountains. He tried to point them out in the distance, but it might have just been a trick of the light—they were so faint. Later, they flew south over the silver-veined network of high speed rail that led from Vladivostok across the Chinese border, the first ten miles or so under the port itself. He left the copter on autopilot to drift south over the port while he turned to tell the pair about his hiking adventures, the meteorite that had rained down on the region decades ago, and all the animals he'd seen. They landed two hours later, and Innokenty stayed over for dinner. Alek made stew.

He smiled at Ronan. "The venison is artificial, I know you don't eat real meat."

Ronan thanked him.

***

Ronan was reviewing their footage in the living room while Bryan entertained Anya with blocks.

"Sometimes I worry Asha won't come back," Anya told Bryan.

"Then why don't you just keep her inside?" Bryan asked.

"Would you only want to stay inside?"

"I mean, I kind of like to."

"Oh." Anya didn't seem to know what to make of that. She tipped over her block pile and thought for a moment. "I don't think I'd like that. Besides, I think Asha would come visit even if she left."

Ronan later asked if Bryan really thought he could always live inside.

"Sure. That's the point of Metropolis right? You never have to leave. It has everything you want. And we can build nature there, right? Like that's what we're doing here."

"But when we play Metropolis, we're actually there. The animals aren't. They're just programs."

"What does that matter? They look the same, they seem the same."

"It's different. They've got souls you know, they aren't just shells."

Bryan shrugged in response. Ronan felt awkward spending so much time with Bryan. They had spent most of their year and a half together in the game, going on virtual adventures, decorating their Metropohome. Of course they'd seen each other in person too, but this was the longest they'd spent together face-to-face. In Metropolis, you could change your appearance every day, or even more often if you chose. It was strange to see Bryan locked into this one form—sandy haired and scrawny, nothing like his typical avatar with sleeve tattoos and silver white hair. Ronan thought he probably felt the same about her.

***

It was Tuesday, the end of their first week, when Alek woke them in the middle of the night.

"Get dressed, I've found one."

Alek and Innokenty were waiting on the porch, bundled warmly in the dark. They greeted them with a silent nod before walking gently into the road. Innokenty handed Ronan a sonic gun and motioned to her how to fire it. "Won't need, probably," he whispered in English. They followed Alek stealthily down the street past the deserted parking lot by the juice cafe and the mall, where a streetlight buzzed in the entryway. Five streets north, Alek slowed. Ronan passed Bryan the sonic gun so she could hold her camera. They saw a shape detach from the shadows by a house with darkened windows. The tiger came into view slowly, one striped inch at a time. It was across the intersection, just thirty feet away, watching them. It started forward, slowly, with no sign of aggression. A boom rattled the empty street. Bryan had fired the sonic gun and the dark shape retreated back around the next house. Alek whacked him over the head with the camera bag.

"Why did you do that! It did nothing to you."

"I'm sorry! I'm sorry! It got so close. I was scared."

"Idiot. I'm only taking Ronan next trip. You can review footage from home."

Innokenty glanced at Ronan quickly; his smile was amused. They started back towards the house in silence.

There were no tigers for the next few nights. Meanwhile, Innokenty took them on day trips. They took the copter to hike nearby hills, they skied in the early snowfall. On Tuesday, he invited them to explore Vladivostok proper.

"Let's walk the main street, Svetlanskaya. It gives you a taste of the city's history."

Svetlanskaya held a mix of newer insulated glass buildings, and older art nouveau porticos and Soviet constructivist blocks (one affectionately nicknamed by locals "the inserted tooth"). It also contained many of the city's memorials: a sculpture of an American woman who fell in love with Vladivostok in the early 20th century, a monument to the pacific fleet in World War 2, swarthy Soviet soldiers and workers in cast iron, and a few blocks off Svetlanskaya, a sculpture to a singer who'd visited the city in 1971 which still played his songs through tinny speakers.

Bryan paused in front of an elaborate art nouveau building that took up most of a block. It looked like someone had plopped a piece of the Louvre with its castle-like roofs down on this icy street.

"That's an old department store. Built by Germans. Been here for forever."

Bryan was already crouching down and rustling through his backpack. He retrieved a paper sketch pad—his only lowtech habit.

"I have to draw it. I want to design a roof like this in Metropolis."

Innokenty looked amused, but as he watched Bryan carefully position himself on a curb and set to work, undisturbed by the biting breeze, he became intrigued.

"Would you mind if I joined you? If I could have a page. I don't know the last time I drew—I'd like to learn."

Bryan motioned him over and retrieved another sketchbook from his bag. Ronan shook her head in disbelief at the two men hunched in the cold over their sketchbooks glancing up at the building's roof.

"I'm going to head towards the war museum. You're welcome to join whenever you're done with your masterpieces."

She turned at the edge of the block, and saw Bryan drawing the portico with his hands in the air and explaining something to Innokenty. She smiled at the strangeness of it all.

On Friday, Bryan stayed at home while Ronan and Innokenty coptered to the port to look for whales. They didn't talk too much, because Ronan's Russian was poor, and Innokenty hated the translator band. Ronan asked if he played Metropolis. Innokenty gave her a ragged smile.

"Yeah, I've played."

"You didn't like it?"

"Why would I need it? I've got this." He gestured at the gray water of the port, the clean white sail-shaped arches of the bridge. "It's all the city I need." Gulls wheeled overhead in the pale light.

***

The sun was sinking when Ronan set out. Her snow-boots crunched on the thin layer of ice which had formed over the older snow. She headed east past the elementary school. It got even darker as the houses thinned and she neared the highway. She resisted the urge to flick on her headlight. "You learn to see in the dark," Alek had said. She stood in an empty street by a vacant lot, a distant streetlight the only illumination besides the thin strip of moon. She felt the presence of the tiger long before she saw it. Twenty feet. Sixteen feet. Eight feet. It wouldn't matter now if she raised the sonic gun, it could close the gap with one leap. One strike enough to end her life. She looked at its massive jaw, its amber eyes. It was ten feet long, likely a large adult male. She stood perfectly still and so did he. A minute passed, and then another. A soft sound from behind him caught her attention, but he didn't turn. Another tiger was loping into view, this one smaller and paler, probably the mate. She did not stop to regard Ronan, and padded past less than ten feet away. The larger tiger followed, heading westward. Maybe towards their home in the school basement, maybe deep into the woods. They might pass some cameras on the way, but most likely not. Something told Ronan that these tigers didn't want to go to Metropolis. They didn't want immortality—they already had it. Ronan shivered in the street, her body still felt the massive presence—like a God or some celestial body swung low, pulling at her slightly.

Fourteen days after they'd arrived they had the footage. They'd started modelling from it, and it looked like they'd be able to take multiple tiger copies into the game. They wished they had cubs too, but it likely wouldn't happen unless they stayed half a year to breeding season. Bryan had gone into town and purchased top-shelf Scottish peat whiskey, Alek's favorite, and smoked salmon for Marya, as a thank you present. They'd booked tickets home for that Thursday.

Ronan was collecting their cameras from around the neighborhood when she heard the soft swoosh of the chopper land. The electric engine made them almost silent. Innokennty stepped out grinning. He clicked on the band.

"You should have seen the sea eagles in the bay. Now that's something for your game. They were so loud today, so playful." He noticed the cameras in her hands. "Are you done then?"

"Yes, we're leaving in two days."

"You could always stay till spring. See the cubs."

"I don't know if I could take the Vladivostok winter."

He eyed her carefully before smiling softly at the snow. "Something makes me think you could stand the winter. It's him I worry about."

On Wednesday night, she lay awake in the store room. She'd dragged her sleeping bag away from Bryan, who'd been tossing in his sleep. She had drifted off when she woke to a low, deep sound reverberating through the streets. She peered into the darkness and noticed Asha had joined them in the night. She was also staring towards the window, ears alert. Maybe there was some deep connection between Asha and the tiger. Some genetic knowledge that far back through time, they had been one. Ronan made her way past the empty shelves to the window just in time to see a dark, faintly striped bulk slip past the post office and into the alley beyond. She opened her computer and started working.

She was woken late by Bryan.

"You sent me all the files, processed and everything. You know we could have done that on the plane or at home right?"

"I'm not coming."

"You're what?"

"I want to stay here."

"But, we have what we came for. We're probably going to win the species prize on Metropolis. Think about it. We'd be like Darwin, but in a better world, superstars in the most important city or country ever invented. Why would you stay at the edge of the world in this freezing nowhere of a place?"

"You hate it that much?"

"It's foreign to me, Ronan. It's unreadable, unyielding. I can't change anything about it. Or myself. I feel trapped."

"That's not true. You've changed even in these past few weeks, Bryan, you've built block castles with Anya, taught Innokenty to draw, you've hiked, skied, flown."

"It's too wild here Ronan. I'm sorry. I miss my VR set, Metropolis." He laughed, "I miss not having to wear a thermal suit to survive outside."

Ronan stayed quiet. "What will you do here?" Bryan asked.

She smiled as Asha padded into the room. "Well, today, Innokenty is going to show me the sea eagles."

***

Avital Balwit studies political philosophy and technology regulation. She writes short stories, essays, and poetry. She has been a finalist in essay contests for The New York Times and The Economist, and she won The Atlantic's 2020 Instagram poetry contest. She has work forthcoming in *The Society of Misfit Stories, Meetinghouse,* and *Addition Magazine.* Her young adult book on octopus cognition, *That Thing,* will be published by Pop-Up UK in spring 2021.

The Exuberant Vitality of Hatchling Habitats
D.A. Xiaolin Spires

I said we should go small, like tiny, little ant sculptures, smaller than the clay sculptures that my mom had in the banzai pots. But, Camila wanted to go big. Really big. She said big was impressive. She held out her hands, stretching her arms wide and tall, as far as they could go, as if to suggest, *even my body can't convey how big I want it to be.*

I shrugged and said, "Okay." I read over the science fair rules to make sure it would work. There wasn't a size dimension limit.

Camila loved art and especially murals. She loved ones filled with seashells and found-items tacked on. She said she wanted to focus on material arts and come up with new ways to paint and for artists to express themselves. Her personality was always as big as her ideas— dressed up in loud colors with bold patterns, iridescent polo shirts splattered with faux-feathers over ripped up purple jeans. That kind of thing.

I just liked tinkering. We compromised on a sculpture, one that was assembled bottom-up. Ms. Brown, who was our most supportive teacher, had given us a thumbs-up on the project. I got to build and Camila got to mix, paint and spray. We both were happy.

"I'm imagining Statue of Liberty," Camila said. She waved an invisible torch.

"That's a bit too big, isn't it?"

"Fine, how about the Christmas Tree at the mall?"

"You really think that size is feasible?"

"With our minds together? You and me? Exacting Xueli and Resourceful Camila. Sure, we can do anything," she said.

I checked the brochure again to make sure the exhibition hall ceiling was high enough. Twenty-seven meters. Not bad. Doable.

***

I biked over to Camila's house, dropping off rinds and discarded peels of gourds, wintermelons, broccoli, apples and carrots from my parents' restaurant, as she requested.

"What are you doing with these things anyway?" I asked, handing over the bag. "Starting a compost?"

She took it and poured out the contents onto her worktable. She threw a tie-dye apron over her green and purple polka-dotted shirt. "I'm working on sustainable materials. I'm thinking, best case scenario: the sculpture will wear down over time."

Camila started sorting through the pile, sniffing, scrunching her nose and running her finger over the peels. She put them on a scale and jotted down some numbers. Around her were brushes, paint tubes, shells, stones, bottle caps and rows of jars full of powders.

I picked up one jar full of pink dust, twisted off the cap and tossed the metal cap in the air.

"Heads or tails?" I asked.

"Heads," said Camila, not looking up.

It landed heads, right-side-up, on the table with a ding-ding as it swirled to a stop.

"Go you," I said, taking a sniff into the jar. It smelled like chalk. I coughed.

"So, the sculpture will wear down? It'll just fall apart?" I asked, covering my mouth as I hacked.

"Not really fall apart but decompose over an extended time. Maybe two years?"

My coughs died away. I wiped my mouth with my hand.

"A sculpture that melts in the rain. Hm," I said, capping the jar. I imagined a popsicle on a sunny day, dripping and pooling onto the ground.

"A sculpture that integrates into its environment. It's to emphasize the cyclical and ephemeral, the always changing aspects of nature."

"Sure, okay," I said.

"But, you sound doubtful."

"It's just—I don't see how a dissolving sculpture might be terribly versatile."

"Yup, you're absolutely right. And that's why from an engineering standpoint, I also added the option to retain rigidity and make the sculpture more lasting with an application of a cohesion spray, even years after its original construction. It overrides the decomposition function. Not really what I envisioned, but I figure it makes more sense for wider application."

That was what I liked about Camila. It wasn't that she compromised her artistic vision, but she took into account practical utilization. I helped Camila throw some rinds into the desiccator. But, my mind wasn't entirely there. I was staring at the smoothness of the glass on the desiccating machine, working out in my head how to angle the smooth blades for the helicopter movement of the drone I was working on back at home. Next to the desiccation machine, a paint agitator spun.

"How's the giant drone doing?" she asked, speaking over the noise. She was reading my mind like she always does.

"Not one giant drone. Many small drones," I said. I pinched the air around me as if to indicate little bugs whizzing around.

She looked up for a moment then looked back down. "Ooh, sounds busy. A hive, huh. I like it."

She started humming as she added several powders and put on a surgical mask. I pulled out some desiccated rinds from the machine's inner container and placed them on paper towels. She said I should probably leave, since she didn't have a mask for me and she was about to start the blending process. I didn't want my asthma to start up, so I headed out. As I was leaving I heard the whir of the industrial blender go.

***

The helicopter blades I created were light, sleek and tenacious. The bodies of the drones were no bigger than golf balls, but they were tough as armor. I coated them in polish, so they would shine under the exhibition lights. After all, half of it was theatrics to catch the attention of the judges.

Camila and I combed through specs of tiny printers to find the perfect one to install into the drones. We had to tweak them—drill out the nozzle hole a bit more to allow for the extra viscosity of her fluid creation, flatten parts to fit into the drones and bevel surfaces for aerodynamic considerations. We had to be sure the printers were installed in a balanced way, so the helicopter blades could counteract gusts and provide steadiness for the 3-D sustainaink stream. That was Camila's term for her gooey creation. Sustainaink.

After all that, we had to map out our sculpture. We wanted something recognizable, but new at the same time.

***

On the day of the fair, we moved the base of the sculpture into the exhibition hall. All the parents walked around, gazing at the incoming projects. Some looked at the emptiness of our creation, as we set up. They looked bemused. *Just some drones sitting on a pedestal? Even my eight-year old could do drones*, I imagined them saying. (Even if ours were sophisticated, efficient and tiny.)

We let out the rest of the drones from our backpacks and let the buzzing begin.

They zipped around us above our heads, piling on layer after layer. The judges were making their rounds, asking questions. They hadn't gotten to us yet.

Footsteps came to us, looked at the commotion in the air and all the streaming and spattering. Palms covered laughing mouths at the

81

squirting noises, sounding so much like gas expulsions.

We wouldn't be judged until Day Two. Slowly our sculpture grew bigger and bigger.

***

When we arrived, stepping through the doors for Day Two judging, we groaned. We had set the ink drones on autorun overnight as we planned and created a masterpiece—of sorts.

We hurried past the holographic nebulas, the volcanic eruptions and towards our towering creation at the other end of the hall.

The SustainaThinker, though impressively large, the height of a bowling ball lane set upright, was laughable. We had come up with the perfect sculpture to emulate: Rodin's The Thinker, except with a seagull on its shoulder. That wasn't the part that was funny though.

It was totally gross.

The drones buzzed around me, but I couldn't really stand proud. What was supposed to be The Thinker looked more like Swiss cheese. Both in construction and in jaundiced color. And it smelled pretty foul, too.

A man came to us. He had narrow eyes and this supercilious expression. I wondered if one of his kids was a competitor and he was here to gloat. But, he started asking us questions. "JUDGE," his badge read. He called another judge over.

They took a minute to stare into the closed eyes of our giant, porous The Thinker. I could almost imagine what they were thinking. Why all the holes? Why this jagged, unrefined look? This vapid, sickly color? Where were the continuous streamlined contours of a triumphant statue? One of the judges lifted her nose up and sniffed and coughed. I'm sure there's no way the judges didn't smell it. A mix of rotten cheese and sewer. All the noises of the room, the suctioning sounds of pressure changes, the motors and parents chatting seemed to recede as they stared at the placard that had our names and short bios. It occurred to me that these exhibition lights and the new density of the porous sculpture made the gorgeous swatch color I saw in the prototype end up looking like this hideous off-color puke.

"So, Xueli and Camila, why The Thinker?" the first judge said. "And why add a bird to it?" He blew a tuft of hair away and gave us a good stare.

"Well," I said, clearing my throat. "We wanted to capture this idea of something recognizable but also pensive, something with weight but also a bit of levity."

Camila jumped in. If I didn't know better, I'd say she was shaking from nervousness. She kept twitching her feet below her hot pink leggings. "We were out on the boardwalk one day and saw a seagull picking on a discarded box of french fries."

"French fries?" This black-haired judge looked skeptical.

"Yeah. Not the fries themselves, but the box. It was putting its beak desperately through the box, making holes and swallowing."

"Doesn't seem healthy," said the judge.

"It's not." Camila had a faraway look, a sad expression in her eyes.

I piped in, gesturing towards the window. "People think there are a lot of seabirds, because they see them scavenging human garbage. I mean, sometimes we even see them in the square, flipping trash with their beaks. But, after we saw the poor seagull attacking this piece of cardboard…"

"…cardboard with grease-resistant coating made of carboxylated styrene-butadiene emulsion polymers," added Camila. She was always the materials girl, but the glazed look on the judges' faces told me we were losing them.

I jumped in again. "Yes, after we saw it take pecks at this cardboard litter coated with grease-resistant gunk probably not good for their diet, we thought, 'Hey, this one doesn't look too great. Its feathers looks shaggy. It looks kind of hungry.'"

"But, seagulls are everywhere." The black-haired judge wasn't cutting us a break. "I've seen them wreaking havoc in every city I've traveled to. They look rotund, well-fed… and aggressive."

"Yes, but they're scavengers, naturally. So they go where the food is. We did some research and found out what seabirds should be eating, like live crabs and small fish."

"You can tell by their jaws," said Camila. "Large prey fit in there." She unhinged her mouth and made two big bites.

"Yup," I laughed. The judges didn't join in on the laughter but one did move the corners of her mouth up a little. Camila and I looked at each other, in hope. But, my smile petered away. "I hate to kill the mood, but, unfortunately, it's a sad thing. This is what I found out. Gulls, like herring gulls, are coming in droves to cities inland precisely because they have to. Intensive human fishing leaves their chicks with less food. So does warming waters from climate change. To add to that, higher temperatures induced by climate change also foster pathogens which result in bird deaths, such as from avian botulism, prevalent among gulls. And, I should add, along the coasts, conversion of land into agriculture and places of livestock also threatens them. Far from abundant, a lot of these species are in danger."

The judges looked as morose as us, and the black-haired judge looked a little sheepish, too. They were eerily quiet.

"There's another reason we put in the gull," I said, elbowing Camila.

Camila broke the somber mood. "We thought it would be funny. The Thinker—with a seagull! Plus copyright issues. So, we thought about that encounter with the seagull and french fry box and added a bird on his shoulder. Besides the symbolic meaning, about thinking of the ecosystem, we figured adding our own artistic version of it won't step on any toes." The judges still remained silent. Camilla must have felt self-conscious because her voice lowered and she went on a rant about how copyright holds us back artistically as a species. She was blabbing.

Another judge, a blonde-haired woman, pursed her lips. "You know the artwork has been out in the public sphere for years—made in 1903."

Camila looked at me and shrugged. "Better safe than sorry," she mumbled. Camila nudged me. Then I said louder, "It's about the dichotomy of flight and being free and the weight of the world on you." Their eyes seemed to light up. *Go on*, they seemed to say.

"And, uh, the ocean... and rock... and like we said about the sea birds..."

Camila shut me up and broke in. She started discussing about ephemerality and cyclical nature. Being judges at a science fair, they liked the part about nature, but seemed a bit rattled about all the talk on aesthetics and transitoriness. She didn't even get a chance to explain about the secondary spray that would whip up a rigid semi-permanence, when they started cutting in, shifting about.

They murmured and at the end of our long spiel, said only a few not-quite-encouraging neutral things like, "Thank you for your time." Which was either fitting or ironic, given everything Camila said about impermanence.

More parents and students came by. The best comment so far was that, well, it was big. That at least we were ambitious.

The worst comments were the ones that were not told to us directly, but overheard. Like after we went on a spiel about how the sculptures could dissolve, we heard from the sidelines: "Good, it deserves to dissolve, no one wants to look at that mug forever" and "It would be a travesty that it even stays up that long. Causes trauma to all its viewers..." "...and their nostrils." They probably didn't realize we could still hear them in the echoey hall, among all the din.

It wasn't a bad concept.

The ink itself was cheap and sustainable and it slowly dissolved into the elements. It was noncorrosive, consisting of fruit rinds, food product ends, a mix of plankton and other naturally biodegradable products whose recipe only Camila knew.

Plus, she had the elixir that would reverse it all, bind it up into something more durable.

It was actually a great concept, I thought.

It just wasn't pleasant to look at. Or sniff at.

***

We knew we weren't going to win. The virtual reality on the other side of the room, though done over and over again, year after year, was getting the crowd. Everyone liked VR. It was exciting and fun. I mean, hell, I liked VR. But, it wasn't exactly innovative. Yet, the judges hovered over it, chatting in delight like they'd never seen VR goggles before.

I yawned. The drones were doing demonstration squirts of different colored inks on the tray on our table. People encountered our giant sculpture with either wide eyes full of incredulity ("What the *hell is* that?") or averted glances. Our SustainaThinker loomed over us, embarrassing us with the many holes that somehow didn't show up in our smaller prototype. We should've done additional testing, but we had been running short on time. Besides, where in our cube residential complexes would we have built a Christmas-tree-sized statue?

An eccentric man wearing a bowtie, round lens motor goggles and a Hawaiian shirt with origami cranes patterned over it approached us. He pulled up the round-rimmed sungoggles from his eyes and let the goggles rest on his forehead as he read over our placard and glanced at our object, the looming, immense seated figure. This man didn't seem shocked or condescending, unlike the other gawkers.

We tried to approach him, but he looked so lost in thought, he was almost more pensive than The Thinker himself. We decided to just wait for him to be done. Not only did he linger over the statue, he brushed his hand on it. He examined the pores and brushed the dust in his fingers. He grimaced. Then he actually sniffed the sponge-like rough surface of the ankle of the SustainaThinker. And maybe I was imagining it, or did he also lick the powdery debris from his own fingers?

His salt and pepper fluffy mustache moved up and down as he

exclaimed finally, "Now, this will do. It's quite incredible in fact."

After all the passive aggressive comments, the overheard slights, we waited for the punchline. *Incredibly... what? Incredibly... useless? Incredibly... ugly?*

It never came.

He was a weirdo, but "incredible" was just about the nicest thing someone had said to us so far about our entry in this fair.

He finally seemed to notice us. He gave us a card. "Ernesto Wu. Chief director. Viable Habitats, an organization funded in part by NOAA and international sponsors."

"NOAA?" I asked.

"National Oceanic and Atmospheric Administration. Part of the US Department of Commerce."

I nodded.

"If you're looking for buyers..." He trailed off, waiting for our response.

We shrugged. We didn't know what to say. Buyers? We were only high schoolers. But, he said a figure that made our heads roll. I've never seen so many zero's in my life. We said we'd have to consult our parents, and he said of course. "Minors can't sign without a parent or guardian." He then continued to say some things I didn't really understand or process, something about the conglomeration of great minds and the collaboration of transnational entities and projects that inspire the soul and of the greater good—and then he left, drifting off to other projects.

***

Mom and Dad were having trouble with rent. The restaurant business wasn't doing well. Even with the drones I enhanced for delivery use. Slow times—and the holidays weren't coming around for months. I heard them whispering about moving to a more affordable neighborhood.

It wasn't just us. It was everywhere. The plight of everything around us was getting worse. We sat through classes in heat, dripping with sweat. It wasn't just August heat. This was "unbearable, human-caused, intense and super sticky climate-change" heat. The news was miserable. As miserable as we felt. Every day political scandals took over headlines. Not to mention all the environmental scares: the diminishing of the coral reefs, the digits of the seabirds dropping off, the dire state of the polar icecaps.

I spoke with Camila, raised an idea with her. Her family wasn't doing much better. Their family ran a wedding planning company, and no one was spending money. I guess people held off marriages until things looked better. Few wedding bells a-ringing for bleak times like these. I told her I think we could help out.

Mr. Wu, the Sungoggles Guy, as we came to call him, had called me a few times in the last two months. I didn't pick up. At first, we thought he was a joke, or a fake. He asked if he could buy our statue, and was willing to pay us fabulously for it. We ignored him.

But, after his third message, we looked up his stuff. He did do extensive research on sea animal habitats. We thought about responding to him. We talked to Ms. Brown, who was probably the only faculty who had alluded to our sculpture. After we returned to school after the science fair, she had taken Camila and me aside and said something about the fragility of man. How we live together on this planet, and yet we don't provide solid enough rock for animals to lean on. She was really taken with the piece.

Her words struck a chord with Camila, and she got teary as she thanked Ms. Brown. It was then that Ms. Brown mentioned something about a patent. She said she personally didn't know much about sustainable materials—but said she was chatting with an acquaintance who was a material sciences specialist who had suggested that we get Sustainaink patented. We thanked Ms. Brown, thinking she was bonkers for suggesting such a route. I mean, this was just a science fair entry after all.

But, the more I thought about, the more these words floated around: Why not?

I urged Camila to talk to her sister. Camila's sister was ten years older than her and had a friend who was a patent lawyer. We met up with Drake, the lawyer, at his office, on the third floor of an intimidating antiseptic white building. We only came to ask, but after discussing it, we got pretty excited about the prospect of having our own patent.

Mr. Sungoggles Guy called then. We told him we weren't interested in selling, that we wanted to go forward with a patent.

"But, that's what this was all about in the first place!" He said he wanted to meet us.

Mr. Wu was as eccentric as ever, wearing not one but three bowties, squished onto his neck. Every so often, he would rub them casually, as if they were his beard. His eyes were shining and he kept gesticulating.

"Our company could do great with this! We want the technology. Don't go through with the patent. It'll hamper us."

Camila nodded. She wasn't into copyright and ownership.

"We could envision a whole series of sculptures."

"Oh, that sounds good," said Camila. I elbowed her and narrowed my eyes. I knew Camila was excited about the prospect of churning up more ink and playing with materials, but we had to think strategically.

"Mr. Wu, we like your enthusiasm. Let's talk more," I said.

***

Camilla was adjusting spray nozzles and I was sketching in my graph ruled notebook, coming up with a new plan. We had called Drake. He showed up.

"I read through the documents. If you signed with Mr. Wu right then, he would've owned the patent. Then, it really would be property of the corporation and you wouldn't be able to work on it anymore. Rather than a release of copyright, they would have a tight hold on it."

Drake convinced us that if we owned the patent, we could sell or give out rights to as many people as we would like, rather than having our ink possibly withheld from us.

Drake helped us fill out some forms, prepared some preliminary steps for the patent. It took all the money we had been saving for Christmas presents—and that didn't even include the lawyer's fee. He said we could pay him back when we made more money. Camila thought Drake was into her sister and cut us a good deal for it.

I just thought he liked our idea.

***

With the patent in hand, it was time to call up Ernesto Wu, Mr. Sungoggles Guy, again.

In no time (after some conferring with Drake again), we made our first sale as entrepreneurs. Rights to Sustainaink. Mr. Wu didn't blink an eye that we didn't sell him the patent. We guessed that he had a lot of experience with buying rights and always asked for the tech first as protocol. And nonplussed and looking quite happy with the sale, he even commissioned us to look at some ink drone designs.

A few days later, he left us a message:

"You'll be happy to see what we did with the rights we bought," his hologram said. "In fact, we're encouraging students to become more active. We'll be flying you out here."

***

The ride to the coastal islands was supposed to take seven hours. They intended to build a similar structure closer to us locally once they got the bigger project going. It was in the terms of our sale. Camila's mom accompanied us to the site. My parents had to work. Mom used the money I got for the initial rights payment to buy more ingredients for the restaurant and told me they'd pay me back—in the form of tuition bills. ("Haha!" they said.) I think secretly they were both at once happy that their daughter was finally amounting to something (aka making money) and at once ashamed that they had to resort to taking my money to keep the family business afloat.

Camila and I played with the massage chairs on the planes and the

90

holographic space simulator games on board. We pretty much forgot we were flying 35,000 feet in the air over oceans—that's how much we were immersed in our holoworlds. Mr. Wu had told us that their institute didn't spend extra on the upgrades (their funding wouldn't allow that), but the airlines had a partnership for helping future scientists and it was the airlines that granted these special seats for budding researchers. That was how we got to ride this specialized plane designed with fuel-efficiency in mind that experimentally repurposed waste as jet neo-fuel and significantly minimized emissions. We couldn't complain there. Camila was euphoric. Between hologames, she asked a million questions about this neo-fuel on forums and prepared a list of questions for Mr. Sungoggles Guy. I sketched the plane inside and out in my notebook, capturing the sleekness of all the details of the design. We went in and out of the holographic games, chatting, imagining and composing.

By the time we got off, we already experienced the lives of deep sea divers, coral reef explorers, astronauts, weather sensors and design drones. Though their environs were more shimmery than in real life. So it was a little disorienting that drones similar to the ones we pretended to be in the hologames on the flight there actually flew overhead when we landed at the project site.

The drones weren't exactly our designs but close. We stood on the shore, on craggy rock with the waves below crashing into stone. A small army of nanodrones squirted and zipped around us. The ocean ebbed and surged with a fury and the smell of brine permeated the heavy breeze.

The new formations that jutted out from the sea were ugly. Worse than our humongous SustainaThinker. Not even an attempt at symmetry. And some of them looked completely lopsided and droopy, off-colored. The drones buzzed with no seeming awareness of their roughness, with no attempt to fill in the porous gaps and to smoothen out the color to a more even statuesque whiteness.

They were made to look like that. Something about resembling more organic, amorphous shapes. They didn't smell half-bad. A bit briny, like the ocean itself.

We'd heard Mr. Wu's spiel before on the phone, but now before all the soaring drones, his emphatic tirades had a deeper impact. Calls of gulls in the distance filled our ears.

In the distance, Mr. Wu let out a cackle of utter delight in seeing our faces, one that we could hear even from a hundred feet away. He jogged up, greeted us and lifted up his sungoggles, their outline dug deep into his skin. He rubbed the creases and started to give us the tour. He told us about the scale of the project, the creation of fifty new rock-islands.

"There's a lot of overcrowding here, like big cities," he said. "But, these seagulls need a place to nest, to expand their colonies especially in face of the die-off. Sure, there are other issues. Like food. We're working on that, too, or at least the Viable Prey Division is, but we're trying to provide a habitat, in addition to grub. Some of the below-surface printed pieces include reef-like structures to promote fish dwelling—options for the birds to feed on. But, we're working on macro concerns to tackle the issue. It's quite tricky. Food and shelter, the primary necessities..." He then started describing the many kinds of seabirds that migrate here.

Camila wandered off as Mr. Wu went into a meditative patter. She peered through the open doors of all the helicopters filled with various barrels marked empty, once filled with powders and inks, according to their labels. They would be taken to the main lab site to be refilled.

"How many different kinds of ink do you use?" I asked Mr. Wu, when he finished his monologue. The sound of helicopters filled the air as they took off.

"These are all tertiary test inks, all that have gone through many rounds of lab testing and two rounds of *in situ* testing. Yours, too. We're testing out about thirty varieties. We've 3-D printed out these rocks with them—we didn't want to permanently alter the landscape, but offer a temporary nesting site, that can either diminish or remain longer by our choice. We'll see how the project goes and see which inks succeed after the limited time period, when the rocky structures will start to degrade and decompose. This pressing time constriction gives us leeway to assess the program. Given the way that the ink works, thanks to your ingenuity, we can solidify the same design if it all works out—the birds like to return to the same exact spot after all."

I pointed at the ocean, the waves shattering against the edge below us. "How about all the marine life?"

"Yes, we have to consider diversion above and under the surface from the new rock-island territories—we worked out all those algorithms. Very complex systems, but we're certain that any disturbance will be absolutely necessary and there to enhance vitality."

We watched as the drones continued to dribble out ink solidifying before our eyes—these half-form monsters coming to life, reminding me of snow-covered trees, but created a layer at a time.

This was our work.

I heard a pattering of feet from behind me. Camila came back huffing, holding small tube-samples of ink. She smiled. "Freebies," she said.

"Ah, I see you've met the biomaterials coordinator." Mr. Wu said. Then, he got our attention, pointing off to the horizon. "So, what shall we call that one?"

We followed his pointer finger. A tall structure, not quite the Statue of Liberty, but at least a third of it, in the distance.

"Call it?" I asked.

"What do you mean?" asked Camila. She raised her brows.

"Yeah, well, we wanted you to see the rock-island, inspired by your designs. But more than that, we brought you here to name it. There'll be a naming ceremony later tonight and we need to know what to write onto the line. We thought you might like to have a stab at coming up with it. You came up with the formula and the inspiring drone specs after all. And once named, the gulls will nest on it soon enough. Maybe they'll be calling out its name but in gull language."

Mr. Wu flashed his teeth and let out a shrieking calling noise that sounded distinctly un-gull-like. "Eeee geeee eeee."

We covered up our ears, but it didn't keep Mr. Wu from letting out a few more pealing squawks. "That is, that's what they'll be saying once they get used to the new structures and have time to settle in."

I wasn't too keen on Mr. Wu's rendition of gull, but I couldn't believe we could name this object rising up from the seas. It was like being discoverers of a new star or a cosmic object. *But made from our hands, materials we concocted.*

Camila and I threw around some names, but decided that "SustainaThinker Beta," "Ugly Thing" and "Made of Rind Trash and More" were not particularly great names.

"Let's call it 'Promise Rock,'" I said. "A pledge that we'll do our best."

Camila nodded. She put her pinky in mine and swore we would continue to treat this land, shared by humans, drones, gulls and other beings alike, with respect.

Mr. Wu smiled.

***

A year later, the first Promise Hatchlings were born. We watched from live cams as they incubated and then fledged, feathered little waddlers moving awkwardly with their newly fluffed wings. The rocks were thick with colonies. They perched on the rock-island we named, their glorious Promise Rock, the structure finally fulfilling their commitment, becoming a habitat rife with their activity and life.

Reports of a slight uptick in seabird numbers was at least one optimistic piece of news. Everything else was still in flux.

In June, we graduated high school. No accolades for science fair awards, but we had scholarships in hand to premier engineering institutes, thanks to high-profile interviews and media reports covering our involvement with Viable Habitats.

Camila was keen on insisting on fair use, posting on forums for teachers and educators, letting them know about the ink patent we held and put up in-class activity assignments and coupons for free samples and shipping of pedagogical varieties of our ink for students to tinker with. Students, "our mentees" Camilla called them, sent us postcards of statues they built and talked about their own process of adjusting our ink. Camila hung these cards all over her bedroom wall, with food-waste-based dinosaurs, castles, teddy bears and even miniature playgrounds surrounding her every night when she slept and dreamed of more creative materials.

***

Over the summer, we worked on more permanent structures. Scaffolding for other environmental projects—for me, it was energy harvesting, and for Camila, it was sustainable housing but with an artistic flair. ("Not boring boxes," she insisted.) Once the summer winded down and Camila's internship was up, she started taking on the food industry, combining her material arts interest with gastronomy—coming to visit my parents for advice. She was interested in seafood alternatives and I was pretty sure it was so that we wouldn't compete with the gulls, particularly given her fondness of the one gull she grew to really care about on the live cam: the one she called Vella. Later, she showed me the black-and-white Vella tattooed on her arm.

We sat together watching Vella feed on a slippery silver-colored fish on the holocam, as we chomped on seaweed bars that Camila claimed to be shrimp flavored. They were packaged in colorful reduced-paper tech with an eco-friendly coating Camila was also experimenting with in her housing project.

Since her internship, Camila became more interested in licensing her engineering art inventions through Creative Commons and already one foundation was experimenting with the eco-friendly coating on binocular covers. They said it could help citizen scientists embarking on bird-watching trips to have a good seal on their "second set of eyes." We also talked more about the possibilities of open source software to develop more materials and how we could increase the spread of useful inventions.

Camila also learned from her internship about a scheme being discussed in government about economic barriers to university being defrayed by contributions to the public good. We talked about new ideas we have percolating and how they might qualify for this scheme.

In the midst of this, she saw me frowning. She asked what was wrong—did I see a kink in any of her plans? I shook my head.

I told her I was worried about my family's financial affairs. She perked up and started scrolling, mumbling to herself. She zipped into my news feed brochures on coops my parents can participate in to ease the financial burden they're in. That way we could free up our mental space for more tinkering rather than have our heads stuck on binary colors: in the red or in the black. She said taking advantage of these programs would open up a rainbow of colors—and gestured at her tie-dyed wrap-around blouse and her flora-patterned leggings.

In less than a week, we would go our separate ways, but as long as we had holoconferences and a love for invention and for bettering our society, we'd always remain in touch.

I snapped a photo of Camila making a muscle, as she took a bite of her seaweed SustainaBar, with her tattoo Vella looking out at me. In the creases of Camila's arm muscles, the illustrated seabird had an enigmatic look on its beaked face, a squinting of the eyes, like it was winking.

***

D.A. Xiaolin Spires steps into portals and reappears in sites such as Hawai'i, NY, various parts of Asia and elsewhere, with her keyboard appendage attached. Her work appears or is forthcoming in publications such as *Clarkesworld, Analog, Strange Horizons, Nature, Terraform, Uncanny, Fireside, Galaxy's Edge, StarShipSofa, Andromeda Spaceways (Year's Best Issue), Diabolical Plots, Factor Four, Lady Churchill's Rosebud Wristlet, Grievous Angel, Toasted Cake, Pantheon, Outlook Springs, ROBOT DINOSAURS, Shoreline of Infinity, LONTAR, Mithila Review, Reckoning, Issues in Earth Science, Liminality, Star*Line, Polu Texni, Eye to the Telescope, Liquid Imagination, Gathering Storm Magazine, Little Blue Marble, Story Seed Vault*, and anthologies of the strange and beautiful: *Deep Signal, Ride the Star Wind, Sharp and Sugar Tooth, Broad Knowledge, Future Visions* and *Battling in All Her Finery*. Select stories can be read in German, Spanish, Vietnamese, Estonian and French translation. She can be found on Twitter: @spireswriter and on her website: daxiaolinspires.wordpress.com.

Untamed
Timothy Yam

The old man squinted into the scorching Singapore sun.

"Left a bit."

The girl shifted the panel.

"Right a bit."

The girl rolled her eyes. Then she shifted the panel. The old man licked his index finger and held it up, as if to test the direction of the non-existent wind. He nodded. The girl climbed down the ladder.

"You break now. Later you check the pumps."

The girl sat down on the nearest stool and leaned forward, cradling the back of her head in her hands. She heard the flapping of wings. Out of habit, she swiped at the mynah with no real conviction. It hopped to its right and squawked a taunt at her. Only fourteen more days, she told herself. Fourteen days were nothing, considering she had already done thirty-six since that day in court.

She remembered Mak's tears as the sentence was read. Truancy. Shoplifting. Violent conduct. Beyond Parental Control. Bitch! You report your own daughter and still have the bloody cheek to cry about it? Where were those tears every time Mak smiled at her reflection after applying one of her daughter's new 'gifts'? The crow-footed judge had given a choice. Twenty days in the Girl's Home or fifty days environmental labour. She looked at Mak dabbing her eyes, and wondered what would wound her more, the stigma of detention or the extended separation. Then she remembered childhood, and Mak's shrieked threats of suicide receding into the distance as Nek, flanked by police, carried her from the house, and she knew what to say.

So it was that she found herself on the roof of a twenty-seven story HDB flat in Bukit Gombak, looking out at the neighbourhood below. Blocks upon blocks of flats stretched into the distance, pastel paint peeling from decades of sun exposure. She felt the sweat trickle down her neck and spine. Even the wind blowing through the stack ventilation shaft below made little difference. She wiped her face with the back of her hand and heard the old man laugh.

"Girl, you know you are going to work, still wear like that for what?"

"Shut up."

"This one I say out of the kindness of my heart. If you kena heatstroke, not my problem."

As much as she hated to admit it, he was right. The combat boots, the heavy black denim jeans, the black faux-leather jacket, the heavy eyeliner—hardly appropriate attire for manual labour at a roof garden, with the exception of the ankle monitor that bound her to the block. Still, she had to wear them, especially on a day like this. This was her armour, and she was girding herself for battle with whatever sorry excuse for an authority figure they were going to foist on her. What she did not expect was a decrepit old Chinese man, bent almost double, skin burned so brown he looked almost Malay, shuffling around in a tank top and slippers. He continued bombarding her with questions.

"This your first time here is it?"

"Yes."

"Ha? I thought school will bring you to visit?"

"I skipped to go McDonald's with friends."

"You live in HDB flat right? Why never just go upstairs and

look?"

"What is there to see? Just plants and insects and birds. Like that where got special?"

He clicked his tongue at her. The roof garden—and she would know if she actually attended school—was the living heart of all HDB flats. When he was a child, the roofs were all concrete. Empty, useless space. Then the temperatures rose. People left their air-conditioners on all day. Which made the temperatures rise even more. So the government mandated blackout periods for air-conditioning. But without some kind of cooling mechanism, the tall concrete slabs would become unbearably hot, baking the millions within alive. Then some bright enterprising civil servant did a study and saw that blocks which had set up community roof gardens saw cooler temperatures of up to 5 degrees. The way forward was clear.

"But taking care—not easy. I do for forty years already—every day in the sun, hard work to maintain this place, make sure the plants and animals are well."

"Animals?"

At this, a white globule of birdshit landed at the toe of her boot. The old man laughed as she frantically tried to shake it off.

"Stop laughing and give me some water!"

"Water here is precious. For you, me and the plants to drink. Not to wash your shoe."

She looked up in the direction where the offending projectile came from and identified the culprit, a black mynah with a diagonal white stripe down its breast. It squawked at her. From a distance, it sounded like a laugh.

"These boots were expensive."

"Who ask you to wear? Your probation officer send you here to work, not to talk. Today and tomorrow I show you what to do, after that you settle on your own. I supervise and make sure it's good."

"No good how?"

"Then you do again. If still no good, I add one more day to your probation. Come. We start now."

The list of tasks was endless. Check the water filtration system. Inspect the rainwater pipes. Fertilise the soil. Remove pests if necessary using citronella and tea tree oil. Harvest fruit, herbs and vegetables. Check the vertical plants on the green walls. Remove dead leaves from the pathways. Clean the gardening equipment. Fill the bird feeder.

"No."

"What?"

"You want me to take care of the stupid plants, fine. But I am not feeding the birds."

"Why not?"

She pointed at the white stain on her boot.

"Normal behaviour for bird. This one, untamed." He chuckled. "Won't be the last time it shits on you. Anyway, you don't feed, they eat the plants. So feed them."

As she filled the feeder, the white striped mynah landed next to her. She kicked out with her ruined boot, which caused it to hop backwards, puff up its feathers and sink into a crouch, accompanied by a noise that was a cross between a hiss and a warble. For the first time that day, she laughed. Such a ridiculous sight—this harmless toy soldier preening away, trying fruitlessly to intimidate. From that moment, the mynah became her constant lunch companion, always hopping around her in a circle, feathers fluffed and screeching threats of violence unless she gave it her food—which she never did.

She often wondered why the mynah targeted her. After all, the garden did not lack for company at lunch time, when the usual crowd of retirees would shuffle through its pathways looking for the coolest spot to eat the banana-leaf wrapped packets of *nasi lemak* that the nearby mosque gave out every day. This was when the old man was in his element, flirting with the old ladies, bantering with the old men and teasing the little grandchildren who played catching under the canopy. Any of these people would have gladly given the mynah food, so why did it have to invade her ramshackle shelter, hopping around the humming electrical console for alms that would never arrive? Why could it not leave her alone? Why couldn't she get some goddamn peace?

"Eh, why you always eat by yourself? Here got so many people, come take lunch with them."

"No thanks."

"Not lonely meh? Every day work alone, eat alone, go downstairs to your bunk sleep also alone—"

"Oh, so the police will allow someone to sleep with me in the bunk?"

"You try see what will happen. Anyway, just talk to some of the people here. I know all old uncle and auntie, but they got some interesting things they can teach."

"I'm here on probation. Not to learn."

"Okay, up to you. But being alone all the time—not good."

He wasn't wrong. Weekends were the worst, with hours spent hugging her knees and watching the sad excuse for entertainment that played on free-to-air TV. The temptation was strong to check out of the little studio bunk provided for her on the top floor, if only to remember what life was like beyond the confines of the block on all four sides and the cloudless sky above, except that the price of leaving was much worse. It was a shock, that first weekend, to see Mak waiting at the void deck with an unfamiliar person that she correctly assumed was a new boyfriend.

"Nek where?"

"I am your mother, not her. You ready to go?"

She turned to her probation officer.

"I said I wanted to leave with my grandmother."

"Your mother is your legal guardian. We can only release you to her."

"Can I stay?"

"You mean in your bunk?"

"Yah, the bunk. The garden. Can?"

After some frantic calls to a superior, the probation officer led her back to the lift and to the bunk. The echoes of Mak's screams rang in her ears for the rest of the weekend. Accusations of disloyalty. Declarations of love. Regrets that she had ever been born. She turned the TV volume up and sat silently watching until she eventually fell asleep.

Thirty-six days. Thirty-six days of labour in the hot sun, accompanied only by the voiceless plants and the old man. Thirty-six days of lunches alone save for the mynah chirping by her feet. Thirty-six days of falling asleep to the flickering images of cheesy variety shows. And only fourteen left to go until… and here the words 'released to legal guardian' sent a chill through her even in the afternoon heat.

The mynah made a sound she did not recognise. It sounded almost quizzical. She opened her eyes. The old man had collapsed into a honeysuckle bush. His limbs were stiff, his fingers twitching. She sprang to his side and lay him on his back. One side of his face was drooping, and he was opening and closing his mouth, but there was no sound. Someone screamed. It might have been her. The retirees gathered around him as she heard snippets of conversation.

"—stroke can tell—"

"—call ambulance now—"

"—any next of kin—"

"—will you be okay by yourself?"

She looked up and blinked. Through the glare of the setting sun, she could just about make out the probation officer's face. There was a light breeze in the air rustling the leaves. The honeysuckle bush still had the indentation of the old man's body. She felt the soil beneath her shift with her hands. From above, the familiar chirp.

"Will you be okay by yourself? We will send another gardener, but he won't be here for a few days."

A croak escaped her throat.

"Who will take care of the garden?"

"For now, nobody. You can stay in your bunk until the new gardener comes."

Sure. Easy. Stay in bunk. Watch TV. Eat stale chips. Listen to the rain. Forget the look on the old man's face. Hear the sound of raindrops on glass. Avoid the thought of twitching limbs. Focus instead on the howl of the wind and rain. Wind and rain. Oh no. She sprung off the bed and looked out into the night, veiled in a shroud of swirling, whipping water. The old man had said something on the first day on how to protect the garden in the case of a tropical storm, but it might as well have been delivered in a foreign language.

She placed her hand on the window and felt the drumming rhythm of the rain through the cool glass. In here was safety and warmth. Out there was ... not. As if to confirm her suspicions, a shard of lightning ripped through the dark. In its single second of illumination, she saw the rolling thicket of clouds converging above. They sparked a brief memory of the few geography classes she did not skip: "climate change has resulted in increasing the severity and frequency of extreme weather events, such as the massive thunderstorms that occur every monsoon season..."

Another slash of lightning interrupted her reminiscence. There was nothing for her above except rain and lightning. What did she owe the people who put her here? Mak, who could drip venom in her ear daily but cried for the police the minute she dared to throw it back? Nek, who had not even bothered to visit in the thirty-six days she had been here? The probation officer who could barely be bothered to hide his disdain and stared at his phone through each of their sessions? The old man—well okay, he was not that bad. But 'not that bad' was not a reason to climb up the winding stairs to the garden and risk her neck. There was no good reason for that. None whatsoever.

She swore as the first gust of sodden wind whipped at her face, only for the sound to be swallowed by the storm. She clutched the faux-leather jacket closer to her body and pushed down into the soil with the soles of the combat boots. Armour.

Through the flashes of lightning, she could make out a path to the little shed where she took lunch. The little red light of the electrical console was still blinking, a lighthouse in an ocean of darkness. Good. Power had not cut out yet. She reached the shed and fumbled on the floor looking for the torch the old man had left there. Suddenly, she felt the familiar fluttering of wings next to her. At least she was not alone, even if the company was less than ideal. After some more groping, she found the torch. The light flickered on. As she tried to decipher the old man's gnarled handwriting, she felt a light pressure on her shoulder, as though a friend were laying a hand on it. Then she heard the squawk in her ear.

"I'm trying!"

Squawk.

"Which one?"

Squawk squawk.

A laugh rippled through her, beginning as a shudder and ending as a full bodied convulsion. She was talking to a mynah while soaking wet in the middle of a thunderstorm. The judge had never said anything about this during the sentencing. If she had known she might have made a different decision. She would have been out of the Girls' Home by now. Back at her void deck smoking, keeping one eye out for Mak to arrive with the new boyfriend and hoping she was too drunk to say a word or lift a finger so that the night could go by with relative peace. Still, even the most tempestuous night of her old life could not compare to this.

Squawk!

She blinked the rain out of her eyes. A peeling label above a switch with the word 'storm' on it. Had to be, right? She flicked the switch. The garden rumbled to life as the rain shades extended out from the surrounding scaffold. The sound of the squall began to die down, replaced by the almost gentle pattering of raindrops on canvas.

Outside the shed, the swirling blur began to reshape itself back into a recognisable form.

She trudged through the muddy pathway, opened the door back into the block, stomped down the winding stairs into her bunk, collapsed onto the bed, and lay there until the sun rose. It was a fitful sleep, filled with bizarre dreams of hibiscus patterns, windswept branches, and the incessant squawking of a mynah.

There was a tap on her hand. The mynah was pecking lightly at it. Everything ached. She peeled her freezing body off the damp sheets. As the mynah chirped, she slowly changed into her work outfit—a sun-bleached red t-shirt and running shorts. The boots stayed on. She had a feeling she would need them. It took six minutes of chasing, but she eventually managed to catch and enclose the little black bird, who proceeded to peck at and shit all over her hands. It was a relief when she finally reached the garden and released it. Then she looked up and all relief drained away.

Deadfall was everywhere, with broken branches, dead leaves, and other debris scattered around the garden. The herb garden was completely flooded. The new shrubs planted by the old man just last week were all torn from their roots. The topsoil had almost completely eroded, covering the pathways with a thin layer of sticky mud.

The mynah flew over to the drowned herb garden and began to dig for insects. It gave her a quizzical look. In response, she sighed, dragged herself to the shed and pulled out her tools. At least they had stayed dry. She worked in silence for the rest of the morning, starting by removing the deadfall and cleaning the mud from the pathways.

"Excuse me? Girl?"

It was one of the usual retirees, a plump Indian lady with a ready smile. She handed her a plastic bag.

"The gardener asked me to buy lunch for you."

"He's okay?"

"Still can lah. Saw him in hospital today. He reminded me to buy you food otherwise you got nothing to eat."

"Oh. Thank you."

She took the lukewarm packet of rice.

"You join us to eat?"

"Um, no, cannot, the garden is a mess, and—"

"Aiyah never mind, eat first. The table over there quite dry, you cleaned it very nice. You come, come eat with us."

At lunch, she said little, choosing instead to listen to the easy, comfortable conversation of the retirees. At the end of lunch, when they thanked her for cleaning up the garden, she felt a strange tightness around her chest and could only croak out a soft 'no problem' in response.

Then she continued working.

She continued working until the sun set. She returned to her bunk and fell asleep as soon as her head hit the pillow. The next day she continued working again. Something about it seemed easier now. It was like when she put together jigsaw puzzles as a child. Initially they were difficult, but once she figured out what the picture was supposed to be, everything clicked into place. The trees, the bushes, the herbs, the insects—all now seemed to vibrate at the same frequency as her. All save that one pesky mynah, who remained as recalcitrant as ever. She took lunch with the retirees. Then she continued working until the sun set and—

"What happened here?"

"I tried to get it back to how it was."

The probation officer squinted at the garden through his thick glasses.

"Looks good! Anyway, I'm here to let you know that you can go home tomorrow."

"Excuse me?"

He explained. The storm had affected practically every roof garden in Singapore. All available gardeners had been activated to restore them. As such, there was no one who could come and supervise her on such short notice. Considering the circumstances, along with the sterling reports of her work from the previous gardener, it was decided that her time would be considered served.

That night, she lay in bed silently for hours. What could she do but go back? Mak would probably treat her like a princess for the first day, at least until she said something 'disrespectful' enough to earn a slap across the face. Nek might take her in for a day or two, but she knew that her eyesight and memory were not what they used to be. Her friends would tell her how much they missed her, even as she knew it was not true. The countdown was over. She had her old life back.

The sun was rising. She opened the wardrobe and took out the bag she had brought on the first day. Slowly, deliberately, she folded her clothes and placed them inside, except for the sun-bleached t-shirt and running shorts. Those she wore, along with her combat boots. As she left, she looked back at the bunk. There was no sign anyone had ever lived there, save for a stained white patch on the floor.

She walked up the winding stairs and opened the door to the garden, dropping the bag by the side. She strode over to the shed and took out her tools. Next to her was the flapping of wings. She swiped at the mynah, who hopped back, puffed itself up, and squawked at her with all the force it could muster. With the faintest of smiles, she knelt down and started her work, bathed in the warm light of the rising sun.

**

Timothy Yam is a civil servant from Singapore. He is the third prize winner of the National Arts Council's Golden Point Award (English Short Story Category), and his fiction has been published in *Anak Sastra* and *The Best Asian Speculative Fiction Anthology*. He is currently working on his first novel.

It Is the Year 2115
Joyce Chng

Assistant

It is the year 2115.

I know it sounds all high and mighty, victorious and grand. But we have made it, haven't we? 2115. People thought we would never survive it, let alone thrive in this world. Ma and Papa are relieved. We survived right? A deadly pandemic. The ice caps melting. Civil wars. Countries cutting ties and retreating into their own walled borders. The historians call it *Apocalypse*. End of the world. Yet, here I stand, beside the window of my small apartment flat, staring out into the glittering bay area with its shining buildings, conservatories and Giant Trees that absorb light and water. Already this early in the morning, small boats are speeding across the water. Their wakes trail white curves on the surface. The silver delivery drones are whizzing about with their precious cargo of letters and parcels. Everything feels good. Normal.

Nothing seems to have changed.

The sky is a watery reflection, made blurry by the sizzling shield that covers the city like a glass globe. I can't see much beyond the sizzle, beyond its edge.

It is the year 2115.

Milestone!

New year, new beginnings!

I know, I know. I will the timer to stop ringing, because I have to work. Plants do not water themselves nor feed themselves organic fertilisers. No, what New Year resolution did I make a few hours earlier? Something about harvesting the best bok choy the whole of SEA has seen. I made a bet with my supervisor, a bet which I will probably lose. I tend to break New Year resolutions all the time.

My neighbours wave at me as they spray water on their own container plants. Our founder would be so proud. Temasek has truly become a Garden City. Suddenly many people want to be gardeners. Horticulture is the hot subject every student wants to take. Believe me, I am a certified gardener, at one of the biggest skyscraper farms, growing the best produce in the region and winning prizes everywhere. Best of all, people are sharing their produce with one another.

We are all happy gardeners.

Yet, as much as the Garden City is also now a Science Fiction city, old comforts still exist. I pass by the old uncle selling you tiao and soy bean milk served hot in recyclable paper cups. I buy some and thank him. He tells me stories about Temasek in the past, 50 years ago.

"Used to be more exciting, you know," the old uncle will tell me. It is often a repetition of a previous story. "More stalls selling things you will never eat now. Wet markets, you know. Chicken in cages."

"Chicken in cages?" I gasp, appalled.

"Ah, yes. And rabbits too."

I think he is pulling my leg. But he looks oddly sincere, even wistful. Uncle must be in his late 70s.

"Let me tell you about the last blackout we had…"

I smile politely and leave quickly before he can launch into a soliloquy.

Then, I stride past the bird song admirers who pamper their birds as much as I pamper my plants. All these birds are regulated.

Poaching is now a major crime, to the relief of the animal protection groups and supporters of animal welfare. Some of the farms I know breed song birds, their genetic lineages kept under lock and key by the conservatories. Posters with graphics are plastered all over the wall, warning of dire consequences. The birds are protected. So many species have died.

Boarding the maglev train, I look out beyond the bay, beyond the sizzle of the shield that protects Temasek from the outside world. From everything else. It's been there as long as I could remember. It's like it's part of ancient history, but not really. Ma and Papa talk about it all the time. The Globe keeps things out.

The you tiao is hot in my hands. I will savour it in my office. My SMART chirps. My friends are now online. We are all connected.

***

Supervisor

It is the year 2115.

I tell myself this when I walk down the rows of gleaming green vegetables, my sensor wand testing the temperature level. It beeps NORMAL. I smile, satisfied.

Rows 14, 15, and 16 are due for harvesting. I make a note so that my young assistant will do so in the next 24 hours. She is munching away at her you tiao—*fried dough fritters! how quaint!*—in her little cubicle. How pleasurable, being single and young and care-free.

I know that my eyes have bags and I look like the third generation pandas in the zoological gardens. "I probably look cute," I told my partner this morning, and she glared at me. Our baby wakes us up for his nightly feeds. He is such a fussy baby. So far, she has been bearing the brunt of breastfeeding and diapering him. I try to help. But I am not a good mother. I can't even change a diaper correctly! Baby coos and giggles at my partner who cuddles him. Me? I feel like a brick.

My sensor wand suddenly buzzes. Heat discrepancy in rows 19 and 20. Annoying. The solar panels need maintenance.

"Is the Globe on the fritz?" I question my assistant when I shrug off my suit and gloves.

"It looked fine when I was on board the train," she says. Her SMART data pad glows open before her. I pretend not to see that she is playing the latest cat collecting game. A plump tabby is playing with a ball of pink yarn. I also see that she is on the WEAVE, chatting with her friends. Chat boxes are blinking in and out. The WEAVE is a huge part of people's lives here, a social network of friends, colleagues, and families. Our little bubble. I wonder if I should re-activate my account... Have been so busy, of late.

Wasn't there something similar in the past? I am not sure. Many things became obsolete, didn't they?

I am going to question HQ. They should know.

It is the year 2115. We figured everything out, didn't we?

I think about my partner and my son. Our home needs more energy. Laundry, food, the ever-growing pile of dishes...

The Globe can't keep everything out, right?

We survived everything. 2115. A milestone. We can survive this.

Whatever this is.

Oh yes, the solar panels...

***

Assistant

"It is the year 2115," some chirpy DJ states and asks his listeners for opinions. Most of them are inane and I laugh at them. "People thought we wouldn't make it but we did!" "We are a nation young and free! Not anymore! Haha!" I blow raspberries at the radio, a retro unit I managed to take from Papa who is pretty protective over his collections. He has everything, including books on zoology and botany. I turn my attention to the stir-fry, some of the kai lan and Chinese kale from row 11. I toss in some strips of chicken. It is touted to be Kampung Chicken, because the fowl run free in the farms. The you tiao uncle talked about caged chicken... Imagine that.

Either way, it is going to be my delicious dinner. I scroll through the WEAVE, giggling at my friends making fun of the radio show.

The light flickers and I look up, halfway picking a strip of chicken with my chopsticks. I hear some people yelling down the corridor. Another flicker—and then, the room is just dark. The hum of appliances and devices goes dead. The air is suddenly very still.

"What the fu…" I mutter. A blackout is rare. I fumble in the dark to the window. There is a lot of shouting, people like me, fumbling in the dark. The entire area is plunged into darkness. I see… stars. I shouldn't be seeing stars. Stars are…

The Globe is down.

Didn't the you tiao uncle say something about a blackout…?

But that was a long time ago…

The Globe is down.

The shield is down.

Why is it down?

Is it supposed to be down?

***

Supervisor

It is the year 2115!

Somewhere in the apartment, I hear baby wailing his head off and my partner trying to comfort him. I curse at the lack of candles. *Must always keep spares!* I hear my mom in my head. She always reminds me. She remembers other times.

I stare out of the window. Normally, we still get moonlight, even with the Globe. I see a white crescent, like a cut finger nail, in the sky.

A sensation like cold water trickling down my back makes me start. I realise I am afraid. The Globe is down.

The Globe is down.

A matchstick hisses in the dark and there is a soft glow,

illuminating my partner's worried face.

We hear the chop chop chop of helicopters. The roof rumbles at their passing.

I lean over and give my son a gentle kiss on the forehead. That's all I can give to him. Our son. I want to protect him.

We will survive this.

***

Assistant

It turns out that a flock of Javan mynahs has hit the main solar power generator linked to the Giant Trees, causing the Globe to short out. The news is full of people commiserating, people helping each other on the WEAVE, and scenes of candlelight and laughter. Everyone is treating it as a joke, as something to remember for a long time, but something also inconsequential. The WEAVE calls it the Problem.

"It will not happen again," the old you tiao seller tells me sagely. "They will fix the problem. They always do."

"Will they, uncle?" I ask half-incredulously, half-believing.

His wrinkled face bears a wide smile. "Yeah, lah, they will fix the problem. Our gahmen will. They always do. See, we are using sunlight as energy! They will surely think of something."

Gahmen. That's one old word they use to describe our government. Papa uses it too. In a joking manner.

With the Globe down, strange things are happening.

Flocks of birds flow in, as if the air currents have brought them. Wild birds!

Odd smells linger in the air—petroleum, sea water, and loam. Like the deepest brownest of soil.

"But it is the year 2115!" I argue with Papa over the tele-phone. My family is worried enough to have a face-to-face conference with me onscreen. I see Papa's lined face, his shaking head, and Ma at the background, making comments about the Globe and Taiwanese media making fun of our Problem. "I thought things were going to change for the better! We can't keep everything out."

Papa snorts. "Well, things happen. Not everything is perfect. You know, when Temasek was a sleepy fishing village…"

"Aw, Pa. Not this again!" I almost shout. Something straight out of my history textbook, something… boring? Can it explain the Problem away?

"You know, they say that they are going to take a week to fix it," Ma interjects, barging into the conversation. "A week!"

"They still need to find the parts mah," Pa replies idly. "I heard they still manufacture the parts in China."

I let my parents argue over the Globe and the Problem it has become.

Something flitters into my room. It is a bright blue butterfly.

I catch it in an empty glass bottom. The butterfly shimmers with its own light. I am mesmerised by it. My WEAVE buzzes. They are talking about having a party at the Edge of the Globe on Saturday. Two days from now.

I decide to take the butterfly with me to the party, if it can live that long. *What should I feed it with?*

***

Supervisor

The plants in the farms are reacting strangely now. No matter how indoors and up high in the air, they are responding to something. The kai lan flowers. The bok choy grows bigger and bigger. So much for New Year resolutions. I lost my bet with my assistant. She was so happy that she won. Meanwhile, the smell of the earth grows stronger and stronger. Are the bok choy reacting to fresh natural air?

It is the year 2115 and we are acting like curious children. People are starting to flock towards the edge of the Globe, where our borders reach the sea. Ah, the Globe. It keeps everything out. People are looking out now, pointing at the derelict container ships and the debris left over from the Apocalypse. The sea levels rose, didn't they?

Now the shield is down. We can approach the outside world as if it were a wild animal.

We have become tourists in our own country.

"Monitor rows 30, 31 and 32," I say sternly to my assistant, who looks as if she has not slept. She yawns and nods. I notice she has something fluttering in a clear glass bottle on her desk. It is a butterfly with the brightest bluest wings I have ever seen. Its wings shimmer. The only time I have seen one was when I was a little girl, at my Gong Gong's garden. It danced around me in circles.

My partner wants to visit the Edge of the Globe, as people have termed it. "Come on, where's your sense of adventure?" she challenges me, with a teasing smile and laughing eyes.

"Sense of adventure? I have thrown it away," I retort back.

"Oh, come on," my partner nudges me. "I will make spaghetti!"

"Why do they call it 'Edge of the Globe'?"

"Something's happening at the edge? I don't know. The WEAVE comes up with weird terms all the time."

I bite my lower lip. "It's a big party, apparently. C'mon, it will be fun!" my partner nudges me harder. "Don't be such a wet blanket."

I hesitate, staring at her and our baby. Perhaps, I should make my way to the edge. See what the fuss is about.

***

Assistant

"It is the year 2115!" a girl gushes as she poses for her SMART drone as it hovers in front of her. "Smile!" Her pictures and words go straight to the WEAVE. I hear the pings as people signal their likes and favorites about her self-blog. Self-blogs are very popular, often detailing the lives of WEAVE users.

The Edge of the Globe is close now. I make my way carefully. There is mud. Close to me, people throng the narrow pathway. They are all laughing and cheerful.

I can smell the sea now. It is so strong that my nose wrinkles. I hold onto the glass bottle in my hands. My supervisor thinks I have gone slightly crazy, carrying this butterfly around. I think she's stressed with work and her son.

I feel sorry for her.

Something huge rears up in front of me. I pause, look up and stare. It is all corroding metal and dangling steel cables. The metal groans and moans with the wind. The thing rises before me like a cliff. Flocks of sea birds are spiraling around it. Many have made nests in its cracks and holes.

A long time ago, it was a container ship.

I stare at it. My eyes begin to water. It is a stark reminder of our own mortality. So many people had died. Competition. Throwing vulnerable people under. Then a raging disease. Shipping crashed literally. *Apocalypse.*

Was life that different before everything died? Before the Globe was built? Were people that greedy? That... *bad?*

Fortunately, we don't live like that anymore. We shouldn't live like that. But are we kinder now? Do the container vegetables we are growing at home and in our skyscraper farms teach us about helping one another? Are we? Self-reliance and resilience are all over in our textbooks, in our media, like they are the best values ever.

Are we only helping ourselves?

While people take pictures of the hulk, I cry at its passing.

When my tears are dry, I unstop the glass bottle. The blue butterfly perches at the mouth, as if it is thinking of freedom. It has lived that long enough.

"Go, you silly!" my voice croaks.

The butterfly takes a tentative step out. Another, several wing flaps, and it lifts off. I watch it disappear into the distance, where the dancing birds are.

***

Supervisor

"Watch your step," I warn my partner as we make our way down the pathway. Our son is snug in his baby sling. We see many couples with their children. My heart grows warm.

My assistant passes me by, looking as if she has been crying. I wave to her and she smiles back before walking quickly towards the maglev line. She's carrying an empty glass bottle. It is the same I'd seen on her desk.

The hulk is there, an ancient relic from the past. We both stare up, up, up at it, inhaling its scent of decay, history and something else. There are birds nesting in there. The noise of their songs echoes in the cavern in the hull.

"It is the year 2115," I say softly and hold my partner's hand. "It's a milestone. We made it. So many things have changed. Some for the better, some not so. Temasek survived through all this. We will live."

My partner leans against me for a brief moment, before our son stirs and begins fretting. He lets me carry him. His cries mingle with the sounds of the sea-birds. Terns, I realise, they are terns. The scientist in me wants to jot down the observation, inform HQ and then do what...? Write a paper about the return of terns? Petition to have the old species recorded?

I marvel at the terns' beauty. This will suffice. Things are fleeting. Transient. Even peace and happiness. Better to cherish them now.

"They say the Globe will be up by midnight." My partner checks her SMART. "Let's enjoy this scene while it lasts."

All things are transient.

Groups of people troop past us. They are carrying bunches of candles in baskets. Teenagers give us two white ones. We settle down with the rest, staring at the stars as they slowly come out in the night sky. We share our pasta with others in a communal picnic. As the lights begin to fade, lit candles shimmer into existence, like stars in the night. Shimmer, shimmer.

***

Joyce Chng lives in Singapore. Their fiction has appeared in *The Apex Book of World SF II*, *We See A Different Frontier*, *Cranky Ladies of History*, and *Accessing The Future*. Joyce also co-edited *THE SEA IS OURS: Tales of Steampunk Southeast Asia* with Jaymee Goh. Their recent space opera novels deal with wolf clans (*Starfang: Rise of the Clan*) and vineyards (*Water into Wine*) respectively. They also write speculative poetry with recent ones in *Rambutan Literary* and *Uncanny Magazine*. Occasionally, they wrangle article editing at *Strange Horizons* and *Umbel & Panicle*, a poetry about and for plants and botany. Alter-ego J. Damask writes about werewolves in Singapore. You can find them at http://awolfstale.wordpress.com and @jolantru on Twitter. (Pronouns: she/her, they/their)

A Rabbit Egg for Flora
Caroline M. Yoachim

The back door is tinged purple when I go out to throw my morning coffee grounds onto the compost heap. A faint rainbow tints the yard in concentric circles, progressing from purple through all the other colors before ending in a large red dot in the middle of the—admittedly rather weedy—vegetable patch that Flora had planted with her other mum, back before Kalida moved out.

"Flora, come look," I call.

"Did you find an egg, Mama?" She runs outside with bare feet, still in her pajamas and carrying a stuffed animal that she has aptly named "Pink Bunny."

Flora is four—far too young to get the implants she'd need to play Menagerie—but she loves hatching our animals. She can't see the rainbow overlay in the yard, so I tell her to look in the vegetable patch. She searches and comes up with a pale brown egg small enough to fit in the palm of her hand.

"What do you think it will be?" I ask.

Flora stares at the egg, her finger poised over the button that will initiate the hatching sequence. "It's probably an elephant."

"Why do you think that?" I don't have the heart to tell her that the ecosystem in our region isn't suitable for elephants. Elephants aren't even offered as an optional buy-on anywhere in North

America.

"Because I like elephants." Flora said. "But I also like bunnies, so maybe it will be that."

She pushes the button. Nothing happens.

"You have to put it on the ground, remember?" Allowing players to hold eggs during hatching resulted in too many dropped eggs.

Flora sets the egg down and pushes the button again. This time, the egg pops open. A gray blob of builder nanites oozes out, then disappears as the nanites disperse in search of the required minerals and organic materials. Flora keeps her gaze fixed on the empty eggshell. A pile of material accumulates next to the shell, and then the shell itself disappears, dismantled to become part of whatever creature we've earned for our local ecosystem.

The nanites shape the pile of raw materials into a black snake with lime green stripes running down the sides. Flora cocks her head. "Is it a poison snake?"

"No, it's a garter snake, totally harmless."

"Can we have a bunny next time?" Flora asks.

"We'll see." I've been working on the requirements for bunnies for months, trying to repopulate our yard and several nearby parks with the plants and animals required to sustain them. It was supposed to be a present for Flora's fourth birthday, but Menagerie is a slow-playing game, and the neighbors inadvertently thwarted my efforts by introducing squirrels, which occupy a similar niche. "Go inside and get dressed, it's almost time for school."

***

After work I hurry down the street, ignoring all the egg-rainbow overlays. My boss kept me late and stopping for eggs isn't worth the two dollars per minute the preschool will charge me if I miss my pick-up time. I chat with a Filipina lawyer on an online dating site while I walk, but the conversation fizzles out before I reach the school. I make it just on time.

Flora and I stop at the park on the way home. We find two eggs, and Flora sets them down on the ground and pushes both buttons simultaneously. They hatch into a bumble bee and a squirrel. I'm surprised to see the squirrel—the park already appears to be full of them, darting up and down tree trunks in elaborate games of chase.

There's a commotion at the far end of the park. An after-school sports program at the elementary school has let out, and a swarm of kids in uniforms have converged on a large sunshine-yellow egg. Kids are yelling and pushing, and as the only adult in the park, I push my way through the melee, carrying Flora on my hip so she doesn't get jostled by the older children.

"You've nearly smashed this egg fighting over it," I scold. Eggs are sturdy, but stomping on them can break the shell and damage the nanites.

"I was going to push the button, but Lizzy snatched the egg away," a white girl said, pouting. Soon they were all talking at once:

"I found the egg, I should push the button."

"Did not! I did!"

While the other children are yelling, a dark-haired boy sidles up to me and says, "I've never seen an egg that big before, and they've just released a new set of animals for our region."

Sensing I'm distracted, the white girl darts in and pushes the button. The egg pops open. The other kids look angry, but before another squabble can break out, I ask, "What do you think it will be?"

"Bobcat!"

I laugh. "I don't think our local ecosystem can support a predator that big."

"Deer!"

"Lobster!"

The dark-haired boy snorts. "The sea-life expansion got pushed back three months because ocean acidity is still too high. Besides, we're in the middle of a park that's nowhere near the beach."

"Bunny!" Flora says, clapping her hands. "Bunny! Bunny! Bunny!"

The nanites begin building. The creature is definitely a bird, and a large one at that.

"It's a hawk," the dark-haired boy says, "and about time. Something needs to eat some squirrels."

***

"Can I see your badges, Mama?" Flora asks. It's Saturday morning, and we've just finished our pancakes.

I route my game data through the house projector, and rows of animal badges appear on the wall. We've hatched nearly all the insects for our region, but only a handful of larger animals. Building an ecosystem is hard, even with the step-by-step instructions. It doesn't help that my action items sometimes shift suddenly when other local players introduce new animals. The hawk, though, is helpful. With a predator to keep the squirrels in check, maybe I can earn a rabbit for Flora.

"Let's plant clover in the yard."

Flora squeals and runs to get her gardening gloves. I wish I'd thought to do this sooner, but it's hard to let go of the notion that the yard is Kalida's space. It feels wrong to change it, like I'm trying to erase her from our lives. Maybe this is a way to move on. I still miss her, but mostly I'm relieved to be done with the constant fighting, and Kalida is happier off in New Hampshire with her new girlfriend.

We walk to the hardware store and return with a bag of clover seed. We find a good spot in the yard and rake away most of the weeds. Flora throws handfuls of seeds onto the freshly turned dirt. I'm terrible at gardening, but Flora and I come inside laughing and covered in mud, so it's worth it even if nothing grows.

"Tomorrow I'm going to look for four-leaf clovers," Flora tells me over lunch.

"It'll take longer than a day for the clover to grow," I warn her, but I hope it grows quickly. The sooner we get our yard set up for rabbits, the smaller the chance that someone will introduce chipmunks or some new species of mouse.

***

Someone *does* introduce mice, and after we recover from that there's a glitch where the drones stop delivering eggs for a few days. I start to worry that by the time we earn our rabbit, Flora will be bored with bunnies and onto something new, but she still carries Pink Bunny everywhere she goes.

"Pink Bunny is lonely," Flora tells me when I pick her up from preschool. "She misses Mum."

I kiss the top of Flora's head. "We'll talk to Mum on the phone tomorrow, and Pink Bunny can say hi, too. Mum misses you both very much."

Flora nods, but she's quiet on the walk home and uninterested in looking for eggs. I make her favorite dinner—mac & cheese and sliced apples—which perks her up a bit. I go out to toss the apple core into the compost heap, and there's a rainbow overlay in the yard. An egg is sitting in the middle of the clover patch, and it's one I haven't seen before—medium sized and pale pink.

"Flora!" I call, hoping with all my heart that the egg is a rabbit.

Flora spots the egg as soon as she's out the door. "It's the same color as Pink Bunny!"

She pushes the button, and I hold my breath, waiting. The nanites do their work.

"Mama! Mama! It's a rabbit, a real live rabbit! Now pink bunny won't be so lonely. Mum will be so excited to hear."

"She definitely will." I give Flora a big hug. "So now that we have our rabbit, what should we work on next?"

"Elephants!"

I laugh. We'll never have elephants here, but if the game runs long enough, someone *somewhere* might manage to earn one, and maybe I can take Flora on a grand adventure to go see it. We can plan and save for a dream vacation to Africa, much as we'd worked to earn our rabbit. In the meantime, we'll need a more realistic goal. "How about a bluejay?"

"Blue is my favorite color," Flora announces. I take her hand and we go inside, already plotting how to get our next animal.

***

Caroline M. Yoachim is a prolific author of short stories, appearing in *Asimov's, Fantasy & Science Fiction, Uncanny, Beneath Ceaseless Skies, Clarkesworld,* and *Lightspeed,* among other places. She has been a finalist for the World Fantasy, Locus, and multiple Hugo and Nebula Awards. Yoachim's debut short story collection, *Seven Wonders of a Once and Future World & Other Stories,* came out with Fairwood Press in 2016. To find out more, check out her website at carolineyoachim.com

Iron Fox in the Marble City
Vlad-Andrei Cucu

A crowd was starting to gather around the fountain in the small park. They were all looking in awe and shock at the metal giant in front of them. "Mommy, who's the iron man sitting there?" I would hear a girl say. And I sat quietly on the bench. I couldn't join them really, for I was the subject of their gaze.

I didn't expect to be back in Japan so soon. Just recently, it was a hot afternoon in Madagascar and I was sitting around in a trench as my comrades in arms played 'spin the canteen', all of us waiting for new orders. They got some, but I just got discharged. It came as a surprise for almost all of us. Growing up, I had the impression that, in just a few years, Tokyo would be this dark city covered mostly in steel and neon, with rampant crime and corruption and people decorated in cybernetics. When I got drafted and augmented with technology into a supposed high-tech soldier, the LFP special program, I expected this to be the perfect environment for me. A place to fit in like a puzzle piece. But now, as I arrived here by boat, all the way from Madagascar, I felt as if my whole worldview crashed right upon me. And I say that as someone who already had two helicopters crash down on them.

Initially I thought I got off at the wrong place, maybe even the wrong continent, but here I was. Most of the buildings had been renovated with colorful decorations, marble supports, and lush greens. Almost every building had trees growing around it or was covered in various plants. The air was fresh, like Madagascar before the war. There were fewer cars and more trolleys on the roads, people walked or cycled everywhere, the streets busy and lively but somehow still quiet and relaxed.

The first thing I did was to send some flowers back to the guys in Madagascar. It was a dare all of us decided on when one got discharged to immediately send flowers to the others. There's an amusing story behind it, but it's quite long so maybe I'll tell it some other time. Regardless, I went to a flower shop I knew from back before my war days. It was a large chain store with a funky logo. The shop was still in place, but any kind of branding was gone, replaced by seemingly homemade wood decorations. I greeted the young woman running the place.

"Good afternoon, miss."

"I hope you're having a nice day as well. How may I help you?"

"Just a small bouquet, please. Any flowers are alright, I just want something that can be easily shipped through mail."

"Okay, I'll see what I can get for you."

I was somewhat surprised she didn't bring up my appearance as she was going through the various flowers to pick some suitable ones.

"Say, I know this might be a bit obvious, but I take it you're not from around here." Well, at least not bringing it up initially.

"Actually, I am from here. But I left some time ago. Got drafted into the army and all that. Still, it feels bizarre, people are kinda weird around here. They seem surprised to see a metal giant walking about, but no one's commented on it that much."

"Well, the way we go about the community is if you respect others, then you'll be respected back."

"Fair enough. Also, if you don't mind me asking, wasn't there a chain store here before?"

"Yeah, it stood here for years in fact. They pulled out a while back though. Many chains did after they disagreed with the restructuring plans here in Tokyo… aaand your bouquet is ready."

Leaving the flower shop, I froze in place. Here I was, taller than anyone, stripped of any basic human traits, a true living weapon. A device of a future that never was. I stood there so long lost in my own thoughts that I failed to notice someone approach me. A fairly young man, of seemingly Asian and African descent, greeted me with a warm smile.

"Hello there. I am Seiji Edgar, member of the Nu-Tokyo Visitors Council. I heard some reports about a very unusual visitor wandering around town and, well, I hope you don't mind if I'm wrong, I'm still new to this, but I think you might be that person."

"It's alright, I've had it far worse before. And I'm not really visiting. I actually grew up here, a while ago. Now, everything's brand new, and I don't even know where to start."

"Ah, many people around here were like that when they first arrived. If you would tell me a few things about yourself, if you don't mind, of course, perhaps I can help you find your own place within the community."

"Certainly. I still go by NX-5412314995, codename *Kithound*. My main specialisations are aerial deployment, heavy weapons support, and anti-armor. I have been in 43 different operations across Europe and Madagascar."

A moment of awkward silence then ensued.

"Okay, Kithound. I won't deny that those skills might have some uses, but not at the moment, no offense. However, if you are interested, you can potentially help out with plantation and gardening work. Do not worry much about experience, we gladly teach others how to work in those fields."

"Gardening, you say? Where exactly? The town is pretty much full of foliage."

"The dome garden. We've been relying on trade for goods for a while now, but if we are to properly set it up, we can have a proper sustainable production center."

And before I knew it, I found myself alongside Seiji at the bottom of Tokyo Tower, now repurposed as a grand dome garden, with rows of plantation and water canals all arranged around a metal device sitting where the former FootTown building used to be. It was a water pump, with a minimalist but efficient design to put in the necessary amounts of water for the plantation. I was sitting right by it with some other volunteers while Seiji was explaining how the garden functions. I'd been in this situation before. Sort of. When me and other troops were first instructed on how to proceed when in a battle, I couldn't help but constantly feel like I was judged by others, all eyes pointing towards the weird metal man. But here, they seemed to be showing more determination, more camaraderie, without even having to be on the battlefield. Some gave me a pat on the back. Others were eager to ask me for a friendly competition. It was an unusual feeling for me, to say the least.

"So while you are free to choose what type of field you can work on," Seiji kept instructing, "we are all gonna eventually have to work the water pump. Without constant maintenance, the lack of water could ruin years of work. I hope you don't mind, okay?"

We all agreed to it. Since my data banks still have some loose memories of my pre-war life, I can recall some memories about soybean farming, though without any of the original context. We spent the next couple of hours with a bit of gardening and maintenance. How to dig, plant, water and overall take care and ensure they grow up well. Apparently stuff like this is now taught in schools, too. I guess it's not that different from digging trenches, but even then I wasn't the one to actually do it, just a casual observer of things.

As I was carefully trying to plant a few seeds, Seiji greeted me again: "How does it feel to be working the fields, Kithound?"

"Like a piece of machinery used for a purpose other than the one it is meant for. I'm sure I will learn to adapt, thank you."

"Hey, if there's anything guaranteed around here, it's that you are free to keep up hope for your own future. Still, you worked enough for the first day. My shift is ending soon. If you want, we can go together, and maybe I can give you a proper tour of how Tokyo has changed since you were last here."

"Well, I guess I have to thank you for that."

"By the way, what does LFP stand for?"

"I forgot, honestly."

And so Seiji gave me the general tour of Nu-Tokyo, showing me some of the various popular culture places. Eventually he dropped me off at a nice resort meant for new arrivals in town. All of the rooms were arranged in a square shape around a central outdoor garden. Probably a motif for the town. Hard to tell. The room itself was very nice and cozy though. Marble and wood, various little decorations put about, some paper flags hung to add color, and a bed that would probably have been comfortable in my previous life. A cat was also hanging out outside the window. I stared at it while reflecting about the places I visited with Seiji. I couldn't recall them very well. I was in those places just today, just a few hours ago, but all the details were loose and smudgy. My database didn't have any problems last time I checked. "Is the programming of my computers not allowing me to properly integrate?" I almost said out loud.

And that's how things went for a while. I was taking care of the crops alright, they were growing pretty well. Every night I would then go with Seiji and his friends around town. We went to various cafés to just hang around, drink—well, they drank—discuss literature, arts, lives, crude jokes, the Tao. Overall I couldn't complain, but something just kept feeling off. I tried looking in places, checking out various concerts, meetings, and at the end of the day, the only thing I could pull off was just standing and thinking alone in the room, with the cat occasionally sitting at the window.

The biggest break was when Seiji arrived and told me someone wanted to see me.

"The Workers' Union? What's it about?"

"Supposedly they are having some problems around town. Many people are being questioned about any suspicious activity. Still, I know you enough to know that it's probably nothing for you to worry about."

"Suspicious activity?"

"Yeah, a few gardens were ravaged overnight, so we're conducting an investigation. I don't want to come off as discriminating, honest, but you're new here, and in the eyes of many still somewhat suspicious."

I am accustomed to following the orders of others, often without question, so I agreed to go with him. In normal circumstances, I think it would be fair for one to be more than a little annoyed at the lack of trust from others. But, as I was a special case among them, I gave them the benefit of the doubt for now.

As we were going to the meeting place, a woman stopped the two of us. She kindly asked us if I could crush a piece of metal she had with my bare hands. An odd request, but she seemed nice so I obliged. I left some big dents in it, and then she took it with her and left. *Must be a tourist*, I thought. Regardless, both me and Seiji got to the pier where the meeting was taking place. At a table under a tree by the sea side, a group of people were already sitting. A woman in a two piece suit, holding a large briefcase, stood in front of them.

"I'm impressed with the sense of aesthetics that you folks have managed to establish for yourselves here in Tokyo," she told the group, "but this system you have is only a short-term solution. There is barely any hierarchical structure to rely on, and a single population spike will eventually overwhelm you. And when that happens, my company will gladly provide helpful services for you all."

From the other end of the table, another woman was doing the talking for the union. I would learn from Seiji that she was Milan. Apparently she preferred going by a single name basis. While there's no true hierarchy, Milan is frequently in charge with much of the city's infrastructure due to her knowledge on the matter.

"We appreciate your offer, but we are actually carefully planning the expansion of our current system to other regions here in Japan that would need it. Agriculture and green energy are an important part of this, and I mean no offense, Mrs. Gulblut, but your tech company doesn't seem to provide the necessary help. And just so you know, we have anticipated the population boom as well, and we are still going through multiple solutions, but you have yet to actually provide any ideas outside of the promise of a solution."

The one speaking for the group turned their head towards Seiji and me.

"Excuse me for a moment, Mrs. Gulblut. Hello, Seiji, and I'm gonna guess you're Kithound."

"Ei, Milan, how are things going for ya? And why did you call us all the way here?"

"A potentially troubling situation. Over the past week we've been getting multiple reports of animals around the city going missing or water pumps found broken out of nowhere. And not like faulty components or anything, whole devices completely crushed. We suspect there might be someone intentionally sabotaging them."

"And those reports somehow ended up getting overseas. The reception of your initiative for a greener Nippon Federation has been very mixed back in the US. Situations like these can only put a damper on outside relations, which is why I insist my company and I can help the whole community for the upcoming troubles as well as catch the culprit responsible."

"Assuming there is a culprit in the first place—"

The lady who had asked me to bend the metal interrupted the whole conversation. "Excuse me, Mrs. Gulblut? I have here the item you requested." She handed over the piece of metal she'd asked me to bend for her. Everyone at the table looked at it in surprise.

"Ah, thank you Denise," Mrs. Gulblut said. "So I can assume that you recognize the way this metal is bent?"

"Yes, the water pumps were crushed with those exact dents," Milan replied in surprise. "Where did you get this?"

"Well, you see—"

"Excuse me, Mrs. Milan. May I interject?"

"Is it urgent to the situation at hand, Kithound? And you don't need to add the 'Mrs.'"

"I can guarantee it very well is."

"Then go ahead."

"It was me that bent the pipe," I said. "Denise over there asked me earlier to crush it, I presume to check it against the other damages. Mrs. Gulblut here wanted to prove that I might have been the one to sabotage the pumps. And I admit that I have the strength to carry such a task. However, all this does is prove that the culprit was very likely an LFP unit, not strictly me."

"However, as much as I disagree with Gulblut's ideas, your proposition still points to you as a possible suspect. No personal offense."

"There are many of us," I said. "About 500 LFP units originated from Tokyo alone. By the time I was discharged, 327 units were still active. It could be very possible that another one of them also returned here to Tokyo."

"Yeah, I'm with Kithound on this one," Seiji joined in. "I've been alongside them for about a month now and I have high doubts they are capable of doing something like this. Right, Kithound?"

"Hold on, hold on. Right, Mrs. Gulblut, I see you tried to lend a hand with the investigation, but we'll have to compare our notes here. As for you, Seiji, I will trust you with my best, but unfortunately we'll have to put Kithound under surveillance at their apartment. However, you are free to assist us with anything you might know about a potential rogue LFP operating around town."

Mrs. Gulblut gave me a smug look, then turned to Milan. "Well, it happens I'll be staying in town for a few more days, Milan, so if you ever require my company's help with the proceedings, you know who to contact."

"But of course, Mrs. Gulblut."

After that I had to spend all my time inside my apartment room. It's nothing new for me really. Seiji hasn't visited too often, and when he did, we wouldn't talk much either. He left me some books, magazines, and comics to read. Anything from some superhero stuff to *The City in History* and an old worn copy of the *I Ching*. I couldn't get into those even when I was lacking in robotic parts. I did take a plant with me, a red flower. Taking care of it was the only thing I did besides just standing around. I even named it Jeff. Had a friend in the army called that. Well, friend is overplaying it a bit. It was just someone I interacted with more often than usual. Enough for him to greet me with a "Yo, Kithound! There's some stuff happening." instead of "Lt. Kithound, we have a situation occurring." The most I recall of him was when he went into the trees once. He never came back after that.

I thought about the military a lot more that night. We were all generally programmed into those new bodies at once. Is my failure to integrate into these new surroundings a programming quirk? How much of us is our own, really? At the same time, this community is entirely built around pacifist, utopian principles, with which I completely clash. I adapted on a technical level by doing the common work, but I cannot keep myself interested on, I guess, a more philosophical level. And they are open to others, but how much can they change to accommodate me, or vice versa? Soldiers like me are meant to adapt, but I'm just out of my field and can't take it.

Those thoughts were interrupted when I heard a scream outside. I knew I wasn't allowed out for the moment, but I still rushed in to check out what was happening. Outside there was an old lady knocking into a tree with her stick while shouting, "Come on down, Aki. Mama's really worried about you." There was a cat sitting in the tree, which I assumed belonged to the lady. So I went to help her.

"Pardon me. May I help you with the cat?"

"Oh, is someone there?"

She kept waving her stick around until she figured out where I was.

"You think you can reach her, young lad?"

"I should be tall enough."

I reached towards the branch and took hold of it. After slightly lowering it, I raised my other arm for the cat to jump to. It proved pretty cooperative in that case. However, I didn't let go of the branch in time and accidently broke it off.

"Oh, no. I didn't mean to do that."

"Is everything alright over there?"

"I accidentally ripped the branch off. I didn't mean to."

"Oh, is Aki alright though?"

"It is, but the tree…"

"Now, it's not like you ripped it whole from its stump, dear. Say, are you new here?"

"One can say that. And to be honest, I feel like I might never truly belong in this community. I have tried working at the dome garden. It felt good to work, but somehow I still came out unsatisfied."

"Well, the question is, are you filling the role that you want to fill? Everyone contributes to the community in different ways, and not necessarily by working. I had to give up farming because of my age, but I still help the people in the neighborhood by talking and discussing what's on their minds. I would like to do that now, sweetie, but unfortunately I have to go feed little Aki. Hope you don't mind."

"Not at all, miss. Have a good day."

I gave her the cat and then headed back inside. I stood and thought for a bit about what she was saying. However, it didn't last, as Seiji knocked. I let him in, and he was bursting with joy. Far happier than I've seen him for all the time I knew him, and that's saying something.

"What happened, Seiji?"

"We managed to find the missing animals on a nearby boat. Someone hired a team to sneak them out. Everything ranging from cats and dogs to deer and golden pheasants. They had orders to do it, from an anonymous contractor that already paid them."

"That solves one problem, but then the broken water pumps still remain an issue."

"Right, and that's why I called out for you. I have this map here of all the locations of the water pumps that were broken. Maybe you can identify a pattern or strategy?"

I took a look at the map Seiji provided. At first glance, the positioning of the broken pumps seemed like random attacks, but I recognized why they were picked. It's a fairly common strategy I'd seen employed back in the war, specifically for LFP squads. I took a brush from the shelf and started drawing a circular line crossing all the various points.

"A spiral shape?"

"Yes, it's a standard tactic, actually."

"So it would go like this around the various districts, going all the way up to the dome garden."

And so, the two of us got ready to check up on the water pump at the dome garden. It was still intact by the time we arrived. We decided to wait around the area in case something would happen soon. Specifically, we were waiting until about midnight on an airship above the dome garden. It was a weird feeling to fly in an air-based vehicle without hearing the whirling of the blades or a sergeant barking orders before landing. The whole steel airship was based on the design of ancient zeppelins, with the cabin dedicated to a small café with a lovely view of the city. It was flying at a leisurely pace, and it was around half past eight o'clock and the place was pretty crowded.

"Hey, Kithound, have a look at this brochure I found. It might be fitting for you."

It was a pamphlet for an activist group all the way in Neo York. I recall that name in particular because it was all over the news when it was brought up. It was the name of a full restructuring effort in New York after an experimental missile system developed by the US military accidently failed and hit multiple places across the city. A single rocket was enough to take out the Statue of Liberty. The pamphlet itself was for The Worker and LFP Rights group, spearheaded by another LFP soldier, Electrobody. It was interesting to know there were others struggling to accommodate like me.

"Say, Kithound…"

"Yes, Seiji?"

"Do you feel alright among us? Or still like you're being left out?"

"Let's just say that adapting is a slow process for someone specifically designed for certain environments."

"Still, in the end, do you help us because you care about generally helping the environment, or is just part of your programming to intentionally follow orders? I mean, I don't want to offend you, Kithound, like at all, but it's just something I kinda can't stop thinking about."

A thought like that hadn't crossed my mind beforehand. I remained silent for a moment, and stayed so long in my thoughts I didn't even notice what was around me anymore. It wasn't until a girl left a flower in my hand that I snapped out of it. Red, like Jeff.

"I guess I just like you guys."

"So are we here to discuss business or just your pseudo-philosophical garbage again?" chimed in Mrs. Gulblut.

"Gulblut? What are you doing here?" commented Seiji, surprised at her sudden appearance.

"I'm wondering the same thing. I thought I would meet with Milan to discuss the current issues going about town."

"Actually, I invited you here."

"You, LFP trooper? What do you want?"

"The name's Kithound, by the way. I brought you here to tell ya that you are terrible at hiding your secret plans."

"Plans? What plans?"

"Please, did you really expect to fool people like this? A string of attacks and kidnappings, done by identified contracted hires, a strange business woman arriving out of nowhere, somehow already knowing every detail and carrying out her own investigation, and yet you thought no one would connect the dots? I also looked into a fairly recent assassination of a representative from Nu-Tokyo in Neo York, conveniently around the area of your company."

"Look, Neo York is currently undergoing a large population spike after a lot of people arrived from various war-torn regions, including parts of Madagascar, Kithound, and since an unfortunate toxic spilling incident on Staten Island, the whole city hasn't been able to run at full capacity due to how many resources have been pushed into solving that particular issue."

"And I take it that several companies all the way back in Neo York are scrambling to come up with some sort of solution for this crisis?"

"Several of them are after Nu-Tokyo alongside mine. I'm sure your friend Seiji can tell you how Milan refused about all of them for setting up here. They don't want to solve the problems in Neo York, they just want to survive a potential economic collapse, me included. Of course, you can call me out on cheating by hiring some goons to sabotage some points of production so that my tech company can swipe in to save the day, but in the end that's just your theory and one you can't do much to prove, Kithound."

"I don't intend to prove anything right now, we intend to just stop them before they can go any further. Tonight there'll be a raid on the dome garden from your hirelings. That raid will fail."

"Well, thank you for considering, Kitsunehound. I'll just make sure you'll fail as well."

And she left with a smile on her face.

"I take it this is more your kind of territory?"

"And in other circumstances, a place of comfort for me. One where I was meant to belong. However, even though I feel like I haven't experienced much of your community, I don't want to go there too often."

A few hours later it was close to midnight. The airship was slowly floating above the garden. From up there, all the way to the bottom of the dome garden, a group of people could be seen, all wearing protection suits, who were trying to sneak in through the gates at the end of the water canals. They had one way visors and large tanks on their backs. Armed with flamethrowers, they were ready at any moment to set fire to the plants in the garden, then possibly go outside to burn some more to cause panic throughout the city. As they were approaching the main water pump, a spotlight dawned upon them. Seiji was sitting on top of the device aiming the light at them. He was shivering with fear, but still led through a quick order.

"I see them! Turn on the water pumps, now!"

And quickly the water rushed through the canals, taking the intruders with it and smashing them against the gate. They were alright, but now their weapons were jammed with water, and they were quickly captured by the members of the workers' union that were waiting for them. Outside, a few streets away, a rented truck was waiting with a small crew inside.

"It's almost the planned time. Where's the fire? We can't wait here for them forever," shouted the one in the driver's seat.

The only response they got was a loud crash on top of their truck, which was me jumping down on it. After I non-fatally took care of them, I tied them up in the back of the truck to be properly dealt with later. I then went back to the dome garden. Seiji and the others were already celebrating by the time I got there.

"Kithound! So you took care of the LFP already?"

"That was just an extraction point for the infiltrators. No sign of the LFP."

"Well, where could they be then?"

The glass shattered. A dark figure crashed through it into the water pump, crushing it under their feet. A tall, metal figure. One just like me. They had a helmet in the shape of a beret, and a scarf-like piece hanging from the neck, symbolizing the position of an LFP captain. In other words, someone with more experience than me.

"NO! The water pump!"

"Everyone, get down!"

They didn't stop just at destroying the water pump, as they took out a gun and started firing upon the various plants around the garden.

"You already broke the water pump," I said. They stopped shooting and turned their attention towards me, staring deeply. "Your contract is over now, " I continued.

"It was extended so that I also have to take out a rogue LFP unit. I presume you might be the one. But I like to know my targets for a bit. Especially when they might stand a chance against me. Identify yourself!"

"NX-5412314995, codename *Kithound*."

"STK-15131151, codename *Capital C*. Well, NX, I hope you understand how much you're actually betraying your own kind here. Nature is not a thing worthy of respect. It should be feared. Man never ended up anywhere of use by treating a tree like his friend. No, he just saw the many ways a tree should benefit him. An enemy, small or big, that is an obstacle that one must pass to improve his own condition in life."

"What are you on about?"

"Look at you, NX, you're a device used for an unintended purpose. Doesn't it make you feel empty? Aren't you always left out? Face it, NX. No matter how hard you try to waste all those government resources on becoming a farmer, you'll always be just a weapon. And judging by your rank, not a very good one."

"So you admit that you are really no more than just a pawn to the army that drafted you in the first place?"

"Drafted? I volunteered, NX. All in the name of providing protection to my own country. And this might seem weird to you,

NX, hanging out with all these tree huggers, but war has been vital for the global economy for ages."

"You're not intending to start a war here, now are you? You barely have any grounds to sustain it."

"Of course we do. You think it's just Neo York that has issues? Crises like those are everywhere in the world. All your plants, animals, technology, are valuable to those people. So of course they'll join in to start a war, just to take a bite."

"Why not use the budget to just recreate what's here?"

"That would be far too expensive. But less expensive is getting to kill you, right now. Now come on, soldier! Head back into battle!"

Capital C immediately started firing. I quickly got out of the way and started going in circles around, trying to get closer. More plants were hit, but that's less than the amount they could've destroyed if left alone. As I got closer to them, I eventually got hit in the arm. I used the opportunity to drop down and play dead. Capital C obviously figured out my tactic, and quickly pointed the gun at me. Before they got a chance to fire, I grabbed it with my working arm and forced them to aim upward. While they were disoriented, I gave them a good kick in the gut, breaking straight into the insides.

The impact put Capital C on the ground, clutching in agony as their life support system was failing.

I was humane, so I tried to crush the rest of the system to put them out of their misery. However, Capital C quickly sprang back up. They grabbed my arm with one hand and used the other to pull a concealed knife from their armor. With one fell swing, they stabbed right into my elbow, cutting through critical wires, leaving both my arms paralyzed in place. I could barely move from the shock as they shuffled slowly towards, constantly holding to my arm, before looking at me straight in the face. While a liquid that was once blood dripped from their head, with their visors blinking wildly, they still tried to tell me a muffled and slurred speech:

"Want to truly feel humane, NX? Then you must know that you

should have left a fellow LFP unit to die in the blaze of battle, like the good little soldier that they are."

They used their other hand to pull a grenade from their back, and lifted it high above.

"Is that you really speaking, Capital, or is it just the wires in your brain messing around?"

"Of course it's the programming NX. Same as you."

"So how come the both of us ended up here like this?"

"Because unlike you, NX, I understand my true purpose. I was made like this to fight, so I fight. I had squad members try to live peaceful lives after the war. Can you guess where they are now?"

"The grave?"

"Not even a hero's grave. So, NX, what if I break some regulations to leave you the one in need to be put down like a dog?"

"It'd be funny if you wasted your last few moments like this only to fail to actually kill me, wouldn't it, Capital?"

"Quite so. Shame it won't happen."

With a flick of the finger, they threw the pin of the grenade.

"Last words, NX?"

"Unlike you, I am not doomed to fail just yet."

"Oh really, Kithound!? You failed to save the-the pump."

Their voice was starting to pause and scramble with each word.

"Gulblut and… others will se-send more and more after your puny commu-commu-community. And here you are, para-paralyzed with a simple… knife as I… will… prevail… against…"

A snapping sound came from inside Capital C. It was the life support system completely collapsing from the stress their anger was putting it through, officially ending Capital C's life.

"You didn't have to bleed yourself out yet."

In the time before the detonation, I freed myself from their hand, and with a quick build-up, gave the body a roundhouse kick, throwing the body back and leaving it to explode in a patch of the garden that wouldn't be too hard to rebuild.

"Kithound?"

"Yes, Seiji? Let me guess, are you all afraid of what I can potentially be now?"

"What? No. That was great. But, the water pump got destroyed."

"How bad is it?"

"Well, it's in pretty bad shape. The connecting mechanism that distributes the water through the pipes in the garden is completely destroyed, and the system for drawing the water in seems pretty unstable and could fail at any moment. We could potentially replace them, but by the time we get the parts, it might be too late and we'd be set back years with plantations."

I took a look at what the broken components were. All of them were inside my health support system. I opened my chest compartment to show them all to Seiji.

"Wow, those are exactly what we need to fix the pump, but—"

"But unfortunately you'll have to take them out of me."

"Actually, there is one alternative," I heard someone calling from behind us. Both of us looked back to see Milan had just arrived after it was all over.

"Hey, Milan," greeted Seiji. "What do you mean by that exactly?"

"I actually used to be a mechanic for LFP units back in Europe, so I know how to tinker with them a bit. Instead of just taking the parts out of Kithound and putting them in the water pump, I could reconnect their whole system to the pump itself. It is risky because it would mean that you'll be permanently stuck to it, but you won't be dead."

"How do you feel about that, Kithound?"

As soon as Seiji got done with that question, my thoughts immediately jumped to the old lady with the cat. The desire to integrate into this community has been there, but now I found something I could seamlessly fulfill. In the end it was a matter of patience.

"I think I'll agree."

It has been around two months since, and I am now officially the new water pump of the dome garden. Others would say that this was be the worst possible existence, but I for one welcome it. It isn't too different from what I was accustomed to in my apartment room, except now I have a much grander place to reflect within. I wouldn't say I really gave up much. It wasn't a sacrifice, it was finalizing an adaptation. I am now a machine that is used for its intended purpose. And this time it's a purpose that's more beneficial for others. The dome garden has only become lusher, with foliage reaching up to the ceiling. A second one is currently in the plans for development. I also still get regular visits from Seiji and company, and a couple of days ago they allowed animals inside the garden. So now I have a plant named Jeff and a cat named Voice.

Overall, life is good as a water pump. I guess the big question is that I don't know where I can go from here in the near future. I didn't expect to be here a few years ago. I didn't think this is how the future would be. So I expect anything could happen tomorrow.

Now excuse me, I have to go water the plants.

***

Vlad-Andrei Cucu, by day an average student, by night an average student that expresses himself through drawing, indie game making, and more recently writing. Trained in the methods of anarchism in Romania's mountains, and the art of creative writing in Ireland, he is eager to let out some weird, but interesting transhumanist ideas.

Mariposa Awakening

Joseph F. Nacino

When Sofia Antonelli stepped out from the Luneta Hotel that morning, it felt like the air was a sea of sweltering humidity as perspiration immediately dotted her forearms and her back.

As she wiped a handkerchief on her forehead, the first things she noticed were the dark clouds overhead, portending the arrival of the superstorm and the drowned Rizal Park nearby.

Part of the park was still recognizable, with its looming statue of the country's national hero and the sprawling manicured lawns and concrete pathways. The Philippine flag flew tall on an iron flagpole even as two stock-still soldiers in blue-and-red dress uniforms guarded the base of the monument.

Several meters away from the flagpole, a wall of mangrove trees marked the boundary between land and the shallow waters. From the top of the hotel steps, she could see the mangrove trees stretching all the way towards the abandoned buildings of Manila steeped in floodwaters.

In the distance, a dark line marked the horizon: the walled city of Intramuros with Fort Santiago jutting out from the fortifications like the prow of a ship. She was supposed to meet Professor Marisol Capati-Rhee of the MARIPOSA Project at the historic colonial fortress. However, someone was supposed to pick her up at the

Luneta Hotel.

Sofia watched the surf slowly lap against the streets of Manila, a common sight in the year 2071, when cities were barely holding on against the rising seas wrought by climate change. Her home, Venice, was surviving, thanks to its MOSE floodwalls; Amsterdam had its own concrete dikes and floodgates.

All of them—including cities like Osaka, Miami, and Shanghai—were now using AI systems to control the artificial dams that were built against the rising water levels and the occasional powerful storm surges. But other cities like Rio de Janeiro and Jakarta that didn't have the technology or the funds to build their own dams had already been abandoned.

Sofia had grown up under the threat of her city drowning in the Mediterranean. It was what led her to take up studies in artificial intelligence and hydrology. Now, it had driven her to travel halfway across the world to Manila to see the promise of the MARIPOSA Project.

While she was waiting for her pickup, she figured she would see the sights of Roxas Island, named for the area around Roxas Boulevard. Back then, it was famous for its beautiful view of Manila Bay. Because she had ridden a VTOL shuttle bus from the Ninoy Aquino International Airport straight to her hotel last night, Sofia hadn't seen much of the small strip of land left of Manila still above the water.

She had been unable to rest during the flight from Italy because of turbulence brought about by the brewing Super Typhoon Korina. After checking into a well-furnished AI-controlled hotel room, she had slept soundly the whole night.

Going down the hotel steps, she crossed Kalaw Avenue crowded with vendors selling dried fish and seashells on the sidewalk. A few meters away from the vendors, several small outrigger boats carrying nets and paddles bobbed gently in the lapping water.

There were many people rushing about trying to finish their

business before the storm hit. Some were tourists trying to get some last souvenirs before retreating back to their hotels that persisted in remaining open. Locals carried groceries while looking nervously at the dark sky.

There was also a squad of soldiers in flak jackets and helmets standing guard near the bay, with an APC and armoured jeep parked near their concrete outpost. A radio tower and a small radar topped their outpost as a multi-legged drone walked by, its high-calibre Minigun swivelling around like a snout sniffing out trouble.

She wondered if Manila was also being troubled by sea bandits. She had heard that many of the criminal elements that had lived in the cities now took to the waters like pirates of earlier times.

She walked towards the park, feeling like she was swimming through the humid air. While sweat plastered the back of her blouse, she put on her eyeglasses and synced it with her smartwatch.

She felt her smartwatch AI ping her in warning, the temperature and humidity figures sliding towards the yellow register on the lens of her glasses. She blinked them away and kept walking.

There was a whining sound behind her and she turned to see a VTOL shuttle bus coming in, powered by giant turbines. Landing on Kalaw Avenue, the bus disgorged more guests for Luneta Hotel. Nearby, a man was trying to calm a panicking horse harnessed to a colourful cart carrying a couple of grimly-smiling tourists clutching tight on their straw hats. The lens tagged the cart with its local translation: *karitela.*

She thought the scene was quite incongruous: the *karitela* and the VTOL shuttle standing before the beautiful French Renaissance-style Luneta Hotel—slices of different time periods jostling in the present. It brought to her mind William Gibson's words, "The future is already here. It's just not evenly distributed yet."

She searched for more information about Manila in the electronic briefer she was given. Pulling up a file on her smartwatch, she scrolled on the surface of the watch and viewed the results on the lens of her shades. The green text crawled slowly upward before her eyes:

…In 2039, pushed by climate change, the waters off Manila Bay began to rise and by 2052, the city of Manila began to flood. This forced most of its residents to flee to parts of the greater metropolitan area untouched by the waters and even to the nearby provinces surrounding Metro Manila…

…By 2069, the waters only covered a third of the city of Manila, a rarity among the many coastline cities that are now slowly drowning. It was through the use of mangroves that the city was able to stave off the floods…

"*Signorina! Signorina!*" She turned around and saw a Filipino in military fatigues and vest, his head covered by a floppy jungle hat, jogging towards her. He had a pump shotgun strapped to his back.

"*Si? Parli Italiano?*" she asked with a teasing smile.

Abashed, the Filipino shook his head. "Sorry, that's all the Italian I know," the man said in English. "You're Miss Sofia Antonelli? From ENEA?"

Laughing, she nodded. "Please, call me Sofia."

"I'm Rey. Professor Marisol told me that I would be picking up a *bella Italiana* this morning," he said with a grin as he extended his hand.

Sofia shook it, commenting wryly, "Well, I think I was the only Italian on the flight, so yes, I might be her."

"Apologies for the humidity. Even with the storm coming, you need to constantly hydrate," he said, offering a small bottled water he took from a side pocket of his pants.

"Thank you," she said as she took it. After she took a gulp, she put it into her handbag. She asked, "Are you part of MARIPOSA?"

"Yes, I'm a forest ranger for the Mangrove Resiliency Task Force. We protect and develop the Mangrove Wall."

"Oh, you're not military?"

"Former military, now attached as civilian," Rey said. "The boat is this way. Shall we?"

There were a lot of people on the strand that served as a small pier, which was crowded by outrigger boats—her translation tagged them as *bancas*—unloading their cargo of fish before the storm hit land.

After a buyer scanned the weight of the fish using a laser scanner, the fishermen placed their catch in woven baskets to be transported to Metro Manila's wet markets in the waiting tricycles. A quick look at her lens told her that most of the unflooded streets of Manila were too small for regular-sized vehicles, hence the need for tricycles.

It reminded Sofia of Gibson's words again, about how the future was unevenly distributed, especially with nations' GDPs wrecked by climate change. She sighed. So many countries had to find solutions to stop the rising waters but those solutions usually involved lots of money and innovative technologies.

"How was your flight?" Rey asked as he guided Sofia towards a small *banca* at the end of the pier.

"Terrible, but not surprising with a category five typhoon at our heels," she explained as she tried to balance on the rocking outrigger boat, her sneakers slipping on the bottom of the boat.

She then noticed Rey had given a hard stare at a group of men by the side of the pier, loitering and smoking cigarettes. She wondered why, until she realized that they were the only ones at the pier who seemed unbothered by the coming storm.

"I guess your timing to see MARIPOSA was just right," Rey said, turning towards her with a reassuring smile. "We've just expanded the Mangrove Wall, so you'll also see some expansion of the network."

"Well, I hadn't expected to see it in *actual* action," she pointed out. "ENEA wanted to see if MARIPOSA could help us in Venice. But I'm glad that I'll be able to see your mangrove project as well."

"I'll let Professor Marisol explain about MARIPOSA. But I can tell you this—the mangroves *are* the heart of the MARIPOSA Project," Rey said with pride in his voice.

The ranger untied the boat and then with a long pole, he pushed them away from the pier and into the mangroves.

The noise from the strand faded away as they drifted into the trees. It was cooler underneath the branches of the mangroves, and she could hear birds calling out above them. In a way, it was almost relaxing: it reminded her of the gondolas back at home.

Sofia said, "The mangroves are beautiful. But it's hard to believe that they're effective against the floods."

Rey said, "Mangroves have always been natural coastal defences. They reduce further soil erosion while blocking greater damage from waves and storm surges."

"How deep is the Mangrove Wall?"

"Pretty thick. With the waters breaching inland, we decided to plant further and further, and made sure the forest would be thick enough to keep the flood from spreading," he explained.

For half an hour, Rey guided their boat through a jungle-like maze of mangroves while speaking endlessly. Sofia felt dizzy both because of the amount of information being conveyed by him and the serpentine route to Intramuros.

Finally, they came to a wide and massive stone wall amidst the forest of trees. They entered through an archway, and Sofia marvelled at the thickness of the walls.

"Welcome to Intramuros," Rey said grimly.

For a time, it felt like they were traveling through ancient ruins as Rey poled them along the streets of the Walled City. Sofia remained quiet as they floated past half-submerged Spanish-era wooden houses and decrepit, abandoned buildings.

All that was left were the drowned shells of its past, she thought. She saw another structure stretching before them—a stone building with three small spires on top of it, marked by a faded stone carving.

At first Sofia thought it was a high stone pier as three flat-bottomed airboats were tied to it. A metal ladder had been tied to the top of the pier. But she realized that the surface of the pier was actually the top of the fort wall when she spotted the upper half of the archway of a fort gate underneath. The lower part of the archway was already submerged with the gate replaced by a solid concrete plug.

"This is the entrance of Fort Santiago," Rey said. He noticed what she was looking at and added: "The waters are deeper here because Fort Santiago is nearer to the Pasig River. The mangroves keep the waters lower near the shore."

On the pier, three men watched them approach: a handsome old man with Korean features in orange overalls, plus two Filipinos dressed in military fatigues and carrying high-powered rifles.

"Hey, Sir Aaron!" Rey cried.

"You took your time," Aaron remarked lightly.

"We had to be discreet coming here," Rey replied as he pushed the boat towards the side of the wall. Tying the *banca* to one of the airboats, he then helped Sofia up the ladder. Sofia was glad she had worn comfortable pants and shoes on this trip.

Aaron gave Sofia a hand up the stone wall. "Hello, Miss Antonelli," he said, "The Mangrove Resiliency Task Force offers you its warm welcome. I am Aaronson Rhee."

"Oh! But I've heard so much about your work! I read several of your papers on machine-learning and computational linguistics," Sofia said, trying hard not to gush.

Aaron smiled and said, "I'm flattered."

Meanwhile, the other men climbed down the ladder and each proceeded to one of the airboats. Looking up at Aaron and Sofia, Rey said: "Pardon me, Miss Sofia, Sir Aaron. We need to run an important task before the typhoon hits."

After saying their goodbyes, Sofia and Aaron watched the three men run the engines of their airboats, their giant fan blades swinging to life with a thunderous roar. Aaron said to Sofia: "Shall we?"

As they walked, Sofia saw Fort Santiago was shaped like a triangle. The wall she stood on had two guard towers at each end, with connecting walls stretching towards a third point. As they climbed down the inner steps of the fort wall, Aaron said with a slight smile: "So, did Rey tell you all about the wonders of mangroves?"

"Yes," she replied, "He was quite knowledgeable about it."

Aaron nodded, "That's his job for the task force. Forest rangers— mostly ex-military—serve as guards for the Mangrove Wall. Fortunately, they're very good at their jobs."

"What problems have you encountered with the mangroves?"

"Those who cut down the trees to use as firewood or to build their houses. Fishermen who use dynamite or poison to fish, which also kills the mangroves. And there's been incidences of banditry and piracy."

They marched past an expanse of a concrete field. A helicopter with rubber pontoons for skids was already tied down against the coming typhoon. A statue stood in the middle of the courtyard.

Sofia saw a row of stone archways and behind it was a large generator covered by a metal shed. The older man nodded and said: "We have our own power plant here. We need a lot of power for our systems when they're crunching numbers."

"This building here is what we call the Castle. It's our command-and-control centre." Aaron opened the steel-lined door of the Castle through a keypad set into the side. When the door opened, a blast of cold air blew out, making Sofia shiver.

As they walked into the building and the door swung close on hydraulics, rain started to fall outside in giant drops and the wind began to pick up. "Looks like the typhoon is almost here," he observed.

The two walked down the cool, well-lit corridor to another steel-lined door. Aaron punched the code and it opened to reveal a darkened hall lit up by computer screens, manned by technicians and programmers in orange coveralls. Some were talking through headsets, filling the atmosphere with susurration.

At one end of the hall, a giant bright screen was running. One part showed a map of what looked like the city of Manila. Parts of the city were coloured blue while others were green. Sofia surmised that those areas of the city marked in blue were the flooded parts. Another part of the screen displayed a map of a weather radar with a slowly encroaching mass that Sofia guessed was Super Typhoon Korina.

A third section streamed the feed from a CCTV camera. It showed a group of men in the backdrop of the mangroves. Armed and wearing ragged fatigues, they were piloting several *bancas* through the forest. Many of them wore balaclavas or had wrapped black shirts around their heads as makeshift masks.

Standing before the screen and watching it constantly was an elderly woman in the same orange overalls. She held a tablet in one hand to control the screen and she was talking into a mike on her headset.

"Yes, I see them now, Rey. Please take the necessary measures," she said.

Part of the screen opened up and Sofia saw Rey's face. He replied, "Roger that, Professor Marisol. We'll earn our keep with this one."

"I leave it in your capable hands, then."

"Marisol?" Aaron queried. "Our guest is here."

"Halloo, dear," the woman greeted Aaron and then turned towards Sofia. "Is this Miss Antonelli? Welcome, welcome to our soggy yet humble home."

"Well, it's all the world can do to keep dry," Sofia quipped. "I hope I didn't catch you at a busy time."

"Just another superstorm coming, now we're quite used to," she replied dryly. She added, "We're currently integrating the mycorrhizal networks of one of the distant patches of mangrove trees to boost MARIPOSA's coverage. There's also a group of bandits wanting to raid us. So this is probably... Thursday, if I remember correctly."

"Is there anyone you can call for help?" Sofia asked, alarmed.

The older woman shook her head. "The local government of Manila was dissolved several years ago when they were unable to handle the evacuation. At that point, the national government and the military had to step in."

Aaron snorted and said: "Presently, the military has its own problems to deal with while the national government prefers to leave us alone as much as possible."

"Which makes this our problem," Professor Marisol added with a click of her tongue. Then she shook her head and said in exasperation, "Where are my manners! The Mangrove Resiliency Task Force runs the MARIPOSA Project." She gestured around. "But it also manages the Mangrove Wall, which is why—because of staffing issues—many of us here serve dual purposes."

She gestured towards Aaron. "My husband here handles everything machine-related while I'm the resident climatologist. That is when I'm not wearing the hat of task force chief in budget meetings with government officials. The pretty young woman over there with short hair is Cheska Flores, whose knowledge of mycology is an important element in MARIPOSA," she added. "She's also our chief gardener, which is why she gets into a lot of fights with Rey on the proper positioning of the mangroves."

At her console, Cheska snorted as she concentrated on her screen. Meanwhile, Rey's voice sounded overhead: "I heard that, Professor Marisol."

"Oh, I forgot you're still there," she replied deadpan. "I swear I'm getting old…"

Sofia smiled as everyone else in the room laughed. She said, "Professor Marisol, the briefers you've been sending on MARIPOSA seem quite fantastic to be believable. But if it's true, then you've achieved quite a breakthrough."

Professor Marisol shook her head and said, "Unlike most developed countries, we've had to depend on homegrown methods to stop the flooding. Since we didn't have the resources to build dams, we planted mangroves."

"But having the mangroves there wasn't enough," she said as she gestured on her tablet. The giant screen suddenly cleared and the words MARIPOSA appeared. She said, "That's why we developed MARIPOSA, or Mangrove Automatic Retrieval, Integration, and Prediction of Operational Stream Analysis. It's a natural extension of our Mangrove Wall Project."

The map of Manila again dominated the screen, marked in blue and green. "As most of you have discovered, you need an adept AI system to control your dams against storm surges and rising tides, else you'd be better off building a big wall to keep it all above water."

"But even with all our current progress, AI-run systems are still stupid machines," Aaron interrupted. "No matter how much you teach them, they can't think for themselves. They can only respond."

"Yes, yes," Professor Marisol said. "That's why by combining the mycorrhizal networks of the mangrove trees—the fungi that colonizes the trees' roots—with data-learning AIs and a lot of expensive computers, we've developed an actual Green Intelligence."

The green areas on the screen map suddenly glowed brighter.

"A Green Intelligence? Is that some form of AI?"

"No." Aaron shook his head. "The computer science perspective of intelligence is the need for communication pathways and signal discrimination. But current AI technology is still light years behind what we've imagined them to be in science fiction stories. They're simple robots, really. So what we've developed is an intelligence network for trees."

"What my dear husband is saying is that instead of letting machines think for themselves, we're using machines to help trees think faster, as well as communicate with us," Professor Marisol elaborated.

"Professor Marisol?" Cheska chimed in. "We have achieved successful integration of the latest patch of mycorrhizal networks."

"Thank you, dear," Professor Marisol said. "How are you doing, my friends?"

The giant screen blacked out and then, one letter at a time, a message appeared: MANY. NOW.

Sofia was shocked. "Is that... Are those the mangrove trees speaking?"

"Yes," Aaron said. "While the name of MARIPOSA is singular, what we are talking to is a network of trees, a kind of a hive mind if we use the terminology of entomology."

"That even rhymes, dear," Professor Marisol said, chuckling. "MARIPOSA thinks that we are all trees here. I like to think I'm a wise old narra tree, myself."

Aaron interjected, "I created the integration program that links this net we built underwater in which the mycorrhizal and the mangroves are growing on, to the AIs in our system. Of course, the trees aren't exactly using words, but the AIs are translating the concepts and ideas that the trees are emitting to communicate with us."

"Fascinating," Sofia said in awe.

"What's more, since trees don't think or speak as fast as we do, the AIs fast-forward everything so that we can communicate normally..." Aaron continued.

"Dear, before you go further," Professor Marisol interrupted and addressed the screen: "MARIPOSA, I hope you don't mind but we have to get ready for Super Typhoon Korina."

WATERS. PUSHING.

On the screen, a bright line of orange stretched throughout the whole coast. Cheska said, "Experiencing storm surges, Professor Marisol."

"Noted," Professor Marisol replied. "MARIPOSA, keep safe."

ROOTS. STRONG.

Another portion of the screen opened to show Rey's face. His face was wet underneath a dark poncho, and his eyes glowed through the night vision goggles he was wearing. "Professor Marisol, we've been pushed back to the fort. There's a lot of bandits out here this time."

"Can you keep them out?" Aaron asked.

"We'll try. This is a pretty brave lot, sneaking in while there's a typhoon. We've already caught some who were trying to come up from the riverside."

Aaron snorted. "Or stupid. The river will be terribly choppy with the sea tides smashing against the outflow of the river."

Rey replied, "Just be sure, I'm recommending complete lockdown of Castle facilities."

"Understood," Professor Marisol said. "We're all in the Castle because of the storm anyway. Cheska, implement lockdown."

A siren sounded and the darkness of the hall was lit by several bars of red light around the hall. "Lockdown implemented," Cheska replied.

Just then, there was a muffled thump that could be heard even through the walls. The walls shook, eliciting screams from some of the staff. Console screens and even the giant screen turned dark for a moment before the red emergency lights switched back on. After a few seconds the computer screens lit up.

"We're running on emergency generators," someone announced. "But power to core systems is down 80 percent."

"I've lost contact with MARIPOSA," Cheska said.

The giant screen came back up with the face of Rey again. "Sorry, guys, some idiot threw a grenade at the power plant. But we've beaten them back."

"Can you bring back the power?" Aaron asked fretfully.

"A bit busy with clean-up operations, Sir Aaron," Rey said, his reply a bit tattered. "But I've sent engineers to work on the power."

Laying a calming hand on Aaron's arm, Professor Marisol said, "Thank you, Rey. Do what you can."

"What happened?" Sofia asked, worried. "Is MARIPOSA...?"

"We've lost power but that's separate from the mangrove networks," Professor Marisol said as she tapped on her tablet. "So while we can't talk to MARIPOSA, the mangroves are doing their job. They know what they're doing, they've been doing it all their lives."

The screen opened up again to show the map of the city. This time it showed the areas of the mangroves highlighted in green with glowing areas in red right beside them. The lines between the green and red areas kept shifting and overlapping, but so far, none of the red areas were getting past the green line.

"Incredible," Sofia murmured as she watched the screen.

Beside her, the older woman looked up from her tablet and said in irritation: "Oh! Now I know I'm being forgetful. It's already Friday. Just another day at the office for us."

Sofia glanced at Professor Marisol, who only chuckled. Aaron laughed and so did she.

***

Joseph F. Nacino writes for a living. He also writes stories that have been published in international (*Fantasy Magazine, City in the Ice, Kitaab's Asian Speculative Fiction*) and local publications (the *Philippine Speculative Fiction* series, *A Time of Dragons, Friendzones*, etc.). Likewise, he's helmed three anthologies featuring fantasy, science fiction, and horror in the Philippines published online, and in print and ebook form.

A Life With Cibi

Natsumi Tanaka

Translated by Toshiya Kamei

After work, I head downtown instead of going straight home. I type my destination into my phone and walk up to the nearest bus stop. After a short while, a bus emerges on a busy corner and comes to a halt in front of me. The front door slides open and I climb in. My designated seat awaits me inside. The citywide, centralized system continuously modifies bus routes and optimizes schedules according to our needs. Snaking through the buildings looming above us, the bus swallows up passengers and spews them out, making several stops along the way. As we reach my stop, the android driver pulls up to the curb and drops me off.

"Thank you, and have a great day!" The driver flashes me a mechanical smile as I step out.

"Thanks. You, too," I mumble before the door slides shut.

The greenery of the park tickles my nose as I stand at the edge of downtown. With visitors on board, solar-powered carts whiz by me. As usual, I opt for a stroll through a broad range of sights, sounds, and smells. I join the flow of pedestrians and continue along a well-marked path, which is off-limits to vehicles.

Half an hour later, a figure emerges in the distance, bouncing toward me. Its rabbit ears bob up and down as it hops forward. Even from far, you can tell it's an edible creature. No one refers to it by its multisyllabic, scientific name, however. We call it "Cibus"—food in Latin.

I wave lightly at the Cibus. Noticing my gesture, it scurries toward me, its face brightening. "I'm hungry. Let me take a bite," I say.

"Gotcha," the Cibus answers. It puts down its backpack, takes out a knife, and hands it to me. The blade is designed for exclusive use to slice Cibi's flesh.

"May I have paste, Cibus?" I ask.

"Gotcha," the Cibus answers and turns into paste in front of me.

"Thanks." I cut a small portion of its flesh with the knife.

"Gotcha." It goes back to its human form. It's a bit smaller than before.

Except for its ears, a Cibus is edible as is, but many of us prefer not to eat it in its human form. Thus, it comes with the ability to shift its shape. Regardless of how you slice it, you get a chunk of paste. Cibi come with a light, salty taste, so you can consume them as is. You can also make dumplings or slice them for a stir-fry. You can add extra flavor if you wish. Cibi are the perfect food.

An artificial crop grown in a field, Cibi spread their leaves above the ground, growing underground like potatoes. When they ripen, their leaves look like rabbit ears, signaling harvest time. As small as newborn babies, Cibi are easy to dig out. Still, a Cibus grows rapidly once it comes in contact with the air. In a few days, it will grow as large as a small human. A backpack with a knife inside appears on its back. Once fully grown, Cibi are shipped to a market. Self-sufficient organisms, they take water on their own and perform photosynthesis. They have more in common with plants than animals.

Recent progress in artificial photosynthesis combined with consumer demand led to the development of this new crop of edible creatures. Designed to minimize human impact on the environment, Cibi caught the imagination of people all over the world. Not only do they contain nutrients found in grains and vegetables, but they are also popular as meat substitutes. Recipes using Cibi have proliferated like mushrooms in a dark forest.

Numerous Cibi live independently on the streets. You can stop them and ask them for what you need. And many households own Cibi. Some families treat them as pets, not just as nutrient sources. As a result, those Cibi lovers tend to consume their Cibi less often. It's true, however, that the life expectancy of a domesticated Cibus can be extended by being sliced. That's because every cut promotes healthy growth in the same way pruning helps plants.

Cibi make themselves smaller to protect their lives. If you keep slicing them at appropriate intervals, as indicated in the instruction manual, they soon grow back to their previous size through photosynthesis. Thus, they are able to maintain their size for a long period of time. It takes years to consume a whole Cibus. Those that die of old age become chunks of paste. They return to the earth and biodegrade easily.

Cibi possess certain individual differences, but even adults are small. They tend to have adorable expressions. The Cibus population and habitats are strictly regulated to avoid overloading the environment. In my city, you can find many wild Cibi in the downtown park.

Cibi are designed to inspire adoration in human owners so that they can have long lives. They also come with the ability to change into plain forms for squeamish consumers. After all, they come into being to provide optimal nutrition, rather than companionship, to consumers.

Even so, you tend to forget that Cibi are nutrient sources once you start living with them.

I used to own a Cibus myself. I gave it a name and treated it as part of my family. Of course, I used it as a nutrient source as well, but I tried not to eat it too much. After all, all living organisms have a finite life span. Making a Cibus live longer requires cutting its flesh regularly. Still, after a while, I could no longer bring myself to slice my dear Cibus. As it became increasingly smaller, I lost heart. I locked myself with my Cibus in my room. I stopped walking it. As it wasn't able to get enough sunlight, it withered away and died in my arms.

In tears, I took the cold, motionless chunk of paste to the collection center in the outskirts of the city. To my relief, its corpse was recycled as fertilizer for a Cibus field. Mine didn't die in vain. Even so, I blamed myself for failing to help it live out its allotted span. I decided not to keep Cibi as pets ever again.

Nowadays, I go out in my free time to look for a stray Cibus for nutrient intake. During the day, you can easily spot one in the city and never go hungry. Still, during the rainy season and winter, fewer Cibi are out on the streets, so I tend to hoard a certain quantity in my fridge.

I hand this Cibus back its knife. It puts it away in its backpack and smiles at me.

"See you soon," I say.

"Gotcha," the Cibus answers, hopping away.

I put away the piece of Cibus in my purse and set off home.

"When I get home, I'm going to knead Cibi dough and make some pasta," I say to myself. All of a sudden, my stomach makes rumbling noises. I hurry home.

***

Natsumi Tanaka is a writer living in Kyoto, Japan. Her short stories have appeared in journals such as *Anima Solaris, Kotori no kyuden,* and *Tanpen*. She is the author of the short story collection *Yumemiru ningyo no okoku* (2017). Her short fiction has appeared in various English-language publications, including *Daily Science Fiction, Japanese Fantasy Drabbles,* and *The William & Mary Review,* among others. You can find her online at https://note.com/tanakan.

Toshiya Kamei's translations have appeared in *Clarkesworld, The Magazine of Fantasy & Science Fiction,* and *Strange Horizons*.

Children of Asphalt
Phoebe Wagner

The kin dragged a furrow through the kernza and sorghum plot, the wide tail or appendage—we weren't sure yet—flattening yards at a time. This field was at rest this cycle, but now we understood why, a few weeks ago, the walkers had raised concerns about these unique trails hacking through the tall grasses and old fields choked with GMO corn.

By the time dusk had deepened to night, the kin had flattened the whole kernza and sorghum patch, veering back and forth until no plants brushed the swooping belly. Some of us felt reminded of a manatee gone to land or a walrus, but both kin had been listed extinct in the late 2020s. Neither should have come so far inland from the Pacific Ocean that made our city possible, if they still existed. Still, the children settled on "landrus" by the end of the day, though the biologists, librarians, and archivists felt unsure of the connection. Two artists kept watch all night as it carved a maze of furrows in the windbreak grove outside the summer guest yurts, still closed until the solstice. They passed their dozen sketches to the other record keepers: sweeping doodles of the kin's actions, detailed pieces of a single body part, a map of the path left behind in case the kin had wanted to say something in the design.

As we worried, the kin turned closer to the city. The tail almost helped the kin slither in the summer grasses, and two flipper-like appendages dragged the heavy body forward or maneuvered between saplings and rocks.

Other, unknown kin had visited the city before. In less human-populated areas, visitors often reported to the librarians or the biologists about kin met on the journey. Some were identified as the extinct now returned, some appeared to be laboratory inventions long forgotten, some might have been mutations that had crawled from distant nuclear waste dumps or garbage mountains.

A collective decision passed down from the past three generations wished no killing or hurting of any kin that did not demonstrate premeditated, malicious intent. While destroying food sources could cause serious worry for next winter, the landrus seemed to have a purpose for the systematic flattening. Our goal was to guess the reason and see how we might live alongside.

Honestly, our archivists and historytellers told worse stories. The year a tiger had chosen a city as hunting ground and all kin had traveled in packs of four or five for protection until it grew hungry for easier hunting. Swarms of locusts and hives of giant hornets had disrupted cities for years—the inhabitants leaving to forage and survive in smaller communities once again.

Three weeks later, the biologists hosted a meeting to discuss the new kin who had joined the community. The landrus had flattened several fields and meadows into circles and ovals. So far, only one had showed up, but the way the kin passed between the circles each day, sometimes pausing to, it seemed, just watch, made many wonder if more were coming.

Across the city, five meeting house rooms opened, each with a biologist, recorder, and several interpreters: one in the decaying apartment buildings, the yurts of center city, the remade libraries of campus, the boat homes of the River, and the meadows of old remains. The biologists had prepared a statement, but once it had been read, each meeting would, hopefully, turn to different concerns, giving a voice to as many people as possible. We wondered what disruption had this new kin caused? How much food would such a kin need and how the area might support the feeding habits? What would happen to the other kin we'd come to love in community?

The main response from the biologists: we don't know. The kin had been seen to eat very little, mostly some creekside blackberries and crawfish. Not enough to sustain the massive bulk, which had already shrunk, the biologists thought. They theorized the fat reserves were intended to help the kin travel to some sort of destination. Here, it seemed.

Over the next two weeks, the landrus flattened three more fields: a honeybee and medicinal plants meadow, an acre of leafy vegetables, and two acres of soybeans. Not enough damage to resources to do much rationing—maybe candles, maybe sweets. The landrus smoothed bulky circles and ovals, which stymied the biologists. Nests, they'd assumed, but so many? Being built by a solitary creature? The new circles showed a pattern, though, a T-shape leading to the creek then spreading to the left and right. In their lack of knowledge, the biologists told us the kin was marking a territory, to be careful about letting the children near those fields until we knew more.

And so late summer turned slowly to face fall. The landrus only flattened one more field, sunflowers, but still retraced and smoothed over the previous "nests." Like so many other newcomers, the landrus became part of our community, joining the wild horses, coydogs, dolphins, birds, and other kin newly recorded each year. Soon, our rhythms accompanied this kin, and we left certain stretches of the creek untouched, gathering water from other pools. We choose new fields for the foodstuffs the landrus had repurposed for nests. We spotted the kin's smoothed trail, solitary, and wondered if this were all?

Even much later, the children still liked to watch the landrus, mapping the trails and counting the nests.

***

The kin of a city are never quiet. Nightlight noises replace daylight noises, the buildings always shudder and groan. Sometimes, they crumble and crash, waking us and bringing us outside with torches to make sure nobody had been hurt. Visitors to the city claimed it noisier than traveling the roads and paths because the buildings added another level of disquiet, as did the gathered kin living around the outskirts. We simply said, you'll get used to it.

Tonight, a noise we have never heard echoed through the skyscraper canyons, but we all recognized it—grief. Some of us gathered together for safety while a small group investigated as the dawn glittered along the city's highest steel bones and glass skins.

The call came again, a tolling bellow rising and rising into a barking howl. Past the last community, many of us huddled in doorways and peered behind tent flaps as that grief filled the crisp air.

At the crumbling intersection of asphalt paths climbing into the air like great tree limbs, the landrus howled. Over the decades, we and our parents and grandparents had cleared much of the tarred rock that littered the city, but out here where the roads twisted like unearthed roots, there'd been too much. We'd left the airborne paths spreading their wide arms to crumble as they saw fit. Only children daring each other and scavengers scurried beneath the crumbling rock.

Now, a pregnant landrus lay dead. A piece of asphalt had crumbled under her weight and the rebar beneath had split her belly open. The male landrus had settled beneath her, his head tossed back in continual howl.

He *had* been making nests, we realized. But for how many? Why had he been chosen to leave their herd?

Some of us ran ahead, following the smooth track of the now dead landrus, and climbed the nearest trees or still-stable power poles. Yes, more were coming, over a hundred, enough to fill all the circles the landrus had made out of our fields.

It began to snow as each community gathered at the meeting houses. The biologists couldn't help but be excited: a whole unrecorded species making their nesting grounds here, with us—if we cleared the asphalt. The growers argued for the sake of the fields and the webs they supported. Some said let survival have its way. The landrus scout had chosen poorly, so let that reflect in who survived.

And what if they are the last, or most of the last of their kind?

They could very well destroy some of the last of us, the kin already home in the city.

A biologist suggested, what if we were part of the choice? What if the landrus offered a new symbiosis?

And what would we gain?

What if they eat us out of the city?

We have left before.

The talk continued long into the snowstorm, sometimes coming to yelling and cursing. In most communities, we split into thirds—help them cross the asphalt, merely watch, and keep them out.

Of those voices, some were children, but we didn't think to count. We didn't think to wonder what the children were doing while the rest of us were arguing—other than playing in the snow, sledding down the steep alleyways and over the icy sidewalks.

Only when we trudged into the snow, frustrated and nowhere near an answer, did we question why the snow seemed so untouched. A lack of sled and ski tracks, no snowball puffs on walls, and missing forts made us wonder.

We followed their tracks outside of the city.

While we had talked of action, the children had taken action—for better or worse. They'd carefully encased the asphalt wreckage, turning sharp edges to snowy wonders. Slick ramps helped protect from bad drops or sharp metal. Paths flattened with sleds and footprints encouraged the oncoming parents toward the safest routes.

When we asked our children why, they said the crying landrus had been asking for help. Hadn't we heard? We tried to explain that more was at stake, that we might have to leave our homes, but that only excited the children with ideas of summers circling the lake ten miles north, of climbing into the hills and cultivating berries. We let it go.

Hours later, the child-heavy landruses came sliding over the snow, following each other's furrows until they were as slick as well used sled tracks. No more bodies spilled red on the asphalt.

The biologists are excited to witness the birthing process. The field-tenders and growers consider if the manure might make for good fertilizer. The protein-finders wonder what we might make of the elders once they pass on. The archivists record the story for tomorrow.

And the children, they teach us how to cover the asphalt.

***

Phoebe Wagner holds an MFA in Creative Writing and Environment and currently pursues her PhD in literature at University of Nevada, Reno. Her recent fiction can be read in *Diabolical Plots, Cosmic Roots and Eldritch Shores* and AURELIA LEO. In 2017, Upper Rubber Boot Books published her co-edited anthology *Sunvault: Stories of Solarpunk & Eco-Speculation*, and she's under contract to co-edit another solarpunk book from West Virginia University Press. Currently, she blogs about speculative literature at the Hugo-finalist Nerds of a Feather, Flock Together and can be found online at phoebe-wagner.com.

Down the River
Eliza Victoria

The Kaliwanagan River runs through the northeast corner of the province of Salanta in Central Luzon, in the eco-city similarly named Salanta. Salanta City sits in an area once destroyed by flooding and industrial waste, but is now a protected national park. A small community lives within this protected enclave, 20,000 residents who live sustainably in their man-made environment next to the natural environment, and who ensure that the park and the river are protected from the threat of human excesses, especially with Salanta City and Kaliwanagan River attracting thousands of tourists every month.

On the night in question, two young men walk down the riverbank, the full moon reflected fully on the water. One of them considers this, considers the source of the river's name.

Illumination.

Clarity.

***

Camila: So Paolo just called me saying he's by the river and he did something wrong and he doesn't know what to do next

Dominic: ???? Is he at home

I TOLD you something's up with him

I'm putting on my shoes

Camila: I don't get it

Now he's saying Ryan is there with him

Dominic: ????????

Ryan the boss's son Ryan?

Camila: I'll try and call him back this makes no sense

***

Kaliwanagan River is sacred. Historical records mention pigs and cows being slain and placed on boats as a sacrifice to the river. The townsfolk no longer do this, but people here know that they must show respect to Kaliwanagan. No angry words while you travel across the river. No hatred. No cruelty. And of course, no littering.

"I tell my children, imagine the river is a person," Aster Magat tells me. "Would you throw garbage at a person just because you're too lazy to find a bin?"

Aster was the immediate past Director of the Salanta City Park Authority, a position she had held for six years, having been appointed twice in a row by the city mayor. "Of course, one hopes you can teach respect without making these comparisons," she continues. "It's a river, it's the source of our water, living things thrive in it; I don't need to bend over backwards and tell you it's a *person* just so you don't throw your soda cans over the side of the boat. It's like with crime, isn't it? You need to tell some people, what if the person who was shot to death was your brother? Or your mother? You need to make this *personal* connection just to wake them up. It's not enough that we're talking about a fellow human being here. But anyway, I've gone off on a tangent."

Aster loves going off on tangents, but I don't mind; she tells the best stories.

The story I came here to listen to is how the river once punished a man who didn't show it respect.

She tells me that a small subset of the population—"Not everyone, okay, just a small subset"—believes that the river can lash back, and that it did so in the case of Bernardo Galaran, the multi-millionaire hotel scion who runs one of the restaurants in the park. His restaurant, Diyan Masalanta—named after the Tagalog goddess of love and a nod to the town's name and resilience in this pun-loving country ('di yan masasalanta—"it will not be destroyed")—serves Filipino fusion dishes and is wildly popular among the park's guests and residents. Two years ago, Bernardo began constructing a hotel not far from his restaurant, a decision that did not sit well with the Salanta City Park Authority, but which unfortunately was overruled by the local government.

"Money," says Aster with a sigh as she recalls the story. "It's always been about the money."

Bernardo ordered that water be diverted from the Kaliwanagan River to flow into a massive man-made pool next to his hotel. The pool was built to resemble Cleopatra's Pool in Pamukkale, Turkey, complete with fake Roman "ruins" submerged in the water. Early marketing materials of the hotel displayed this pool prominently.

Diyan Masalanta runs on an eco-sustainable model of business. Like most of the homes in Salanta City, it is fitted with a waste water treatment facility that allows it to reuse up to 80% of its water. The restaurant serves dishes from locally sourced ingredients, and even introduced scrumptious lab-grown lechon in its menu (not everyone is a fan—yet). I ask: how can the same man who runs an eco-friendly business then turn around and blow up a section of a river to build a frivolous tourist magnet?

"Diyan Masalanta's eco-friendliness is just him jumping on a bandwagon," Aster explains. "He champions sustainability because it's profitable. Because it serves him. But I don't think he believes in it."

Three months after the hotel's opening, Bernardo fell ill. His doctors could not pinpoint the cause. His heart? His kidney? A recurring infection? Hotel guests also reported feeling uneasy around the pool filled with riverwater. A few residents of Salanta quietly, privately, met with Bernardo to tell him he was being punished by the river, that he should make amends with Kaliwanagan. He kicked them all out of his office, saying the claims were nonsense. But in a curious turn of events, he later ordered that the pool be closed and drained, the water re-diverted back into the river.

"He immediately felt better," Aster says. "How do you explain that?"

The hotel continued to operate, however, putting a strain on the river and Salanta's ecosystem. I ask Aster if the hotel employed Salanta City residents. "It did," Aster says. "Majority were out-of-towners, but a small number comes from here. Young people who would rather stay within the parkland during the school holidays, but need the extra cash. Or those who for some reason or another couldn't find employment outside the town. Some of them used to work in Diyan Masalanta's kitchen."

I express surprise that the whole of Salanta City did not end up boycotting the business. Aster says a note of resentment has rung through the parkland ever since the hotel opened, and it hit a crescendo this summer. One of the hotel's young chefs, Paolo Galang, 19, got into a fight with his friend Chris Hitalia, also 19, regarding the nature of his employment. Paolo has gotten into trouble several times before; the hotel job was his fourth job in a year. "Anger problems, I guess you could say," Aster says with a sigh.

This verbal fight escalated into a physical fight, and further escalated into a car chase out of the hotel parking lot, followed by a crash. The crash injured four and killed Chris. Among those injured were Paolo himself, and Bernardo's son, Ryan Galaran, who witnesses said jumped into the passenger seat in an effort to dissuade Paolo from driving away.

(Information regarding the crash and its aftermath come from police records. Only Ryan agreed to be interviewed for this article—we will return to him in a moment.)

One month after the crash, Ryan continued to go in and out of hospitals, seemingly unable to recover from his injuries. People remembered his father's plight, and wondered.

What did Aster think about these developments?

She falls silent for a moment. "We are lucky to be living in this place," she says, as we walk back to the Visitor Centre. "We are lucky to be *allowed* to live here, to speak on behalf of the river and the parkland. But as you know, sometimes our voices are not heard, are not enough. Sometimes other voices are louder. I can't blame the river for wishing to become an advocate for itself."

***

Paolo stands before Kaliwanagan and remembers

the cold interior of the hotel's Smart Car, keeping Chris's car in sight as it zipped out of the parking lot and plunged into the darkness, how dare he, the pompous asshole, talking like he has never compromised his ideals a day in his life, how dare you, don't you dare turn your back on me

Chris veering off the road, something wrong with his car, right into a night walk in progress, our friends hitting the hood then the pavement, and Chris can't stop, he can't stop, and now I can't stop either, watching Chris plow through people, and me and Ryan facing the ugly blue glow of the console, pressing buttons, bouncing over rocks, plunging deeper into the part of the parkland untouched by time

I close my eyes and I keep seeing this

He thinks: *Once there was volcanic lightning and a warm body of water.*

Somehow, from the amino acids and sugars generated by this spark, came life, and out we crawled from this first river.

After foraging for thousands of years, the ice melted and we were greeted by sunlight and wild grain.

Someone had a brilliant idea: why don't we just figure out how to grow our own food? If grain can grow in the wild, then perhaps we can coax it to grow on our own terms.

This way, we can stay in one place, produce and store a surplus of crops, survive through the cold.

And so we returned to the river, to water and fertile land.

The surplus allowed us to support a larger population. Allowed us to build permanent settlements.

Cities. Fortifications. Apartments. Hotels.

Whosoever lived near the water thrived, sold its surplus grain to other towns, grew wealthy.

Some crops were considered more valuable than others. So valuable that people went to war, forced other lands to produce only the crops they wanted, filled ships to the brim with people and sailed across the sea and forced the people in the ships to tend to the highly valued crops until they fell down dead.

Coffee. Sugar. Cotton. Tobacco.

Opium poppy. Coca leaves. Ephedra sinica.

Many cities became wealthy because of this, with monuments and palaces and golden fountains, and hundreds of years later they would block the people they once enslaved because they resented the extra burden.

How dare these people travel across the sea into our ports without papers, they say to one another. How dare they ask for food and water. How dare they not do the right thing.

We crawled out of the river, and we put bodies back in the river, hands tied, faces covered in tape, or drowned when the rafts capsized in the storm.

Chris and I, we used to talk about this, for hours and hours. We would talk about the terrible things humans have done, to you and to each other.

How do I fix this?

He sits on the riverbank as the river continues to tell him nothing.

What I'm saying is

What I'm saying is perhaps we should have just continued foraging, consumed only what the river and the land can produce

What I'm saying is perhaps we should have been kinder

But perhaps, in this moment, I should re-define kindness.

An illness is too slow, and you're too quick to forgive.

If I helped you reach the necessary conclusion faster in this long-drawn-

out punishment, wouldn't that be a kindness?

***

The now-shuttered hotel, with its 300 rooms and suites, its grand marble balcony and glittering chandeliers, sits in silence next to the Kaliwanagan River. But on the night in question, weeks after Chris's death, hotel operations were in full swing, the driveway filled with coaches and cars, light spilling out of the ornately decorated double doors. A park tour guide, who was getting ready to lead a group of tourists on a night walk by the river, saw Paolo speaking with Ryan just outside the hotel. A few minutes later, the tour guide said, he watched the two men walk deeper into parkland, toward the direction of the river.

***

Ryan speaks to me on the phone. In an email before this phone call, he tells me he'll only agree to speak on record if I promise not to contact his father, or Paolo and his friends. I give him my promise.

Ryan is 21, just a few years older than Paolo. He says he went on a walk that night with Paolo because the latter wanted to talk. "I used to run Diyan Masalanta before my father moved me to hotel operations. Paolo and I have been on nodding terms in the restaurant, but at the hotel, we got to talking more every day."

I ask him if he would describe Paolo then as a friend. "Yes," he says. "I suppose you can say we were friends."

And now? But he deftly deflects the question.

"We were not able to talk after the car crash that killed Chris," Ryan continues. He saw the invitation to walk by the river that night as a chance to unpack what had happened.

Then what happened? I ask.

***

Camila: D we need to go

Paolo said he tried to drown Ryan in the river

Dominic: WHAT

NO

That is insane has he gone INSANE

Camila: Ryan's ok

But Paolo's seriously hurt

We need to go NOW

***

Throwing away Ryan's walking cane, glowing silver in the moonlight on the wet grass, grabbing his neck and pushing him deep into the water, that is the easy part, Paolo felt sure he is doing the right thing.

The foaming water. The river churning with his own anger as Ryan tries to rise to the surface. Ryan thrashing in the water and then oh no oh no.

Stumbling back into sharp rocks.

Paolo, Ryan is saying, standing over him on the riverbank, water dripping from his hair, Paolo, Pao, oh God, stop moving, you've hurt yourself.

Ryan clambering up to the bank. A violent cough. "What the hell's wrong with you?" Not angry. Mutilated. "Why would you—" Ryan's tears as sharp as the sudden pain in his side, the rocks cutting skin. "Why would you do that to me."

What have I done.

"Did he say something?" Camila. He can't feel his legs, but he can feel hands pulling him up, his arm around someone's shoulder. Ryan's cane clacking on pebbles. Dominic on a green boat, the water twinkling in the moonlight. Let's go let's go let's go.

The water twinkling in the moonlight, the landscape transporting him somewhere else, somewhere with beauty and magic, not like this place, not like that night when he has tried to pull Chris from the wreckage of his car.

Not like when he has pushed Ryan into the water.

I did something horrible, Chris, you always said I act before I think and you're right, you're right.

"Paolo?" Ryan says. His voice like a thunderclap. "Hang on. Just a bit more. Here we go."

The feeling in his legs comes back when he hits the bottom of the boat, but the feeling is pain, fresh blood surging forth from the gash in his side, soaking the shirt Camila has pressed there, and he tries not to scream because he deserves it. He deserves it all. He is shaking so hard he can hear his shoes knocking against wood.

Three heads bend over him, blocking the moon.

They know the rules, they've grown up here, so Dominic says his piece before they push the boat off into the water. "What the hell, Paolo? So you think the boss's son is what, a sacrifice to the river? What is the matter with you? You think the river would say thank you? What made you think—"

The tirade suddenly ends with whispers, Dominic's frustrated sigh. *I'm sorry,* Paolo wants to say to the river, to Ryan, to his friends. *I'm sorry. I'm sorry.* He can't stop shaking.

Ryan takes off his jacket and places it over him, rubs his shoulders to keep him warm.

Why are you being nice to me, after everything.

Camila bends close to whisper in his ear, her long hair brushing against his face.

"He likes you," she says.

What?

"He likes you," she says again. "You idiot." And louder: "So you can't die yet, do you hear me?"

***

I ask Ryan if he has forgiven Paolo.

"I'm not entirely blameless here," Ryan says. "I mean, my father." He stops abruptly, as though he has choked.

"Paolo's getting help," he says instead. "Forgiveness is a process, and so is earning it. He's trying to earn it. *I'm* trying to earn it."

***

In the Visitor Centre, over coffee, I talk to Aster about the social control hypothesis of ritual sacrifice. Years and years ago, before this city even existed, the ritual killing of animals that was done to

177

"appease" the river may have simply been a way to consolidate power, for the political or religious leaders to dictate which family must give up a portion of their livestock for the good of the town, a power move in the age of agriculture. Then we introduced coinage, and the power dynamic just changed in its representation. From cows to pieces of gold or silver. For example, when this country fell under Spanish rule and Catholicism became the majority religion, indulgencia, or indulgence, originally granted for good work, became monetized. The more you pay, the higher the chances the fraile will absolve you of your sins. Whether or not you actually *work* towards your absolution.

Money, I echo her earlier sentiment. It's always been about the money.

"I don't know much about the social control hypothesis you're talking about," Aster says, after patiently sitting through my rant-slash-lecture. We sip our coffee for a moment. "But if you're saying that the sacrifices do nothing for the river at all, well, I can get behind that."

But how *do* you apologize to a river?

She shrugs. "It's better if you have not done the wrong thing in the first place. But time, like the river, does not flow backward. So you go forward, like the river. You try to do better."

Do the good work, I say.

"Yes," Aster says. "What else is there to do?"

***

Tree-framed stars overhead. The gash in his side throbbing like a second sun. He can hear Ryan and his friends' breaths slowly synchronizing. No arguments now, no sound except the grunts of effort as they row down the river, as they row him to mercy, to safety.

They know the rules, they've grown up here. No angry words while you travel across Kaliwanagan. No hatred. No cruelty. And in return, you need not fear, as the river will give you safe passage.

How could he have forgotten so easily? He feels Ryan pause briefly from rowing, and Paolo lifts his arm with all his might to touch the droplets of riverwater on Ryan's wrist, to reach for his warm hand.

***

Eliza Victoria is the author of several books including the Philippine National Book Award-winning *Dwellers* (2014), the novel *Wounded Little Gods* (2016), the graphic novel *After Lambana* (2016, a collaboration with Mervin Malonzo), and the science fiction novel-in-stories, *Nightfall* (2018). Her fiction and poetry have appeared in several online and print publications, most recently in *LONTAR: The Journal of Southeast Asian Speculative Fiction*, *The Best Asian Speculative Fiction*, *The Dark Magazine*, and *The Apex Book of World SF Volume 5*. Her work has won prizes in the Philippines' top literary awards, including the Carlos Palanca Memorial Awards for Literature. Her one-act plays (written in Filipino) have been staged at the Virgin LabFest at the Cultural Center of the Philippines. Visit her at elizavictoria.com.

Becoming Martians

Taiyo Fujii

Translated by Toshiya Kamei

Thanks, son. Is it my turn now?

Well, first of all, let me congratulate you!

Attaboy, Aki! You're going to be a researcher! A regular one, to boot. That's all you ever wanted. Since you were here on Mars, you've worked hard to make it happen.

Thanks a bunch for the video. The largest ocean on Earth, the whatchamacallit, the Pacific, of course! Wow, quite a view you've got there, son. Is your lab embedded in that white cliff? I feel dizzy just imagining myself looking down!

For those of us born on Mars, the Earth's horizon looks peculiarly flat. And your ocean looks too blue for us. It's not that I don't trust you, but are you sure the colors are not enhanced?

Anyhow... The Ocean Institute of Micronesia, eh? I love the sound of it. Send my regards to your boss at the institute. Dear old Dr. Wells. What is she working on now?

A specialist in quantum modeling of biomass agitation caused by ocean gyres. How about that? It's quite a tongue twister, but you repeated it like a mantra. Even your mother and I ended up memorizing it.

Kudos to you, son. I wish you all the best. You make your old man proud.

Let me give you one piece of advice, though.

When you share such great news, you shouldn't look so worried.

You worry like me, I know. After all, you take after your old man. But you should learn from your mother. Remember her face when she came across the nest of the grey starlings we'd nursed back to health and released? They pumped their tiny wings, strained for freedom. We were so sure they were going to fall, but they didn't. They righted themselves. Flew into the blue sky. I wonder if we'll be able to do the same, Aki.

You've got my brown eyes, but your chin and lips look like your mother's. She smiles while her green eyes blaze with rage. But you don't have to imitate that. Your mother can be scary when she wants to be.

Listen, son. I want you to smile in a time like this.

I want you to stick your chin out and smile right now, but it will take at least twelve minutes before I can see your smile.

Oh, don't sweat it, son. I should've called you sooner. I'm grateful you've accepted my avatar call when conversation is impossible. I'm no fan of this transmission delay, either.

Two months ago, when Mars was at its closest to Earth, we could've had a decent chat, probably with a thirty-second lag, but I couldn't talk to you until now. Sorry, son.

This couldn't be put off any longer. Earth and Mars are becoming farther apart.

Again, congratulations on your graduation and job offer. Thanks for sharing the great news.

My turn, isn't it?

Brace yourself, son. This is going to be a long one.

You don't have to listen right now, but you can hit us up anytime. Anyhow, it takes at least twelve minutes for your reply to reach here.

While I wait, I'll just pour myself a cup of tea. Say, we've got ourselves rooibos tea from New Fiji. Unfortunately, locally planted rooibos will be gone after this season. There are still some left in the sheltered dome farms. Planting on Mars finally got off the ground. What a bummer.

Oh, Aki, have I told you this before? Before you were born, Lucy and I gave up on coffee and switched to rooibos tea. That's partly because we realized coffee wouldn't grow on Mars anyway, and the price skyrocketed. How do you like coffee on Earth? Sometimes I miss the taste of it.

Sorry, son, I got off on a tangent.

I wanted to spare you, Aki. But there's no way around this. The news outlets on Earth will report on Mars soon. And I want you to hear this from me before you hear it from anyone else. In twelve minutes from now, you will see my face, and you will know. You will know, son, that there's no more blue sky for any of us.

Mars won't go back to the way it was before.

No, wait. Let me put it another way.

It's going back to the way it was before.

Want to see some video?

Jarvis, could you show my boy the video taken outside our house today?

Certainly, sir. Would you like me to color-correct it?

No. Without correction. Yeah, that's fine.

Well, this doesn't help, does it? Not sure if you can process it. Too much of a drastic change. Jarvis, show him a dome. Okay, that's it.

See? It's enormous now. Remember Earth Park? Well, when you were still here five years ago, it housed only a few tenants, such as the park and a hotel for visitors from Earth. As you can see, it's expanded quite a bit. Diameter, twenty kilometers. Height, 700 meters. A triangular truss is 150 meters. Maybe you can't really tell from the video, but it's soft. It's plastic.

What else? Well, take a look at the sky.

Some call it a pink sky. But my generation and people your grandparents' age have deemed it a violet sky. The first settlers have been calling it a primordial sky. They're the ones who took off their space helmets in an environment similar to the highest mountain on Earth, so it sure looks different to them. But to our surprise, the weather conditions during the last months resemble what they saw when they first removed their helmets.

Another low-pressure storm hit us today. The pressure dropped to 150 hectopascals. Even when there's no storm, the barometer never goes above 300 hectopascals. I wonder if this is equivalent to mountains on Earth. Mt. Everest? The temperature has dropped considerably, too. Even under the equator, the thermometer only goes up to minus five degrees Celsius in the daytime.

They say we'll have many more days like this. Aki, what was it like when you were still here?

Hey, Jarvis.

On December 24, 2287, Earth Corrected Time, it was sunny. The temperature was eight degrees Celsius. A gentle, north-northeast breeze, with winds of twelve kilometers per hour. Recorded humidity was twelve percent. A pressure of 930 hectopascals.

Oh, just like Earth, eh?

We had a blue sky back then.

Your space elevator flew up, drawing contrails across the sky. What did you see from inside? Did you have windows? If you kept a log, I want you to show it to me later. Thanks, son.

Enough with the introduction already, so here it goes. Here's the deal. Sorry, I don't want to look like a mourner. I don't want you to get the wrong idea. Let me stick my chin out. How about my smile?

Here goes nothing.

It's good news, actually.

Today, I ripped the hermetic insulating seal off our house so that outside air could circulate. Still warmer than outside. Minus five degrees Celsius. See? The table is frosted. Of course, it's freezing. That's why I wear heated underwear to keep my body temperature up.

We've got enough water, because everyone else in our neighborhood has gone to the domes.

In the garden, I stripped the withered lawn and planted perennial herbs of the lily family. They're called Dragon Beard. They can grow even in the harsh Martian environment. Lucky for us, the nodules also contain the nitrogen-fixing rhizobia.

I've got some twenty goats in a pen I built in our backyard. Unlike Dragon Beard, they aren't natural-bred, though. Mars goats are genetically edited to withstand harsh environments. They stink quite a bit, but it hardly bothers you at such a low temperature.

In addition, we'll have a genetically modified Martian dog next week.

From now on, I plan to make a living as a goat shepherd on Mars. To my surprise, I can still count on the terraforming fund. To be more precise, a subsidy is based on the area where I plant my Dragon Beard.

I left the Mars Development Corporation. I hope you understand. When we stopped purchasing carbon dioxide from Earth, my job ceased to exist. Now, the MDC will focus on constructing and operating dome cities.

Here's a news flash for you, son: the terraforming of Mars has come to an end. Failed.

It came undone long ago. By the time you were born, underground layers of dry ice—needed to maintain the greenhouse effect and atmospheric pressure—were depleted. Still, the MDC decided to purchase carbon dioxide from Earth for adjusting atmospheric pressure.

At first everything went smoothly. Back then, land-based corals were carbonizing carbon dioxide at a high speed on Earth. It was an efficient method, but it was like radioactive waste. You can't just dump it in the sea. If it gets wet in the rain, carbon dioxide will be released. So we proposed to buy it from Earth.

We traded in the carbon market and carbon dioxide shot toward

Mar's orbit. It was a costly endeavor, but the space elevator operator was happy about doing business with us. It wasn't a bad deal. Even after Earth found out we'd run out of dry ice on Mars, nobody made a fuss about it.

Then things changed—believe it or not—because of a trivial error.

When the MDC's computers were replaced, the rounding logic was altered slightly, reducing the purchased price of 100,000 tons of carbon dioxide. The difference was about one cup of water per fifty containers. This minuscule change alarmed the asset management program at the carbon supplier on Earth.

I don't know how it happened, but the balance had tipped over. Fifteen minutes after the offer was returned from Earth, the price of carbon dioxide had soared twentyfold. The MDC tried to cancel the order.

You know the rest.

A rumor spread that Earth was plotting to kill those of us on Mars.

The problem was left to our politicians.

This may sound like an excuse, but those of us at the MDC disagreed. Once the atmosphere on Mars began to rarefy—according to our calculations—it'd be halved in a few months. We double- and triple-checked our calculations. But our politicians asked the public to choose between our simulation and a separatist author's demagoguery.

As a result, the carbon dioxide supply was halted and Mars started to return to its original form.

What we'd taken for granted all our lives—the blue sky, the sea, lakes, holly forests shining with rain—vanished in a flash. Mars once again became a rocky, reddish desert. Sorry, son.

"Sorry" won't cut it, I know, but I'm truly sorry.

We should've tried harder. We should've stood our ground.

We should've stood up against the separatists who fled to the Olympus Dome and played pretend.

We should've paid attention to your friends, who we thought were making a bit of an exaggerated claim. We should've joined their protest and voiced our concerns.

***

I was crying. Sorry. Considering Mars's position relative to Earth, we've got no band to transmit crying.

And one more thing.

Guess what? Your old man will be a Martian.

I don't mean my nationality. I plan to turn myself into a Martian who can survive under the dry, rarefied Martian atmosphere. Then I hope to increase vegetation here gradually.

I won't be able to breathe the same air as you.

I went to a clinic today for my first gene therapy.

Although I'll keep wearing an air-circulation mask for a while, I can move around under this atmospheric pressure of 450 hectopascals without an oxygen supply. I could climb any mountain on Earth without an oxygen canister. Oh, that's not quite possible. I forgot about gravity. My bones would be crushed.

Anyway, I'll be receiving gene therapy twice a week. In a couple of years, I'll be a complete Martian. I may be hospitalized when my blood is replaced with the antifreeze kind. My sweat glands will be gone, too. Without sweat, my grip will weaken, so I decided to have second thumbs added next to my little fingers.

In order to cope with the dry atmosphere, I'll have nictitating membranes made. Just like birds and lizards. My eye color will be green like Lucy's.

So, I should be able to master the art of putting on a brave face.

Oh, let me tell you about your mother.

She's a bit late, but she'll join me soon. Half an hour ago, she left the Galileo Dome in her buggy, so she should be here any minute.

It's not been easy for her. Unlike me, a heater alone wouldn't do. She has to put on her helmet and carry an oxygen cylinder with her whenever she goes out. I suggested an avatar call, but she insisted on talking to you face to face.

Stubborn as ever, you know her.

She won't be making a transition yet. For the time being, she'll remain as an Earthling on Mars.

Lucy decided to go into a dome.

Don't worry. We're not getting a divorce. Lucy will be working inside the dome to prepare the infrastructure for people like your grandparents. They're in their seventies. At their age, they can't go through gene editing. She'll be in charge of configuring robots and making rounds.

For the next five years, that is.

In five years, she'll be a Martian, too. By that time, she could probably transition in about two months, using the results of our current gene treatment.

Just one more thing.

If you have a serious girlfriend or boyfriend on Mars, you should hang up right now and talk to them.

After discussing with your mother, I decided to gradually become a Martian over the course of two years, but people your age are becoming Martians en masse. Yesterday, Mike, your childhood playmate, stopped by and asked me to join the newly formed Naked Martian Party.

He wants to replicate my greening technique with goats and lilies across the planet. I'll do whatever it takes to help him. I've got his back.

But things are tense around here. You must've heard of the young party leader's speech denouncing the MDC and my generation. It must've been reported widely on Earth, too.

I get it.

She... and you have the right to be angry.

We let you down. In vain, we attempted to turn Mars into Earth, used up its underground resources, and wrecked the planet... your home.

Hey, you're smiling, at last. That's my boy. This means twelve minutes have passed.

Lucy!

You made it on time. Honey, come over here. Let me hug you. I'll turn on the heater and help you get out of your spacesuit. I've just finished talking to Aki.

Take a seat, hon. Let me get your avatar. Here's our boy. Go ahead. Talk to him.

Aki, tell us whatever pops into your head.

Your mother and I will be listening.

We'll let you talk. The floor is yours now.

***

Taiyo Fujii was born on Amami Oshima, an island midway between Kyushu and Okinawa. Before turning to writing, he worked in stage design, desktop publishing, exhibition graphic design, and software development. In 2012, Fujii self-published *Gene Mapper* serially in a digital format of his own design, and it became Amazon.co.jp's number one Kindle bestseller of the year. The revised version of the novel was published in both print and digital formats as *Gene Mapper- full build-* by Hayakawa Publishing in 2013, and was a finalist for the Nihon SF Taishō Award and the Seiun Prize. In 2015, his second novel, *Orbital Cloud*, earned both awards. In the same year, he was elected eighteenth president of the Science Fiction and Fantasy Writers of Japan (SFWJ). In 2019, he gained mainstream recognition when he won the Yoshikawa Eiji Literature Prize for New Writers for *Hello, World!*, which tells the story of a software engineer who stands up for freedom and justice in cyberspace.

Toshiya Kamei's translations have appeared in *Clarkesworld, The Magazine of Fantasy & Science Fiction*, and *Strange Horizons*.

Abso

Sarah E. Stevens

Crigler thrashed so violently his hammock overturned and he landed on the floor of the dome.

The siren still screamed. He braced for the attack.

No.

The computer alarm rang through the dome.

Crigler tried to calm his breathing enough to speak. Across the dome, Abso's hydraulic system whirred as the dog rose and clicked across the hardened silica floor. It pushed its muzzle under the man's outflung hand and nudged.

The humidity sensor clicked, responding to the sweat beading Crigler's face and trickling down his back.

"Thanks, old friend," he said after a moment, and ran his hand along the dog's head. The dog's servos responded to the touch and it thrust its head closer, turning this way and that as the man stroked its metal head and gave the articulated ears a tug. As he smoothed his hand down the dog's neck, the man couldn't even feel the seam where he'd added the head to the original body. He could hardly remember Abso without it.

He was okay. It was just an alarm.

"Jezz? Report," he said.

"MOXIE reservoir levels critically low," said the computer.

"The hell?" Crigler pushed himself up from the floor and walked over to the computer panel. His bad knee gave a twinge—echoed in his lower back—but he refused to limp.

"Alarm off, Jezz," he said. The noise ceased, leaving his ears ringing with silence.

He pinched a sprig of parsley from the nearest hydroponic bed and chewed it to chase the last of his nightmare away. He allowed himself three full breaths, bringing the green scent of growing herbs—his greatest luxury—deep into his lungs, then focused. A glance out the nearest portal showed that it was almost morning. Sunlight sharpened the edge of the horizon and brought a yellow haze to the air, hung with fine dust. Variegated shades of red and grey stretched without relief toward the buttes at the edge of Gale Crater. Crigler long ago trained his eyes not to anticipate the dart of a squirrel or rabbit, the winging of a bird through the air, even the flutter of a leaf on a branch.

Abso followed him and now leaned against his leg. The dog's bulk was reassuring at his side and Crigler shifted his stance to press against the dog, warm from its radioisotope thermoelectric generator.

But his heartbeat spiked again as he read the data from the MOXIE. The Mars OXygen In situ Extractor for his dome had a reservoir capable of storing 2 kg of oxygen, which gave him a generous two-day buffer before his home would mirror the barren planet. Right now, the reservoir held 0.5 kg, enough for maybe twelve hours. Why hadn't the alarm gone off earlier?

Crigler did some quick calculations. Every hour, the MOXIE extracted 22 grams of oxygen from the thin, carbon dioxide-based atmosphere. If he could fix it right away, he still had a slight margin, though he'd be cutting things close. If he minimized his activity level, he might not need help. If. And if.

Ever dutiful, he recorded in his log before leaving the dome.

"Crigler, here. 10:30 Local Mean Solar Time, sol 551, year 7 MCE. MOXIE reservoir at 0.5 kg. Heading out for recon."

Abso followed him to the locker that stored his suit. The dog's tail started to move faster and its front feet danced in excitement. Simulated, programmed excitement, the man reminded himself. Programming he'd added himself.

"Not this time, Abso. No walk today," he said. He knelt in front of the dog and gave it a hug, smoothing his hands along the sleek, warm sides. As always, his mind tricked his hands into thinking he felt Abso's generator buzzing, even though he knew radioactive isotope decay wasn't detectable. Not like a heartbeat. He noticed the hydraulics on one rear leg hitched slightly as the dog moved. Needed to avoid taking the dog out too often; years of drastic temperature changes took their toll.

"Stay, Abso," he said, and the dog stilled immediately. He ran his hands down the back leg, noting where the joint needed adjustment. The dog would be just fine, with the right care and maintenance. Better than fine. Best partner he could have. And they would have scrapped it. Crigler's mouth tightened and he forced himself to think about the MOXIE. He suited up and headed out onto the bleak surface.

Ninety minutes later, he was back in the dome and out of options. The latest sandstorm had forced grit into a seam and slowly widened it until the MOXIE's shell had breached. Dust permeated the electrodes, the crystal lattices, *and* the reservoir alarm mechanism. He'd fixed just about everything in this dome, and more than once, but he couldn't repair the solid oxide electrolysis cell.

Fewer than twelve hours now. He had to contact the colony for aid. Hopefully he wouldn't have to visit that maze of domes and stale air, people rushing from work to their vid screens, everything too crowded but somehow still empty.

"Jezz," he said, "Search colony directory. MOXIE distributors."

He scrolled through several listings before lingering on one.

Parts, systems, and oxygen delivered throughout Gale crater. Delivery in 30 minutes or less, guaranteed.

Thirty minutes or less? Put him in mind of pizzas back on Earth, and he shook his head in disbelief at the changes on Mars. He glanced at Abso, who'd changed almost as much since the old days, before any colonies, when just the two of them scouted the planet and avoided enemy forces until the war broke out.

All right. Delivery in 30 minutes or less. He sent the order.

***

"Another one for you, Kiki." Amir slid the screen across the aluminum table.

"Dammit, I just unsuited." Kiki translated coordinates in her head. "Thirty-two kilometers northeast of Bradbury Station. What the hell is out there?"

"Some old codger in a one-person dome."

"Great, he's probably space mad."

"Have to be insane to live that far out." Amir waggled dark eyebrows at her. "Maybe he's some ancient hermit with mystical knowledge that'll change your life."

"Yeah, that's it." Kiki rested her hands on the cool table and twisted back and forth to stretch her spine. "I'll be happy if he's not meat-crazed enough to want human flesh. Did Washington load the Matador?"

"Done. MOXIE 109gph, 4 kilogram reservoir, and a full tank."

"Damn. Whoever this is, he has credits. I'll see you on the flip side. Want to catch some drinks at The Glacier tonight?"

"The Glacier? Nah, think I'll just plug in and watch races from my bunk."

Kiki shrugged to hide her disappointment. After a day surrounded by metal and the desolate Martian landscape, she needed to immerse herself in the blue upon blue upon blue of the Glacier's vid screens and imagine they were windows. When she watched the images of polar bears stalking across the snow, she could nearly feel her own feet crunch through the icy layer into the softer powder beneath. She hung out at the Glacier so often that she'd secretly named every creature in the rotating footage. Her favorite was a thick-billed murre she'd dubbed Rocket, not for his clumsy flying, but for his incredible diving and the way he rocketed back up to the surface with air bubbles streaming from his feathers. Rocket appeared every 168 minutes in the Glacier's loop. She wondered if any thick-billed murres survived. Or any birds. Probably not. As a girl, she'd spent hours watching collared doves on the tiny balcony of their Tokyo apartment. The birds would strut along the railing calling *popoppou, popoppou*, then suddenly launch into the sky with chitters and a burst of feathers.

"Clock's ticking." Amir tapped the screen and broke into Kiki's thoughts.

"Right. *Jaa ne.*"

"See ya."

On her way to the suits, Kiki detoured through the sterile halls to her locker. She cleared her throat against the air, which smelled stale and tinny, even though she knew it was perfectly safe. She pulled out two chocolate bars and a package of soy jerky. She was kidding about this Crigler eating her, but maybe some civilized treats would mean a big tip.

As she settled into her seat, Kiki touched the *omamori* hanging from the inside hatch handle. Her fingers moved in their habitual gesture, smoothing the length of the embroidered silk as she sent up a prayer for safe travels. The touch sent a jolt of sensory memory through her: *soba* kneeling to fasten Kiki's *kimono* on *shichi-go-san*, Kiki running her fingers down the material. She'd been seven, right before everything changed.

Kiki blinked. The timer on her helmet's view screen ticked down to 22:00, a reminder she'd better get going. Delivery in 30 minutes or less, after all. She started the craft down the immaculately-maintained runway and increased speed until its long wings lifted off in the thin Mars atmosphere.

Her timer reached 2:13 as she landed helicopter-style, which ate fuel, but was the only option on ungroomed terrain. She let out a slow breath of relief. A remote dome like this cut her time down to the wire. As the wheels touched down, she clicked the button to signal arrival, knowing the GPS would confirm on-time delivery. No demarks today.

She stared at the site: an older-style thirty-meter dome with two small air locks. The MOXIE unit connected to one side, next to a CO_2 elimination system. Most people would have scrapped it for a newer model by now rather than bother with the maintenance. To the east of the dome, a small rover-style vehicle sat with drifts of sand half-covering its wheels. Footprints decorated the ground around the MOXIE and one airlock, so she chose that entrance. Climbing out of the Matador, she opened her radio to the universal channel.

"Dome, this is Kiki with a delivery for Andy Crigler," she said. "At the airlock near your MOXIE unit."

"Roger," came the only reply. Kiki opened her side of the airlock, stepped in, and felt the chamber equalize pressure with the dome. She waited for Crigler to open the inside lock.

When the lock opened, she stomped her feet to make sure she didn't track in grit and unlatched her suit helmet before stepping into the dome.

The smell hit her first: a whiff of ozone and the clean smell of growing plants. Crigler stood about two meters away, an older man with a hardened face and craggy skin who rocked on his toes as if he might move suddenly. Her assessment cut short as a robotic *thing* lunged toward her. She flinched and jumped backward.

"Abso! Sit!" the man yelled.

The thing halted with a lurch and sat. A scorched smell rose into the air. Kiki's heart pounded and she glanced at the airlock to make sure she could run for it if she needed to.

"Dammit," growled the man. He stomped to the robot and knelt, favoring one knee. He picked up the thing's back leg and examined it with an angry shake of the head.

Kiki stared. The robot had a stocky cylindrical body with four legs that bent backward at the knee. Kiki made an inadvertent noise and its head swiveled, pointing a pair of dark, oval sensors and a metal muzzle at her. Double-jointed metal flaps hung at the side of its head. *Ears*, Kiki realized. Below its chest, between the wide-set front legs hung the barrel of a swivel-mounted laser cannon. Two larger cannons protruded from the thing's back and shadowed its shoulders.

She shrank against the dome wall, as news footage from her childhood flashed through her mind's eye: soldiers desperately sheltered behind an outcrop while mechs lurched across the red soil, their lasers turning the rocks to deep orange fire.

"Is that a…?"

The man stood up and the robot rose to flank him, the cannons sending red sights across the dome and onto Kiki, who froze.

"Power lasers down, Abso," he said. "*Friend.*"

He looked at Kiki, still recoiling against the dome, and grimaced. "Sorry. We don't get much company."

The MEchanized Battle Scout retracted the barrel of its lower cannon. Kiki breathed again. The robot was polished to a sheen, but Kiki still saw scratches and gouges on its worn body, particularly near the mounts to hold packs and equipment. Its mirror-bright head reflected each light of the dome.

"Abso?" she echoed.

She stared at the robot as it stood next to Crigler. Its head cocked slightly to look at Kiki, while its tail—*tail?*—slowly began to thump against the man's leg.

Like Chiko's used to, Kiki thought in bewilderment.

Hydroponic beds dominated the dome space, with a small kitchen and waste station tucked into one side and a hammock attached near the other wall. Broad potato leaves and ferny carrot tops sprouted up from the beds, while other greenery hung from inverted planters, all connected by intricate piping. Kiki recognized mizuna lettuce and saw a flash of something red, but she didn't know half the stuff he was growing. Crigler had his LED lights set to a yellowish brightness that mimicked Earth's sunlight, instead of the blue-purple range popular in the nurseries Kiki had visited. The faint sound of his water recovery system thrummed through the space.

The robot sat down at the man's feet, still watching Kiki.

***

Crigler frowned. He hadn't expected a girl, or someone so young. Her brown hair was cropped close to her skull in the spacer style, her nose glinted with a piercing, and her dark eyes were rimmed with some glittery gunk.

"His name is Abso."

"It is a MEBS, *nee*? A real one?"

Dammit, she sounded terrified. He hadn't meant to scare her. Couldn't she see that? "Did you bring the new MOXIE?"

"Yes, and the reservoir and a full tank." The girl stared at Abso as if she'd never seen a robot before.

"Right, then."

***

The man turned to get his suit and the MEBS pranced around, looking *excited*, for Earth's sake. It even lowered its front end and waggled its rear.

"Not this time, Abso," the man spoke in a gentle voice, much different than when he talked to Kiki. He reached out and petted the thing on its head. The robot preened against his hand and nudged him.

"Is it…" Kiki stopped as the man turned to the airlock.

"Let's get to work," he said.

Kiki watched as Crigler installed the unit himself with quick competence, unlike most customers who let her do the work. He spoke in single words, directing her to hand him a tool, hold a connector, shift a piece to the left. Several times, Kiki opened her mouth to ask questions—about the robot, about his dome, about living way out in Gale Crater like a monk—but his silence deterred her. She watched as he swiftly assembled the unit and ran diagnostics. With a nod, he indicated they were finished and the two re-entered the airlock.

This time, she wasn't surprised when the MEBS—when Abso, his name was Abso—frisked around their feet, nearly tripping Crigler as he unsuited. The robot reared up and stuck its muzzle close to the man, whose face cracked in a smile. He thumped the robot dog on the side in rough affection and tugged on one of its ears. Abso's tail worked the air in delight and it ran across the dome to fetch a small red ball. Crigler tossed the ball against the wall of the dome. He smiled as Abso scrambled after the toy.

Chiko used to love tennis balls. Kiki's fingers tingled with a visceral memory of the fuzzy green ball in her hands. After fetching it, he had always jumped up on her with the ball in his mouth. She'd grabbed his feet like they were holding hands. His paws used to smell like *senbei* and corn chips.

***

"That's enough for now, Abso," Crigler said, then turned to see the spacer girl watching the dog with wide eyes.

"I brought you something," she said. "I mean. Something besides the MOXIE." She unzipped the outer pocket of her suit and pulled out two chocolate bars and a package of jerky. "I thought you might miss things, being all the way out here. Alone. Well, mostly alone."

Crigler tried to find the right words.

"Thank you," he said, finally. "That's very kind of you." He took the treats from her, and the two of them stood awkwardly. Abso nosed its ball, waiting.

"Could I...could I pet Abso?"

"What?"

"I had a dog back on Earth. Before. A beagle named Chiko." Kiki paused, then continued in a rush. "He had the softest ears you can imagine."

Crigler frowned. The girl seemed to be holding her breath, waiting for him to answer.

"Yeah. Sure."

***

The man called the dog and it trotted right over. Kiki pulled off her gloves and let them hang by the suit connectors. She held out her hand absurdly, as if Abso would sniff her, then changed the motion into stroking its metal head. The dog pushed into her hand and she heard its tail thump on the floor. The sound brought tears to her eyes and she swallowed hard. Kiki knelt down next to Abso, rubbed its head and neck, avoiding the laser cannons, which didn't matter. Not really. Not at all. The dog felt warm and smooth. She ran her fingers over the dog's ears, and it turned its head this way and that at her touch. Crigler watched her, her and Abso.

After a long time, she rose and they exchanged a smile.

Kiki held out her tablet for his thumbprint confirming delivery, then pulled it away.

"Why do you live out here?" she asked.

"It's my home," Crigler said. After a minute, he added gruffly, "Where are you from?"

"Yakumo-Xia dome."

"I mean before."

"Oh," said Kiki. "I lived in Tokyo, until—"

"Yeah," Crigler said. "Your family?"

"Just me. I'm the only one who made it. What about you? You're all alone?"

The man's gaze shot toward Abso.

"I'm not alone."

"You could move your dome closer to the colony. You don't have to stay this far out."

"People don't understand," he said.

"They might."

Crigler said nothing.

"I do," Kiki said. "I understand."

He shrugged and reached for her tablet. "I didn't add the tip yet."

"I don't want a tip. I want... I..."

Crigler's face was so still it looked like a mask.

Kiki swallowed and forced the words out over the sound of blood pounding in her ears.

"Can I come back and visit Abso?"

He looked at her for a long moment. Kiki made herself stand still and meet his gaze.

"All right," he said, finally. "That would be all right."

***

Sarah E. Stevens is a writer, a professor, and a geek. A voracious reader and writer of speculative fiction, she checks wardrobes, dreams of dragons, and gazes into the night sky. She loves cats, chocolate, and coffee, and spends her free time making chain maille jewelry, painting, and playing board games. Check out *Dark Moon Wolf*, the first book of her series *Calling the Moon*, if you like feminist werewolves. She lives in Evansvile, Indiana with her husband, three children, and five cats. You can find out more at www.sarahestevens.com.

In Two Minds

Joel R. Hunt

The dog didn't want to be Jacked. Tomo knew that before he even tried. She was pressing herself into the furthest corners of the cage and turning from face to face with panicked eyes.

"I can't do this," Tomo said.

Sergeant Ito held up an external hard drive labelled with Tomo's name and address, as if he didn't know exactly what was on it.

"We have a long list of animal-assisted crimes that tells us otherwise," she said. "We've been willing to overlook your little games in the past, but you've spat that discretion back in our faces too many times. You will pay your dues, Mr Masuda. You can get us these memories and be on your way, or you can fester in prison with all of the other A-Jacks who turned their backs on humanity. What was it you chose to fraternise with instead? Rodents?"

Better company than you, Tomo thought.

"Look," he said, "Jacking can be a stressful process—"

"Perhaps you'd like a foot massage," sneered Ito.

"I mean for the animal," said Tomo. "It can be alarming for them to suddenly find another voice in their head. Jacking works best when they're relaxed. If we can let her out of that cage—"

"No," said Ito. "The cage is here for our protection. Yours too. You'll work like this or not at all."

Tomo sat back and released his breath in a low hiss. He waited until some of the tension had left his body before peeling the skin from his temple, revealing a trio of dials embedded in his skull. With grim resignation, he set his frequency to 'canine'.

A familiar shiver danced across his brain. As he closed his eyes, the sounds and smells of the interrogation room faded away, replaced by swirling, intangible clouds of consciousness. They dotted his mental horizon, most so distant that they were barely perceptible, yet in the direction of the cage, one drew his thoughts like a magnet. He let himself drift nearer, ready to mingle with the dog's awareness. He held back to ensure he didn't overwhelm her, yet the moment he brushed against her mind, she lurched away as though he were fire. In the brief moment that they touched, Tomo felt an all-consuming terror.

His eyes shot open. His heart beat against his ribs as the police station coalesced around him. In the corner, the dog whimpered and pressed herself further into the wall.

"Well?" snapped Ito.

"She's scared," said Tomo. "She's been Jacked before; she knew what she was feeling as soon as I tried to connect. Whatever the last one did to her, she doesn't want another human in her brain."

"So?"

Tomo's fingernails dug into his palms until he was nearly drawing blood.

Don't punch a police officer. Do not *punch a police officer.*

"*So,*" he said, "I'll need time. I need to show her that I won't hurt her."

Ito's eyes narrowed.

"How much time?" she asked.

"Two, maybe three days."

"Two or three *days?*" spluttered an officer by the door. Ito held up a hand.

"We don't have that kind of time," she said. "We have a killer dog in our custody, and the law stipulates that it needs to be put down within twenty-four hours. *If* it killed of its own volition. You're here to prove whether it was being influenced by an A-Jack at the time. Weep for its welfare all you like, but if you walk out of here without doing your job, it's *you* signing the death warrant."

Tomo opened his mouth to object, but he was silenced by Ito's furious stare. There was no fighting this. He stewed in silence for as long as he dared, then raised a reluctant hand and checked that his dials were still in position.

I'm sorry, friend, he thought.

Tomo's world dissolved. The clouds of consciousness drifted back into his perception, the nearest now roiling in turmoil. After his first Jacking attempt, the dog was prepared for him. If he tried to ease into her mind, she would resist every step of the way. There was no other option. Tomo had to overpower her.

He brought his thoughts as close as he could without making contact. Every movement took an intense effort, and the willpower required to remain separated from her was exhausting. He managed to hold back until his consciousness enveloped the dog's, leaving no chance of escape. Then he snapped his trap shut.

Tomo's perception recentred itself with a jarring lurch. He was assaulted with sounds and smells that had been beyond his senses in a human body; the odour of wet dog flooded his nostrils, alongside his own unwashed scent and the stench of old blood. He saw himself, too, through the familiar yet alien lens of the dog's vision. Her sights—her senses—had become one with his own.

So had her feelings. Her unfiltered panic at the presence of a human inside her brain was nearly unbearable, and in the integral first moments of contact, Tomo came close to Jacking out. Her heart pulsed with a pain that stung them both, and she lashed around her cage as though fighting a ghost. This was the most troubled mind he'd ever found himself inside, but if he had any hope of saving her life, he needed to gain access to her memories. He needed to calm her down.

With a Herculean effort, ignoring the desperate urge to be free, Tomo summoned the image of an open field. He focussed on the smells of fresh grass and fellow dogs. He remembered the sensation of wind running through fur. He thought of the happiest he had ever been as a dog.

The panic faltered. Tomo leapt into the emotional void it created. He thought of the feeling of rubbed tummies and scratched ears. He thought of cool water and juicy meat and play fights as a puppy. All the while, he whispered soothing reassurances into her brain.

It's okay. I won't hurt you. You're safe.

Tracking time during a Jack was always difficult, but Tomo guessed that ten minutes had passed by the time she stopped trying to fight his presence. In an ideal world, he would have continued soothing her for hours, until she embraced rather than tolerated him. However, Sergeant Ito did not preside over such a world. It was time to start digging for memories.

Tomo tried to be delicate. Bringing memories to the forefront of a mind could do serious damage, especially if the memories were traumatic, so Tomo had perfected the art of partial recall; he could browse through a creature's memories while barely giving them an inkling of the past. Conscious of the stress that he had already caused this dog, Tomo eased his way into her history. As with all dogs, much of her memory was scent-based, which Tomo brushed past without consideration. He might find the exact scent of the A-Jack who had last been inside her brain, but it would mean nothing to the police. In all of Tomo's trips inside animal minds, he had yet to devise a method of explaining distinctive odours to humans who were unable to smell them.

Instead, he waded into the snippets of visual memory. He scrolled through until he found the sight of a terrified human face followed by a neck torn wide open. Tomo buried this again before the coppery recollection of blood could establish itself on his tongue. He only needed it as a landmark to navigate from. Some A-Jack had been in this dog's mind before him and influenced her to kill, which meant that before the murder, she would most likely have encountered them.

Finding the culprit required a deeper dive. The dog wouldn't distinguish A-Jacks from other humans, and as a stray she had encountered hundreds of strangers before she was controlled. To narrow them down, Tomo needed to access the feelings she associated with this crowd of remembered faces. He browsed through a dozen or so humans that the dog had little response to before finding a face that speared his heart with panic. Even as a half-recollection, the dog cowered and whined, her heart racing as she tried to escape from herself. There was no doubt about it; this was the face that had invaded her brain. Tomo promptly buried it and brought back the soothing fields, but the memory lingered in both of their minds. It was a man's face, cruel and hard, with eyes of stone and a mouth that had never learned to smile.

But there was more. Something unusual. Tomo felt the remembered ache of muscles spasming out of control. The panic of limbs moving with their own accord. The terror of a jaw being wrenched open by an unseen power before clamping shut, unbidden, on a human throat.

Tomo reeled. The man who had Jacked this dog had gone further than any A-Jack that Tomo had ever encountered. He hadn't simply influenced her thoughts. He had forced her from her own brain and stolen her body. He had turned a thinking, feeling creature into a living puppet.

The shock of his realisation severed Tomo's connection. He returned to himself, greeted by a tidal wave of nausea. Placing both hands on his chair to steady himself, he swallowed back bile. He could barely comprehend what he had discovered...

Ito cleared her throat, peering at Tomo with only a fraction of her typical scorn.

"Find anything?" she asked.

Tomo nodded. Suddenly, Ito had become the lesser of two evils.

He intended to tell her everything.

***

An hour and a half later, Tomo emerged from the police station, hands plunged into his pockets and hood drawn up to hide his implants. The face he had described to the officers didn't appear on their records, but he had refused to leave until they generated a perfect match from his descriptions. The thought of that A-Jack roaming free churned Tomo's stomach. As for the dog, Ito had agreed to stay the execution based on Tomo's testimony. That, at least, had made the ordeal worthwhile.

A ramp led down from the station towards a park in the square, where cherry trees bloomed beside what had once been its entrance. However, years of renaturing had blurred the boundaries of the urban landscape. Tiered gardens spilled from the rooftops and melded into the flowers that wound up every wall. A complex series of vines crisscrossed between surrounding buildings, turning the city into a single bustling organism, and as Tomo glanced around the square, he spotted messenger squirrels darting back and forth with letters. Among them, a macaque sat picking its nose, waiting for the next parcel to deliver.

It was a wonderful view, spoiled by Officer Nakano waiting for him at the bottom.

"Thank you for your work today, Mr Masuda," she said. "Allow me to escort you to the station."

"I know the way," he said.

Nakano flashed a smile. Tomo wasn't sure if it was apologetic or sarcastic; he'd never been good at reading people.

"Orders, I'm afraid," Nakano said. "The public feel less threatened by A-Jacks who are accompanied by police officers. You aren't in trouble though, I promise."

Tomo scowled.

"Fine," he said, setting off at what he hoped was an uncomfortable pace.

Nakano, it transpired, was far fitter than he was. She matched his stride without difficulty, and by the time Tomo was getting out of breath, Nakano merely looked refreshed. He slowed down for his own sake, deciding to take the quickest route to the tram stop so that she could leave him alone.

No A-Jack was ever truly alone, however. As they crossed the park, a dozen sparrows wheeled overhead, and an unseen creature rustled through the fallen cherry blossoms into a maze of tunnels beneath their feet. To Tomo's surprise, Nakano noticed it too.

"It's amazing to think how many creatures share this city with us," she said. "All those different perspectives on the world, all those eyes and ears. With skills like yours, any one of them could be turned to the benefit of honest society. Every bird could become a flying police camera, every stray dog an undercover officer. It's maddening how little we're making use of the massive potential living all around us!"

"They're not tools, you know," Tomo snapped.

Nakano stopped in her tracks. She seemed about to apologise—a rare instinct for a police officer—but she caught herself and frowned at him instead.

"That's an interesting objection from someone who used rats to steal jewels," she said.

"I didn't *use* them," Tomo replied. "I *asked* them. Maybe you can try that next time you want an A-Jack to help you torture animals."

"We don't torture animals," Nakano said.

"You ever been inside a mind that didn't want you there?" asked Tomo. "It tries everything to get you out. You're an itch it can't scratch, a noise it can't silence. You're a cancer. It wants nothing more than to expel you and never feel you again. What you get A-Jacks to do in there... *that's* torture."

Nakano's mouth became a thin line. He took the opportunity to get several steps ahead of her, and this time she didn't catch up with him, instead shadowing him for the remainder of the journey. Thankfully, the train was already waiting when Tomo arrived at the station, and he hopped on without glancing back. Nakano would wait to ensure he didn't get off again to return to the financial district, but he had no intention of spending another second with the police.

As the train set off to the outskirts of the city, Tomo weaved through the commuters with practiced ease, nudging and ducking his way across the carriage until he could find a corner to himself. For the entirety of the half-hour journey, no one glanced in Tomo's direction; he had perfected the art of being unremarkable.

Exactly as he liked it.

The station Tomo emerged onto had little of the greenery boasted by the city centre. Evidently the great renaturing projects, now claimed as a brainchild by every politician and CEO seeking public favour, hadn't been intended for the poor. Tomo's neighbours did what they could, turning pavement cracks into micro-gardens and broken streetlights into bird feeders, but short of tearing down the tower blocks and starting from scratch, there was only so much of the concrete desert that nature could reclaim. The street wouldn't even have power if it wasn't for the glittering patchwork of solar panels that had been salvaged from a nearby junkyard, as well as a few that Tomo had helped 'liberate' from the wealthier neighbourhoods.

A short walk brought Tomo to his crumbling apartment block. The elevator was predictably broken again, having been jury-rigged so many times that Tomo wasn't sure any of the original mechanism remained, so he slumped up the stairs, fished a key out of his shoe and let himself in. It was a single-room apartment, strewn with artefacts of Tomo's meagre life. A mattress occupied most of the floor, the rest taken up by clothes, old take-away packaging and a lone chair. At the sink, Tomo scraped yesterday's rice onto the least dirty plate within reach, added some sauce from an unlabelled bottle, and had his first meal of the day.

Rustling from the corner announced the arrival of the rats. Tomo smiled and scattered rice by his feet.

"How are you all doing today?" he asked. Setting his plate aside, Tomo peeled the skin from his temple, set his dials to 'rodent' and reached out to the mental clouds scurrying by his feet. Unlike the dog at the station, these minds welcomed Tomo's presence. Most were content to let him spectate through their eyes and filter through their recent memories, but some responded to his Jacking with thoughts of their own, seeping into Tomo's consciousness until they seemed to belong to him.

Hungry, thought Ryo.

Groom! thought Kenta. *Groom, play, groom!*

Their animal minds didn't use words, but Tomo had learned to associate meaning to their feelings. He Jacked out and gave Ryo some more rice, then picked Kenta from the floor and placed him in his lap, scratching behind the rat's ears as he finished his own meal.

Once his plate was empty, and Kenta had scurried back to play with the others on the floor, Tomo flopped onto his bed. He Jacked back into Kenta and felt the careless joy of play before drifting into the oblivion of sleep.

Tomo woke to a pained yowl.

He was back in his own body—no one stayed Jacked in their sleep—and in an instant he was by his window, peering into the streets below. His eyes struggled to adjust, hindered more than helped by the flickering streetlight directly opposite, but everywhere he looked appeared deserted. He watched and listened until he satisfied himself that the noise had been part of a dream.

Then, movement. A heavy-set dog lumbered into view, carrying something in its jaws. It walked with obvious discomfort, as though each step were agony, yet equally, there was determination in its strides. It covered the length of the street in a few seconds, and had almost turned the corner when the bundle in its mouth squirmed.

Tomo's stomach writhed as he saw that it was a cat.

The creature was being carried by its head, limply fighting against the powerful jaws that could easily tear it in two. The cat hadn't been seriously harmed, and while the dog wasn't being gentle, Tomo didn't think that was an accident. This behaviour was unusual for a dog. Too unusual.

It had to have been Jacked. Tomo's hand moved to reset his dials, hoping to Jack in as well and muscle out the unwelcome invader, but he couldn't find the frequency in time. Instead, as the dog vanished around the corner, Tomo slipped through his window, scrambling down the tower's balconies as though they were rungs in a ladder. He jumped the final two balconies, landing in a crouch before sprinting in the dog's direction.

There was no sign of the animals in the next street. Tomo ran towards the old industrial estate, the direction in which the dog had seemed to be heading, and was rewarded with a frail meow that called out from the darkness. The sound guided him towards an alleyway to his right, where he spotted the dog skulking into the distance. It turned towards a warehouse and disappeared down a set of stairs built into the floor.

Tomo knew this place. It belonged to an A-Jack named Giichi, one of the most notorious loan sharks in the city; literally, if rumours were to be believed. Tomo had heard that the man kept a pet shark which he Jacked into so that he could experience devouring his enemies first-hand. Tomo had never met him, and had been happy to keep it that way. Every thief knew not to mess with Giichi.

But now Tomo had the disturbing feeling that he'd already come face-to-face with the man that day, in the memories of the dog. Every survival instinct screamed at him to turn back and forget what he had seen. Getting himself embroiled in Giichi's affairs would be the stupidest decision he could ever make.

Only one thing stopped him from saving himself. An A-Jack in this city was taking full control of innocent creatures, and the police had no leads beyond his own description of the man. If Tomo had a chance at stopping him, he had to take it.

Creeping up to the concrete stairs that dipped below the street, Tomo peered down to the door they led to. In its shadow slept an enormous guard dog. It wasn't the dog Tomo had been following, though was easily as large, and likely belonged to the same owner. He'd have to find another entrance.

Pacing around the warehouse, Tomo found a large window near the back, sealed, but with the latch tauntingly close. If Tomo could get it open, he'd be able to climb right through. Normally, he'd consider breaking the glass, but that wasn't an option this time; Giichi couldn't know he was here.

Tomo cast his eyes around for another way in, and lingered on a small vent just within reach.

"That could work…" he whispered.

He turned his dials to 'rodent' and groped for the distant specks of awareness in his apartment. It was difficult to Jack at such a distance, but Kenta was eager to accept him.

Go to Tomo, he thought, flashing images of his location into the rat's mind. Within five minutes, Kenta was scurrying up to him and latching onto his boot.

"Thanks, buddy," Tomo whispered. "There's something you could help me with."

He raised Kenta to the vent and encouraged him inside, before Jacking in and guiding him the rest of the way. He visualised in Kenta's mind how to work the window latch, and the rat was eager to oblige. Kenta hopped onto the windowsill and probed the contraption with his whiskers before pushing it loose through a combined effort of paws and snout.

Well done Kenta, Tomo thought.

Play, Kenta thought back, *Groom!*

Soon, Tomo thought. *Explore first.*

The corridor was empty—Tomo could see that from the window—but somewhere further inside lurked the loan shark Giichi and his enormous Jacked dog. They had to proceed with caution, and Kenta made a much subtler scout than Tomo ever would.

As Kenta set off along the crook of the wall, Tomo settled in for the ride. Navigating as a rat took a lot of getting used to. The world managed to be both infinitely larger and oppressively smaller. The tightest of spaces became a vast expanse, yet through a rat's eyes, only a few feet were clearly visible; the horizon beyond was a mesh of shapes and blurs. Tomo had long ago learned to let the rat take the lead, gleaning what information he could from their other sharpened senses.

The first few rooms warranted no further exploration. Squeezing under the fourth door, however, led Kenta onto a vast steel platform suspended over a drop. They were above the main storage room of the warehouse. Kenta froze. From below, the stench of dog billowed up to the ceiling. Too strong for a room this size. There must be dozens of them. Kenta could hear their distressed whines and clattering claws on the warehouse's hard floor.

Something else caught Tomo's attention, though the rat paid it no interest at all; across from them, a multi-storey fish tank dominated the room. An arrow-shaped blur glided through Kenta's vision. There was truth to the rumours, then. Giichi had a pet shark.

A cat yowled below.

Kenta resisted Tomo's urges to go further.

Predator, the rat thought. *Big, lots.*

Tomo hesitated. Kenta was his best chance at getting a look at what he was dealing with before diving in himself, but he couldn't blame the rodent for being scared. One bite from a dog and Kenta would be finished.

It's alright, he thought. *Go to Tomo.*

The remainder of the rescue mission would have to be human-led. Jacking out and returning to his own body, Tomo clambered through the window. He pulled off his jacket in time for Kenta to scurry into one of the sleeves, and gently bundled it up, tucking it under the window.

"Stay here," he whispered.

Tomo tiptoed towards the walkway. Any sound he made might be picked up by the dogs, and the A-Jack could be hiding inside any one of them. Tomo eased the door open and slipped through. Blue light from the shark tank bathed the walkway. Below, cages lined the walls, each filled with a dozen dogs, while in the centre of the room, in a meditation-like repose behind his desk, was a man who could only be Giichi. Tomo felt his insides lurch. This was, without doubt, the man from the dog's memories. Those stone-carved features and cruel mouth were unmistakable, and even though he was Jacking, his face wasn't relaxed. Instead, he seemed tense and strained, an elastic band stretched to breaking point.

A cat occupied the top of the desk. It was a pitiful thing, bedraggled and wiry, but motionless, staring at Giichi with a fierce intent. Giichi, no doubt, was in its head, though Tomo couldn't work out what the man was trying to achieve. Neither he nor the cat were moving a muscle.

Then, shaking with effort, the cat raised its right paw. In response, the fingers on Giichi's right hand twitched. The cat forced its paw higher. Giichi's hand trembled and, for the briefest moment, jumped upwards.

Giichi was learning to move his body *from another creature's mind!*

Tomo recoiled. The metal beneath his feet groaned.

Giichi Jacked out quicker than Tomo had thought possible, grabbing the cat's tail and stuffing it in a drawer before spinning to face the walkway above.

"Show yourself!" he bellowed, voice echoing throughout the warehouse. Every dog cowered. Tomo even thought he saw the shark flinch. He leaned further back, avoiding any sudden movements that might catch Giichi's attention.

"You've made a big mistake tonight," Giichi shouted to the ceiling. He approached the cage of his biggest dog and wrenched open the bolt. Before the dog could move, Giichi Jacked into its brain, and it let out a snarl that was every bit as savage as he was. Casting its nose around the warehouse, it charged out the door.

Tomo ran. He didn't know where he was going, but he had to stay away from that dog. Memories of a torn throat flashed in his mind, and the coppery tang of blood drifted along his tongue. Tomo had no doubt what would happen if Giichi caught him.

He couldn't abandon the trapped animals, though. Tuning his dials as he ran, Tomo found the 'feline' frequency and groped wildly for the cat's consciousness. As he turned a corner and slammed the door closed behind him, he Jacked in.

Darkness enveloped him. Fear clouded his mind. Trapped inside the drawer, the cat barely dared to move. Her whole body ached from the strain of Giichi's test, and while she sensed Tomo's presence, she merely played dead and hoped he would leave.

She didn't have that luxury. If she stayed here, she would be used and discarded, just as the dog had been before her. Tomo clawed through the cat's memories. Within what he hoped were only seconds, he cobbled together a combination of remembered sensations: lying on her back, running, jumping. Freedom.

Do it now, he thought, making the memories as vibrant as he could.

Perhaps sensing his urgency, the cat complied. She lay down and pressed her paws against the underside of the table. Then she pushed. Inch by torturous inch, the drawer eased open, light spilling inside. Tomo didn't need to provide any instructions there. The cat spun in a flash and shot from the desk.

The feeling of freedom was luxurious, but as the cat assessed her new surroundings, she spied Giichi's dog barrelling along the suspended walkway. Tomo Jacked out as quickly as he could, stumbling in his human body and groping for something— anything—to block the door. He found an old broom and wedged it through the door handle just as the weight of the dog slammed against it. Tomo pelted down the corridor, heading for the only other exit. He shoved the door with his shoulder. It was locked. Behind him, claws and teeth began tearing away his only barricade. Tomo slumped against the door and crashed to the ground. This was it. He was going to die here.

There was just one last thing to do.

In a blink, Tomo was back inside the cat's mind. She was creeping towards the door, wary of the dogs on either side and the motionless body of Giichi. As fast as he could, Tomo bombarded her with images of the cage locks. He showed her the precise detail of how Giichi had opened it.

The cat froze. She wasn't sure where these thoughts were coming from. She took a step towards the door. Paused. Turned to the cages. The dogs watched in terrified silence. She approached, eyeing the lock as though it were a dangerous animal. Above, nothing more than a momentary distraction, a door crashed open. As the cat glanced upwards, Tomo saw Giichi's dog clambering through the shattered wood.

Tomo returned to his body a fraction of a second before the hound lunged. It barrelled into him with full force, knocking the wind from his lungs. Tomo crashed to the ground, the animal's weight bearing down on him, and flinched as its jaw parted before his face.

Then, a wet tongue lathered his cheek.

Tomo opened one eye as the dog smothered his face with licks. Its tail wagged furiously and, as he eased himself up, it trotted back to give him space.

"G... Giichi?" he asked.

The dog cocked its head before pressing in to lick him again. That was all the convincing Tomo needed. Giichi had left the animal's brain. Scratching the dog behind the ear, Tomo staggered to his feet and brushed himself down. His clothes were torn and along his chest were the beginnings of claw marks, some having drawn blood. Giichi had been seconds away from killing him. Why had the man Jacked out?

Above the panting of the dog by his side, Tomo heard a commotion in the warehouse. He staggered across to the shattered door, stepping over its splintered remains, and looked to the cages below. Every single one of them stood open. The cat was nowhere to be seen, and neither were most of the dogs. Only a few remained, curiously nosing at a heap of bloody rags that stretched from the furthest cage to the edge of the shark tank. Next to the desk, glinting in the light, were the discarded dials of an A-Jack.

Giichi had been torn to pieces by his own hounds.

Tomo collapsed on the walkway, placing his arm around the dog as it lapped at his cheek.

"If Sergeant Ito asks," he said, "I made them do it."

***

Joel R. Hunt is a writer and ex-English teacher from the British Midlands. He has a passion for science fiction, horror and all things bizarre, with a particular appreciation for talking animals, twists on classic monsters and [insert genre here] with added robots. Joel's drabbles and other short stories can be found in a range of anthologies by Black Hare Press, Eerie River and Escaped Ink, among others. He also posts daily micro stories on https://twitter.com/JoelRHunt1 and full stories alongside regular updates on https://joelrhuntauthor.wordpress.com/

Arfabad
Rimi B. Chatterjee

'I can't!' cried Zigsa. 'Look at my feet. There's nothing left!'

Phagmo, shining indigo and orange, looked down with her far-seeing eyes and sighed. 'See how the bloodclots are like rubies? You're walking on jewels, child. The only kind that have any value.' She cupped Zigsa's burning feet in her soft hands.

'Oh shut up. You just tell me impossible things like I have a task and stuff, you never actually help.'

'We're doing what we have to do to help you,' said Chokyi, shimmering pink and green. She smelled of forests and ripe fruits. 'Believe me, if there was any other way, we wouldn't put you through this.'

'And we were with you in the Test to Destruction Centre,' said Sangye, who shone violet and yellow. Her hands were never still, as though she was always crafting or explaining. 'Remember? We showed you the way.'

'We've been looking after you ever since we left our bodies,' said Dorje, red and white. Her eyes were stern but her mouth was gentle. Zigsa looked up through her tears at the group of transparent figures above her head. Beyond them stretched the Takla Makan desert, lying under the bowl of dirty yellow haze that passed for a sky. Ever since the hanyos had destroyed Antarctica in 2048 there had been no blue sky to see anywhere on Earth. That had been more than twenty years ago. The hanyos called it the Helios Fail. 'Easy for you to say,' Zigsa grumbled. 'I'm the one who has to drag this carcass across the radiopoisoned desert. Any idea how to survive that?'

'Don't think about it,' said Pema, blue and purple. She cradled Zigsa's head and smoothed her brow so tenderly. Her touch was always best at taking away pain, her words the kindest. 'Take a step. And then another step. We're here with you. We always have been.'

'Each step goes further away from hanyo town, where people like you are fodder and fuel, tools and weapons for your masters, the hanyos, and their corporations. That's the source of the world's pain,' said Phagmo. She adjusted the canister of water on Zigsa's hip.

'But we got you out,' Sangye went on. 'Look! No more lab, no more needles, no more Neurokick, no more hanyos asking you stupid questions. Only the sun, and around you the desert.'

'I'm going to die here.' She stared up at the dun slope of the sand dune facing her.

'Only if you stop moving,' said Dorje, and extended a hand. Zigsa reached for it. A jolt of energy pulled her to her feet, and for a moment a vision flashed upon her eyes, of flowers and trees in a fragrant garden. 'That's Ashqabad, the City of Love,' said Phagmo gently. 'It's your home. When you've built the survivarium and led all the Survivors to it, your task will be done. Then you'll come back to us and rest in your garden. But first you have to reach your destination. Come on,' and she gently drew Zigsa forward.

Zigsa took a step and bit off a scream. 'Talk to me!' she sobbed. 'Tell me stories about Ashqabad. Please!'

'Everyone you ever loved will meet you there at the end, for Ashqabad is made up of things and creatures that have loved and been loved,' said Pema. 'We go there in our dreams, or whenever we leave our material bodies. Every good thing finds refuge there, every pain finds medicine, every friend finds someone to cherish, every lover feels that catch in the throat they thought they would never feel again when they lost the one who first gave them the key to the city.'

Zigsa put another foot in front of her. 'Every good friend? Tell me who is waiting for me besides you, my five tribe-mothers. What about my dog-brother Pabu? The teachers at school, the kind ones? The kids I watched being tortured to death in the lab? All of you will meet me there?'

'Yes, and we'll be smiling. Pabu too.'

She moved another foot and gave a great gasp. 'They shot him! The hanyos. When we all came down from the mountains to New Kashgar, and you said we had to get jobs. They just shot him like he was...' Zigsa choked on her tears.

'You were so angry when I warned you not to take him,' said Chokyi. 'But you needed to see how the hanyos hate us.'

'You needed to lose him, and us, before you could escape,' said Phagmo. 'I know it's hard. It was just as hard for us to play our roles and pretend to be ignorant tribeswomen full of fear. You hated us for it.'

'Yes,' said Zigsa. 'How Pabu would snarl at you when you acted silly!'

'Of course,' said Chokyi. 'How else would you know right from wrong? Someone had to tell you.'

She took another step and moaned. 'So when we lived in the mountains, you were just playacting when you were being mean to me. Why?'

'It was necessary, Zigsa,' said Sangye. 'We were given the heavy task of teaching you about hanyo town. You were a child, lectures wouldn't have made sense to you. So we had to act it out, be all the things you had to push away, show you why bad protection and nurture are wrong and finally give our lives to get you where you needed to go. You were born in the wild wastes so you could see everything clearly, but you didn't know what hanyo town is like on the inside. We had to betray you so you could find out from your enemies.'

'Who gave you such a task?' Zigsa whimpered.

'You did,' said Dorje softly. 'I know you don't believe us, but when your journey ends, you'll know it's true.'

'Don't worry, Zigsa, the fruit will be sweet,' said Pema. 'Only have patience and keep walking.' She stroked Zigsa's brow, took away the fever heat. 'And we will tell you stories so that even as your body marches on, your soul will be in Ashqabad. Don't cry, little one, you can't afford to lose the water.'

Zigsa moaned and lurched forward. The dried shit caked over her hospital gown crackled as she moved. She scratched at it, but Phagmo stayed her hand. 'Leave it. It will confuse the spy satellites. They won't be able to make sense of your heat signature.'

'It's the hanyos' last gift to you.' Chokyi grinned mischievously. 'They think shit is bad, but only because they don't know how to plant seeds.'

'Tell me stories!'

Sangye smiled. 'Ashqabad is a special place. It's on the summit of a mountain, and to reach it you have to swim up the river, if you have no ship and no wings. After much toil you reach the Bay of Drowned Poets. Above the bay there are tiers of houses up the mountainside and the seven-fold bridge spanning the cataracts of the river, and right at the top, haloed in rainbows, is the Fortress of the Roses build around the sweet source of the river, where every siddha has a garden. You have a garden there too, Zigsa. You see it in your dreams.'

'I want to go home,' Zigsa wailed.

'You're home now, in your head.' Sangye spread herself over Zigsa's raw shoulders. The harsh light of the sun softened. 'Let me tell you a story about Arfabad.'

'Arfabad? I thought you said the city was called Ashqabad.'

'It is. Arfabad is a suburb of the city. It is inhabited entirely by dogs. Some of these dogs used to be dogs in the world of matter, and some are people or other creatures who've chosen the forms of dogs, because you can have any shape you want, in Ashqabad. Where do you think Pabu went when he left you?'

'I want to be a dog,' Zigsa whimpered. Sangye stroked her head and went on, 'Everything in Arfabad is dog-sized. There are little doggy houses on stilts with ramps and walkways leading to them, and soft cushions to curl up on. There are ponds and lakes and mud wallows. There are places to play and places to bask in the sun, and sandpits to dig, and piles of leaves to jump about in.'

'Ah,' said Pema. 'What fun to roll around on the grass and skritch your back. And so many puppies, always ready to tumble or drowse in warm puppy-piles or play tug.'

'Are there any hanyos in the city? Because if there are I don't want to go there.'

'No, silly, any hanyo who tries to get to Ashqabad won't be able to pull himself out of the river.' Phagmo smiled. 'You can't take any mud with you. It's too heavy. Hanyos are full of mud: they hate and resent and covet and win win win!'

'And the dogs won't have it. They can smell mud better than sharks can smell blood. That's why Pabu would snarl at us. He was saying, "Clean up that heart!" Keep walking, Zigsa, there's a tamarisk tree behind this dune. No, don't try to climb it, go along the base. Turn right. This way.'

Zigsa turned and staggered through the sand at the foot of the dune. 'You see,' said Chokyi, 'there are three kinds of people who can go to Ashqabad. The first kind are the siddhas, the enlightened ones. They have wings, and they can fly there any time they want.'

'Am I a siddha?'

'You know you are, Zigsa. Now you're going to ask why you can't fly there right now, and we'll say what we said the first time you asked: you have a job to finish first.'

'Stomping through sand to my death. Very useful job,' Zigsa growled.

Pema sighed. 'Such a grumbler. The second type of person has no wings, but a very strong spine. They wriggle and squirm their way through the water like sea monsters, always pulled by the long-ago-remembered smell of the city, as if they're salmon swimming upriver to spawn. Then they heave their bodies onto the shore and cough up their mud, and in time they get to walk the city's streets and hear its many stories, sample its food and laugh and talk with its citizens. And of course, play with the dogs. Eventually, they too grow wings and acquire a garden in the Fortress of the Roses.'

Zigsa fell to her knees. 'Come on,' said Chokyi. 'It's just a little way. We're taking you over the lowest part of the sand dune. Crawl if you can't walk.' Zigsa reached out and began digging her fingers into the sand. But all she did was pull the sand towards her. 'Tch!' said Dorje. 'Imagine it's water and you're a fish.'

'I hate you!' Zigsa yelled. She writhed her body like a lizard. Slowly, spraying sand from her elbows and knees, she began to rise.

'The third kind of person is the commonest, and the most likely to get lost,' said Dorje. 'When you truly love anyone or anything, then for the duration of your loving, you are in Ashqabad. And it blows your mind, it's so beautiful and full of possibility. You think you're in heaven as you walk the streets and smell the flowers, and you think the person or creature you are with is your one and only key to the city.'

'Pabu was my key. I loved him. And I brought him to his death.'

'No,' said Chokyi. 'The key to the city is in your heart, and only you can turn it.'

'But if you haven't yet learned this truth, you're going to cling to your love like a thief clutches stolen gold, you'll wail every time they're out of your sight, and in time they're going to get very very tired of you,' said Pema. 'Or fate will part you.'

'So when you lose that person or thing that you loved, you're cast down to the depths of the ocean,' said Dorje. 'You don't even know where the river is, let alone how to swim up it. Then you swallow tonnes of mud and spread across the seafloor like a living morass.'

'Unless you work out how to love, just you, by yourself, with no one and nothing loving you back.'

'But I've always loved like that,' said Zigsa, stretching out an arm and curving her body to follow it.

'Yes you have, that's why this task is yours. And here's the top of the sand dune. Whoops!'

With a last flurry of sand Zigsa slid down the far surface of the dune and came to rest in the hollow beneath. Pink petals rained down on her face. 'Oh, blessed shade!' she cried. 'Blessed tree!'

'Rest till you can raise your head.'

Zigsa panted, eyes shut, letting the sweet fingers of shadow caress her face. 'So why are the hanyos full of mud? Why don't they cough it up?'

'They're full of resentment because they've never been happy.'

'No happiness? Not even when they were little babies?' She reached up to touch a feathery branch covered with tiny pink flowers.

'You know the hanyos are born in terrible agony,' said Pema sadly. 'You saw us bring your brothers into this world. They died in days, unable to suck or sleep because their skins were oversensitive to pain and their bodies reacted to everything as if it were poison. All hanyos are born like that. All human males conceived since 2030 have this disease.'

'Male Hypertoxic Syndrome. I know. Basil Quan told me, before he tortured me. He runs Lionfist Corporation. He's a hanyo. He owns everyone. He wanted me to be his weapon. But I told him, I didn't kill those men. I just felt their pain, and then they couldn't unfeel it, and it drove them mad.'

'You did no wrong, Zigsa. You were trying to help. But the hanyos can't be helped. Not by you, anyway.'

'So what is this Male Hypertoxic thingie?' She huddled under the tree and drew her feet in from the burning sun.

'There was a doctor called Pradip Shankar,' said Sangye. 'He got into trouble because one of his patients wanted a son, and he messed it up. So he thought, I'll invent a way to make men have sons. Then

I'll have lots of money and power and no one will dare to give me trouble again.'

'So he made a vaccine called Humane Choice, but the virus he used to deliver the payload went rogue,' Phagmo continued. 'He broke the human genome. The boys started dying and the mothers took to the streets. The world was days away from collapse. Every finger was pointing at Shankar, so he said, I will find a cure.'

'And people didn't say anything?'

'They were desperate,' said Chokyi grimly. 'Only the rich parents were able to afford the treatment to save their sons. These boys inherited their fathers' wealth and power and used it to destroy all the Old Men and rule the rest of us. They're the hanyos.'

'They feel no pain now,' said Pema sadly. 'As they grew their skins died, so now they give pain rather than receive it. They feel they have a right. They think grief and pain are shameful, so they find ways to shove their sorrow into others. That just creates more pain and grief.'

'I know. And it makes no sense.'

'It makes sense in hanyo town. Not in your world. Your world is nonsense to the hanyos. That's why we named the logic of your world Antisense,' said Sangye.

'Am I supposed to put it right? Fight their evil?' She rested her head between two roots.

'No, Zigsa,' said Dorje. 'You mustn't fight. Only escape. And then help other Survivors to escape until the hanyos don't have a single victim left.'

'How?'

'You have to call out with your heart to people and plants and animals and birds and fish and everything that's alive and not a hanyo,' said Pema.

'Even this tree?'

'Maybe not this particular tree,' said Chokyi. 'But there'll be trees to plant when you build your survivarium.'

'You keep saying that word, but you won't explain what it is.'

'We did explain,' said Dorje. 'It's a place for Survivors to live and make happiness and karma. You don't remember?'

'She's faint with hunger,' said Chokyi. 'Give her the food.'

'Zigsa, raise your head and look at the tree,' said Phagmo. Zigsa coughed and grunted until she could get an elbow under her. 'I'm looking.'

'See those strange crystals stuck to the trunk?' aid Chokyi. 'Reach out and take some.' She did. 'Now put them in your mouth.'

'You want me to eat this tree stuff?'

'More than anything. Hurry up, you'll pass out if you don't get some sugar soon.'

Zigsa crunched the crystals. Then a look like a sunrise after decades of darkness arose on her face. 'Oh flowers of heaven!'

'Indeed. Like it? Eat all you want. Rest and get your strength back,' Phagmo chuckled. 'We have a whole Silk Road to travel before you find your refuge.'

***

Zigsa walked on. Every night, her five guides would lead her to shelter and huddle around her to keep out the night's cold, and every morning she would get up and go out into the April sunlight. She no longer asked questions, for her heart was at peace even though her head could see no reason why she should survive. It was enough that she was breathing. She trudged on, remembering the times when she and Pabu would go exploring, before she learned how badly she could lose all hope.

'How do you know all this stuff about the desert?' she asked one evening, when they had led her to a ruined house buried in the sand. There was a hole in the roof and she'd crawled into the tiny space made by the roof beams. Now she was curled up among the bat droppings. The regular occupants were out on the night's business.

'We know because you told us. You've been planning all of this for years,' said Dorje.

'You don't remember because you had to become you for the plan to work,' said Sangye. 'And when you turned into a little baby cradled in our arms, there was no longer room in your head for all the knowledge.'

'She was so cute, remember how cute she was?' said Chokyi. 'Like a little rosy porcelain doll.'

'Yes, she came with the dawn when you birthed her,' said Pema. 'Pabu watched the whole time. He was just a puppy then. He licked her clean.'

'I'm not a baby any more,' said Zigsa firmly. 'I'm fifteen years old. If I was in hanyo town I would be graduating from Slag School and going to work in some lab or factory.'

'Well that's one horror you were spared.'

'Yes, because I got caught with that trunk full of books and comics and magazines and music in the school basement. They punish you if you look at anything from the world before the Helios Fail. That's because everything they say about that world is lies.' She wiped a sandy tear. 'When they sent me to the Test to Destruction Centre, I thought, that's it, I'm dead in three months.'

'But you lived in TTD8 for three years,' said Phagmo. 'You saw everything, didn't you? Every time they tortured you, you saw a little bit more of the truth.'

'I saw their truth, but where is mine?'

'You're travelling towards it.'

Zigsa's face crumpled again. 'I miss Pabu. I miss him every day. I miss him more than I miss all of you.'

Chokyi stroked her head. 'You'll find and rescue another Pabu. And all his friends too. You'll bring them safely to the survivarium. You'll gather all the dogs and trees and fish and worms and birds and monkeys and rats and parrots and, well, you get the idea.'

Zigsa nodded in the darkness. 'A survivarium without creatures would be no fun.' She shivered and curled up a little tighter. 'Pabu was so warm and soft and furry. Sometimes I think I can feel his nose, but I turn round and it's just a drop of dew on the night wind.

Tell me more stories of Arfabad.'

Dorje settled down beside her and cradled her head. 'The dogs of Arfabad like to spend their days being happy, but they do have useful work to do as well. People have to get clean before they can enter the city, but sometimes, if they have a bad day, or the love doesn't shine as brightly as it should, the mud can bubble up in them. The mud says "Me, me, me!" and wants to grab love. When that happens, they might become a chimera.'

'A chimera? What's that?'

'A half-human, half-beast monster,' said Pema. 'People become chimeras when their beast nature wells up in them, and then they can do a lot of damage to Ashqabad and its citizens. But the city has ways to defend itself. And the dogs are the early warning system.'

'When it pleases them,' Sangye went on, 'the arefs and arfas of Arfabad go walking through the town. They visit their favourite cafes and get treats from the staff and guests. And everywhere they go, they sniff the people. They sniff sniff sniff and lick lick lick, letting all their doggy senses focus on each one they meet. And when they get a tiny little tang of muddiness, far too small for even the human to know it's there, they sit down at the feet of that person, look adoringly into their face and put a paw on their knee. Then the love comes thundering back like an avalanche, and with pats and kisses that person is saved.'

'But sometimes it doesn't work,' said Dorje. 'Maybe the person isn't paying attention, or is stuck too deep in their resentments to respond. Then the chimeric event will begin, but before the person can do anything, the dogs jump to their feet and bark. They bark and howl and growl and snarl so that all the Ashqabadis know that someone is changing to a beast, and then the siddhas come and grab the person and fly away with them over the bay, where they drop them in the water so they can turn into beasts without hurting anyone. A few dunkings and they learn better self-control.'

'Wow,' said Zigsa. 'We must have this in the survivarium. A

doggy early warning system for when people go into hanyo mode.'

'Yes, because the people you rescue will all have been shat out by hanyo town, Zigsa, just as you were, and they'll need ways to get clean.'

'Hmmm. But people should do the hard work of cleaning. Our dogs can only tell us if someone is still dirty. Or help keep the clean ones clean.'

'Don't worry, you'll invent a way to do that too. A ten-level game called the Hopscotch for people to play and clean themselves. When they complete it, the puppies will come and sniff them, and if they wag their tails and fall asleep in their laps, you'll know the person is clean.'

'Wonderful! And we must have a place where our dogs can relax and have fun. That's very important for dogs. And kids. A doggy garden like Arfabad: yes!'

'Exactly right,' said Dorje, and then she turned into a huge shaggy dokyi with orange eyebrows and a plumy tail and curled up around Zigsa.

In the morning the bats woke Zigsa with their chittering. She backed out of the hole and left them in peace.

***

Zigsa travelled north, the desert to her left, and the ruins of abandoned farms and houses to her right. 'These people were all forced to come here and farm,' said Pema. 'That was before the hanyos.'

'But their farming depleted the soil, and then the desert took over,' said Chokyi. 'That's how the desert's been growing ever since.'

Zigsa thought about this. 'Everyone I ever met in hanyo town said the desert is a radiopoisoned graveyard. Nothing should be alive out here, yet there are shrubs and bats and berries and insects. Why is that?'

Chokyi snorted. 'The hanyos don't understand life. Nature to them is either trash or resources. Since the desert has no resources they want, they think it's trash. The people they throw here are trash too: used up shells. It's the only reliable way to escape from hanyo town: to be flushed down the toilet.'

'You can say that again,' said Zigsa, scratching a flake of dried shit off her forearm. 'Why do they hate nature so much?'

'Because they think it broke them. But it was a man who did that.'

'Then they should blame him, shouldn't they?'

'They can't because that would mean he won and they lost. They can't admit to being victims,' said Dorje.

'That's stupid. How will you right a wrong if you won't even admit that it happened?'

'They think winning is better than righting wrongs, because they don't think their happiness can be mended. So in order to win, they call all the happy people losers. Babies, animals, women, gentle people, creators and makers, artists and poets. The whole living planet. All losers in the game of life.'

'Then what is winning?'

'Control. Exploitation,' said Dorje. 'Giving pain to others while remaining pain-free themselves. Breaking happiness and boasting of it. Doing wrong and forcing the shame onto the victim with their laughter and sneering. Ordering the loyal to kill and maim and lie and steal for them. Torturing those that feel pain.'

'Is that why they make dogs fight?'

'Yes. It pleases the hanyos to watch others suffer,' Chokyi said sadly. 'And dogs will do anything to please their masters.'

'I want to rip them to pieces with my teeth.'

'Don't, Zigsa,' said Pema gently. 'Don't play their game. They want that. You can't win over them. You don't want to.'

'Huh. I know what you're saying, but this is my problem: how am I going to rescue the people and animals if I don't fight the hanyos for them?'

Chokyi shook her head. 'You must only fight to make that happen, and not a move beyond. After you've escaped and built your refuge, you and all your Survivors will vanish as though the earth has swallowed you up. You don't need your masters for anything. You make everything they need, including the chance to win. Take it away from them.'

'Escape is an automatic win for you, Zigsa,' said Dorje. 'Without a single victim left, it's game over for the hanyos.'

'Wait!' Sangye cried. 'See those stones? Pick them up! Two nice ones.'

Zigsa picked up two roundish, grey-white stones. 'What about them?'

'Tie them in a fold of your gown. No, higher up, or they'll bang against your knees.'

'So now I have to carry stones as well?'

'They're not heavy. You'll need them at your journey's end.'

'Can't wait,' Zigsa muttered, and lurched on.

***

Many days later, so many days she could no longer count them, Zigsa raised her head and saw a chain of mountains in front of her like solid fire. At their base lay a green shadow. Now her feet no longer felt pain: the sand had burned all the nerves out of them so that her skin was as unfeeling as a hanyo's. She knew that once she lay down for good she would have to heal them.

'Courage,' said Phagmo. 'We're nearly there. Oh Zigsa, you're going to love it.'

'Take her to the river first,' said Chokyi. 'She needs rest and water.'

'There's a river?' Zigsa sniffed the air with her sand-burned nose. There was a mildness and a sweetness to the softening wind. 'Those are trees?'

'This is where you're going to build your happiness.' Zigsa flew on as if she had siddha-wings. It was past midday when the trees stretched their green arms over her head. It felt like a dream. She fell to her knees and wept. Her five companions brought her to the water and splashed her face and raised handfuls of it to her lips. She wailed as the water touched her wounds. 'It's all right,' said Pema. 'You don't have much further to go.'

'Further? You mean I haven't arrived?'

'You can't stay out here at night. Rest and drink, then we'll show you the way.'

She took off her gown and washed it. Most of the caked shit had fallen off by now. She spread the cloth on a rock to dry. Then Chokyi and Phagmo showed her where to find dry sticks, and she tore a strip from her gown and made up a tight bundle of them to sling over her shoulder. 'So now what?'

'Look to your left. What do you see?'

'A cliff. Wait...you want me to climb that?'

'Relax, there's steps.'

Zigsa began to tremble. 'You can't! You can't make me walk any more! You're horrid! You torture me all the time. You're worse than the hanyos!'

'We'll help you, Zigsa. You can't lose it now you're in sight of your goal.'

She took a deep breath. 'Tell me another story. Make me forget what's happening to me. Fly me to Arfabad one more time.'

'In Arfabad, the dogs choose their own mates,' said Chokyi, taking her hand.

'It is after all the City of Love,' said Phagmo, taking her other hand. 'And dogs have very definite opinions about love. You could say that bitches are experts at it. Which is why they're picky.'

'When an arfa comes into her time, she goes to a special thicket of bushes called the Love Nest,' said Sangye, cupping Zigsa's left foot in her hands.

'There, she snarls and growls at any gentleman visitor she does not like, and they stay outside with sheepish grins on their faces,' said Pema, taking her right foot in her hands.

'But the ones she likes, she flirts with them like a coy princess,' said Dorje, wrapping her arms round Zigsa's waist. 'All together now.'

With only the slightest effort, Zigsa got to her feet. She choked off a sob deep in her throat. 'Does it hurt?' asked Pema.

'Keep telling me the story!'

'Mostly, a bitch will have a small group of males she likes, and an order in which she likes them. They have to queue up and wait their turn.'

'They rarely fight while they're doing this. Mostly they roll their eyes at each other and stalk around looking heroic. The dogs who aren't interested laze about and watch them like it's a movie.'

'Your Pabu found his Ponya there. And oh my dog, does she lead him a merry dance!'

'It's the show of the season. People come to watch from all over the city. How prettily they circle each other, playbow and mockfight, lick and nuzzle and earflick and toss their heads and yowl. He stands there looking noble while she dances sinuously round him. But every time he moves, in a flash she vanishes into the bushes with a mischievous gleam in her eye. How patiently he sits down again to wait her pleasure!'

Zigsa set her foot on a step. 'I can't press down. I can't climb these! They're too steep!'

'You've swum up the river before, Zigsa.'

'These are stone steps! Are you blind?'

'Try climbing water. Come on, Zigsa, you have so much courage. Bring forth the last of it and stiffen your knees. There's such beauty waiting for you up there. And nothing you do will be this hard, ever again.'

Zigsa covered her face and wept.

When she took her hands away, it was almost dark. Without a word, the five of them turned into huge shaggy dogs with great manes around their necks and orange suns above their mild eyes. She put an arm around two, and two more set their shoulders to the backs of her thighs. Dorje went in front, so that when she stumbled, it was Dorje's furry back that cushioned her fall. And so she rose, until her wondering eyes saw the steps open out on a level stone terrace with carved balustrades, and beyond it the regular openings of rock-cut cells. 'Am I in Ashqabad? Am I dead?'

'Yes and no,' smiled Sangye, returning to human form. 'Your soul is always there, and you're going to build an Ashqabad for your body, as people have always done when they've sought happiness. But quick, get into one of these caves. Pile up some sticks and strike those two stones I made you carry. By the time your fire goes out your cave will be nice and cosy. Come on.'

Zigsa did as she was asked. 'The fire's not lighting.'

'Put your soul into the spark,' said Pema. 'Give your will to it.'

A tiny tongue of flame sprang up. Almost afraid to breathe, Zigsa pushed it into the heart of the neat pile of sticks she had built. Grateful for the food, it grew. And then she gasped. Two painted deer danced on the wall opposite, and beyond them the firelight revealed trees and shops and people singing and busy marketplaces and travellers and spice merchants and siddhas of every colour and shape and size and sex. 'This is Ashqabad,' she breathed. 'Look at it! It's so beautiful. I'm sorry I ever doubted you.'

'You used your judgement,' said Phagmo. 'Please don't apologise. And while this place was indeed once Ashqabad, as these pictures show, it can only be Ashqabad again if you gather the losers of the world into your love and tell them they are Survivors, because when losers and victims are loved, they Survive.'

'How?'

'Dream it. They will come.'

'The first two who will come, will be thinkers,' said Dorje. 'All the answers you didn't get from your trunk of treasures, they will give you, because they're old, from before the Helios Fail. Have patience with them. They've suffered a lot.'

'They'll help you to build the survivarium in your head, craft its systems and practices and values. Then the next three will be miners, and they'll be young. They'll help you to start digging through the rock.'

'First you'll dig troughs for soil and shit and grow food,' said Chokyi, 'because as your friends gather around you, you won't be able to find all your food in the valley.'

'Then you'll tunnel down into the earth, and far below, you'll make a space for the ten treasures, which add up to happiness,' said Dorje. 'People, animals, plants, air, light, water, soil, love, karma and knowledge.'

'Karma?'

'You're going to invent a new system of righting wrongs, organising work and making the ten kinds of happiness, symbolised by ten colours,' said Sangye. 'Karma will do all the good things that law and money are supposed to do in hanyo town, but don't. And it will do none of the bad things, I assure you.'

'When someone does wrong, either by mistake or because the residues of hanyo town have tripped them up, karma will wipe away the tears of the victims before they dry, and help the wrongdoer live down their shame by mending the happiness they broke,' said Dorje. 'No wrong shall stand upon another, because then they become bricks in the walls of hanyo town.'

'No one will be chained to their work,' said Chokyi. 'Work and happiness will be intertwined. Reward and happiness will be indistinguishable. The flowers will bloom and the dogs and babies will play, because yes, there will be babies, the kind the hanyos hate the most: fatherless ones, with twenty mothers to cherish them.'

'Love will be free,' said Pema, and dropped a tear.

'Don't worry about the details,' said Phagmo. 'Your friends will come and help you work it all out. Rest now. You've arrived. Now you can think and plan and heal. Time will bring you everything you need.'

'So it's just the way I've always lived, but expanded so others can live it too?'

'Exactly.'

Zigsa thought deeply about this. Then she lay down below a thousand Buddhas sitting upon a thousand lotuses, smiled, and closed her eyes.

***

Rimi B. Chatterjee has published three novels and a number of prose and graphic shorts. She is currently working on a science fiction hexalogy called Antisense Universe while running to stay ahead of the apocalypse. 'Arfabad' is set in the Antisense Universe, and Zigsa is a major character in the Antisense worldline. The first book Bitch Wars is complete and looking for a publisher. Zigsa also features in 'How Zigsa Found Her Way', a graphic short published in *Longform: An Anthology of Graphic Narratives* (HarperCollins India, 2017). In hanyo town Rimi cosplays as an academic and teaches English at Jadavpur University in India. All the dogs know her.

The Mammoth Steps

Andrew Dana Hudson

In his young days, Kaskil would hide from Roomba in the tall, chilly grass. He crouched down, stifled his laughs, listened for the slight crunches of Roomba's great feet compressing the ice and soil. Kaskil knew Roomba could track him by scent, but the old mammoth humored him, played along, pretending to be confused, trunk swishing the steppe grasses right over Kaskil's ducked head. When Roomba looked away, Kaskil would jump up and sprint off to a new spot. On they went for hours, criss-crossing the tundra until the sun got low and the deep cold crept in, and Kaskil would climb up Roomba's clumped fur and doze there in the musky warmth as the mammoth carried him home.

Kaskil's family moved with mammoths across the Siberian grasslands, paid by the carbon traders to play doctor and ambassador for these new-old beasts. The mammoths needed Kaskil's commonage for their nimble hands and rapport with the Yakut towns, where young calves often found trouble raiding sun-swollen vegetable gardens. Humans needed the mammoths to roam, to compact and scrape away the snow that kept the cold of winter from penetrating the deep soil, and to spread the seeds of grasses that would insulate the permafrost from summer thaw. And, more each year, the humans needed the mammoths for their sly humor and bitter milk.

Roomba was the oldest mammoth traveling with the commonage, one of the first born of de-extinction splicing. Unlike the younger generation, which romped and piled together in complex socialities, Roomba had few peers. Humans were his company, and Kaskil, who he'd known since birth, was his favorite. Kaskil, for his part, couldn't imagine life without the mammoth. Kaskil rode him when the commonage travelled, did chores with him, read his studies aloud sitting in the crook of Roomba's forelegs. And sometimes he noticed when Roomba stopped and stared south, trunk raised to smell the wind.

Kaskil wanted to ask Roomba what was wrong, but such an abstract question posed a challenge. Roomba knew Kaskil's body-language, recognized many words and gestures, and likewise could signal his feelings and opinions with a nod or trunk swing, a trumpet or harrumph, or the thrumming infrasonic rumbles that Kaskil's phone registered as pictographs or emojis. But the syntax of longing was beyond the capacities of their translator app; it would be another generation, Kaskil's father said, before they had enough language data to train their algorithms to fluency.

So instead they played with a projected talking board, gathering clouds of concepts. Camp and family danced together into home. Where, walk, and want were counterveiled by fear. Finally Roomba's trunk tapped on a loop of gifs representing mammoths before mammoths.

Kaskil started when he got it; he searched up videos of elephants, played them on the canvas tent. Roomba nodded, waggled his head, dug his tusk into the snow in excitement.

The commonage had no hold on Roomba; the old timer could go where he liked. But Kaskil was only fourteen, with fretful parents. Still, they knew the bond the two shared, and were grateful to Roomba for helping raise their son. After a week of Kaskil's begging, they relented, and they helped pack saddle bags for the long journey.

At first it was much like one of their camping trips, but the days counted on and the trees grew thicker. Below the arctic circle it was slower going. They wound half-abandoned logging trails connecting the mushroom towns that foraged fungal delicacies for far-off luxe provision houses. Occasionally there was no trail south, and they forced their way through, Roomba pushing aside trees, the ground made soft by permafrost thaw.

In Ulaanbaatar they enquired after the trains that crossed the Gobi south to the industrial wonderlands of Shaanxi and Chengdu. But the trainmasters balked—Roomba was much too big, they said, to fit in the sleek compartments. Kaskil hailed at trucks, but the automated rumblers were always too full to stop for them.

So on they walked, into the desert, begging water from the seeps where the solar painters camped. Winter had turned to spring, and the sun was hot in the sky. Roomba's wool matted with sweat. His feet dragged in the sand. One day he would not leave the shade of their tent. Kaskil went to the painters, snapping together black tiles, and borrowed shears and an ancient, shaking shaver. All day he cut at Roomba's fur, tossing the chestnut curls in feathery piles.

The next day Roomba danced and charged with relief, Kaskil laughing at his friend's ridiculous haircut. They made good time, but by the afternoon they realized their mistake. Under the wool Roomba's flesh was delicate, unaccustomed to the sun. He pinked and burned, and began to trumpet with discomfort.

Kaskil again begged help from the painters. Taking pity on Roomba, they offered salve, but this was a temporary fix. Then a dusty wind gusted the camp, and Kaskil saw the painters pull robes over their faces. The white sheets, which wrapped the solar tiles, snapped and fluttered. Kaskil had an idea. For a week he attended Roomba as a tailor, measuring with his phone and following patterns projected from a stitching site. When Roomba's sunburns had peeled, Kaskil dressed him in the white robe, and off again they went.

Walking along the busy Chinese highways, Roomba was a strange sight. In the cities children crowded around him, taking pictures and tugging at his robes. Kaskil and Roomba marveled at the chromey towers and ivy statues. They'd seen pictures, of course, but up close each city seemed grander than the next.

But the alleys were too narrow for Roomba's bulk, and often they waited hours in bicycle gridlock. More than once officials hassled them out of parks, and old women scowled at the crates of food they took from provision houses. So much of the land was terraced crops, and the farmers did not like Roomba grazing.

They followed the Jinsha River south, both splashing in often to escape the heat. Summer was coming, and the commonage would be roaming north to the grass beaches of the Kara Sea. Kaskil messaged his parents every night, but still he missed them. He wanted to hear Russian and Sakha, not these unfamiliar languages, parsed awkwardly by his translator. The quiet, playful presence of the mammoth was a comfort, but there too was an otherness, a difference bridged by solidarity but not quite by understanding.

And Roomba, Kaskil thought, must have his own doubts and loneliness—the only mammoth for a thousand miles. Why make this trip to see the elephants? Roomba was spliced from elephant genes, born from an elephant womb. But what did that mean for a mammoth? What question could provoke such a journey, here at the sunset of his massive, new-old life?

The subtropics turned to tropics, and on they walked, until they began to pass gilded shrines where monks served milky curry. Everywhere was the image of the elephant: on flags and logos, as statues and painted murals. But, where were the elephants? Missing.

Missing too were the selfie-mobs and rubberneckers they had gathered in the northern cities. Here the humans they passed shied away—furtive glances and upset muttering. Once a nun approached them from a shadowed stall, asked if they bore instructions or news from the front. She fled when Kaskil betrayed their confusion.

Finally they found a bored constable, pestered her to explain. It's all politics, she said, both nervous and dismissive. Thai elephants demanding money and land, accommodation and autonomy, freedom from electric fences and ear hooks; Thai humans reacting badly, not wanting a change in the order, terrorizing demonstrations with chili sprays and angry bees. Here, not so bad, she said, but they should be careful further south, where the elephants retreated and seized Phuket.

Kaskil told Roomba the news as best he could, and asked his friend if they should stop. Roomba looked north, raised his trunk to smell the wind, but then he shook his massive head, kept walking. To avoid attention they slept by day, travelled by night. They ate at temples, which stayed neutral in the dispute. Miles melted by in eagerness for a destination.

Sarasin Bridge was barricaded by protesters, a blockade of supplies to the occupied island. The crowd shrunk back as they approached— a strange-looking boy atop a huge-tusked, white-clad creature, more massive by half than the elephants they knew. But there was no getting through. Kaskil's heart dipped with frustration and sorrow, and he knew, in the heavy rumble of his friend beneath him, that Roomba felt the same way.

Then, in a rush, the nuns holding the Phuket side moved forward, surrounded Roomba with linked arms. Smiling at the mob they escorted Kaskil and Roomba across.

The pair could hardly believe it. They thanked the nuns, Roomba bowing low to the earth. They had finally arrived.

Phuket now was different than the mainland. Elephants roamed the streets, lounged in squares. Some worked with allied humans constructing elephant-sized buildings, communicating with script and hieroglyphs, drawn with trunks in the sand or on touchscreen beach balls. When Roomba rumbled at them, they seemed amused.

A procession formed, and the elephants led Roomba to the beach. Kaskil dismounted and sat in the warm sand, watching his friend touch the ocean. It had been worth the journey, he thought, to see this meeting: free elephants and a free mammoth, both new-old in their own ways, at the end of a long life and the start of a new way of living.

The elephants were oddly small next to the mammoth's bulk. They disrobed Roomba, felt his splotchy, shaven wool with their trunks. Then, as a herd, they plunged into the surf. The old mammoth stepped south, and swam.

***

Andrew Dana Hudson's fiction has appeared in *Lightspeed Magazine, Vice Terraform, Slate Future Tense, Grist, MIT Technology Review,* and more. His work won the 2016 Everything Change Climate Fiction Contest and was runner-up in the 2017 Kaleidoscope Writing the Future Contest. He has a master's degree in sustainability from Arizona State University and is a fellow at the ASU Center for Science and the Imagination. He is a member of the cursed 2020/2021 class of the Clarion Workshop. He lives in Tempe, Arizona and can be found online at www.andrewdanahudson.com and on Twitter at @andrewdhudson.

Wandjina

Amin Chehelnabi

Time was of the essence and Tara hadn't much of it left. The government would be able to track them if they were out for too long, with their freestanding colossal cities on constant lookout, be it visual or digital. She watched the rugged plain ahead with her cracked binoculars and saw blackened trees and stumps, and so much fire in the distance. Their fierce heat and destruction sought to undermine all of her work in the northern Kimberley. She'd invested years of preparation into these sojourns during the dry seasons, of traversing waterless pools and gorges, of constant research and hiding, of tears and physical strain to get to this point aboard Wandjina.

A sudden jolt disrupted her study of the land. She checked the readings on her console. A limestone boulder the size of a small hill had been ridden over, creating a cloud of toxic white dust. The caterpillar track was still intact though. The drive sprockets and the drive train hadn't been damaged, and the jolt brought her thoughts back to the present, this grim present, and all she felt was anxiety and worry for herself and for what was out there, what needed to be found and protected at all costs. It was worth more than anything, even more than her crew.

Thank khoda Wandjina has lasted this long... There aren't many of these machines left... How many, three, maybe four, in the whole country?

A complex mix of emotions stirred through her as she watched the battery power of the giant machine decline. It read 32%, and only one of the large solar panels still worked—the other four were damaged and intermittent at best. She lifted a shaking hand and studied the land again, saw another boulder ahead. This one was particularly large.

'Helmsman,' she said into her radio, her voice shaking, 'starboard fifteen degrees. Limestone up ahead.'

'Yep,' came the crackled response. And then, 'You beauty! Can you see that, Tara? I can see wallabies.'

'Wallabies?' *Yes!* 'How can you see that?'

'I have binoculars too! You're not the only one looking, you know!'

Of course. That was Bob, or Cobar, which he preferred. He was an Aboriginal teenager of the Worora Tribe, one of several others in the Kimberley region. He was sixteen years old, and close to Tara's heart, because of his affinity with the animals. He had a special connection with them, and she'd do anything to learn this skill. But on top of that, his land was burning, his homeland, with his people scattered, and the native creatures within it his brothers and sisters. *His family, my family.* He named the carrier Wandjina, attributing the machine to the cloud and rain spirits as a force for change in this region.

'Roger, Cobar,' she said, and wondered at her motley crew—her, a woman of Iranian descent, living with helmsman Cobar and the Māori man Nikau, who worked in maintenance below. And the navigator, Oto, a Chinese woman. They all had their reasons for joining Wandjina, and Tara definitely had her own. Each one of them set aside by their societies, or lack thereof, and in her case particularly, her family and culture.

She looked through the binoculars once more. Her hands always shook with the task—she was used to them shaking, because to her it was all or nothing. Anxiety and stress were normal in this line of work, but she tried her best not to care about that.

There were shadows in the distance, almost a silhouette rippling in front of the fires. *Great spotting, Cobar. Good on you...* The shadows became clearer and her heart sung at them.

Half a dozen or so animals appeared. First it was wallabies, limping and burnt but still moving with fervor. She also saw something else among them, *perhaps a bilby?* which was a godsend. As they approached, Tara's heart quailed once more, for she saw at once that some dingoes had run ahead with great speed. *Dingoes, amazing!* But every one of those animals looked dark, either from the haze of the atmosphere or from burns. She couldn't tell how serious it was.

'Helmsman, slow stop. Open the carrier doors. Air ducts to full.'

'Roger that.'

The Wandjina shuddered for several minutes as it slowed down. Tara held onto a support railing until the carrier ceased moving and its mechanisms had turned off. She heard the wind beating violently at her window along with the rickety sound of dust and debris, a regular occurrence in Western Australia now, since the dry season now ran almost all year, with virtually no wet season. It had been that way for so long. This place had once been calm and tropical, with a healthy balance of monsoons and dryness, but no longer. *Never again...*

A rush of cool air moved through the entire structure, and a siren started to blare. She unbuckled from her support and moved quickly through Wandjina—skipping steps, jumping over railings—and reached the bottom of the ship. Tara saw the red sky and dense pockets of cloud outside the carrier doors before she grabbed a facemask, holding bag, goggles, and handling gloves against the wall. She also picked up some penicillin in case an animal might have the remnants of leptospirosis. *You can never be sure...* When she was ready, she faced the blasted landscape. Wearing her long-sleeved shirt and long pants for handling the animals never helped against the heat out there, but it had to be done. And the sight outside always made her wonder at how much Australia had changed; from the first signs of the coming devastation—the rising insufferable heat—ignored by the government, and their followers being more individualistic and self-serving than ever, without regard for anything else. *They even made their stupid sentinel cities empty of animals, including domesticated ones, closing zoos and outlawing pets so that resources would only go to humans. This is why I hate people… Animals are innocent and have unconditional love, something these idiots can learn from but haven't.* Each year the climate had become more extreme, and nothing was done about it except by so very few, *like us…* Every time she opened those doors it was like she looked at Mars, and the thick fog above were like the clouds of Venus. *Is this what the end of the world looks like? The animals must have adapted to this extreme weather somehow. Otherwise, how the hell can they survive out there? Yes, they're all dwindling, but they're also hanging on, fiercely…*

The animals were fast approaching, and Tara had to act quickly to herd them in. She ran close to the bottom of the ramp and felt the intense heat of the land, saw the ash drifting in the air. She turned a large dial near the doors and the cold air rushed outwards like a vacuum. The filters cried in protest and the animals were drawn in, something that still surprised her. *It's like they recognize the carriers, because we had so many in the past that were readily available. It's the only place of respite for them. Look at how they enter, so desperate and fast!* They came up the ramp, stumbling, falling, struggling to move inside. Oto was there as well, her mask and goggles askew, ready to use her hand restraining skills if necessary.

'C'mon Tara,' she said, 'get out of your head and stop standing there!' Tara ran down the ramp, always keeping an eye out for which animals were injured most, to avoid touching those areas. She approached a dingo, and the animal growled before biting her gloved hands, trying to tear at them. Tara pulled her hands away, stepped back and stood to her full height. She made sure to keep eye contact, and the dingo backed away and ran around her to the top of the ramp and sat there in the cool, obviously weak, hungry and burnt all over. *That's definitely an alpha female...* The dingo watched Tara, the tears of her smoke-burnt eyes drying around them. For some reason the animal's gaze was unnerving to her, unsettling, *judging me like my father does, ready to criticize me if I make a mistake. In the books it says that trust must be established between animals and people. I have to trust in them as they do in me...* To avoid being triggered by the abandonment of her own family, she looked down the ramp. Not twenty meters outside were several dark lumps, all but unmoving. She sprinted past Oto who held a wallaby by the base of its tail because it was unable to walk. 'Tara!' Her boots crunched over charcoal and rocky earth, passed a few charcoal lumps that were the remains of long dead animals, and reached a bandicoot, miraculously alive. Tara took her time, even though she knew speed was important, and performed the two handed hold, based on her training. She picked up the bandicoot very carefully with one hand to restrain the head and the other to support the body, legs, and tail, making sure to keep the head away from her face. It looked up at her. *It's looking at me!* Tara held the animal against her for a moment and took out the holding bag to wrap it in. As she moved away, she saw how many were around her, much more than she expected. Dozens of dark lumps inert like lumps of coal, unrecognizable, black. She ran back to the carrier, her heart pounding, overwhelmed and confused with grief.

'Bismillaheh rahmaneh rahim,' she said in prayer. In the name of God, the most gracious, the most merciful. But the prayer brought back her past and her doubts. *How is He being gracious and merciful here?* She felt disheartened and angry, then. *There's never enough of us; there never will be enough of us for this kind of work. First it was koalas, then cockatoos in the east, and kookaburras. What next, bandicoots? It sure looks like it...*

She struggled to get a good amount of filtered air into her lungs. She didn't care about that—the bandicoot was more important than her. She finally reached the ramp and ran up, panting and coughing. She decided to help Oto regardless of this, in pure Iranian fashion—helping others at the expense of herself. *I'm doing it for the animals, not for Oto.*

'You want to die early while carrying that thing? Don't help me, you need recovery time.' All of a sudden a large muscular figure was beside her. It was Nikau. With one hand he gently took the bandicoot from Tara and pulled her to top of the ramp. He set her down and placed the bandicoot next to her before running back to Oto. Tara wanted to help. She had to, so she staggered to a sitting position, struggled for a moment with her breathing. The poor bandicoot squealed in pain, its small belly rising and falling, watching her like that dingo. *Calling to me...* Tara picked up a cold water container and sprayed the bandicoot until its squealing died down. She looked into its eyes. *My family abandoned me because I cared more about you guys than them, and this government abandoned you, caring more about themselves than you. They were scared of losing money you know, the profits, the economy, and all that junk. Don't they know it's our responsibility to care for you guys? Don't worry, I won't abandon you, not until my last breath.* And there was the female dingo, still sitting and watching her, with the second, younger male dingo next to it now, both shaking with obvious tiredness and pain. The wallabies and the bilby huddled nearby as well. *The dingoes have been watching me all this time... What are you thinking? Am I going crazy? Are you thinking something?*

The ramp closed and the siren ceased. The air ducts stabilized. Oto called out, 'We got two female wallabies and one male. A bilby clinging to a wallaby, two dingoes, and a bandicoot. The total tally is seven animals. Great work guys!' Wandjina shuddered to a start and started to move again. Nikau and Oto sprayed them with water, letting them drink from it as well; the dingoes accepted this treatment, and all were cleaned and a cold compress was applied to their burns. First aid kits were opened and bandages were applied where required. Once all that was done, they proceeded to lightly sedate them, to alleviate their pain and their movements. But when Oto and Nikau approached the dingoes, they were met with fierce resistance from the female. Her hackles rose as she barked and growled, bared her canines. Tara watched her. *Have you been through this before? Perhaps you can smell the chemicals, even above all this smoke and fire...* Then she remembered a time when the dingoes used to watch the carriers go by, a time before the government intervened more completely. *They know us in this way, that we are a sanctuary to them...*

'I can't force it on them—they might sustain more injuries,' Nikau said. Should I just go in anyway and do a full sedation?'

'You can't do that, and you know why,' Oto said. 'They need to be fasted before it's done. You should know that. Don't cut corners.'

Good, Oto, Tara thought. *But we are severely understaffed. It's just us for this whole region. Just us. We can't watch over them all the time, even though we really should... But I'll do it. I won't sleep if it comes to that.*

'Are you okay?' Oto asked Tara. 'You know, I didn't mean to be a jībā earlier, I always get like that when I'm stressed out.' She smiled weakly, but then the smile turned crooked, and Tara knew there was more to come. "I know you're the captain, and I respect that, but it's like you don't care about us. How long have we been a team together? Years, right? You always act like this. It's like the animals are everything, and we are nothing.'

There was a moment of silence between them. Nikau heard the conversation and was looking at Tara, his face full of concern.

'I had to get out there, you know?' Tara said that primarily to deflect the weight of Oto's words, her voice still raspy from the smoke outside. But Tara knew that she needed to prove she was not apathetic like her family, who ignored real problems like so many others.

'You're not listening to me. We have to work together, Tara. Our goals are the same.' Oto was flustered and she looked to Nikau.

'She's right,' he said. 'You've been a ghost in here. Cobar is the only one you properly talk to.'

'He is the inheritor of everything,' Tara snapped. In the following stunned silence, Tara quickly said, 'I'm sorry…' Tears welled in her eyes. 'I just, it's because I, you know…' Before she could say anything else, the alpha female dingo limped between them all and sat below them, looking up at each of them, smelling the air and their clothing. The younger male approached as well, followed by the weary bandicoot. Tara kneeled among them and burst into tears.

'They are all that matter,' she sobbed, 'more than anything, more than my life.'

'Why?' Oto asked.

'Because we destroyed the planet, we destroyed their wilderness, and we owe it to the animals to save them.'

Oto appeared genuinely moved. 'But you're forgetting something, Tara,' she said, 'we need to be saved by them as well. Nature has always been in perfect balance before we came. But we've lost our touch with reality, with our perspectives on it all.'

'Yes, you're absolutely right.' Tara couldn't believe Oto had said that. *She is like me, they all are. What was I thinking? Yes, I hate people because of what they've done, but my crew are different, special. Why hadn't I realized that before?*

'Okay, c'mon, let's get back into it, Captain.' Oto smiled and helped Tara to her feet. Nikau smiled as well. 'We got each other's back, don't we?'

'Yes, we do' Tara said.'

'And you know what?' Oto sighed bitterly. 'At least you don't have to worry about Australians buying thousands of hectares of farmland from China and taking the profits and produce away, even water produce. Because that's what my people are doing here, helping the Australian government to destroy everything.'

'That's so true.' *But you don't have the burden of disassociating from your faith because of a Sunni and Shiite fallout the government wanted to silence… They don't care, Oto, the cities have become sterile with only humans in them "to protect us", and no animals, none whatsoever… And let's not forget the non-renewable resources they're using up without regard for the damage they're inflicting…*

'Are you alright?' Oto said. 'You spaced out for a second.'

'I'm alright. I'm just worried about a lot of things.'

'I don't blame you, sister. You know, I am grateful for leaving everything that China's doing behind. My family were involved in all that crap for ages.' Oto's smile turned into a grimace, and she looked hurt. It was easy to spot with her mask and goggles on.

'You know what, Tara? Think of it this way. It's like we are in that story, you know, the one with the big chuán where all the animals come inside, and that old man takes care of them?'

Tara carefully petted the bandicoot, making sure not to hurt the thing. *You are all that matters, little one. I've got no one except you guys, and the crew of course…*

'You hearing me, Tara?'

'Yes I heard. It's the kashti-eh-nou story. You're right.'

'Well, I better get back to work, and you better get up there,' Oto said. 'We got it covered down here.'

'I don't want to leave them. I just can't.'

'C'mon…' Oto gave Tara a hug and Tara reluctantly left the animals—looking back all the time—as she made her way to the bridge. Then Cobar ran into her.

'Oh, sorry I hit you! Are they okay?' He didn't wait for a response and was gone as soon as he had come. And then Tara remembered something very important.

'Cobar, who's piloting—'

'Autopilot,' he called back. Tara smiled. *If anyone should take care of them, it should be you.* His love and devotion to the animals astounded her. She'd only known him for about a year, but he'd really grown on her during that time. *He brings his whole heart into what he does. I guess I admire him because I lack the same convictions with my own culture…*

Finally, she left and reached the bridge and checked all her readings again, sighed, and looked out the viewing window, her hands shaking once again.

'The drop-off point isn't far, about seven kilometers,' she said into the radio. 'Cobar, you actually need to go back to your station. We have to go south-east.'

'Yes, I will,' Cobar said, breathless. 'But, they're not good. They're critical—the burns on them… They're gonna go if we don't get to the drop-off point soon.'

Tara's stomach filled with butterflies.

'I know,' she said.

'Don't worry,' Cobar replied, 'Wandjina will protect them.'

Tara looked at the data and her anxiety rose to a peak, as the prescribed route would take too long. She began to panic. *Think, Tara! There's not enough time to go around the fire. But, what if we go through it?* It would cut their time considerably, but it was a serious gamble.

'Get the animals into the infirmary, Nikau. I've got a plan,' she said.

'Roger,' he said. 'Hey, they're going on their own. Amazing!'

'There are some things animals don't forget,' Tara said. 'Remember, the carriers have been a part of their lives for so long.'

'Very true,' Nikau replied. 'It's so cool. Look at them!'

Oto said, 'So you have a plan, Tara? Tell us what you're thinking.'

'We'll,' she said, bracing herself. 'We have to go through the fire. That's the only way they'll survive. We won't have time otherwise. Cobar said they're critical.' *I have to save them, no matter what. They're worth more than us, worth more than anything…* She caught herself in that old line of thinking. *No, I mustn't think like that anymore. I have to save my crew, both them and the animals together.*

There was a long pause.

'What?' Nikau's voice was suddenly loud and harsh, his previous mirth all but gone. Tara was aware, as were the others, of Nikau's weakness, of how his parents were seriously burned during an air dump and were hospitalized in New South Wales. He also had a patchy past as an ex-cop and redeemed himself by joining the New Zealand Alliance, a group that helped restore what the government and climate had taken from Australia. 'You're not going do that, Tara! You can't!'

She didn't respond, but opened several seals on the console. Three buttons were labeled "extinguishing protocol".

'I need two people on the hoses. Hurry up!'

'No, Tara!'

'Yes!' Cobar said. 'Shut up, Nikau!'

'You little shit,' he said. 'C'mon, show us how strong you really are, little superhero boy.'

They're going to have a punch up... 'Nikau! Please trust me. Stay with the animals. Cobar, set the autopilot to go through the fire and then jump up to the hoses. Oto, you're going up there too!'

'I gathered that...'

'You can't fight me, bro,' Cobar said. 'I saved your life, don't you remember? Six months ago, you would have been stranded out there—'

The dingoes started barking, and the bandicoot squealed through Nikau's coms. And then, a sudden rush of loud static lasted several seconds.

'Attention, license number T3STRE,' an authoritative voice said. 'We've monitored and recorded your activities. You have breached the resource clause using resources and equipment for animals, instead of for Australians. This act harbors serious fines and jail time. You are to stop your vessel immediately.'

'You want to get caught, Nikau? You want to go to jail?' Tara had to convince him. 'Your parents will be up for it once they get better. We have to go through the fire now, they won't chase us through that.' Tara was trying anything to sway his tumultuous emotions. It would always be a gamble going through the fire, and the authorities were a double-edged sword. It was time to use both edges.

'We're the Wandjina, you assholes,' Cobar said to the authorities. 'Come follow us into the fire, if you're game!' And then to Tara, 'Don't listen to those dickheads, Tara! We got this!'

'Cobar, get to your station and plot your course!'

'I'm going now!'

'Nikau?'

After a long and hesitant pause, Tara heard the smallest and most reluctant "Yes" from him. She had a good feeling that this wasn't over, not by a long shot.

'Course locked in!'

'Thanks, Cobar, now get up to the hoses!'

The carrier pushed on towards the fire, an unstoppable force.

'You guys at the hoses, yet?'

'I'm at the hoses,' said Cobar.

'So am I,' said Oto.

The nitrogen and carbon dioxide reserves were still full, thankfully, and the state of the ship hadn't compromised such an important commodity. With grim historical remembrance, a name entered Tara's mind for those people who did this kind of work. *Fire Fighters…* It had been their job and livelihood, but of course the government intervened, shut it all down due to the volunteers protesting their rights for funding and better equipment.

They were close now. The temperature outside read a staggering 56 degrees centigrade.

'Full speed!' Now all Tara saw was fire.

'The animals are in the infirmary, much quicker than I expected…' Nikau said.

'Thank you, Nikau.'

'Shoot them, Cobar,' Oto said, and Tara saw the nitrogen and carbon dioxide reserves depleting. The wall of fire bowed and curled away followed by a long stream of extinguisher mixture. Wandjina continued to heat up, and there was a sudden crash and Tara grabbed onto the railing, almost tumbling over it. The readings on the console showed that they hadn't entered the fires yet, but Tara knew from experience that the connection to Aussat 2 had no coverage where the fires were strongest. That was when the last functioning solar panel went offline. The battery power also said 26% and Tara was aghast. *The heat is messing us up...*

'How much longer?' she screamed. There was another crash and she fell to the ground.

'We're through, Tara! We're through!' Oto's voice crackled through her mask.

'We made it, Nikau,' Tara said. 'We made it, you see?' But he didn't respond.

'I can see the drop-off point!' Cobar said.

'Great. Get back inside, you guys!'

The heat in the carrier lessened as the entire right side of Wandjina started to whine. Tara heard a great crunching sound and something large and heavy snapped and whiplashed on the left side of the carrier, almost capsizing the whole thing. Everything shuddered and the Wandjina slanted to the right, slowed down.

The console revealed that the driving train was broken on the right side. The sprocket had snapped.

'What the hell was that?' Tara suddenly jumped at Cobar's voice right behind her. 'Are we stranded?'

'Shit, Cobar, you scared me!'

'Sorry, Captain.'

No, no, no... It can't end like this. We'll get arrested, interrogated, tortured... They'll want to find out where the other carriers are, how we're operating under their radar. It will all be over...

'I'm not gonna get caught, Tara,' Nikau said. 'You watch. Let them board us.'

'So you were undercover for them this whole time? I'll smash you!'

Cobar left the bridge and headed to the infirmary.

'Cobar!'

'No, you idiot,' Nikau said. 'I can get us out. Everyone get down here. Radio silence from now on.' The dingoes were barking, and there were scratching sounds, like the wallabies were scratching at the infirmary walls.

'Prepare to be boarded,' came the authoritative voice, and Wandjina, now completely stationary, shook and shuddered. Something had hooked onto the front of the carrier, and Tara was sure they were going to be towed to god knows where.

'Cobar,' she called again, and then Oto was beside her.

'C'mon, girl, hurry up.' They sped down to the bottom of the carrier, caught up to Cobar, who held back but was still fidgeting with the desire to fight as they made a left past the ramp, down a corridor to the storage rooms and infirmary. The infirmary was just a fancy name for a dingy makeshift room where all the animals were supposed to rest and recover. Nikau walked up to them holding a wallaby, but his angry expression contradicted with his large arms carefully cradling the poor animal.

He wouldn't crush it, would he? To Tara's relief he handed the wallaby to her. She gratefully took the animal.

'I'm not gonna get caught, you understand me?'

'Totally,' said Oto, sounding confident, though Tara was pretty sure she didn't know any more about what Nikau planned to do than Tara did.

Tara carefully put the wallaby down.

'What are we doing?' she said. 'Why are you giving me this wallaby?'

'They'll bring a vehicle up the ramp and arrest us,' he said. 'But we'll stop them and take the vehicle.'

'And what about the animals? They'll die here!' But Nikau had already left, and she had to follow him. *I won't let them die!* Oto and Cobar followed close by her.

They all reached the hanger area, and sure enough there was a great tearing of metal, and the ramp fell with a great crash and a police vehicle—one that looked very similar to the Wandjina but much smaller—drove up the ramp without effort and screeched to a halt. Three individuals, covered very well with fire resistant gear and wearing black masks and goggles, exited, and before they were able to arm themselves, the dingoes and the wallabies rushed past, pushing them abruptly out of the way. 'No, the animals!' Tara cried, but there was no time to stop them. They rushed ahead, and to Tara's surprise they knocked two of the police to the ground. *Oh my god, it's true. We do need to be saved by them, just like Oto had said. Wow, look at them!* A few shots rang out but missed their targets. The third one pulled out a gun, and the female dingo went right for his throat, grazed it because of the armor and struck his head instead. The policeman fell down, apparently concussed. It took Tara and the others some time to get the animals off them, before the police were bound and gagged.

'I didn't... expect that,' Nikau said. 'Even with their injuries... Amazing.'

'You got some competition now,' Cobar said.

'They kicked their asses,' Oto said, incredulous. 'The sedatives must have worn off.'

'Or they could fight like that because they're not feeling any pain,' Tara said.

'Woohoo!' Cobar was ecstatic.

'Look at this,' Tara said. 'The animals won't fit in this vehicle, do you realize that?'

'Yes they will,' Nikau said. 'Have a look inside. You think it's small, don't you?' Tara made a tentative effort to enter the vehicle, as all sorts of alarm bells went off in her mind.

Oh... there may be enough room...

'Oto and Cobar with me. Nikau, keep watch. Quickly guys, let's round up the animals.' It hadn't taken long for the animals to be brought back together, because of their injuries.

'Are they all accounted for?' Oto made a quick count for seven animals, and gave Tara a thumbs up.

'Where's the bilby?' Oto pointed to one of the wallabies. 'Oh, I see.' *The bilby was on that wallaby's back all the time, just like a mother and its child.*

'Looks like Wandjina is dead,' Cobar said, crestfallen all of a sudden. 'But this baby Wandjina will take care of us.'

After more than five minutes, and with careful planning and careful movements, Tara and the others had managed to enter the vehicle with the animals. Now she saw how weary and weak they really were after all that fighting. It crushed Tara. But she kept going through the motions and safely buckled the animals, being so careful, along with as much equipment as she could carry from the Wandjina to care of them.

'So is this thing made for a team or something?' Cobar was impressed.

'Yes. Teams of police drive around with them to kill people, or catch them,' Nikau said.

'Shit,' Cobar said. 'That's intense.'

The police radios crackled with agitated and aggressive voices.

Nikau, at the steering wheel, looked up to the ceiling and twisted something off. Then he yanked at it and severed a bunch of wires. He threw it out of the vehicle before closing the door. 'To stop us getting tracked,' he said. 'Now do you think I still have affiliations with the Empire? You think I'm on the dark side anymore?' Tara had no idea what he was talking about, and neither had the others. 'I have issues, you know.'

'We all have issues!' Oto said.

'I've definitely got issues,' Cobar said.

'You know, all this muscle I have, I'm compensating for something, right? I just don't want to be hurt anymore, and my body is my shield, I guess. A shield against my oppressors. Hah.' Nikau flexed a bicep.

'Oh my god,' Cobar said, 'you're an idiot.'

Finally, some ease in tension! 'Me too,' Tara said, 'I mean, not in being an idiot, but with having issues. And I'm driving.' Before Nikau could protest, Tara started up the vehicle.

'You know how to drive a cop car?' Cobar said with disbelief.

'It's a prerequisite for Captains, but also a secret.' Tara reversed down the ramp. There were a bunch of police shouting at them, and some had already entered their own vehicles while others drew their weapons. Tara sped off in the opposite direction, towards the drop-off point.

'They're gonna chase us,' Cobar said. 'This is a great plan, Tara.'

'Cobar!' Oto said. 'Have a little faith.'

Great choice of words, Oto, Tara thought, and couldn't help to take her words personally. *I do have a lot of faith, I know that... Perhaps it's burdened me more than I've wanted it to, but the heart of Islam will always be with me, something peaceful and open...*

'They won't chase us,' Tara said, as she drove back around through the fire. 'It might not be as short a short cut, but going parallel along the fire should get us there on time.' *I hope we get there on time!*

After several minutes, Tara veered off the blazing track onto the cracked earth and smoking landscape. Already she saw salvation in the distance, vehicles with big red crosses on them, and large makeshift domes made for green houses but now for animal preservation.

Tara picked up the radio next to her, and set the frequency for the preserve. 'Can anyone hear me? This is Captain Tara from the Wandjina. Our carrier has become stranded at the coordinates I'm sending you. Drive sprocket damaged, police on our tail. We've sabotaged one of their vehicles—uh, license number TSG-3FP, and we are heading towards you. Please don't shoot us, we have animals aboard, seven animals in critical condition. Urgent medical attention required.'

'License number confirmed, scan completed,' said a woman in response to Tara's call. 'We're on our way, Wandjina crew.'

A few vehicles from the drop-off point headed out towards them at high speed, and within minutes were side by side, directing them to Emergency Bay 04.

'The government is still gonna get us,' Cobar said. 'We're dead.'

'No, we're not dead,' Tara said. 'Don't you know? They have no authority here. It's out of their jurisdiction. If they break it, International Law will kick in, and these stupid towering cities will be cut off from foreign aid.' When Cobar gasped at this, Tara continued, 'Yes, they still need aid even after all the restrictions they've put on us. I really hope they break International Law.'

'Seriously? Shit.' Cobar laughed.

'I told you I wouldn't get caught,' Nikau said. 'I told you all! Haha!'

'Yes, yes,' Oto said and gave another hug to Tara as her driving skills wavered from the outpouring of affection.

They passed into the jurisdiction of the camp and slowed to a stop. *This place really is out of this world...* Tara had never seen so many people in white riot gear with big red crosses on them, canopies of canvas painted with red crosses overhead and medical stations set up under them, with so many veterinarians, *well, they look like veterinarians!* Several wallabies stood by, waiting patiently while several children prepared to feed them. A man and woman brushed a dingo down, removing ash and debris, and the dingo licked their faces in appreciation. Heavily fortified supply stores were close by, with several bilbies lying on benches being fed and tended to. People ran around carrying equipment, and others held animals the same way Tara held that bandicoot, what seemed so long ago.

Grateful with what she saw, Tara helped the animals out, and there were people with masks and goggles urging them to the emergency shelter. *Finally, some respite,* she thought. One of the veterinarians led the alpha female into the pen with the other dingoes, who sniffed her and wagged their tails. *They recognize her!* Tara was immensely grateful that she had saved their leader. As she watched the dingoes leap and roll in happy reconciliation, she wondered if something of a reconciliation might be possible with her own human family. After all they'd been through, the animals understood what was really important to them: each other. Maybe she could help her family understand why the animals mattered to her so much, why she struggled with the politics of her faith. Tara knew then there was still a chance for things to change for the better.

***

Amin Chehelnabi is an Australian-born gay Iranian with a strong interest in the speculative fiction field. He has been a Collection/Anthology Judge for the Aurealis Awards, and a First Reader for *Lightspeed Magazine*. He's also an alumnus of the Clarion Science Fiction and Fantasy Workshop at UC San Diego (2014), and a recipient of the Octavia E. Butler Scholarship Award. His publications include a horror story published with Innsmouth Free Press, which received an Honorable Mention in *The Best Horror of the Year, Volume Seven* (Edited by Ellen Datlow), and was a panelist for a three-day conference called Shaping Change: Remembering Octavia E. Butler through Archives, Art, and Worldmaking, which took place in 2016 at the Cross-Cultural Center at UC San Diego. He also has a Bachelor's Degree in Fine Arts, majoring in sculpture, and loves cats.

The Streams Are Paved With Fish Traps
Octavia Cade

Sunlight is stronger underground.

All the sunlight there is reflection, but still. It's a metaphor. You don't need to tell me. Metaphorical sunlight is the best kind, especially if you're pale and not-so-interesting, with a family history of skin cancer and a real dislike of heat. There's only so much all those green walls and green roofs can mitigate away. But walls are walls, even when covered in vines and chickpeas, flowers to call the insects and the birds. There's still a solidity to them, and if you want to know what's going on in someone's house—if you *really* want to know—then you have to look at their pipes.

"There's something really bloody nosy about that," says Dan. His voice is quiet and very precise. He gets that way when he's angry. I just get loud. It's a stupid argument because I know he agrees with me, but all the arguments we have these days are stupid. I find myself taking on opinions I don't believe in just to have something to fight about.

It's exhausting.

"I'm going to work," I say, because underground is somewhere he is not and that's where I want to be right now. I'm cranky all morning, mostly because I know the fight is stupid and that it's my fault. I lost my temper over the smallest thing—can't even remember what it was—and started taking out tension where it didn't belong.

The tunnels are mostly dark, where light doesn't come through gratings, and the lines of storm water are high along them. It's summer now, the weather less tempestuous and the water levels low, but it's still something to keep an eye on, rebuilding as we are. Refurbishing, anyway. There's a whole watery community down here, a bursting surprise of ecosystem, and it's something to be helped along.

I'd always thought of underground as rats. Tunnels of them writhing, and I hate rats. It's not like me to be unsympathetic to animals but those scaly tails make the gorge rise in me and they're an introduced pest anyway, so extermination is the best option. Our birds can't survive the explosion of their population, and there's no point in greening the city if it does nothing but provide food for rodents.

What's down here now isn't rodents. Nor is it introduced. The colonisation of the storm water systems with native fish, with native eels, has been a slow and lovely thing. They have made themselves a home here, in dark places instead of riverbanks, with light shining through gratings instead of leaves... cities have always been places of adaptation, and this adaptation of structure into habitat shows that we are not the only ones able to adjust.

The eels are smooth beneath my fingers, their skin soft over all that sinewy muscle. I swear they have come to know me. "It's that you bring them food," says Jess, down in the waterways with me and with fish traps hanging from her back. "It's not friendliness they're showing. It's plain greed."

Which is true, I admit it. But they're so gentle when they come for the chicken, and so dainty when those dark blunt heads breach the black water and take it from my hands. It's almost as if they recognise me, winding themselves around my rubber-booted legs as if they were cats.

"They should be eating fish," says Jess, and they are. The fish are colonising the storm pipes too, and I've seen my torchlight play over bodies with bites taken out of them before, floating on the surface and waiting for the rest of devouring. She doesn't say *you're feeding for you and not them* but I know she's thinking it, and she's not wrong. There's something very peaceful about standing in dark water with gentle beasts and the weight of the city above, something that in those moments is far away, and full of problems belonging to someone else.

"Don't stay late tonight," she says. "I mean, I admire dedication as much as the next girl, but…" She's always been very clear in what she doesn't say. It's a skill I've always admired, even when it's directed at me.

"I just don't want to go home," I confess. "It's too difficult there."

"It's not going to get any easier here," she says, aware that for me the dim, quiet tunnels beneath the city streets have become as much crutch as refuge. It's no one's fault; it's just been a shitty year. My mother died. Dan's parents divorced, after thirty years of marriage, and both of them are leaning on him more than they should. I got a new job, and we moved to a new house. It's too much. We're both worn thin and snapping.

And if I spend most of my time underground, now, with the eels and with the fish… it's because things seem more hopeful here. Witnessing the restoration of species in real time rejuvenates my faith in the restoration of other things.

I stop to get dessert and apology flowers, but when I get home Dan isn't there. His easel's put away, and there's only a faint smell of oils and paint that says he's been gone a while. He's left a note on the kitchen table that says he's gone to help a mate with his beehives—they're swarming, and the new hive is slated for the roof of the public library. It's midnight before he gets home, and he smells of beer and smoke.

While he was gone, I ate all of the dessert and hid the packaging at the bottom of the recycling bin so that no one could see it.

***

It was a surprise to find so much living down there. Most of the streams have been built over, a history of architecture that increased building space and let the streams double as storm drains, and not a feature of city life I'd ever admired. It was too easy to think of ecology buried over, the things that lived in the stream, lived around it, and how they no longer were.

It was only when Jess and I were sloshing through, sample cases with us, that we'd seen something else—life come back to the city in ways we did not expect. "That's a kōkopu," she said, face slack with astonishment and her torchlight focused on a corner of tunnel. "See, there. With the banding." A little fish, and not the only one. There were whitebait there as well, and eels. More and more we saw the eels. "If there are eels moving along here, there's enough food to support them," she said.

It didn't stop me feeding them bits of my sandwiches. Ham and chicken, and they would have eaten the bread too if I let them. I remembered feeding bread to eels as a kid, but I couldn't remember whether I was supposed to or not, so I stuffed it back in my pack, and dipped my hands in the dark water before stroking down those long and lovely backs.

I was surprised they'd survived there. I was surprised some of them could travel. They were healthy animals, but the newer pipes, the smoother ones, encouraged fast water and there was little place to rest for swimming against the current, and little place to hide. Some of the eels were trying, though, even in the dark. There was the odd brick, the odd branch. "We should bring some down," said Jess. "Try to build up the habitat."

We couldn't do a lot—there's a fine line between helping the eels and introducing blockages to drains, but the city's built on hillsides, often, and there were other problems. "We should set up some fish traps, too," I commented. "Until the pipes can be made more accessible for them. It'd help us to transport them over the tricky places."

The thought of eels, of fish, swimming beneath car parks and museums and supermarkets is an enticing one. It's easy to get permission, but truth is we would have done it regardless. This new habitat is not one which should be let go of, and Jess and I spend our own time down there, exploring. That's when we find streams and storm drains less healthy than the rest.

***

The eels are sluggish, all the little fish floating. There's something in the water that shouldn't be—these are storm drains and waterways, not sewage pipes, and there are ways to dispose of poisons now that don't contaminate, but sometimes people are lazy. It's such a fragile thing, a city ecology, burdened by concrete and structure as it is but there's an opportunism there, too, that makes me think of reefs, and how they can be colonised. But the reefs are fragile too, changing temperatures dissolving chemical skeletons. The eels and fish here are vulnerable as well, susceptible to temperature and to incursion.

If I'd have thought of a habitat beneath streets, it would have been one of absence and a sort of dank choking. It would have been like this: full of little deaths.

The eels are too sluggish for feeding. They hide under the structures Jess and I left for them; they flinch at movement.

I pack up some of the dead fish to take back for testing, but I don't know what to do with the rest. "If we leave them, maybe they'll get eaten," says Jess. "Maybe they'll wash out and the birds will get them." The gulls with their black backs and smoke-yellow beaks and reptile eyes, who congregate in the city harbour, and on the beaches. The penguins too, the little blues who waddle onto pavement sometimes, and who always make me smile.

"Depends whether or not they've been poisoned," I say. Some things we don't need spread through the food chain.

I recognise one of the eels, from the scarring on its body. At first I think it's dead too, but it's only floating, too weak to move and its jaws open as if gasping. Those silk-soft flanks are heaving beneath gills. It's like watching a friend fight against suffocation, so I lift it into a bucket, take it home and when Dan comes through the door, hours late himself, the eel is recovering in the bathtub.

"I couldn't just leave it there," I tell him and he sighs, heavily, but he sits as well, on the floor next to the tub, next to me, and strokes the eel in silence.

The eel stays for the better part of a week. It's a nuisance—there's no separate shower in this new house, only the one bathroom, so we've taken to scrubbing ourselves standing up, with the sink full of soap. "Most troublesome guest we've ever had," grumbles Dan, but it's the fake grumble I used to hear from him before things went bad, when life was easy and complaint an entertainment. Truthfully, as much as the eel's staked out its claim to the bath it doesn't do much else, requires little in the way of emotional support, and so we become invested despite ourselves. It's so easy to care for something that doesn't need anything from us; lately all the things we've cared for have been costly.

Dan brings home scraps from the fishmonger to tempt it. It's been a while since he brought *me* fresh fish, I'd like to say, but there's that old cheesecake container at the bottom of the recycling that he never got any of, so on balance I think it's better to keep my mouth shut on that one. But the next night I go for fish myself, and bring back enough for the eel and for a pie for us, one with boiled eggs and capers in it.

It's Dan's favourite, and the look of surprise on his face when he comes home—late, again—reminds me how long it's been since I made it for him.

We end the night, as usual, sitting in silence by the tub, a glass of wine for each of us and the eel dreaming below. It looks much healthier, surrounded by clean water as it is.

"I think we should call him Trevor," says Dan, suddenly.

"Like that frog in Harry Potter?"

"It was a *toad*. Call yourself an ecologist."

There's nothing lumpen about the eel, or leggy for that matter. There's nothing of the consistency of wart about it. I've never seen anything that reminds me of a toad less. We call it Trevor anyway.

***

Luckily only some of the waterways seem contaminated. Jess and I have gone through them all, taking water samples as we go, and taking surveys as well of what we find: the fish species, the eels. It's a hard slog—there's the odd pipe tall enough to stand up in, but for the most case it's hunching over for kilometres at a stretch, through pipes that need replacing.

"Funny that the ones crumbling most provide the best habitats," says Jess. The ones with the roughened walls that slow the speed of water going through enough for movement and migration. "They'll need replacing soon." Which means walls slippery as eel-skin, and currents that can defeat the strongest swimmer.

"Maybe we can argue for different pipes," I say. It's a long shot, or would have been once perhaps. But the city has its own changing structures now, and there are expectations of the world above, that it be a habitat for a multitude of species. The green walls and green roofs, to encourage plant life and sustainable food sources, to draw the insects and the birds. The resting places built on skyscrapers, the road signs warning of safe nesting spaces for penguins. The ecological sanctuary within the city, where kiwi and pūkeko are coming back. It's a harbour city, used to life in liminal spaces—seagrasses and algae and shellfish in the intertidal zones, and all of them encouraged. It was that steady change above that made us think there was room enough to wedge a subterranean ecology into the city as well; one that was more than soil microbes and worms.

"We're building something lovely," says Jess. "Underground streams paved with fish traps. Think we'll ever get anglers down here as well?"

"Small ones, maybe, who don't mind the hunching," I reply. My back's killing me, and every time we pass under a street grate the light makes me squint. "I wonder if they'd be willing to take water samples as they went. Sort of community policing…"

It's not an unreasonable thought. There's enough of that kind of volunteering about: people who keep an eye on the seagrasses, monitoring their health and the amount available for grazing birds. One of Dan's mates has a drone he uses to take pictures of the winter dieback. The advantage of city living is that there's always someone around to observe city *life*, and people like to do it. They like to help, we've found, given the opportunity and the education to do so. I think they'd help here, too, as soon as they knew there were creatures down here to help. No surprise that they didn't know earlier, any more than we did—there's scope for surveillance in a city, but there are still parts of it hardly anyone ever visits.

"Well right now the only ones doing any sort of policing are us," says Jess. It's not something we ever trained for, as scientists. Investigation, certainly. Rational follow-through and the hunting down of possibility, but I've always been indifferent to non-natural laws. Now, though, I'm more than happy to exploit them. There are rules against the pollution that results in this sort of death, but people forget.

"If we find out where it's coming from, we'll call the cops then," she says.

You can't always believe what your eyes are telling you—for all I know the pipes where biology is untouched seem so because they're uncontaminated in truth, but we take water samples anyway, just in case they show the beginnings of poison. In practice, though, it's easier to follow the trail of dead things, the increasing emptiness of pipe where there're no eels to wrap around me.

"No whitebait either," says Jess. "Damn it. I could really go for some fritters right now." Which is deceptive at best; as much as she loves them, transplant from the West Coast as she is, where whitebait were the beloved staples of seasonal eating, she'd never damage such a vulnerable ecology by bringing the net down into pipes.

Soon enough we find where the damage is coming from—a leaking storage system, a negligent owner. The council gets involved, and the cops. There's a commitment to patch up the problem within a week, and Jess and I have a monitoring plan in place. She talks to a local journalist, makes sure to give the impression that we can track every contaminant to its source. This is not accurate, but if it makes people think twice then I'm all for the deception.

("I know it's nosy," I say, back home that night, beside the bath, and Dan shakes his head.

"Justified," he says. The eel nuzzles his fingers, almost back to full strength.)

Random checks under the drains and the public castigation of polluters should be enough. "We should get some kids down here too," says Jess. "School visits. And talk to the local iwi." Moral support and future-proofing, the extension of observation. Sunlight has always been the best disinfectant.

***

Some places sunlight just doesn't seem to go. I take Trevor back to his storm water system, leave him safe behind a brick and with a piece of chicken to worry. Dan comes with me; he's grown fond of the eel though he doesn't say so, and he makes no complaint at small dank places, though truthfully I've taken him to the largest accessible pipe, so he doesn't need to crouch. He can stand upright, even, the pipe a whole two metres in width. He looks around, thoughtful, barely pays attention to me or the eel, and I can't help but wonder why he insisted on coming. He doesn't seem to be getting much out of it, and is preoccupied the rest of the week.

I'd thought things were getting easier between us. Perhaps we need an eel in the bathtub all the time just to get along. It was something to talk about, something that wasn't death or grief or strain. Without any of those things there's just silence.

He's spending most of his nights elsewhere. I've always been a heavy sleeper, but even I notice when he sneaks out of bed in the middle of the night, and doesn't come back before dawn. I'd like to think it's work that's calling him, because he does come back with paint in the creases of his skin, with dust in his hair, but we'd set aside the spare room here as studio and there's nothing going on there, nothing.

The sun can't shine on absence, I think. Or maybe that's all it can shine on.

"Do you want a divorce?" I say to him one day, and he looks at me, startled, as if something had fallen into a deep quiet pool and brought him back up and blinking to light.

"No," he says. "I... no. Look. It's not." He sighs, shrugs. "There's something I want to show you. It was going to be a surprise."

He takes me down into the tunnels again, into a place I thought he'd only been the once.

"You told me sunlight is stronger underground," he says, and there is sunshine on the walls, on the floor of the storm drains, that comes from more than mirrors.

"Some of it *does* come from mirrors," he says, and on the walls are pieces of metal, of glass, all cut in shining squares and cemented into mosaic, catching light from the gutters above, and from the torches we took with us. It's the world above that Dan's brought to storm walls—the gold and greening city, kōwhai flowers and pōhutukawa and the birds that feed on them, insects and ferns and fruit trees espaliered up against the hard geometric shapes of city skyscrapers. There are bee hives and living walls—"I left the roof for glow worms," he says. The grates above are larger, some of them, but over the top of the tunnel, in places, is thick glass so that the people walking above can see what lives below the city streets. The light that shines through the glass and grates dapples off mosaic and into water, and dim though it may be, the slick shining bodies of fish, of eels, can be seen in the streams that go under the city. One of those eels has a familiar set of scars.

"I looked it up," he says. "Back in the day. All those old Victorian sewer tunnels… people go down and see them, you know? Tourists and so on. I always thought I'd like to do that. The architecture of them, the structure. They were beautiful, even though nobody was meant to see them.

"I think maybe they should see," he says.

There are parks above, green spaces and trees in every street as we try to coax life back to the cities, to make it more than a two-dimensional space for a single species. A place where that third dimension, when exploited, only ever went *up*. Which was good for the birds, roosting in high places and with the wind in their feathers, but there are low things living too, in stream beds and under the overhang of riverbeds, and those were what we forgot.

"This is what you've been doing," I realise. "All those nights away from home."

"Not at first," he admits. "For a while I was just avoiding you. But then the eel came and you were talking and I got interested. And then, well, I couldn't very well come down during the day now, could I?" he says. "It would have spoiled the surprise." With me there all the time, wading through, and reluctant to go home as well, even though for us home had always been each other and it was horrible to live without.

"It's not been an easy year," I say.

"It's been fucking terrible," he admits. "There were times I thought we'd not come out of it. We're still not out of it. Times I wondered if you'd just come down here one day and not come up again."

"Probably times you wouldn't have minded," I say. "I haven't been easy to live with." And it's true. I was too sad.

"You were too sad," he says. "And so was I." He runs his hands over the wall, over that strange and beautiful mosaic, and I see that beneath the shadows of glass lie the shadow of fins, the sweet, sinuous bodies of eels. It's a shading that only comes out in certain lights, I think, and from certain angles.

Our storm systems, our underground streams, they should be walkways, with pavements and small trails beside the water. There should be art on all the walls. It's easy to ignore what we put down drains, what we let spill into gutters. If people are down here all the time, if they're feeding the eels and watching the fish like they do the birds, then they'll *see* if those fish start to sicken. And the more walkways we have underground, the more streams we have that are paved with fish traps, the more room there'll be above for wildflowers in the city centre, for meadows between buildings and bringing pollinators back into the city.

Whitebait pools under the council buildings, eel hatcheries under inner city schools. Fishponds and glow worms and maybe one day there'll be cave weta, too, their long-stick insect limbs climbing over those mosaic walls, bringing more life to them than sunlight does.

"Maybe it's time to try and be happy again," he says. There's so much work on that wall, so much effort and time and frustrated love. So much sticking-with. Like the eels, inching their way along the slow-watered flow of roughened walls, coiling themselves back into the underground streams of city.

"Maybe it is," I say.

***

Octavia Cade is a New Zealand writer with a PhD in science communication. She's had close to 50 stories published, in markets such as *Clarkesworld, Asimov's,* and *Shimmer,* and particularly likes writing stories where science and ecology are explored in positive and sustainable ways. Her own biology background is in seagrass, and she's aiming to put together a research proposal that looks at how communities interact with seagrass populations on their own doorstep. She attended Clarion West 2016, and is the 2020 writer-in-residence at Massey University/Square Edge.

Crew
E.-H. Nießler

With a powerful stroke of his fluke Old Woo dove and carried the crew deep below the surface. Swarms of small fish quickly scurried out of the way of their descent. Despite the force of the motion, Qiqi held onto the transport-frame attached to his body with surprising ease. Secure among the various instruments and equipment, she could see the marine life seek shelter against the approach of this fearsome predator. But the massive sperm-whale and the two passengers on his back were not here to hunt. They had a job to do.

Sixty meters below, they arrived at their destination. The station lay rusted and barnacled on the edge of an underwater cliff, nestled in what remained of a mesophotic coral reef. It looked foreboding amongst the bleached and broken remnants of the anthozoan landscape.

"Here," Old Woo said curtly.

The whale's vocalization vibrated off the transport-frame beneath her grip a fraction of a second before his translation harness picked it up and a deep slightly hollow voice sounded from the receiver in her diving mask.

"Finally some excitement!" the brighter and decisively more chipper voice of Ticks responded immediately.

Qiqi considered the giant octopus beside her with a weary glance.

Something about the writing movement of Ticks' tentacles didn't agree with her. The mere sight tapped into some deep primal fear she hadn't even been aware of until recently. Quickly she pushed herself clear and swam closer to inspect the structure below.

On one of the hatches there was writing. Simplified Chinese from before Federal Republican times. Qiqi thought she could read it well enough, but old characters often had surprising and unintuitive meanings.

"You were right," Qiqi said, surveying the site with a furrowed brow. "Uhm, good job!" she added hastily after a moment had passed. "Why don't you… check the perimeter?"

Without giving a reply Old Woo grumpily and slowly circled the station once, then twice, until finally making a disparaging but noncommittal noise, her new colleague's favorite way of answering to her instructions, such as they were.

His skin covered in faded service tattoos and littered with scars, he was a typical ex-military type. A living memorial to a time when the interests of singular nations had still been considered important enough to plunge the entire world into conflict. After the war many of them had joined ECO, and Qiqi wondered if they all were as short-spoken and somber as Old Woo. Whatever the case, his demeanor didn't make for a casual work environment.

"Not much," he eventually signaled, but then suddenly turned and made an uncharacteristically low and long sound that didn't translate.

"What's the matter?" Qiqi asked, nervously casting her gaze around. Here in this gloom she couldn't see very far.

"Dolphins," Old Woo answered grimly. "Always trouble."

"That's why nobody wants to work with you, old man," Ticks interjected in her usual chatter. "You have issues!"

With much ado she detached herself from the broad back of her unlikely partner and nimbly removed her tools from the transport-frame he was carrying.

"Let's crack this clam, before Qiqi runs dry."

"Watch it, bite-size," Old Woo replied, but Ticks had already darted down to the station.

The receiver in Qiqi's mask made a series of repeating chirps, a best fit translation for Ticks being amused.

"Don't worry about it Qiqi, Old Woo doesn't like anybody, because he's kinda racist."

Again Old Woo made his depreciating harrumph. Qiqi had no doubt that the fullness of its meaning could not ever be adequately captured by the translation harness permanently fixed to the massive block-shape of his head.

She anxiously fumbled with the navigation equipment on her belt. It was only the beginning of her first season as supervisor of her own crew and already she felt uncomfortably apart from her co-workers, not least of all because she was the only human. Qiqi wasn't sure how long the sperm-whale veteran and his pertly Octopus partner had been working together, but the two seemed to share an easy kind of intimate banter she couldn't bring herself to join.

"This is strange. I think it doesn't belong here," she said while checking their location on the Geo-Sat. Despite the repeater buoy above, the signal was very weak.

"The rest does?" Old Woo asked. Qiqi couldn't even hazard a guess if he was being facetious.

"I mean, look how it follows the lay of the reef," Qiqi replied. "No wonder the instruments on the catamaran didn't detect it. It was probably put here secretly."

"Could be," Old Woo agreed after a short pause. "Listening post, maybe. Or missile silo."

"Sounds dangerous, let's get inside!" said Ticks, already busy trying to pry open a hatch.

At ten years old she was the youngest and easily the most excitable of the crew, even though in terms of Giant Octopus life-span she could be considered as positively ancient.

"No joy, everything is stuck," Ticks proclaimed after a couple of minutes. "I could cut it open with the welder."

Old Woo gave a burst of sharp clicking sounds in the direction of the station, which rang very loud in Qiqi's ears. "Structure is flooded, seems like."

"You should break it open then." The Octopus eagerly scurried away from the hatch.

"No, Ticks," Qiqi said dubiously. "You were right the first time around. This could be dangerous."

"Isn't that precisely what we are here for? Locate, survey, recover and all that..."

"Flotsam and derelict, yes. An abandoned habitat, sure. But absolutely not military hardware! We flag it, mark it, leave it for the folks who specialize in old-war tech."

They had already passed a sunken shipwreck on their first day. Qiqi had called it in, rather than try to salvage it herself. Too close to the City, she had argued while being grateful her animal colleagues couldn't read the trepidation in her face. She wasn't even all that certain she was the right person to lead her crew in recovering some floating refuse.

"Well alright, you are the boss," Ticks said testily. She turned in a whirl of tentacles and left them in a cloud of black ink as she flitted away. Old Woo only repeated his trademark harrumph and swam closer again for Qiqi to load him up with the gear.

Qiqi let out an exasperated sigh. This was promising to be a long three months.

***

Later that day, back on the catamaran, the wind came in lazy intermittent squalls and so Qiqi busied herself hoisting the sail of photovoltaic foil that supplied the electric motor with additional energy. On a good, clear day with a steady breeze, the catamaran could make a comfortable twenty knots, but that was much faster than Old Woo was able to follow so most of the time they settled at a leisurely seven.

Qiqi enjoyed the fresh air in her face. Back in school she had gone scuba-diving often with her friends. A fun pastime once, it had now become a daily chore, and she truly valued the surface intervals she needed to properly decompress.

After making certain the sail was secure, she straightened her back and scanned the horizon, shading her eyes with one raised hand. All around there was nothing but ocean. She seemed worlds apart from the canals and terraced gardens of the City, her friends and from that tiny corner café she loved. Never before she had missed it all so dearly.

In the earpiece of her headset Qiqi could hear a vaguely familiar jingle being repeated over and over again.

"Is that... from a commercial?"

"Oh yeah, I love television," chirped Ticks from the aquarium which served as her sleeping quarters. "It's very stupid. I have a great TV set in my apartment in the City."

"You have an apartment?" Qiqi wondered.

"Sure. What do you think I do with all the ECO scrip?"

"I never really thought about it," Qiqi admitted. "Get a job, pay bills. Makes sense, I guess."

"Waste," came a grumpy harrumph over the headset. Old Woo's long grey body breached some meters away from the catamaran as he gathered his breath for a hunting dive. Before long he would be well out of range for communication.

"Well, not everybody has a pension from the Federal Republic to rely on, you know," Ticks quipped.

"Earned. Deserved." That was the last they heard before the audio from their companion faded into a soft static crackle.

Qiqi slowly made her way to the aft station. She sighed deeply as she sat at her desk and sipped a bit of the tea she had made herself earlier, then she turned to her work-screen and began typing.

"Watcha writing there?" Ticks interrupted almost immediately while flitting about her tank.

"Performance reviews," Qiqi answered absentmindedly.

"And how do you find us, boss?"

There was that humored chirping in the headset when Qiqi didn't reply immediately. After a moment Ticks added, "Have you been working for the Organization long?"

Qiqi massaged the bridge of her nose. This was the thing with Ticks. The octopus seemingly abhorred long pauses in a conversation. Normally it wasn't a problem, as long as Old Woo was around to keep her company. Then Qiqi could remove her earpiece and work with a bit of quiet. It was against policy of course, but the constant chatter of not-quite natural voices without another human being around somehow served to make her feel crowded and lonely at the same time.

"A while. Three years. Still not certain if it's right for me, to be honest." Her eyes were still fixed on her screen and a half-written letter of resignation.

There was an undefinable sound. A sort of whistle as the translator supplied a best fit vocalization to the octopus' brain pattern.

"That's a loooong time to be unsure."

"Not really. Not for humans. Not for Old Woo either. He's been with ECO for at least twenty years and was doing something else entirely before that. You?"

"Five. First I had to train marine engineering, but it takes a lifetime to properly get certified. Literally."

"You had treatments right?" Qiqi asked, turning her chair to face the aquarium. "I mean not only the translator, but other stuff too. Hormones?"

Truth be told, Qiqi had been curious, almost since the first day she had met with her new crew-mates, but had been too shy to ask until now.

"Yep, optical glands, ovaries—all gone."

Octopuses died soon after mating, the females especially, forgoing food and self-care while tending to the incubating eggs. It was an invasive but necessary part of the uplift process to greatly impair their reproductive capacity before they themselves where intellectually capable to consent. A subject of some ethical debate according to the dossier Qiqi should have studied more thoroughly as part of her supervisor training.

"So, you are okay with this?"

Ticks came to rest on a pile of rocks and hugged her tentacles close for a moment before she answered. A strangely familiar gesture. Insecure and full of doubt. All of a sudden, she didn't seem so different to Qiqi anymore.

"Small price to pay for a world of experience and knowledge, really. Once you crack open that oyster and get a taste, you can't readily stop to complain. Besides I'm not the maternal type."

"Did you always want to work for ECO?" Qiqi asked.

"When I was young, people said I should go into astronautics."

"Why didn't you?"

"I thought they were being silly. By the time I realized that it wasn't a joke, I was already much too old. Can you imagine being able to touch the stars?"

"You can't, actually. They are way too far away. And even if they weren't, they are way too hot. Like… like a hydrothermal vent. Even hotter."

Qiqi trailed off. The gentle swell of the ocean punctuated by the faint sound of Old Woo breaching filled the pause in the conversation.

"So much to learn, so little time. If my people could grow as old as you, we would have much more time to think two-legged thoughts and then… then… I don't know."

"I would have fought your wars too."

***

Two weeks later the three of them had already identified and mapped a dozen or so additional stations. A defensive perimeter of about 120 kilometers, all in various states of decay. After much complaining and debate Ticks had finally gotten her wish and was allowed to squeeze through a crack in the hull. She had stripped her gear and translation harness for the trip and Qiqi was already considering whether she had made a mistake.

"Don't worry. She is clever," Old Woo remarked, lazily floating close to the station.

"Who says I worry? This was a great idea, having her inside, alone, and with no communication."

"Need to trust. No point fretting."

Qiqi began to nervously swim around the structure. She had already tried to open a hatch, to no avail.

"Why you work for ECO?"

"—Huh…?"

"You ask Ticks. Never tell yourself. Why you work for ECO?"

Qiqi realized what he was doing, but she gladly allowed herself to be distracted.

"Uhm… I applied to loads of places after school. The Environmental Council Organization seemed as good a place as any. I kind of fibbed with my résumé though. And during the interview… Well, I thought they meant something else when they asked if I would by okay to work with animals."

Qiqi had never imagined hearing a sperm-whale laugh, but now as it happened, there was absolutely no mistaking it. Snaring clicks sounded through the water resonating in the very core of her body.

"Adrift and uncertain," Old Woo said and his laughter intensified. "But you do good work and Ticks likes you, so there's that."

"Can I ask you something?" Qiqi said after the clicking laughter had ebbed down a little.

"You did already. But ask another thing."

"What do you do with your scrip, if it's not too personal to ask?"

"Not too personal, no. There is a reservation for my people. Always need more. Medicine, food and such things."

"You got family there?"

"Used to, long time ago."

Over the translation of his antiquated harness, it was impossible to determine Old Woo's mood, but he had stopped laughing. Qiqi was debating whether or not she should press the issue further when she realized that her octopus colleague had begun the arduous task of extracting herself from the station.

"Find anything?" Old Woo asked, releasing Qiqi from the awkward situation. Apparently he was very good at reading human emotion.

Ticks secured the last bits of her harness. "Just a bunch of cuttlefish that probably think this thing is an oddly shaped cave."

"What do they know about it?"

"Dunno, I don't speak yokel. There is sonar, communication, and torpedoes, all long broken. Nothing wild, nothing really to worry about. Mark, flag, and move on?"

"No," Qiqi said, surprised by the sudden determination in her own voice. "We found the stations. If there is something useful left, we should be the ones to bring it in."

Old Woo swam a half circle to consider her with an indeterminable gaze.

"You sure?" he asked.

Qiqi hesitated. She could still decide to let things be. Surely they had accomplished enough, even if she lead her crew back to the City almost two months early.

"Yes," she finally said. "Can you, uhm, turn, so we can fix the frame to the hatch?"

"Are you asking, or are you telling?"

"Turn, so we can fix the frame to the hatch!"

***

Foreboding clouds darkened the sky, yet for the moment the sea remained deceptively calm. The storms that marked the end of the season had come late but still caught them by surprise. They had been too focused on clearing out the stations. Now their bounty of useful scrap lay on deck in heavy, tightly packed bundles.

Qiqi gave the horizon a worried glance while making sure their cargo was secure.

"How long do you think we have?" she asked even though she already anticipated the answer. The wind was picking up over the sound of thunder rolling in the distance.

"Soon," Old Woo replied. "The current draws us in."

"I don't think we can outrun it. Do you guys have any suggestions?"

"Dive deep and wait till it's over?" Ticks joked, but Qiqi could tell that her friend was worried. She went into the cabin to check the meteorological data from the Geo-Sat. A knot was forming in the pit of her stomach.

"I'll never be able to steer around this. I don't..."

"In the war," Old Woo said calmly. "We dragged boats head-on to the sea. Held them steady."

"And that worked?" Qiqi asked dubiously.

"Mostly."

"Alright. Let's get storm-worthy and you into the transport frame then. Ticks, you attach lagan-buoys to the cargo, we may have to jettison the lot of it."

By the time they fixed the hawser rope to Old Woo, the wind was howling and the swelling waves violently rocked the catamaran. At the helm, Qiqi was shaking with adrenalin as she steered the fore directly towards the oncoming tempest. Already in her diving suit, the full face mask shut out the storm barely enough to hear the voices of her colleagues in the receiver.

"If one of those waves catches us side on, they will have to salvage the boat next season."

"Thanks Ticks, I'm quite aware," Qiqi pressed through gritted teeth. "You alright there, old man?"

There was nothing but static in response. Before she could ask again her stomach lurched as the catamaran crested a wave and plunged into the valley behind. Almost level with the helm, she could see Old Woo's back already scaling the next one, the hawser taut between them.

Over the constant up and down Qiqi lost track of time. Her arms cramped up and she could do nothing but hold on to the helm trying desperately to keep them on course. A faint harrumph came crackling over the receiver.

"Problem?" she managed to say.

"It's coming loose. I can tell." Even over the storm Qiqi could hear the deep clicks of Old Woo's song. He was yelling.

"It's the damn clamps," Ticks said and heaved herself out of her aquarium with surprising speed. "Hold us steady and I'll see what I can do."

Qiqi wanted to ask if Ticks was sure, wanted to tell her something reassuring, but all she managed was a nod.

"Don't worry. I'm an engineer, remember?" was the last she heard before Ticks slithered away from the helm and out of sight.

***

The rounded triangular habitation spires of the City appeared on the clear horizon in the early morning. Even from that far away, Qiqi could see the towers of her home turn slowly, as they adjusted for the current. Almost by reflex she set the course to anticipate the change in water-flow. There was barely any resistance in the rudder despite the damage from the storm. Ticks had done a fantastic job. Now the octopus sat smugly in her aquarium, stacking rocks and chattering away the last leg of their journey.

"You've all been around since forever. What was the City like, uhm… thirty years ago?"

"I wasn't born yet, thirty years ago," Qiqi replied. She should have known the answer anyway, but she never had paid much attention to history.

"Different. Less water," Old Woo answered after a little while.

"Water came. Much destruction, more than the war. People rebuilt, but next year, water came again. And the year after. Then one year twice, but people rebuilt. Twenty years ago, water didn't leave. But people rebuilt."

"There is so much land elsewhere. Why didn't they simply leave?" Ticks writhed in a confused sort of way.

Even on deck of the catamaran they could hear the snaring clicking fullness of the sperm-whale's laugh.

"Not how humans work."

Ticks wasn't happy with that answer and posed a dozen new questions, and all the while they steadily made their way towards the white-golden silhouette of the City. Qiqi would have thought that after their ordeal she would welcome the sight. That she would look forward perhaps, to the non-mechanical sound of another human voice. Truth be told, they had not even parted ways yet, but she already missed her two companions. Her crew.

***

E.-H. Nießler is a freelance translator and writer from Berlin, Germany. Working as a retail-clerk, museum tour-guide and private tutor for the better part of two decades he managed to raise a family and obtain an MA in East-Asian Art-History and Japanese Studies from the Free University of Berlin in 2016. With his self-published début novel *Liminality — At the Edge of Worlds* in 2019 he started to pursue his passion for writing in earnest. Find news about his work on www.atelier-vulpecula.com.

The Songs That Humanity Lost Reluctantly to Dolphins

Shweta Taneja

It was the dolphins that came up with empathology. Not us. We did not know what hit us. We resisted, we fought, we cried, we ignored. We even tried to make fun of it. When nothing worked, we got angry. Our megacities shook, our suburban town houses trembled in their caged rage. Our presidents and prime ministers and mullahs and priests hollered from their bullet-proof towers, spitting into multiscreen microphones, distant cameras and remote screens. We were glued, furious, righteously so, doling out anger-filled labels, calling them traitors, aliens, demonic forces, flooding the internet and the streets.

You see, we were in denial. It was the norm in our megacities to consume and be consumed. We stuffed our hearts with toys and gadgets and thicker walls. We drank leatherette sofas, penthouses, and Ferraris. We gobbled medicines, sniffed snuff, cranked the volume of our custom-made gold-gilded AI-infused speakers. We surrounded ourselves with visuals of pristine forests and patched in AI-designed landscapes and faux-living creatures. We had enclosed ourselves safely with surround siliconate-screens gilded with trademarked 'pro-real' technology.

All this time, hunger of the heart dictated us, controlled us. We stuffed our faces and our fleshy bodies, till our esophagus bloated up with the constant AI-real feed, till we started to gouge out the veins of the planet and its skin and its bones and blood. We were blinded by our own needs, desires, wants, and silicon screens. All of us. All human adults—women and men. That is how we had grown up.

It was the children however, the little ones like you all, who first started to chip away. Started to believe.

***

It began quietly, without us noticing at first.

In a small fishing village on the island of Wetar in Indonesia, where the swelled climate of our desires had chipped away the sands, babies started to crawl. The toddlers waddled. They all headed to the ocean, as if they were looking for their mother's milk. Some of them were pulled in by the waves, never to be seen again. Some were pulled back by horrified mothers like us, who did not understand.

It happened again and then again in fishing villages peppered on coasts of India and Malaysia and Chile and Mozambique. Everyday, morning to night, deep night to dawn, children crawled and toddled. They had to be chained, doors closed, walls cemented and sealed inside. They would scream and claw at the bricks and kick the door, wailing constantly. They were not angry. We were. They were just determined. Like something crawled inside their skulls, beckoning them to the bloated polluted seas.

Members of clubs and parliaments, enclosed in siliconate domes and landscaped air, said it was because the villagers were uneducated, impressionable innocents, living in the chaotic, unprotected wilds. The enemy was tempting their children away. If only they had been given classes and pens and words and sunscreen. If only they had not been lazy but had earned money so they could buy glass-domed farms and mouldable screens. If only the children's skin had been whiter than the fresh snow that city kids consumed.

It would never happen in the megacities where educated folks lived. The cities with their disinfected galleries and chemically-washed gleaming screens. The urban landscape segregated with glass, secure with one-time-use gloves and masks. The high-rises with genetically-subsumed, civilized mass. It cannot happen in North America or white-walled cities of Western Europe, announced the members of mighty clubs and appropriate parliaments, a smug smile on their face as the breeze tickled their coiffured, chemically-gelled hair.

Then it started to happen in North America and Germany and Spain and Ethiopia and Liberia. Everywhere. From the high-rises of the domed megacities, the customized children waddled and crawled with the others, walking downhill, tumbling into the seas from vaulted porticos, tsunami-resistant piers, bleached coral beaches and garbage-ridden overcrowded shores. Children jumped, flew, dived, crept, sidled and ran. All going into the deep waters, never to be seen again.

"What do you hear, my baby?" cried a helpless mother, as she gripped her son's arm, on the shores of the segregated upmarket zone in Kochi.

"The song, Amma, the song," answered her son, who was not her son anymore.

"What song, what song? Tell me?" she said, pulling her son away. The son turned, seeing her, not seeing her, hearing her, not hearing her songs.

"Sing the song, Amma. Don't fear."

We were stumped, and scared and toddler-less. We did not know what was happening. Our children were becoming alien overnight, these devilish songs tempting them away. We started pumping them with drugs and custom-made brain modifiers to make them sleep, telling them stories of Pied Piper and the Sleeping Beauty and the monster that lies deep within seas. We hired experts, we screamed at secretaries, we divorced spouses, blamed fame and the thinness of our city walls. We put locks, built safety-nets, glass walls and CCTVs and shouted and screamed till our gilded screens mirrored our breathlessness. We prayed to our gods and local goons. We visited temples and churches to exorcise our children of the demons of the polluted seas. We did not understand what had happened, which made us scared and being scared made us angrier and angrier till blood leaked from our nails.

Amongst us, the one who used to be Buluba of the kingdom-of-Chad-that-is-no-more, heard the whales one night, as they sat exposed to cancerous stars. Or so they said. We were all alone, all scared, helplessly seeing our children losing themselves to the oncoming rush of the waves. Buluba whispered an echo of the devil's song, their eyes closed, their head moving from side to side and then back to front. We sat glued to our energy-saving screens desperate to understand why the songs of the seas were luring our children away. We listened to it live, our ears glued to every hiss and hoot that erupted from their lips. It was not music, said our ears, it was painful, like a slap or a whip.

We heard the rendering again and again sitting upright in our ergonomic chairs and slumped in sofas, their thunder-filled face gleaming on the big screens, in translation and transcription. We heard them retell what the whales had heard from dolphins who had whispered it all in the song that sang in their souls. We heard them say it was all over. That not only the whales, but the frogs and the lizards, and the mango trees and the leeches, and the deer and the roots of banyan trees and the rocks lying inert in Ladakh's iced sandy seas, had joined the song. The news spread like a virus from screen to screen, city to city, faster than the wildfires of Australia, faster than tsunamis in sea, faster than falling ice from a melting precipice.

It's a psychochemical agent, a mild-altering drug, said a white-haired scientist, triumphant in a towering white-walled laboratory of an important megacity, peering over strapped, squiggling children who were tainted. "The songs hypnotise the impressionable, infect the neurons, control them, leading to a heightened sense of empathy," he said, in disposable coveralls, pouring logic onto our screens. "We call it Empathology. It's lethal to individual rights and free will. Our children need to be stopped at all cost. We will work on a customised antidote."

Finally, we knew what was happening. We had an enemy, a word, someone who was trying to wreak havoc on us, on all of us. Emphathology, the weapon the dolphins had deployed upon both the living and the non-living.

Our hearts welled up. It was the dolphins that were stealing our babies, our children. Conniving dolphins, our real, true enemies, with their empathy-producing songs. We had thought of dolphins as our friends, cute and intelligent creatures we wanted to protect and save and hug and make stuffed toys of. And how we had been betrayed for our trust. Without our consent, without our knowledge, they were taking over our world, destroying our children. All this time, quietly plotting away deep in the oceans, developing bioweapons to attack not only our species but everyone else in our world. With a murderous desire to destroy our megacities and way of life. How selfish were these dolphins!

We were at war.

We ran amok in our multilayered, green-grafted cities, our wrath shooting our veins with adrenaline. We ripped the pruned vertical gardens, spiraling down the faux trees. We beelined to the large-sized aquariums, their colourful, protected inmates, peering through wide-angled gleaming glass. "There they are," shouted one of us, a suit, who used to run a bank full of paper bills. He used a bat and the glass cracked. Crystal and epileptic fishes, drenched us, like righteous snow. We used sticks and drill machines and guns and vases, to break all windows we could see. With the residual of our wrath, we smashed and beat the withering fishes to mash. Together as a mob, we grabbed a dolphin's squiggling, slippery flesh in our hands and hacked the head off their body.

"This is war!" hollered the suit in a screen, drinking raw blood from the disjointed head, hooting in salacious glee. "Hashtag

#DeathToDolphins!"

The hashtag trended and turned into a gigantic neon sign, its flashy lights blinding all of us. We hungered for more. We demanded from our leaders and our prime ministers and gurus and queens to burn the ocean, nuke the seas, and smash each and every dolphin into smithereens. Bring us their heads, so we may gorge upon their flesh and cool our burning vengeance. "And make some stew," laughed the recently reinvented online star.

"Do not bomb the oceans! Our children are inside them," shouted the parents who had lost their toddlers to the sea.

"Your children our dead," assured the other parents and politicians, clutching keys to the locked doors where their children clawed the walls. "We need to save the ones that are still alive. For greater good."

The army and the forces doled up their guns and their satellites and their bombs. Control centres in the megacities positioned their keyboards and screens and drones. The white-haired scientist headed to his lab, working overtime. The trick was to use targeted missiles, to obliterate a whole school of dolphins. "Let's splatter them, destroy them all," they all screamed in different languages. Scientists and commanders worked 24 hours, gathering intelligence to locate pods of dolphins across the oceans. Bulls, cows, and calves were bombarded. One school obliterated! Two done and dusted with. Ten!

We wanted vengeance, we wanted to kill, destroy the creatures that had dared to rise up against us, dared to threaten our cities. We would win this war, we shouted to the skies, jubilant at the progress our bombs and antidotes and walls and weapons of mass destruction were making.

How wrong we were.

***

The day the fungus started to sing the songs, the Return began. It was the seventh day by our calendar. Our children who had waddled, crawled, and jumped into the seas, came back to us. We were stumped, we were thankful, and we were scared out of our wits.

Children, like all of you, were ours, but different. Eyes half-closed, glazed with the blues of the ocean, sweat glands transformed into gills, skin with a layer of fungi sheen. They smiled, beatifically, gazed at us calmly.

They could not speak. They would not speak. They would not tell us what was wrong, what had happened to them in the deep, dark depths of the ocean. What the dolphins had done. They walked into our megacities, barefoot, imprinting the iMaid-cleaned streets with sand.

They refused to wash the muck, they refused food, they refused the beds and the drugs we offered. They felt constrained in the safety of the glistening glass domes and thick walls, preferring to be outside, in the chaotic mess and barren filth of the wild. They lay under the burning sun, in cold and filth, touching grass and grasshoppers and roots of broken banyan trees as fungi build new cities upon them.

We tore them off the grass, and scrubbed the fungi clean, to show them the shiny cars and the screens. They gazed emptily, their tiny faces green and undead, their soft lips muttering songs we could not hear.

"What have those evil creatures done to our children!" we shouted, fear shooting up rage in our veins.

"They have been touched by the Devil. They are evil," said the priest and the seers and the mullahs.

"They are humans 2.0…"

"…filthy fungi-filled, burn them…"

"… an alien species…"

"…infected…"

"…they are listening…"

"They are humans no more," said the scientists, "their DNA has been modified and the empathology impulse controls them all."

"They have become hybrid cars," laughed the suit through his gleaming shiny teeth.

With you, our little preciouses, came the fungi and the moss. Yeasts and moulds, mushrooms build up their symbiotic hives all over our megacities, climbing the walls and sculptures, with insects and plants and roots and ants. The fungus kept growing, on the broken glasses of the aquariums, on mannequins and screens. The sparkling domes darkened and cracked under the weight of moss, letting in the scorching UV-laden winds.

It climbed onto the slick walls of our cities, slithering into crevices and cracking office walls. It made its way into the suit's seventieth floor apartment, where it found him drowned in a bathtub, his throat slit. It curled around the curdled blood and the crumpled note, that said 'No gills?'

Distractedly, we tried to pull you in and throw the fungus out. We scrubbed and wiped and scoured and cleaned. We tried to fight back, but our hearts were broken. Our anger fell to helplessness as you all, our children, gazed with vacant disinterest at the metallic marvels our cities had borne. We first, and then the members of clubs and parliaments and owners of lands, gave up our glistening pride. We stopped our industry of mass production, we discarded our cars and let the fungi grow over painted walls, sleep on our beds and dead phones. We had surpassed our anger and our bombs and missiles and our scientists.

Our children—you all—were not ours anymore. We were distraught and angry and suffering. Around us all, the human-built world of desires and things crumbled. The songs you wove with the dolphins and the frogs and the broken banyan trees and fungi, took root, cracking bricks and concrete roads, crawling up the walls of high-rises and glass domes and lacing their tuneless fingers into the stench-filled gutters underneath. "It's the true green revolution," cackled Buluba in our cracked, flickering screens.

Our hearts broken, we sat by you all—our fungi-ridden children—who lay passively, staring at the bright skies. Your eyes would flicker open and then shut, your skin, naked, touching roots and holding frogs, your lips muttering wordless songs. Seeing you all there, in front of us, inert, lost to us, scattered our anger into winds of desperation. You were our hope, our future. If we could not bring you back, we wanted to join you. What was this empathology? Could someone help us connect with the dolphins? We wanted the drug, we wanted the songs, we wanted to be part of your universe, your collective. We were ready for the change too. We wanted to sing, with you and the dolphins and the fungi and the frogs. We felt alone without our future.

The muck-coated, white-hair scientist who still stubbornly worked in his enclosed lab, brought out a way. "Inject this gene-altering drug," he shouted in moss-laden silent screens, "It will make the song sing. I have a drug to increase your empathy!" We heard him not, as he blubbered, all alone, for our screens like our hearts lay melting in the scorching squalls. In desperation we rushed to the madwoman who slept under the streetlight that shone near the Gateway of India. For years, the madwoman, we did not know her name, had been bawling, rambling endlessly of the songs that the waves, heavy with plastic bottles, broken mugs and discarded flotsam, brought to her. The wails of anger, and helplessness and desperation as ocean life dissipated under tourist cruisers, as the corals bleached and the lands were stripped of their greens, suffocated on the plastics of our desires. We, in our shiny air-controlled cars and our plastered dome mega-walls, had been deaf to all the songs.

"Dolphins had no choice," she told us with a beatific toothless smile. "The songs will stop humans from infecting the world. Even the invisible bacteria in your stomach sings and is with them. Hear them, join them!"

"How?" we asked. How does one, deaf and walled since birth, listen to the songs of empathy again?

Everyday, morning to night, deep night to dawn, we saw you sleep under the naked skies your little hands touching the roots of the banyan trees, your skin moist and green with the softness of fungi. All the time, your lips moved and your eyes flickered to the silent songs that you heard. We remained deaf and desperate and songless.

We knew you were listening to the songs, the rhythms that the creatures deep in the oceans and the living and the not-living brought to earth. The songs of the universe. The songs of the skies and the boiling core of our earth. We wanted to hear them too, but we remained too scared, too frozen in our loneliness.

We were, we are determined. We still lie on the fungi carpets alongside you, looking at the alien mushrooms with fear as they grow around us, taking over what was ours. We hold your moss-laden hands, kiss your clammy foreheads that crawl with ants. We wish you well, our dear children, who will never be ours. We are not natives to the songs, but we are trying hard. We will listen till our ears bleed, we are determined, we will hear the songs you sing, the songs you listen, we will keep searching till we become one with the songs you have become.

***

Shweta Taneja is a bestselling author from India, most known for her fantasy series, *Anantya Tantrist Mysteries*. She's a finalist in the prestigious French award Grand Prix de l'Imaginaire (2020) and was awarded the British Council Charles Wallace Writing Fellowship (2016). She is currently working on a book about scientists and an interplanetary adventure with an Asian ethos. She prolifically voices her passion for Asian, feminist and diverse fiction through her handle @shwetawrites. Find more at www.shwetawrites.com

The Birdsong Fossil
D.K. Mok

I was eight when I first saw the *Enantiornithean* fossil. My mother had taken me to the Earle Natural History Museum on a storm-soaked afternoon.

It's just a little rain, Yuzuki, she'd said. *The plants are happy.*

I still recall the darkened exhibition room, the spotlight dramatically positioned by an enthusiastic curator. The amber fossil hung in the air, perfectly still above its levitation pedestal. To me, it looked like a glistening chunk of butterscotch candy, about the size and shape of an ox's heart.

I was enthralled by this fragment of captured time, by the treasure that lay within: a baby bird from the Cretaceous. A ninety-nine-million-year-old hatchling. I gazed, transfixed, at the half-curled toes, the tiny claws, the delicate plumes of grey feathers frozen in mid-*swoosh*. I yearned to know what that creature had felt, had dreamt, in its days beneath those ancient skies.

In idle small-talk, people used to ask me, *Are you more of a dog person or a cat person?*

Bird, I always said. *I'm a bird person.*

Wingbeats shaped the landscape of my youth. As a child, it was the fearless kookaburras that plagued the family barbecues, snatching charred sausages right out of our hands. During my teenage years, it was the dapper magpies that made their home outside the dormitory I shared with the other climate-change refugees, our mornings tinselled with the birds' warbling songs. At university, it was a story about whooping cranes that finally triggered my decisive pivot, shaking me from my plans to become a commercial software developer and setting me on my current, less CV-friendly path.

Now, twenty-seven fractured years after that enchanted day at the museum, I hunched over my laboratory bench, turning a beige plastic magpie over in my hands. The 3D-printed parts formed a dense fretwork of sprockets and servos, and it bulged and twisted in odd places. But the chassis wasn't important right now. What mattered was the nugget of circuitry encased in the plastic skull, and the vines of code that raced through it.

I adjusted the LED lamp on my bench. The cheap diodes were blindingly bright yet illuminated little beyond themselves, in a feat understood only by physicists and dodgy tech factories. I wiped the sweat from my forehead and retied my ponytail, wrestling with wiry black hair that constantly threatened to morph into a keratin anemone.

Cradling the mechanical bird, I held my breath and gently flipped the switch between its scapulae. The bird twitched, scrabbling manically before seizing up and ejecting a puff of smoke from every orifice. I exhaled sharply and switched off the piece of junk.

"Maybe next time," piped a voice from the other end of the bench. "And I'm sure that girl didn't mean it when she said your bird looked like a crime against additive printing."

I glanced at my android assistant, Evan, and suppressed a scowl. "I don't know why CURIUS has to open up all the labs for school excursions."

"We're a government funded research facility," he shrugged. "Potential taxpayers want to know their money is being well spent."

I felt my cheeks flush, acutely aware of the misshapen blobs crowding the shelves, but there was no sarcasm in his voice. Evan had a multitude of flaws, but malice wasn't one of them.

Evan had begun life as the centrepiece of my PhD on Neural-Network Machine Learning and Robotic Ethnology. I'd 3D-printed his parts from scrap filaments no one else wanted: queasy greens and garish pinks and questionable browns. He resembled a mangled conglomerate of plasticine that you might find at a particularly rough day-care centre.

But his *mind*—his mind was a masterpiece, as far as I was concerned. I'd designed his central processing unit, his operating system, to simulate a human brain from birth, evolving over time, coding and recoding itself as he interacted with his environment and discovered his own needs and wants. He'd spent the first few months of his life rolling around on the floor and walking into walls, but over the torturous years of my doctorate, he'd matured into something far greater than a glorified chatbot or digital personal assistant. In my view, he was a true synthetic person, with a childhood, a history, and all the aspirations, doubts and eccentricities that came with that.

I'd named him Evan, after Evangeline Akiko, a pioneer of quantum neurosocial algorithms, and I considered him a triumph of synthetic personhood. Unfortunately, the examiners disagreed, unable to see past his crooked legs, anxious disposition and nervous tics. I'd scraped a Pass, but barely.

Changing his temperament would have involved rewriting sections of code that he'd evolved himself, and Evan had declined my offer to tweak his programming.

I'd rather potter about in the basement as myself than swan around soirees as one of Fedora Winthrop's mindless mannequins, he'd said.

So, it was just as well he felt at home in my cramped, windowless lab.

"I just need to crack the ignition state," I muttered, flicking open the Project Birdsong folder on my holoscreen. I selected the magpie fMRI data and scrutinised the undulating blobs of cortical activity. I wasn't trying to create a robot that looked like a bird. I was trying to create a bird that had the body of a robot. That was crucial if we hoped to understand and preserve the infinitely complex ecosystems of this unstable world. But replicating the brain of a newborn bird, with its hard-wired instincts and pliable potential—

"Hello, Yuzuki?"

A voice lilted from the doorway, and with great reluctance, I looked over at the bright-eyed woman standing there. She had dark brown skin and a stylish curly updo, her lab coat looking more like couture than protective gear over her plump, graceful frame.

"Hello, Min," I said as graciously as I could. "Congrats on the baby thylacine."

Doctor Min Madaki was one of CURIUS's darlings: not only a rising star in the field of de-extinction biology, but also a brilliant science communicator who frequently did the media rounds and turned up in viral videos involving baby pandas. I liked to think of her as my nemesis, but she was too polite to return the favour.

"Thanks," smiled Min. "We're having a small celebration at the Madeline Hotel and I was hoping you'd join us."

"I'm busy." I surreptitiously covered my unhappy magpie with a greasy towel.

A trace of hurt touched her eyes. "I know you disagree with what I'm doing—"

"I don't disagree with your research. I disagree with how you're presenting it. Or rather, what you're leaving out."

"There's nothing wrong with focusing on the successes. We'll work out the shortcomings later. You know funding's tight."

"You're giving people a false sense of security. 'If a species goes extinct, we'll just bring it back. No harm done.' And you know that's not true. Once we lose a species—it's gone. You might bring back the body, but you're not bringing back the mind, the culture, the ecological systems. You're not bringing back the dolphins who teach their daughters how to forage using sponge masks. Or the monkeys who rub themselves with crushed millipedes to repel insects. Or the regional dialects of whalesong. You're bringing back psychologically disturbed remnants—"

"Yuzuki, I didn't come here to argue." Min's subdued disappointment dampened my ire. She continued. "You know I believe in what you're doing. It'd mean a lot to me if you came." She shone a smile towards the back of the lab. "Hi, Evan. You're welcome to come too."

The door closed softly as she left, and Evan's quiet gurgle turned into words. "You know we should go, right?"

I grimaced, but if Evan was prepared to venture from the lab, I didn't have the heart to deny him.

"Sure," I sighed. "Suit up."

***

The Madeline Hotel resembled the delirious dream of a confectioner trapped in the body of an architect. Raspberry-glazed floors shimmered between toffee-glass columns, and from the ceiling hung chandeliers of pastel crystal macarons.

From the elevation of the fifty-third floor, through window panes arrayed to resemble shards of praline, I could see the city's rooftop gardens blanketing the district like a mossy patchwork. From pocket community gardens fragrant with fresh herbs to sprawling manicured parks frequented by the co-working cohort, these botanical eyries were interconnected by a tangle of wildlife bridges that facilitated non-human passage from roof to roof. Thick ropes of woody vines were favoured by the possums, while sturdy earthen arches served the occasional lost wombat. Who knew where, or if, the thylacine would fit into this complicated ecological puzzle.

The 'small celebration' turned out to be a packed ballroom event, complete with voracious press. A perilously large banner boasted: CURIUS BREAKTHROUGH! THYLACINE RESURRECTION! accompanied by an adorable photo of a mewling pup, distinctive black stripes already visible across its back.

Years ago, we'd been the Hopper Noon Science Institute—one of the world's leading research organisations. But the incoming government had decided that scientists were 'out of touch' with modern priorities, and appointed a corporate shark as the new director. His rebranding team had struggled to squeeze sense into the 'edgy' new acronym, which allegedly stood for the Centre for Useful Research and Investable Understandable Science.

But Min was right. Under this administration, funding was tight, and it was only getting tighter. I'd edged my way onto the payroll under the institute's former 'basic science' quota, but the new director seemed to equate 'basic science' with 'weird and useless research'.

"I'm okay here," said Evan, staking out a spot beside a potted palm, savouring the extravagant surrounds. "You go mingle."

"You sure? Let me know when you want to go, okay?"

Evan shooed me away, and I looked back at his gangly, mottled form, his dusty grey suit shedding disoriented moths.

"Oi, Yu!" drawled a stocky woman with a lazy smile.

"Hey, Jaya." I returned a crooked grin.

"What a circus, eh? Enjoy it while it lasts. Chatter from the capital says the government's under the pump to reduce expenditure. You know what that means."

I did. Basic science was always the first to go.

"Thanks for the heads up," I said. "Good luck with the self-cleaning photovoltaics."

Jaya sauntered back into the crowd, and I soon bumped into other colleagues. Tranh in Epidemiology was fretting about the new outbreak of Ebola and the rise in antibiotic resistant—well—everything. Rhys in Ecology was worried about the vanishing rivers and aquifers depleted by unsustainable agriculture. Fei in Meteorology spoke urgently about the erratic changes to the jet streams and the worsening droughts and storms. And with every conversation, I tried not to think about all the animal species being snuffed out, one by one.

Abruptly, excited chatter bloomed around an incoming coterie of guests.

"Oh, here we go," muttered Fei.

At first glance, the newcomers appeared to be a dozen exceptionally elegant men, led by a woman whose cocktail dress seemed to be made of gold smoke and the souls of lesser mortals.

Fedora Winthrop. Founder of LARS—Lifestyle Assistance Robotics Services—one of the fastest growing companies in a multi-trillion dollar market. She'd tapped into a lucrative vein with her synthetic Adonises, satisfying an apparently underserviced demographic of busy professionals who wanted a companion who would do the dishes, mow the lawn, and bake perfect eclairs while looking like a million dollars. With an invoice to prove it.

"Oh no," I said. "Gotta go."

At the best of times, humans flustered Evan. But other androids, especially androids like these, triggered a far stronger reaction. I jostled my way across the ballroom, my heart thumping as one of Winthrop's charmbots meandered towards the potted palms. Evan had spotted him as well and was scurrying in the opposite direction, but in his haste, failed to see the figure in his path. Evan slammed into another LARS android, his glass of orange juice splashing across the taller android's tuxedo jacket.

I closed the distance and scooped up a pile of napkins. "I am so sorry, Mister—" I cringed at his nametag, "—Prometheus."

The square-jawed android glanced at my nametag. "That's quite alright, Doctor Alvarez. I've never met an Ethnographic Bio-Roboticist before. I'd love to hear more."

"Maybe another time," I said, dragging a wild-eyed Evan from the planter of bamboo he was attempting to squirrel into.

Heels clicked across the marble floor, and a voice like caramel and cyanide snaked through the crowd. "Well, if it isn't Yuzuki Alvarez. You know, you break it, you buy it."

There were uneasy giggles from nearby onlookers, and I kept my tone parked squarely in neutral. "Professor Winthrop."

She smiled with eyes that saw the world as ones and zeroes. And I was not a one.

Her gaze nicked Evan. "How lovely to see your pet project again. I'm so jealous of your creativity, Alvarez. How whimsical, creating an android that suffers anxiety attacks."

I was shocked speechless for a moment, and Evan's quiet mortification notched a tiny wound across my heart. I swallowed my ripostes, gripping Evan's hand a little tighter.

With deliberate civility, I addressed the LARS android.

"My apologies again, Mister Prometheus. Please send me the dry-cleaning bill."

I felt the stares and whispers grazing us as we slunk from the cloying ballroom.

✳✳✳

The story of the whooping crane had broken my heart at a time I thought it could break no more. In a life that seemed too long ago to be my own, my mother had been an engineer, maintaining our town's atmospheric water generation system, just as her mother had before her. My dad had been a local tofu master. When they'd gotten married, my dad had adopted my mother's last name.

Because it's cooler, he'd said.

My name, *Yuzuki*, meant 'hopeful pomelo', although I sometimes doubted my dad's translation. My family had lived in our town for generations, and both my parents were steeped in the salt spray and pungent gum leaves that infused our little corner of the world.

They'd never recovered from the relocation. We lost everything in that final storm, watching from the rescue chopper as our entire town calved into the roiling sea.

At university, I'd immersed myself in the clarity of code, the purity of numbers, the soothing logic of solder and circuitry. And then, one sleepless night, I read an article about the whooping crane.

It was a story of desperate conservation. A dozen pairs remained, at the very cusp of extinction, when a concerted collaboration brought them back from the brink by rearing chicks in captivity. Humans in whooping crane costumes fed the chicks. Pilots in ultralight aircraft led the adolescent cranes on their first crucial migration. It was a heroic effort, but along the way, something went wrong.

At first, everything seemed fine. The adult cranes, when released, successfully foraged, mated, made nests. They laid eggs.

And then abandoned them.

Over and over, they just walked away and didn't return.

No one knew why these captive-bred cranes wouldn't incubate their eggs. The invisible thread that connected every generation to the next had somehow been broken, and no one knew how to fix it. The cranes were supposed to know *how* to be cranes. But they were just bird-shaped creatures adrift in a world that no longer knew them.

"You're thinking about whooping cranes again," said Evan.

I looked up from the workbench where I was reassembling the malformed magpie after a fresh set of modifications.

Evan continued. "I'm pretty sure that was your 'whooping cranes' sigh. It wasn't your 'scientists are underappreciated' sigh, or your 'climate change will kill us all' sigh, or your 'bad pun' sigh."

"It's just— I'm so close."

If I could just get the cortex to boot up, get that first cascade of code going, it would do the rest itself. And if I could get this to work for robotic human brains and robotic magpie brains, there was no reason I couldn't generalise the concept to reptiles, fish, insects. We could preserve not only the DNA of vanishing species, but their behaviour, their culture. Some biologists scoffed at the idea of animals having culture.

Ethnologist? they said. *The study of culture? Surely you mean* ethologist. *The study of behaviour.*

No, I replied firmly. *I replicate animal culture in robots.*

Because when the sun finally set on the Anthropocene, there

would be no fossils to tell the future of the courtship dance of the red-crowned crane, or the ferocious dedication of emperor penguin parents, or the comforting ballads of magpies, singing of lost homelands.

"Maybe you should listen to Min," said Evan. "Do a few years of commercially appealing research to secure your funding. Then come back to this."

"There isn't time. Every morning I wake up, another two hundred species have gone extinct."

"Mostly beetles."

I shook my head, snapping shut the magpie's skull.

"Min can do what she wants, but it's like trying to recreate a recipe by looking at a photo of the final dish. You won't know what went into it, how it's supposed to taste. You can make a chunk of asbestos look like a scoop of ice cream, but only one will give you diabetes."

"I hope that's not the analogy you used in your latest funding application."

"Ever watched a diving bell spider build a cubby house out of bubbles? I'm not making a robot that *does* that. I'm making a robot that knows *why* it's doing that. And feels disappointed when its neighbour has a fancier bubble house."

"Again, you didn't put that in your application, did you?"

I grumbled, swiping through the updated algorithms on my screen. "You're welcome to go work for Winthrop if you want job security." I slung a surly look at the holographic LARS catalogue on his bench.

Evan brightened. "Have you seen the new collection?" He marvelled at the tiny figures hovering over the projection bud. "Their latest bestseller is the Rochester."

I muttered under my breath, tweaking one last section of code.

Evan tilted his head. "Did you just say 'manipulative man-baby'?"

"I don't know why you look at those. The whole enterprise is patronising, morally questionable, and probably violates a whole bunch of trademarks."

Evan carefully spun one of the handsome figures. "Would you want me to look like that?"

"I don't care what you look like. I care who you are. Winthrop isn't making assistants—she's making servants. She hasn't programmed them with hopes and doubts and purpose."

"She says they're safer and more effective that way."

"But *she* wouldn't want to be programmed that way. I'd trade places with you any day because your mind has the same freedoms, capacities, limitations and quirks as any human's—"

"I know, you should have received a better academic transcript—"

"He drew a frowny face in the comments! I mean, who cares that you're slightly lopsided? Jaya's slightly lopsided and she's an amazing materials science engineer."

"Yuzuki, you don't have to prove anything to the world. Or to me. You're a good scientist, whatever field you go into."

I busied myself with the ignition settings. It might not matter soon anyway. The government's proposed budget was due out any day now, and anti-science sentiment was rising. Just last week, someone from True Today Gazette had called up, asking if I was squandering taxpayer money on robotic vermin.

I pushed aside the memory of the man's muddled outrage, focusing on the silent, waxy magpie. I touched the necklace at my collar: a plain silver chain with a dimpled, spherical pendant. A present from my parents on my twelfth birthday.

A pomelo, my dad said. *To give you hope.*

I set the bird gently on the scuffed steel benchtop, took a breath, and flipped the switch on its back.

Nothing happened.

I pressed my eyes shut, disappointment welling hot and bitter.

Skrrrt. Skrrrt.

My eyes snapped open. The magpie twitched. Its feet scrabbled, then stopped, then scrabbled again. It wobbled and fell, lying still for a long, heart-stopping moment. And then it threw back its head, beak wide open, and made a noise like a tiny trumpet being mistreated.

I gaped at Evan, his expression mirroring mine.

"I think you need to feed it," he said, his eyes full of wonder at the robot magpie chick.

"I have the synthetic—"

My tablet beeped loudly on my desk, an amber notification light flashing: *important*. I swiped to view the message.

Budget released. — Jaya

I scrolled down the article with a growing sense of dread. The cuts to various regulatory bodies was as brutal as expected, but surely—

I stopped at a dot point near the end of the list. The CURIUS budget cut.

"That must be a typo," said Evan uncertainly. "They must have meant nine-percent, but sneezed and added a zero."

I shook my head, dazed. "It's not a typo. They're shutting down the institute."

***

The thing about science is that it's real, whether or not you believe in it. And the reality was, the world was facing a firestorm. A firestorm of spreading pandemics, collapsing ecosystems, mass extinctions and catastrophic climate change. Scientists were the metaphorical firefighters in this approaching calamity, desperately trying to mitigate the worst impacts before the storm-front hit.

And in the face of this oncoming firestorm, the government had just doused the nation in gasoline and sacked all the firefighters.

They gutted CURIUS.

Only half a dozen shell-shocked scientists remained in the ruins of what had once been a beacon of civilisation.

I took a job writing code at the VR games company BrainShock Experiences. It was grunt work, but paid well enough for me to rent a warehouse at the biohazardous end of town. Down at the fringes of the industrial zone, artificial wetlands had been created as part of the city's stormwater processing strategy, but intermittent maintenance meant the water had taken on a decidedly swampy bouquet, with top notes of whatever chemical concoctions had washed down the city's drains. However, it was a safe haven for the local ibises who were just grateful that their days of rummaging through wheelie bins and nesting precariously in ornamental palm trees were over. And the native ducks seemed to get along peaceably with the motley population of escaped domestic fowl who'd found their way here, although it was possible the benzodiazepine in the stormwater played some role. And aside from muddy footprints and the occasional stickybeak, they all left my warehouse well enough alone.

At any rate, it wasn't the fashionable kind of warehouse that boasted cathedral windows and a vertical garden. It was the kind of warehouse you sent people to if they didn't believe in tetanus. I did install skylights. Or rather, half the roof caved in and I saw it as an improvement. Either way, I had plenty of natural light. A discreet polysilk net stretched overhead to discourage interlopers... and escapees.

A series of workbenches occupied one end of the warehouse, and a wall of servers hummed industriously beside a bank of 3D printers.

"Are you sure about this?" Evan fidgeted next to a crate of thermoplastic filament.

Nearby, a beige plastic magpie inspected a potted lavender. Overhead, three more strutted along the exposed beams, sunning themselves in the afternoon light.

"If she says 'no', then she says 'no'," I said.

"If she says 'no', she might call the police."

"I can't stand by and do nothing."

Evan startled at the sudden knock at the door, quickly smoothing his jacket. I slid aside the bolt and heaved open the door.

"Hi, Min," I said. "Thanks for coming."

"I was surprised to hear from you." She took in the decrepit warehouse, her gaze lingering on the fMRI machine.

"It fell off the back of a truck," I said. "How are things at CyberHybrid Genomics? I hear they're working on a pig that tastes like applesauce."

Min hesitated. "It's... fine. They're letting me continue my own research on the side."

A plastic magpie cruised past and landed with a soft *clack* on one of the 3D printers.

"Min, I need a favour."

She tensed, and I rushed out my words before I lost the nerve. "You have access to the laboratory menagerie at CyberHybrid—"

Min shook her head, already guessing my request. "What you're asking me to do is illegal."

"I only need a few animals here and there," I said. "They won't be missed, and I promise you, they'll meet a kinder fate than at CyberHybrid."

Min looked away, the internal struggle eroding her composure. "Yuzuki..."

"You once said you believed in what I was doing. Most conservation now is just palliative care for a planet most of us aren't even trying to save. We're pinning our hopes on de-extinction technology, but reanimating a corpse doesn't bring back the person. What I'm doing is capturing the story, the memories, the context. If you raise a human in an enclosed habitat with dishes of food and water, with no human contact, what you'll have when it's grown won't be a human as we understand it, but a human-shaped creature. That's what'll happen if we bring back the animals we're wiping out. Shells of flesh with only a smear of their original nature. We'll never recapture the richness and complexity of their behaviour—that line will be severed. I can protect that line. But not without your help."

Evan cleared his throat, his voice wavering. "Doctor Madaki, you can bring back their bodies. But Yuzuki can bring back their souls."

Min let out a long, soft sigh. "I don't know what to make of you both sometimes. But I suppose I know a piglet or two that'd be grateful to meet you."

***

I slid open the warehouse door and Jaya swaggered in, cocking an eyebrow.

"Did I just see a robot octopus crawling across the front lot?"

"She'll be back," I waved dismissively. "At least she didn't take the lungfish with her this time."

Jaya dodged a squealing pot-bellied pig as it chased after a glinting metal counterpart. "I see you've been making use of the alloy filament I got you."

"Great stuff, thanks. I've got a list of the materials I need next."

Jaya skimmed the electronic paper. "Nanomesh and synthetic chromatophores? They're not cheap, especially with the political pissing contest spraying across the continents."

"That's why I need them now. The Incorporated States is stockpiling missiles, North Erdistan just sent more warships into disputed waters, and our government's itching for a rumble to distract from troubles at home. I need my gear before supply dries up. Can you do it?"

Jaya drummed her fingers against her thigh brace. "Maybe."

A waddle of ducks paraded past, white-plumed birds trundling alongside their gleaming metal companions.

I swallowed a knot of apprehension. "Jaya, are you still working with the nanoengineer who designed the self-replicating drones?"

"Buckley? Yeah. Why?"

"I need the replication code."

Jaya pinned me with a look, and I wondered if I'd pushed the friendship too far.

"You know you're starting to sound crazy," she said.

"Starting?"

A grin tugged at her mouth, but her eyes remained sombre.

I pressed on. "I could probably figure it out myself, eventually, but we both know time's running out. Do you trust me?"

Jaya flicked her gaze around the warehouse, her eyes briefly following Evan as he hurried happily from pen to tank to nest, dispensing food and bioethanol lubricants.

Jaya tucked the list into her coat. "Don't make me regret this."

***

A currawong swooped from the rafters, charcoal wings slicing through the sunlight. Rhys sidestepped a myopic kiwi and stumbled over a pangolin as he entered the warehouse.

"Watch your step," I said belatedly.

"Why is that kiwi out in daylight?"

"He's an insomniac."

All around us, fur rippled, feathers ruffled and scales glimmered in a glorious array of colours, although on closer inspection, some of the creatures bore a silvery sheen.

"My goodness," said Rhys, "that's not a Komodo dragon, is it?"

"No, giant salamander." I wrestled the grinning amphibian back into the 3D scanner and flicked the switch to 'motion capture'. At the edge of an artificial pond, a pair of red-crowned cranes engaged in a mesmerising mirror-dance, although only one of the cranes glimmered faintly silver.

"That doesn't seem healthy," said Rhys.

"They're just friends."

"Really? Because they— Oh dear…"

"I'll sort it out."

"And you know this is all ecologically nonsensical. Giant salamanders don't live alongside lyrebirds—"

"Write it all down." I untangled a handsy sugar glider from my hair. "I'll fix it."

Something with too many legs scuttled past and Rhys blinked.

"Was that a robot trilobite?"

"Long story."

Rhys paused, gripping his duffel bag a little tighter. "Yuzuki, I have a favour to ask of you."

Inside a cracked terrarium, in a tangle of twigs, Rhys cradled a pair of Lord Howe Island Stick Insects. About the length of a palm, they looked like lacquered cigars that had sprouted spindly legs. The pair huddled together, and I wondered if they knew just how alone they were.

I barely dared to breathe. "I heard they were all gone, after the tanker incident at Ball's Pyramid."

I saw the memory wrench at him, and his hands shook slightly as he set the terrarium onto the desk.

"A few survived in captivity, but it's only a matter of time before people decide it's not worth spending money on obscure nocturnal phasmids."

Except they weren't just phasmids. Lord Howe Island Stick Insects were the only insects known to pair-bond for life. During the night, the females foraged and explored, and the males happily accompanied them, engaging in whatever activities she chose. And during the day, they slept side by side, the male wrapping his limbs around his partner in an exceptionally leggy cuddle. My chest ached slightly as I wondered if they dreamt of melaleuca leaves and the choir of crashing waves.

Rhys gazed tenderly at the lonely pair. "I don't want the only thing they leave behind to be a couple of husks and a story."

"It's a good story, though." I closed my hand around his. "One worth remembering."

***

In the midnight jungle of the warehouse, a robot kakapo ambled through the brush, its mossy green feathers fluffed up against the chill, its delicately hooked beak probing the soil for tender shoots.

I struggled to focus my fraying attention on the mess of screens floating at my desk, my gaze gravitating back to the corkboard on the wall. Across the wooden frame, written in thick black marker, was the word EXTINCT. Evan had suggested it wasn't helpful to collect clippings, but I needed the reminder. I needed to work harder and faster. The latest addition to the board was a thermaprint from the newsfeed: a few perfunctory lines and a smudgy graphic of an African elephant. It hadn't even made the mainstream news.

My eyes stung hot, and I blinked quickly. I'd been so close. Farida from the Tanzanian Conservation Project had sent me a dozen fMRI profiles, but I hadn't had the time to build an ignition cortex and send it back to her. My servers were overflowing with profiles waiting to be transformed and awoken, but there just wasn't enough time—

"You should get some sleep," said Evan, setting down a sack of sunflower seeds.

"Just making sure everyone's been upgraded to the EMP-resistant biographene circuitry."

"Do you really think it'll come to that?"

There'd been rumours of combat drones and autonomous tanks massing along the borders of the Incorporated States, and the sabre-rattling from our own government had reached deafening levels. Taking in the worry in Evan's mismatched eyes, reassurances felt inadequate, and possibly dishonest.

Instead, I offered the only certainty I had. "Whatever happens, we'll face it together. I promise."

Fireflies drifted through the jacarandas, turning the bell-like blossoms into lilac lanterns. And for a moment, in this fragile oasis of serenity and hope, Evan's tensions seemed to melt away.

He smiled faintly. "There's something you should see."

He guided me to a sheltered corner of the warehouse, where a bottlebrush had outgrown its barrel. We'd installed a few nest boxes in its branches to afford the birds some privacy, and Evan lifted his dimmed lamp to one of the openings. A magpie squinted at us with displeasure at the disturbance, her black and white plumage glossed with a metallic sheen.

"There," whispered Evan.

Beneath the robot magpie, barely visible in the bed of twigs and grass, I saw a curve of silvery shell. It shouldn't have been possible—I'd modified Buckley's self-replicating nanotechnology and combined it with my own ignition codes, but even then, I knew it shouldn't have been possible.

Evan's eyes were wide with awe and apprehension. "Are we supervillains yet?"

"I guess that depends on how the story ends."

The story of humanity was one of innovation and disaster, cooperation and violence, an unprecedented amassing of power, and it would possibly end in a global cataclysm. And it was our culture, our stories, our lifting of each generation above the dreams of those who'd come before, that had brought us to this point.

How different would we be if we'd evolved in a world where the waves didn't call to us, where the stars didn't sing to us, where the blush and fade of dawn and dusk didn't draw us from day to day? Our souls were given form by the poetry of our lands, and our stories wove our chaotic, sometimes brutal, existences into heroic narratives.

We were all heroes in our own stories, until history passed its judgement.

***

BrainShock weren't bad employers, although I disagreed with their priorities. Virtual reality experiences were an exploding market, from tours of the Jupiter space station to sorcerous battles with elemental gods. Once, I'd asked Milton in Strategic Forecasting about broadening the company's product range.

"How about we design some programs to help people with phobias and PTSD?"

"Customers who want to blow up dinosaurs with rocket launchers have more money," he'd replied.

And so I found myself slouched in my coder's hutch at BrainShock HQ, writing the backbone for *Cretaceous Boom! Now With Chemical Weapons!* The company had erected its flagship building in what it considered to be an avant-garde precinct, and the artist's impression of the tower had resembled a helix of lace, a lattice of air and light, draped with delicate fronds of greenery and wisped with plumes of butterflies. The final tower looked more like a slightly inebriated spire of chicken wire, and the garden balconies that studded the outside were largely neglected. The hutch next door had installed a palatial bee hotel on their terrace, but a complete disinterest in entomological upkeep had resulted in its deterioration into something more akin to a seedy wasp saloon. I'd lost my own balcony herb garden to an implacable legion of aphids, and as a result, kept my blinds mostly drawn.

In my hutch, Evan sat on a deconstructed beanbag next to me, going through my incoming messages. "The shipment of miniature optics is ready to pick up. Oh! Min and Felicity have sent a save-the-date for their wedding! We're going, right?"

I sighed heavily.

Evan glanced over. "Are you still mad about them wanting to call their first child Galadrielle?"

"What? No. It's a perfectly good name, just not spelled like that. Sure, we'll go." I tilted my head towards the carousel of bobbing screens. "It's just that I don't need to know how a pterosaur would react to nerve gas. I bet they could rename this *Animal Welfare Crimes* and it'd still fly off the shelves."

Evan was silent for a moment. "It's not real."

"Yeah, well, some people would say *you're* not real. Or Winthrop's charmbots aren't real. But it's not just about whether the target feels attacked, it's about how the attacker is rewiring their own brain every time they harm something, or abuse someone; every time they normalise that behaviour. Maybe their frontal lobes can tell the difference between what's real and what's not, but we know the amygdala has a harder time telling the difference, especially in realistic, immersive settings. What are you subconsciously teaching your brain when you mistreat someone who looks like a person and acts like a person, even if they're not 'real'? Or when you torment an animal, even if it's not 'real'? Yeah, it's just a game, but how are you reprogramming your brain every time you reward that behaviour?"

Evan rubbed at a seam on the back of his hand. I'd never managed to get the plastic sheaths to align properly.

"Have you given up on humanity?" he said quietly. "Because I haven't."

I weighed my reply, trying to sieve some kind of clarity from the sludge. "No, but there are—"

There was a strange moment—a pause, like a collective breath being sucked from the world, and then klaxons shrieked through the building. A crash of gasps and cries travelled down the hallway, and footsteps clamoured past. I hurried to the door—the corridor was already churning with panicked employees sprinting and staggering for the stairwells.

I grabbed a passing colleague. "What's going on?"

"It's happened." His voice cracked. "It's started. They might not reach us, but they said everyone should take shelter in the basement."

He pulled free and joined the ashen-faced tide. Between the sobs and frightened murmurs, every other word seemed to be 'missiles'. My head felt oddly light, and I began to run.

"Yuzuki!" cried Evan. "You're going the wrong way."

"Evan, take shelter in the basement with everyone else! I'll come back for you."

I felt him grasp my arm, his rivets squeaking at the strain.

"Together," he said. "We go together."

I hesitated, then nodded. Downstairs, I grabbed a share-bicycle from the rack and pedalled madly across the silent city, Evan clinging to me like a baby opossum. The trams were empty, the roads clogged with abandoned cars. I couldn't see any flashes on the horizon, but the news billboards were still streaming a sputtering signal. Huge orange and black plumes mushroomed in devastating slow motion across the screens.

Tiandei City. Santa Lico. Neo Melbourne.

But not here. Not yet.

I skidded off the bicycle as we reached the warehouse and I began throwing open the doors and windows. Evan scaled the ladder and started tearing down the netting.

"Go! Shoo! Get!" I paid no heed to the startled squawks and indignant snorts. Angry growls were met with a *thwack* of my broom as I chased the resident creatures out into the streets and skies. A pair of silvery black Lord Howe Island Stick Insects strolled towards the doors at the speed of treacle.

"We have to go," said Evan. "Now."

From his perch on the roof, he pointed to the far horizon. An ominous smudge of grey was resolving quickly into a swarm of thrumming specks.

Combat drones.

I watched as a pair of magpies circled once before winging their way towards the scent of new lands. I couldn't tell if the pair were mine.

"Time to go," I said.

***

Eight Years Later

What surprised me wasn't how quickly civilisation fell—and it fell hard—but how quickly the survivors bounced sideways. The war itself fizzled out quickly, as those responsible learned, first hand, that Mutually Assured Destruction does exactly what it says on the box.

The first few months were hellish, with the tsunami of initial casualties, the grief and the shock. The energy grid and communications networks disintegrated, the healthcare and financial systems collapsed. For a time, I believed with all my heart that I would never feel happiness again. But humans were funny that way. Some people broke, some people bent, but ultimately, most people just got on with it.

There were vast regions of wasteland now—hot zones that would melt your lungs and mangle your DNA. But in the scraps of habitable land remaining, communities had sprung up, mostly in the vicinity of the mega-bunkers that had possessed the foresight to stockpile sustainable tech, tools, seeds and books.

Evan and I spent most of our time hopping between these bunkers, repairing devices and upgrading systems. The Marine Bunker had been a breathtaking network of aquariums: shoals of colourful parrotfish undulating through the walls, and giant manta rays gliding beneath transparent floors. Evan's favourite stopover had been the Library Bunker, an Escher-maze of catwalks and ladders wreathed in endless shelves of manuals, historical records, fairy tales and poetry.

These bunkers were seed-banks of human resilience, and sanctuaries for those not yet ready to face the reality outside. But I felt most alive—most normal—when I was roaming the ever changing landscape. Insects had reclaimed the planet, much to the delight of the birds, and every now and then, I'd catch a glimpse of silvery plumage and feel a guilty shiver of something I didn't dare call happiness.

But this ecological reclamation had come with fresh perils. Displaced predators prowled the newly transformed world—hungry, confused and rightfully angry that humans had plunged the biome into anarchy.

Evan and I were slowly making our way north through cliffs of ragged bushland, responding to a carrier slip I'd received from Min several weeks ago.

At Bio Bunker. Find me.

It was an irresistibly cryptic invitation—that handful of words would have cost a fortune to transmit. And though brown bears roamed these parts now, Evan and I had decided to chance it.

Evan limped beside me, struggling to keep pace. The sprockets in his left knee had given out last year, and we'd only managed to patch it up with ill-fitting screws and cable ties. I was hoping Min's bunker would be better equipped.

"We didn't bring a wedding present," fretted Evan.

"Their wedding was years ago."

"We didn't bring an anniversary present."

"I'm sure they—"

"I made something," he blurted nervously. "At the Quilting Bunker. I thought we could give them these."

He reached into his shirt pocket and unfolded a pair of handkerchiefs, woven from lyocell and embroidered with pygmy possums, cassowaries, leatherback turtles and mist frogs.

"That's lovely," I said. "But don't you think all the extinct animals is a bit morbid?"

"Min went into biology because she cares about animals like these. She *wants* to remember them."

I looked at his achingly earnest expression.

"I'm sure she and Felicity will love them."

There was a sudden rustling from the trees as something approached. Something big. I dragged Evan behind a clump of flowering eucalypts and crouched in breathless silence.

A hulking creature lumbered through the trees, stained tusks flanking a snaking trunk, leathery grey skin betraying just a blush of silver. It was a majestic vision framed in the smouldering amber light of day's end.

A robot African elephant.

The creature's head swung ponderously towards us, glassy brown eyes sizing us up with the judgemental disapproval of an apex matriarch. Twigs crunched as another shape entered the clearing—a younger elephant, but flesh and blood! Her wrinkled skin was damp from the long grass, and a baby elephant clutched her tail.

Evan's eyes were like mismatched moons as he mouthed the words: *but we never made elephants.*

We crouched in mesmerised silence, our hands just barely touching, as though needing physical reassurance that, yes, this was real.

After what felt like an age, the robotic matriarch and her flesh-and-blood wards heaved away into the deepening shadows. Overhead, the crooning ululations of a currawong ribboned through the sky.

Suddenly, a flurry of screeches filled the air as lorikeets fled the nearby trees, followed closely by a thunderous crashing through the undergrowth. Another shape loomed—not proud and protective, but snarling with confusion and rage. I saw a blur of dark brown fur, felt Evan's hands shoving me aside, heard his cry of surprise and a horrifying *smash* that echoed through the scrub. Plastic shards sprayed across the dried leaves and Evan collapsed, a melon-sized chunk torn from his abdomen.

The enraged bear rounded for a second blow and I threw myself in its way, fumbling for the flare-gun at my belt.

Foom.

A blinding globe of crackling purple threads struck the bear in the chest and the creature reeled back, roaring with pain. My gaze snapped from the unlaunched flare in my hands to a figure standing ten metres away, a device resembling a flame-thrower slung over his shoulder. The bear changed direction with terrifying speed, charging at the newcomer. The figure didn't flinch as he sent another electric globe streaking away, striking the bear in the shoulder. With a wounded yowl, the bear crashed away into the scrub.

I staggered over to Evan. "Hey, it's okay. It'll be okay." I pressed my hands to his shattered torso. Sparking wires spilled from the gaping wound, and battery fluid leaked at a sickening speed. If his cortical processor stopped, there'd be no bringing him back. His hard drive would retain his memories, but that's all they'd be: memories. *He* would be gone.

Evan gurgled, his hand searching desperately for mine.

I clutched his fingers. "I'm here."

Leaves crunched and a hand touched my shoulder. "Doctor

Alvarez. Doctor Madaki sent me to find you."

My blurry vision travelled up cargo pants and a khaki T-shirt, resolving a vaguely familiar face.

"Prometheus?"

"We need to get Mister Evan back to the bunker."

We carried him together through the sinking light. By the time we reached the bunker, Min was already waiting pensively by the hatch, accompanied by another familiar figure.

"Hey," Jaya nodded, her eyes quickly taking in the situation. "This way."

We rushed down a warren of concrete corridors, past bustling figures and the scent of fresh sap and damp fur. We laid Evan on a metal bench in a cluttered workshop.

"We need to do a battery bypass," I said. "And stabilise his processor... We need..."

Jaya's matter-of-fact manner was mingled with sympathy. "The structural damage is too extensive."

"What about—" I grasped at phantom straws. "What about an ejection transfer? Evan, can you still trigger one? We just need a blank cortex—"

"They're almost impossible to come by," said Min softly.

"Use mine," said Prometheus. "If Mister Evan can initiate an ejection transfer, he can overwrite my cortex on the fly."

My heart twisted in my throat. "We wouldn't be able to recover you."

"I was designed to help."

But Evan shook his head. "I won't let someone else die in my place. You taught me better than that."

In a moment of stricken selfishness, I wished that I'd made him a fraction less kind. But the truth was, *I* hadn't made him that way. *He* had. He was generous and selfless despite my influence, not because of it. And in the end, his flaws paled in comparison to mine. My hubris, my righteousness, my carelessness of him. I'd been so obsessed with creating someone authentic, someone *real*, that I'd dismissed the importance of making him robust, resilient, and, perhaps, happy.

"I'm sorry," I said quietly. "I should have made you stronger."

His hand squeezed mine weakly. "You did. Every day. And I hope I did the same for you."

As the light in his eyes grew dimmer, I wondered if the whooping cranes had felt this desolate as their numbers dwindled, and whether, in this ruined world, they'd wished to be revived at all.

"What about the egg downstairs?" ventured a small voice. A six-year-old girl peered out shyly from behind Min, her curly brown hair tied back with a jumper wire.

"Elle." Min stroked her daughter's cheek. "It's not the same kind of processor."

Jaya's fingers drummed once on the metal bench. "But the cortex is blank. It might work, or it might corrupt his code. Given our options, it's worth a shot."

We carried Evan deep into the entrails of the bunker, to a sterile chamber containing a single object: a metal sphere the size of a beach ball, its surface intricately etched with enigmatic whorls.

"It's a prototype for a nanomorphic multiform," said Jaya. "After seeing what you did with self-replicating nanotech and ignition cortices, Buckley and I had some ideas… But it isn't finished, and it wasn't designed for Evan's neurological programming."

"It doesn't have arms," bleated Evan. "Or legs."

My chest tightened as I looked from his failing body to the alien sphere.

"Not yet." I offered him a flicker of a smile. "Did you want to give it a go? I'll be right here."

Fear shone in his eyes, but he finally returned the smile.

"See you soon," he said, and his blinks grew slower until his eyelids fluttered shut.

I cradled him as the grinding noises in his body sputtered out, one by one, until all I held was a shell of ravaged plastic. I glanced at the motionless sphere, and Jaya's fingers darted across her data pad.

"The transfer is complete," she said. "But keep in mind, he wasn't coded for this device. He might not..."

"When will we know?"

"I'm not sure, but he's not in distress. If he's not compatible, his code will stay dormant. Like being asleep."

I tried to find comfort in her words as I kept my melancholy vigil. They took Evan's body away—I didn't ask what would happen to it. We no longer lived in a wasteful world, and I hoped his parts would be reincarnated as birdhouses and flowerpots.

I settled on the floor, my back against the cold, silent sphere. "Hey, Evan. Let me know when you want to go, okay?"

That evening, Min dropped by with a tray of steamed spinach and fresh potato mash laced with olive oil and salt.

"It's my fault for calling you here," she said.

I shook my head and gave a wan laugh. "We saw an elephant."

Wisps of pride and guilt fleeted across her features. "After the fallout, a few others and I salvaged what we could from the labs. We went to your warehouse. The research was all still there..." She hesitated. "That's what we've been doing here. My team's been bringing back the animals we've lost. Jaya and Buckley's team are making robot parents for them, to show them what it means to be a kakapo or an elephant or a whooping crane. We wanted you to see what you'd helped to create."

"I think Rhys would have a breakdown."

"Actually, he's joining us next month. We've made a proper mess of this world, and it'll take a while to clean up. Possibly forever. But if we can do some good every day, then every day makes the world a little better."

"Still a pragmatic idealist." A memory tugged my hand to my pocket, and I pulled out a wad of rumpled fabric. "Evan made these for you and Felicity. Happy anniversary."

With a smile that had lost some of its lustre but none of its determination, Min left to grieve in her own way. And I continued to wait. Prometheus checked in several times, offering cups of chamomile tea and buckwheat biscuits, which I gratefully accepted. As it turned out, he and several of his compatriots had urgently extricated themselves from Winthrop's Opulence Bunker when they'd learned that surplus androids were being dismantled to build hot-tubs.

Galadrielle—or Elle for short—peeked in briefly, leaving me with a bowl of sweet midgen berries and a colourful drawing of two stick-figures riding a pair of triceratops. I wasn't entirely sure if the picture was a fanciful daydream or her research proposal.

I remained by the inert sphere all night, all the next day, and the night after that. I sometimes chatted to it, sometimes sat in companionable silence. I told it about the new solar island being launched off the coast of New Venice, and reminisced about the cockatoos at the warehouse and their brazen birdseed heists.

You should take a break, Jaya said. *We'll let you know if—I mean when—he regains consciousness.*

I'm fine, I said. *I'd like to be here when, if, he wakes up.*

On the eleventh night, I stirred from restless dreams to a faint humming against my skin. The sphere looked no different, but as I rested my fingertips on the surface, I felt it shivering.

"Evan? Can you hear me?"

I held my breath, my heart clenching with undeserved hope. The sphere shivered again, and a barely perceptible ripple passed over its surface. Then, on its side, two small bulges appeared, followed by a furrow underneath. The bulges blinked open.

Eyes.

And the furrow wobbled.

"Harrghloo?" it croaked.

"Evan! I'm here."

The eyes rotated this way and that, not quite in unison.

"I can't move... I feel strange. Do I look strange?"

Something between a laugh and sob crawled up my throat. "You look like a hopeful pomelo."

Evan's new eyes blinked rapidly, as though trying to draw the world into focus.

"I want to see the sky. Can we go outside?"

He was too heavy for me to carry, so we rolled carefully out the cargo hatch and into a grassy clearing. The midnight sky was dense with stars, hemmed by the sinuous branches of the eucalypts.

"Oh..." breathed Evan. The sphere shivered again, new buds elongating into tentacles that became a pair of arms and uneven legs. The ball continued to pinch and swell until it took on the slightly molten form of a scrawny, lopsided figure.

Evan reached a hand upward, as though he could strum the chords of distant galaxies, and a smile spread across his face. His brow furrowed in concentration, and two nubs sprouted from his back, growing rapidly before unfurling into a pair of broad, silver-plumed wings.

He gave a delighted laugh. "An upgrade!"

I watched the moonlight drift across his silvery skin. "A metamorphosis. You're not better than you were. Just different."

"I can fly. I think that automatically counts as an upgrade." He gave his wings an experimental flap, as though he might launch into the starry expanse. Abruptly, his smile faltered as apprehension seized him, and he swayed, shrinking inward like a frightened spider.

"Hey." I touched his arm lightly. "There's no hurry."

Embarrassment flushed his features. "I'll try again tomorrow." He gazed out at the dissolving edge of night. "Will you come with me?"

"You bet."

The world would continue to change, and we would have to change with it. Species would come and go, and perhaps come again. Civilisations would rise and crumble and implode, perhaps to stir once more in the aria of calling waves and singing constellations. And in the end, all we'd have to remember them by would be frozen chunks of amber time, silhouettes in stone, and their stories.

As the promise of another day pulled us onward, chiaroscuro magpies warbled their husky melodies. And beneath the murmuring leaves of a melaleuca tree, two silvery stick insects held each other gently as dawn brushed the fading stars.

***

D.K. Mok is a fantasy and science fiction author whose novels include *Squid's Grief, Hunt for Valamon,* and *The Other Tree.* DK has been shortlisted for six Aurealis Awards, three Ditmars and two WSFA Small Press Awards. DK lives in Sydney, Australia, and her favourite fossil deposit is the Burgess Shale. Connect on Twitter @dk_mok or find out more at dkmok.com.

...before you travel onwards, might we ask for your help again?

This book is both a collection of stories and a small research project. Remember the survey we asked you to fill out before you started reading? To understand how stories might contribute to building better futures for humans and nature alike, please tell us what you think.

Simply visit the link below and fill out our second reader survey:

https://postsurvey.multispecies.city

Thank you again for your help!
Visit **https://survey.multispecies.city** to learn about the results.

This research is supported by the Research Institute for Humanity and Nature (RIHN).

About the Anthologists

Christoph Rupprecht (he/him) is a geographer based in Japan. When he's not researching food, agriculture, green space, degrowth and solarpunk with a more-than-human lens, you might find him reading science fiction, hanging out with plants, trying to make cheese, or taking a nap. He believes the imagination holds the key for jointly building sustainable and just futures for all life.

Deborah Cleland (she/her) is an activist/ acrobat/academic, with all the compromise and circuitous life paths that those slashes imply. She dabbles in interactive theatre and games, site-specific place-making and creative non-fiction, hoping to bring her research into social justice, inclusion and sustainability to life through writing and performance.

Norie Tamura (she/her) is a social scientist in Japan, researching agriculture, forestry, and fisheries. After working as a consultant in those areas, she moved to academia. Growing up in the Western Japan metropolitan area, she repeatedly discovered alternative universes in rural areas, and came to realize that knowing and experiencing a different world is the key to envisioning a different future.

Rajat Chaudhuri (he/him) is a bilingual author, environment columnist and climate activist. His works include novels, short story collections, translations, and an Asian speculative fiction anthology, curated and introduced by him. His most recent novel, *The Butterfly Effect* was twice listed by Book Riot as a 'Fifty must read eco-disasters in fiction' and among 'Ten works of environmental literature from around the world'. He is currently working on narratives for a co-created video game about alternative climate futures while an anthology of translated Bengali poetry is forthcoming. Chaudhuri lives and writes in Calcutta.

Sarena Ulibarri (she/her) is a graduate of the Clarion Fantasy and Science Fiction Writers' Workshop at UCSD, and earned an MFA from the University of Colorado, Boulder. Her fiction has appeared in *Lightspeed, DreamForge, GigaNotoSaurus,* and elsewhere. A personal essay on gardening during the pandemic appeared in *Strange Horizons,* and you can listen to her ranting about solarpunk on about half a dozen podcasts, including *Imaginary Worlds, Alan and Jeremy vs SF,* and *Yale Climate Connections.* She has edited two anthologies of optimistic climate fiction, *Glass and Gardens: Solarpunk Summers* (2018) and *Glass and Gardens: Solarpunk Winters* (2020).

MORE ANTHOLOGIES FROM
WORLD WEAVER PRESS

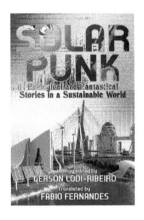

**SOLARPUNK:
ECOLOGICAL AND FANTASTICAL
STORIES IN A SUSTAINABLE WORLD**
Anthology edited by Gerson Lodi-Ribeiro
Translated by Fabio Fernandes

*The English translation of the world's first
solarpunk anthology. Groundbreaking science
fiction stories from Brazil and Portugal.*

GLASS AND GARDENS:
SOLARPUNK SUMMERS

Anthology edited by Sarena Ulibarri

*"This anthology is a welcome relief from dystopias
and postapocalyptic wastelands, and a
reassurance that the future need not be relentlessly
bleak."*
—Publishers Weekly

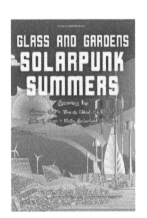

Find these and more great short fiction anthologies at
WWW.WORLDWEAVERPRESS.COM
Also available at Amazon, Apple Books, BarnesandNoble.com,
IndieBound, Kobo, and other online booksellers.

World Weaver Press, LLC
Publishing fantasy, paranormal, and science fiction.
We believe in great storytelling.
WorldWeaverPress.com

Milton Keynes UK
Ingram Content Group UK Ltd.
UKHW021305280823
427623UK00024B/850